LOVER'S

With Nick's arms around her and their bodies touching, their laughter subsided. Fancy looked up to search his face. Was he, too, feeling the funny, tingling sensations that ran through her like liquid fire.

He was, indeed, feeling a hellish torment which he had not meant to inflict upon himself, and now he had a devilish ache in his groin. He burned for her with an agonizing yearning.

Her cheek rested against him and the sweet fragrance of her hair tickled his nose. His arms felt the exciting curves of her young body burning into him, and when she moved back just enough to look at him with those dark eyes and her lips were only a couple of inches from his, he was lost.

"Kiss me, Nick," she whispered softly. "I want you to kiss me." She was serious, not playing a parlor game.

Dear God, she could not know what she was asking!

"Oh, my sweet innocent Fancy," he murmured huskily and let his lips meet with hers. As his lips took her, he swore he'd never make her regret asking for that kiss. He was only a mortal man and he knew this could not end with just a kiss. He was not that much of a gentleman . . .

RAPTUROUS ROMANCE
by Wanda Owen

ECSTASY'S FANCY

WANDA OWEN

ZEBRA BOOKS
KENSINGTON PUBLISHING CORP.

ZEBRA BOOKS

are published by

Kensington Publishing Corp.
475 Park Avenue South
New York, N.Y. 10016

First printing: November 1984

Printed in the United States of America

This book is for all my devoted friends and readers who urge me to keep writing my stories.

A special dedication to all my special blessings: Sandi, Nikki, Angie, Joy Dawn, and Mikie.

Prologue

She was a miracle to behold, old Raoul thought to himself, as he hobbled toward the bank of the muddy Mississippi River. The black man's heart ached for the precious child sitting there on the old plank wharf with her legs dangling over the side and a pensive look on her lovely face.

He shook his fuzzy gray head and cast his sad eyes skyward, mumbling, "Oh, my sweet little Fancy—if only I had it within my power to make your lot in life more beautiful!" That was the futility of it for he was only a blacksmith on the grand plantation, Willow Bend.

The poor child had no chance at all, despite the glowing promise of the ravishing beauty she would soon become. She was not born of the gentry and old Raoul saw heartache, pain, and peril in the future ahead. It could not be otherwise for a girl like Fancy.

The twelve-year-old girl sat there with no awareness of the black man's adoring eyes watching her that bright summer day. She heard the melodious songs of the birds and the rustling branches of the tall trees. Her black onyx eyes beamed brightly when she spied a fish close to the surface stirring a gusto of bubbles in the rippling waters. A gust of lilting laughter erupted from her. She loved all of God's creations. God's gifts were Fancy's toys and companions. These were gifts wealthy parents could not have given her. Her wealth consisted of a vivid imagination which allowed her to see things and to explore places in ways the ordinary person did not. She had a sense of whimsy and of fantasy which made up for the material things of this world.

Raoul ambled slowly down the bank thinking that she'd been blessed with that light tawny skin of satin which produced a glorious golden hue. Her dark brown hair looked like glossy velvet in he sunshine.

Daughters of the gentry sure couldn't, and wouldn't, sit in the sun like that with their gardenia-white skin exposed. A fancy bonnet or parasol would be necessary.

Her sensitive ears heard his shuffling footsteps; Raoul's feet were a source of discomfort to him. She turned around. "Wondered if you were goin' to come down this mornin'?"

"What you say—me not come down? Why, Miss Fancy!" he laughed. "I ever disappoint you, huh?"

She shook her waist-long hair from side to side. "Nope, Raoul — you never have." She hastily told him her mother was going to be up at the main house all day working on Miss Roberta's fancy gown.

"Then I guess I just have to put up with you, child." He gave her a broad smile, which concealed his true feelings. Raoul felt very protective toward Fancy, and he constantly feared that some river boatman would venture near the cottage where she and her mother lived and catch the young girl alone.

A bond bound him to this girl for he had been the one who'd delivered her the night Fleur Fourney had gone into labor all alone in that little shack down by the river's edge. That no good Louis Fourney was away getting drunk, and before the night was over he'd ended up dead, leaving his wife and newborn baby to the mercy of the owner of the Willow Bend Plantation.

Being of a generous heart, Charles Kensington had allowed his former overseer's wife and child to remain at the shack, and later Fleur had gone to work at the main house. Alicia Kensington had deeply resented the kind consideration her husband showed the young, beautiful widow, and she had not made life pleasant or easy for Fleur. At the time all this had taken place — twelve years ago — Alicia had been expecting her third child. Her daughter, Roberta, was four and young Chris was three. The twelve years that had passed had not mellowed her.

Roberta was now sixteen and a self-centered haughty young miss, but her brother Chris adored Raoul as Fancy did, and he loved to hang around the smithy shed or the stables, having inheriting Charles's love of his thoroughbreds.

Raoul's wife, Chessie, was also fond of young Fancy and felt sorry for her. She was constantly bringing castoffs or food to give to the Fourneys.

Over the years Raoul and Chessie had grown fonder and fonder of the little black-eyed child. Both had noticed that lately she was blossoming and both knew that would bring problems they could no longer protect her against. Each had a troubled, heavy feeling for Fancy.

And so on this summer day Raoul noticed her bare feet and teased, "You go git your slippers and I'll take you to the marketplace, huh?"

"All right! Be right back, Raoul," Fancy exclaimed, leaping up to run across the wharf. "Meet you up by the oak tree!" She dashed like a gazelle up the path to the cottage, stopping only to wave at the paddle wheeler tooting its whistle three times.

Before dashing into the cottage, she waved and waved until she was sure Captain Jack had seen her. When she returned with the slippers in her hand, Raoul chided her, "They to be worn on your feet, Fancy, and not on your hands." They both laughed as she hopped on one foot and then the other to put them on without breaking the pace of their striding walk.

As they made their way along the manicured grounds surrounding the plantation house, Fancy saw the two elegantly dressed Kensington ladies getting into the carriage and she called Raoul's attention to them. "Look at that gown. I'll swear it's the same shade of yellow as the pretty wild jasmine blossom you put in my hair the other day."

"Yes, Miss Fancy—I'd say it was." What he did not add was how much prettier the gown would have been on the dainty little Fancy instead of the horse-faced Roberta. What a sight that would make, Raoul thought, envisioning sweet Fancy in a yellow silk gown, her deep brown hair flowing down her back. Now that would be a pretty picture to see.

As they skirted the magnificent lawns surrounding the sprawling plantation house to move on to the barn, Fancy chattered away about the many-colored flowers and about how soft the verdant, thick carpet of grass looked. She pointed out that the long rows of taller poplars lining the drive were the exact same size. The old black man never ceased to be amazed that the girl missed nothing within eyesight.

Once they entered the barn Raoul busied himself harnessing up the team as Fancy roamed around. Suddenly he heard her blurt out, "Oh, hell!"

"Missy, what's that you say?"

She repeated it and Raoul wanted to know where she'd heard that. Fancy answered him,

11

"Momma's friend."

"I see," he mumbled with disdain.

This was just another thing neither he nor Chessie could do anything about so he had to accept it. As he turned back to the harnessing and dropped the subject, his wife rushed out of their quarters, an old straw hat in her hand.

"That child needs this, Raoul. Just a minute." She rushed around the wagon to hand the coarse straw hat to Fancy, and gleefully, the girl flopped it onto the top of her head.

When they'd traveled about a mile away from Willow Bend Fancy insisted that Raoul stop so she could pick a cluster of the wild verbenas growing by the roadside. As she scampered back up onto the seat beside Raoul, she placed the red and purple verbenas in the faded band of her hat and, pleased with herself, declared to Raoul, "Mine's as beautiful as Miss Roberta's hat!"

"You right, Miss Fancy," he laughed. More than ever he knew there was something special about this girl sitting beside him as they journeyed into Memphis.

The marketplace was a beehive of activity carried on by a hodgepodge of people from all stations of life. Vendors busily peddled their goods while a parade of rough-looking river boatmen moved idly by. Raoul knew that pickpockets flourished in such crowds, as did other unsavory characters, so he held on to Fancy's hand with a tight grip.

Even a few of the gentry milled around, drawn

by curiosity since they could have sent servants from their fine houses to do their marketing. And because of the forests that flourished outside the city, fierce husky lumbermen were also in evidence. Indeed it was a busy day here in the market square.

Raoul made his purchases, and loaded the flat-bedded wagon, leaving the stop at the Dubose Warehouse for last since it was in the direction they would travel to leave the city. Fancy sat on the seat enjying the fresh peach he'd bought for her.

He reined the team toward the alleyway that led to the loading dock of the warehouse. Once he'd picked up the cases of the special imported brandy Mister Kensington had ordered and the cases of champagne for the approaching ball, his purchases would be all through for another couple of weeks.

The wagon came to a halt, and while Raoul attended to his chore, Fancy jumped down to stretch her legs and roam aimlessly about the street. Raoul was not aware of what happened next for he was busy and did not see a gusting breeze take her hat from her head and sweep it down the street. As Fancy ran after it, a fine carriage came rolling directly toward her. Raoul looked up just as the carriage came to an abrupt stop and a handsome young man leaped out. He was a striking young dandy in a bottle-green coat and cream-colored pants, Raoul observed, but the black man was impressed by the warm smile the youth gave Fancy as he gallantly rescued her straw hat and placed a

13

hand on her shoulder. Raoul heard his deep, rich voice caution her, "Whoa, little one. Granted the hat is a beauty, but it is not worth your getting trampled by my bays."

Placing the hat atop her head, the young man was rewarded by a grateful smile from Fancy and a polite thank you.

The gentleman stood, awed by the magnificent loveliness of the young girl. Fancy stood, too, staring up at his handsome face and thinking that he reminded her of the Prince Charmings in the fairy tales Fleur had read to her.

A shrill feminine voice from inside the carriage broke in on her illusion. "For Lord sakes, Nick, will you quit wasting time on white trash. I'm going to be late."

A black eyebrow rose disgustedly and his eyes flashed green fire as he darted a furious glance over to the carriage. But his expression mellowed when he looked back at the lovely child he'd just encountered and he bid her, "Farewell, little one."

Fancy told him goodby and then rushed back to Raoul's side. Raoul told her to jump up onto the wagon.

The twenty-two year-old scion of the Dubose family took a seat beside his younger sister, Denise. Through flashing white teeth, he hissed, "You, my dear, are a heartless little witch, and but for the fact that we share the same mother I would not be so kind. It would not have been witch I labeled you." He gave an angry yank at his white

14

ruffled shirtsleeve.

He sat thinking how different his other sister, Doreen was. She would have been so impressed with the girl she would have wanted to capture that rare breathtaking beauty on her canvas.

Raoul always readily answered Fancy's questions, as numerous as they were. However, as they rolled out of the city toward the outskirts, she prodded him, a serious look on her face, "What's white trash, Raoul?"

He thought for a minute before telling her, "A very dirty word."

That seemed to satisfy her. "I thought so 'cause that nice man looked real mad." She leaned back, a pleased smug look on her pert little face.

"He was a nice man and he like you, Miss Fancy."

"I know." She smiled up at Raoul. How easily she'd been appeased this time, but what about the next time? Raoul woefully mused. That's when the heartbreak begins!

Part One
My Sweet Fancy

Chapter One

She sat under the spacious, draped branches of the willow tree. To Fancy, the willows were like giant umbrellas, protection from the rain or the sun, and the plantation had come by its name, Willow Bend, because of the number of them thriving down here by the river. Today, they provided the refuge she sought, a safe place to shed the river of tears that welled up in her when she'd heard Alicia's harsh words to her son Chris. Why had she said those awful things, Fancy wondered?

Four years ago, she'd heard those dirty words, but today they'd stabbed at her in a hurtful, painful way. That summer day in the past they had not seemed so harmful. What made them so different at sixteen she wondered?

Something had told her, when she'd allowed Chris to help her up on Sugarplum, that she shouldn't go for that ride with him. But Chris had wanted her to go, and he'd always treated her so kindly, just like Mister Kensington.

What fun they'd had for that marvelous hour! How utterly enchanting the woods had been! When Chris had halted the amber-colored mare he'd named Sugarplum because she'd reminded him of brown sugar and they'd sat there on the ground and leaned back on an old fallen tree trunk to talk, it had been nice. Wild ferns and violets grew profusely there, and it would not have surprised Fancy if a gathering of fairies had danced out before her. But she dared not voice this to the seventeen-year-old Chris who seemed so much older than she.

It amazed her to realize how tall he'd suddenly become and how good-looking too. His eyes were the brightest blue, and his hair reminded her of cornsilk with its pale yellow hue. Yet she'd known him all her life.

As she sat there with him and her busy fingers played with a thin blade of grass, he took her hand in his and turned it over. "Mother works you too hard. Look at that red roughness. Someday, it won't be that way, I promise. Someday, you'll have what a beautiful girl like you deserves." He brought her fingertips up to his soft warm lips and kissed them with a tenderness Fancy found sweet and to her liking.

"You're always so nice to me, Chris. You always have been. I'll never forget when Momma died with the fever and I came to live in the big house how you and your father made me feel so welcome." She was not dishonest enough to include Alicia and Roberta Kensington.

"It's easy to be nice to you, Fancy. Why, you're the sweetest, dearest person I've ever known." Chris Kensington spoke with complete sincerity. Dear God, he thought, if there were such a thing as an angel it had to be Fancy. He had come to detest his own mother and sister these last two years when he'd seen how badly they treated her. Fancy hadn't picked her parents, Chris realized.

Alicia would have been mortified if she'd known the thoughts possessing him lately, but Chris did not care. He'd apply patience, and when the time came he planned to remedy Fancy's plight here at Willow Bend. He was in love with her and his seventeen-year-old heart wanted to cry it out to her.

When his friends teased him and spoke crudely about the beautiful young orphan living so handily under his roof, he bloodied more than one nose and received some blows in return. However, he'd managed to keep any knowledge of these fights from his mother, although his father knew and approved of them.

When Chris and Fancy had returned from the woods that afternoon and Alicia had spied them together, a horrible scene had taken place. Fancy had been ordered to her room and Chris had been told to remain in the sitting room with Alicia. But Fancy had not gone to her room. Instead she'd rushed down to the river, to sit under the willows.

She'd cried and cried until she could cry no more.

At first, she'd intended to go to her room as Alicia Kensington had told her to do, but the woman's fury had so shocked her that she'd stood for a moment outside the carved oak door to the sitting room and had heard Alicia's cruel, cold voice shout to Chris, "Dear boy, you don't go riding with white trash."

Chris's voice had screamed back, "Fancy's not white trash, Mother!"

"Your father is going to know about this, Christopher! I can assure you of that. I knew something like this would happen when we moved her in here."

"Nothing *did* happen, Mother, other than a ride in the woods. You'd better not worry so much about me and Fancy. Instead you should look into what Roberta enjoys doing on the veranda with her latest beau," Chris's angry voice cried out.

Had Fancy not rushed away at that point, she would have known that he'd bolted out of the room in defiance, leaving his mother gasping with shock at her son's behavior. Indeed, Alicia decided then and there that she must rid Willow Bend of Fancy Fourney at once, regardless of what Charles said.

That evening during dinner, Alicia Kensington used her womanly wiles. She was unusually sweet and mentioned nothing about the late afternoon episode. The sullen-faced Chris, disgusted, saw through her and left the dining table as quickly as he could.

"What's the matter with Chris tonight?" Charles inquired.

"Growing pains perhaps, dear," Alicia said soothingly. "You know the moodiness of the adolescent."

"Huh, I guess so," Charles quipped, not completely sold on that explanation where Chris was concerned. Charles knew his son to be an intelligent young man, never given to moods like Roberta or Chad. He knew Chris possessed an even temper and a cool head. Something had plagued Chris tonight, and Charles intended to find out what it was even though he gave Alicia no hint of his intentions.

Fancy sequestered herself in her room, drowning her hurt within the pages of a book. She knew no better way to sweep happenings of the day from her thoughts. Nothing relaxed her more than reading.

She thought back to when she'd been allowed to join Chad and his tutor, Mister Lacrosse, in the classroom at the plantation. That had been Mister Kensington's idea and she'd blessed him for the privilege. How sad a life it must be, she thought, for someone unable to open a book and to explore all the knowledge recorded there or to live vicariously through the adventures of the tale on its pages.

Mister Lacrosse had told her she had an amazing talent for learning. She knew he'd not mentioned to the mistress that she'd surpassed Chad months ago. Never should she let it be known even to Chris that she was smarter than Chad. Vanity did make her want to know a little though, she secretly confessed. Only Chessie and Raoul knew.

Everything that had happened today seemed to provoke thoughts about her future. She knew one thing: Willow Bend would be a lonely place once Chris left to go East to school come autumn. She knew Raoul would miss him too, and certainly poor Sugarplum.

She knew it was time to lay the book aside and to go sleep when she'd read the same line for the third time. She had no doubt she'd pay a mighty high price in chores for the ride today. Oh, yes, Alicia Kensington would delight in releasing her resentment—whenever her husband was away from the house.

Hatred was a feeling alien to Fancy, for she was too full of love for everything. She felt perplexed and puzzled by her mistress's hostile feelings for her. As with anything, there has to be a reason, she told herself.

Next morning she had no time to ponder because the main house stirred with a flurry of activity. The mistress's widowed sister was arriving from Natchez, her first visit in five years. Fancy and the house servants weren't allowed a minute to catch their breaths during the morning hours.

At one in the afternoon the Kensington carriage

pulled into the long winding drive with their guest, Alita Dumaine, her little lady's maid, and a mountain of luggage. Fancy just happened to be out on the upstairs veranda shaking a coverlet when the entourage arrived. She watched the group come up the steps.

The lady had to be the mistress's younger sister, Fancy thought, and such a shame she was a widow already. But then her own mother had died far too young. When she could see them no longer she flung out the coverlet one final time before going back to the bedroom and finishing up the bed. After that Chessie had told her to go have her lunch and she was more than ready for it. Her stomach growled with hunger.

When she finally descended the back stairs, a strange feminine voice resounded with laughter, and Fancy listened for a moment before descending to the pantry. She sighed at the pleasant thought that maybe the arrival of Alicia's sister would cause the happenings of yesterday to be forgotten. At least she hoped so.

As she sat so weary she could hardly munch on the food, aware of her frock clinging to her back which was damp with sweat, Fancy thought about how nice it would be to cool herself down in the river. She must have had a wistful look on her face. A hand tapped her slumped shoulder and a voice teased, "Penny for your thoughts, Fancy." She turned to see Chris standing behind her looking handsome in his fine attire. The deep blue of his coat made his eyes appear darker. It was the first time she'd noticed how broad his shoulders had become in contrast to the rest of his trim body.

Playfully, she teased him back, "Oh, you wouldn't want to know."

He took a seat across from her at the little square oak table where the servants took their meals. There was nothing ostentatious about Chris, and this was a quality that endeared him to the servants milling about in the kitchen.

A pale blond wave of hair fell casually over his forehead as he leaned across the table to say to Fancy, "But I would want to know, Fancy. I'm more interested in your thoughts than you know."

Her dark eyes looked into his. Something she couldn't fathom stirred within her, but some inborn instinct told her the carefree camaraderie they'd shared was swiftly moving into something else. It rather frightened her—that startling new awareness that had come the day in the woods when Chris's warm lips had touched her fingertips in a kiss. She felt it now as his blue eyes warmed to her and she adored the feeling, strange as it was.

Chris had no way of knowing the mystery Fancy's sweet innocence was pondering for it was no mystery to Chris. For over a year her blossoming loveliness had affected him so overwhelmingly that he had spent numerous sleepless nights lying in his bed.

Fancy was his first love, and he swore no other girl in the countryside could compare to her in beauty or sweetness.

Fancy finished the food on her plate, and with no desire to be at odds today with her mistress, she started to get up from the table. Chris stopped her, urging, "Don't leave just yet . . . please!"

"Chris, I should. I . . . I don't want your mother to get mad at me again today."

"Oh, you won't have to worry about that for a while. Aunt Alita will keep her occupied, I assure you! She's a very good influence on Mother. I welcome her visit. Lord, I find it hard to believe that they're sisters."

Fancy found herself easing back down into the chair. Funny that Chris should say that because somehow she'd gotten that impression just seeing the lady enter. There was a softness about her face, whereas Alicia Kensington's face was always tense, and there was a lively beat to her step which indicated that she enjoyed life. God knows, she is certainly a lovelier-looking woman, Fancy thought. Even the sisters' coloring wasn't the same, for Alicia was as fair as Alita was dark.

"I think my aunt finds Willow Bend too dull to visit often. Widow or not, she leads a very active life in Natchez."

Fancy forgot about how tired she was or that she could get into trouble with the mistress as she listened to Chris talking about the city of Natchez, where his Aunt Alita lived, down the Mississippi River. How many times she'd sat on the bank of that river looking up and down it and dreaming about those faraway cities.

How wonderful it would be to stand on the upper deck of one of those paddle wheelers — like Captain Jack, who was always waving to her!

Even now in the kitchen where she and Chris sat, she could almost feel the cool breeze along the river at night and imagine how the moonbeams would play across the waters. What fascinating people would be aboard!

She was so deep in thought she didn't hear Chris's voice as he talked to her. Fancy's thoughts were drifting gloriously. She saw herself walking down a gangplank in the most exquisite gown of pale green silk and carrying a parasol of white cambric. In the breeze, her lovely bonnet rose from her head but was caught by the handsomest man she'd ever seen. Oh, he was truly magnificent! So tall and impressive he took her breath away.

His face was known to her . . . every finely-chiseled feature. She'd seen it a million times in her girlish dreams, ever since that day four years ago.

Even though she now sat with Chris at the table, a part of her was back in that other place and time. It was not Chris's face her eyes were seeing. These were the greenest eyes and the hair framing his face was the blackest hair she'd ever seen.

"I — I must ask you to excuse me, Chris. Really, I must," she stammered, moving with an awkward clumsiness and plagued with something akin to guilt because she'd been thinking of another man instead of dear, sweet Chris.

As muddled as her mind was, that day and that moment had come to her as clearly as if they had occurred only yesterday, instead of four years ago. Should she ever chance to gaze into those eyes again, she knew she'd know them instantly!

Chapter Two

Alita Dumaine had already made up her mind that one more week would find her ready to return to Natchez. The last seven days had begun to drag and Alicia's officious air played on her nerves. She didn't need her sister's advice or counsel. For her legal problems, she had a very capable lawyer and had already decided to keep her house in the city and to sell the country home now that she was alone.

Her devoted, competent housekeeper, Claudine took excellent care of her home and of her. Dear Lord, in her wildest nightmare she wouldn't consider living at Willow Bend as Alicia had urged her to do almost daily since she'd arrived.

The one thing missing from Alita's life since her beloved Henri had passed away a year ago was the presence of her niece, Cindy, who had married in the spring. The vibrant eighteen-year-old girl had brought life and spirit into Alita's life when she'd needed it badly. While Alita had called her a social secretary, she'd really been more of a companion for the lovely widow, with whom she'd attended numerous social events around the city.

All day Alita's dark head had been whirling with a most outrageous idea that might provide what she needed in her life, an idea that she was at the point of discussing with Alicia. Oh, Alicia would think it ludicrous.

The girl was a trifle young agewise, but her lovely body was that of a young woman. She was neat and clean in appearance. Around Alita, she'd been gracious and soft-spoken as she'd done her job. Indeed, the poor little thing walked around as if she feared her footsteps would rile Alicia. It wouldn't be that way in my home, Alita reflected. Dressed and coiffured, given a little bit of kindness and encouragement, the girl could take on a whole new image. Unlike her older sister, Alita was a woman of vision, and she could see the dark-haired Fancy as a ravishing beauty when the girl reached the full bloom of femininity.

"Why not?" she murmured thoughtfully. "It would solve the problem Alicia has conjured up in her mind where her precious Chris is concerned, and it might just prove to be interesting for me." She gave a sly smile and her eyes flashed brightly. Tonight, after the dinner hour, she'd mention the possibility of this young girl, Fancy, returning to Natchez with her when she left next week.

The Kensington household was run by the clock whereas Alita found it hard to adapt to a fixed dinner hour and specific times for doing this or that. Still, she did try her best to descend the winding stairway at the hour appointed for dinner to be served. This night was no different from the other nights she'd been here except that Charles had remained in the city on business and Alicia was in an impossible mood.

By the time the other members of the family had scattered throughout the house or gone to their rooms, Madame Dumaine was sure that her idea had been a sound one. She'd taken special notice of the dainty miss that night. Fancy moved her petite body with grace, and although ill-at-ease around Alicia, she maintained a certain dignity and poise. Alita liked that.

God knows, Alita had seen enough gawkiness and ill manners displayed by the youth of her wealthy friends in Natchez. Something told Alita Dumaine this young servant girl was never meant to live out her life this way. She felt that very strongly.

I'm going to give her a chance, the lovely lady decided, sitting there in the Kensington's lavishly furnished parlor that was decorated in white and Wedgwood blue.

When she and Alicia were alone, Alita strolled over to Charles's elaborately carved teakwood liquor chest. "I feel like a brandy, Alicia. How about joining me?"

"Oh, no . . . no, I don't think so, Alita dear, but help yourself," Alicia replied, disgruntled that Charles was still not home at this late hour.

Alita filled a glass, strolled back to the over-stuffed blue velvet chair, and took a seat. "Alicia, I told you I thought I'd sell Dubonnet, didn't I?"

Her older sister nodded for her thoughts were elsewhere, but suddenly she came to life and started to admonish the younger woman. "Alita, a woman alone needs to be around her loving family. Dubonnet and the house in town should be sold, and you should move back here to Willow Bend. Rooms are going to waste here."

"Willow Bend is your home, Alicia, not mine. My friends and my life are in Natchez, and that is where I shall continue to live. That is my final word, but I do have something else to discuss with you." Without hesitation she told Alicia the idea she'd had about Fancy.

"Are you crazy, Alita? Dear God, would you take white trash into your home and travel with her? Mercy!"

Alita would have sworn her sister had become so pale that she was on the brink of fainting. "Oh, Pooh! Some of the trash residing within the walls of our most palatial homes in Natchez would put that girl to shame. At what point did you become such an obnoxious snob?"

Alita saw that her statement shocked Alicia.

And it brought back a flush of color to her sister's gardenia-white skin. For once, Alicia Kensington was dumbfounded and speechless.

"I am quite sincere. The girl could be a big help to me, and you find her a pest — so why not? No longer would she be here to tempt young Chris. Could anything be more perfect?"

The more the idea sank in, the better it sounded to Alicia. "Well, it's just that it was the last thing in the world I would have thought of, Alita dear. 'Course, you understand I'll have to discuss this with Charles?"

"Of course, dear," Alita smiled, reading her sister like a book.

Moments later, Charles arrived and Alita excused herself, intending to retire. She was about to get into bed when there was a rap on her door. She was overwhelmed with surprise when she saw her nephew standing there, his good-looking face tense with anger.

"May I come in a minute, Aunt Alita?"

"Oh, of course. Has something happened? You look upset." She clutched her sheer wrapper around her and motioned him to have a seat. Chris was deeply angry at his favorite aunt for the first time in his life.

"I hate you, Aunt Alita, for wanting to take Fancy away from me. I love her," he blurted out as soon as he sat down. Alita saw the pain on his handsome youthful face so she was not hurt by his acid words. Deep in his heart he did not truly mean them, Alita knew.

"Just a minute, my dear, before you firmly convince yourself of that and maybe—just maybe—you'll be glad I have suggested to your mother that I might take your pretty Fancy with me. I would not do anything to hurt you, Chris, and if you care for the girl at all you must listen to me. I may be doing you and her a favor."

Chris started to protest, but his aunt quickly hushed him, demonstrating an authority that made him obey her. "The girl is not going to be staying here, Chris. I mean this as no disloyalty to your mother for she is my sister, but her mind is made up. Far better I take the girl with me, as my companion, where she will be treated kindly. You would know where she was, eh? Think about it."

Chris was quiet and he did think about it. He didn't doubt for one minute that his mother was capable of such an act. He knew his mother and sister had resented Fancy.

"You see? You are a smart young man, Chris. The smartest of all my sister's children. You can't provide for the girl yet, but when that day comes then I would not stand in your way, Chris. You surely see the logic of this now?" Her dainty hand closed over her nephew's. He could only nod his head dejectedly.

Poor Chris! Such a sweet young man, with a kind heart and gentle nature. Alita wanted to ease his hurt and the pain of his heart. Didn't he realize that his parents would never accept a girl like

Fancy as their daughter-in-law? Time could cure so many of the ills that were plaguing Chris. He was very serious for a seventeen-year-old young man.

When he bid her goodbye she realized that she had calmed him and that he seemed to accept her advice about Fancy. At any rate, autumn would soon be here and he would be leaving Willow Bend to go to school.

Everyone noticed a remarkable and pleasant change in the mistress of Willow Bend the following week. But Fancy went about her chores unaware of the change about to take place in her own life. Chessie and Raoul had heard the gossip whispered by one house servant to another, and their hearts were heavy. The thought of not seeing Fancy again broke their hearts but they could do little for the young girl. Age was taking its toll on them and they were aware they wouldn't always be around.

For Fancy's sake Raoul thought she would have a far easier life under Madame Dumaine's roof than here at Willow Bend. The woman had impressed the old black man favorably. It was easy to see that she was kindhearted and more pleasant than her sister. Raoul knew this, just from his chance encounters with her on the grounds of Willow Bend. He and his good wife, Chessie, agreed about that.

Alita's persuasive power had even charmed a reluctant Charles Kensington, and by the end of the week Fancy seemed to be the only one at Willow Bend who was unaware she'd be departing from the place she'd called home all her life.

She was cognizant of the nice Mrs. Dumaine's eyes observing her intensely at various times for the last few days as she served her in different ways. The woman's smile was so friendly and warm that Fancy found it easy to respond. It seemed to the young girl that Mister Kensington was observing her too. Yet, Fancy assured herself, their looks had been approving and the good lord knew, Alicia Kensington had been in rare form. For this, Fancy was grateful.

When the right moment presented itself, Alita chose to talk to Charles about the girl's background. She felt he would tell the unbiased truth.

They had their little talk and Alita learned that Fancy's roots were right there at Willow Bend, that her father had been Charles's overseer and that her mother, Fleur had died of the fever. At the end she had no qualms whatsoever about taking the girl to Natchez to live with her.

"I assure you, Charles, it would be best for everyone, the girl included." Alita Dumaine rose up from the bench in the garden where she and Charles had sought seclusion for their talk.

Charles Kensington stood up, smiling at his lovely sister-in-law. He admired this lady very much, to the point of wishing Alicia had more of her qualities. "Shall I tell her or would you prefer to?"

"The girl seems friendly enough toward me, and I would like to, Charles. Is that all right?"

Feeling greatly relieved, Charles readily replied, "Oh, just fine. Absolutely!"

So Charles Kensington walked away from Alita, responsibility for Fancy Fourney now taken from him. Dear Lord, it had caused enough tension between him and his wife the last two years, he lamented. What would Alicia find to plague him about now? She couldn't use poor little Fancy anymore.

Chapter Three

The *Memphis Belle* plowed through the water heading southward. The gentle breeze and the turning of the paddle wheeler made Fancy feel dreamy. A spray of mist caressed her face as she stood by the railing. She could have sworn the lovely smile on her face was frozen there, for she still could not believe all the strange wonderful things happening to her the last twenty-four hours.

Companion to a fine, lovely lady like Madame Dumaine! Her . . . Fancy! She had, indeed, pinched herself to prove this wasn't a dream, although her pinch had been a gentle one. She'd also clasped her arms around herself, as if in an embrace, and giggled when she was alone. It wasn't a dream! She was actually going to Natchez to live with this nice lady, Alicia's sister.

How many times she'd touched and felt the luxurious softness of the gown Madame had given her to wear on the journey to Natchez. It was the prettiest thing Fancy's eyes had ever beheld and it was all hers! So was the little bonnet that dripped with rainbow colored ribbons. It reminded her of her favorite spring flowers. The fancy slippers had fit perfectly. When Fancy had slipped her feet into them, Alita had laughed lightheartedly. "See, my dear, we even wear the same size slipper. Ah, Fancy, I'm so happy to have you coming to Natchez with me."

Fancy's heart swelled with warmth for the charming woman she'd be serving. How wonderful it was to be truly wanted! Natchez could only hold happiness for her, she mused, since Madame Dumaine would be her mistress.

Her only regret about leaving Willow Bend was that she would not see Raoul and Chessie. Chris would soon be gone anyway, she reminded herself.

Alita, sensing Fancy's excitement would never permit her to sleep, gave her permission to take a stroll around the passenger deck before retiring. However, she did caution the naïve girl, "Don't talk to strangers, dear. A beautiful young lady like you can't be too careful, eh," She gave Fancy a smile before leaving her by the rail to go to her quarters where Dahlia was attending to her luggage.

"Yes, ma'am, I promise to be careful. I've dreamed of doing this for so long," Fancy declared, her face glowing with radiance.

* * *

No one could imagine the pride churning in the girl because of her new position and station in life. It burned with a rosy glow, and her spirits soared for she was so blissfully happy. All the world seemed to be hers in this golden moment. She was a stunning image to behold. More than a few pairs of eyes saw her and admired the beauty of the young lady standing there alone.

The silvery moonbeams seemed to be shining just for her and the dappled shadows they cast on the rippling waters were a glorious sight to behold. She arched herself forward against the railing, looking like a magnificent masthead, like a goddess or mermaid whose hair blew wildly. The effect was intoxicating and exhilarating.

On the upper deck of the boat, a young man leaned over the rail and caught sight of this enchanting vision. "Good goddamn!" He took a deep breath as wild sensations affected his body. Heavy consumption of wine had not left him as numb as he'd thought. He wobbled along the rail, determined to go below to meet this charmer. But that hope was dashed.

"Miss Fancy," Madame Dumaine's maid called to her from the doorway. Fancy turned to answer the tall, willowy octoroon, Dahlia. "Madame Dumaine say it's best you come in now for we'll land early in the mornin' in Natchez," Dahlia informed her and stood waiting for Fancy to come with her.

"I know. Guess it was so nice I forgot the time,"

Fancy sighed, going along with the girl who was not much older than she. Dahlia smiled, agreeing with her that it was a nice night. Being about the same age, Fancy found herself thinking of Dahlia as a friend, someone to talk to. In all her sixteen years she'd never had a girl friend to talk and laugh with. There had always been Chris or Raoul or Chessie. But with them she could not talk the way one sixteen-year-old girl did with another.

Back in the night, the young man stood, looking over the railing and feeling discontented and riled that the little "moonlight maiden" had vanished. Suddenly he grimaced, remembering why he had been ordered by his father to take the boat from Memphis and to stay down in Natchez for a while until the atmosphere cleared and cooled where a certain Memphis lady was concerned.

Somehow, his little escapade had not come off as he'd anticipated. Claude Dubose had a way to go, he realized, before he'd possess the cosmopolitan veneer and suave personality of his older cousin, Nicholas. Maybe, that had something to do with living in the wicked city of New Orleans instead of up the river. The gods always smiled on Nick, it seemed.

He wasn't exactly looking forward to this month's stay in Natchez, but when old Albert Dubose gave an order, Claude and his twin sisters, Cecile and Clara, obeyed. Still, there was one bright spot on the horizon. Nick was at their uncle's plantation, Magnolia. Maybe, Nick would take him in hand and teach him some finesse with the ladies fair. Good Lord, they all adored him! Claude wondered what caused their adoration when Nicholas was so cool and aloof toward them. Yet, Nick's attitude seemed to draw them to him. Claude knew that every female in the vast Dubose dynasty adored him. Even his own two sisters, Cecile and Clara, worshipped Nick, as did his cousin Yvonne.

In his rather drunken state a devious thought came to Claude as the paddle wheeler plowed closer and closer to Natchez. Maybe it wasn't his Uncle Andrée's fine race horses that drew Nick to Natchez. Maybe it was their vivacious cousin, Yvonne. Poor Uncle André had his hands full with her now that he was widowed. At least, his older son Daniel was the quiet scholarly type.

His uncle, André was the leading authority in the sport of racing. The city of Natchez buzzed with crowds and excitement during the spring and fall meets at which the fine Dubose thoroughbreds made a showing. It had galled his uncle that his only son, Daniel, had no interest in the stables or in his horses. Nonetheless, although Daniel had lacked enthusiasm, Nick did not. Yearly, he made several trips to Natchez from his family's home in New Orleans. Now Claude wondered what had prompted Nick's early arrival this time.

Claude's family was one of distinction and prestige. Their vast wealth was concentrated on their flourishing shipping business, in exports and imports, in banking, and in race horses. Yet, each branch lived in a different city along the Mississippi.

Claude's father, Albert, was a banker who resided in Memphis, Tennessee, where he had an interest in the vast lumber business. Alain Dubose, Nick's father was the owner of a shipping line in New Orleans. Uncle André was the youngest of the Dubose brothers and his interest lay in horse racing, along with raising cotton on the acres of land he owned outside of Natchez.

When Claude finally ambled to his quarters on the *Memphis Belle* and laid his head on the pillow of his bunk, he fell into a deep sleep forgetting about the lovely young girl he'd seen back there in the night's blackness.

Fancy's sleep was deep that night, too, for all the excitement of the day caught up with her when she finally lay down. Morning seemed to come all too soon, and she reacted slowly when Dahlia gently nudged her. "Git up Miss Fancy. We goin' be landin' soon now. Git up!"

Fancy sat up, but she just gazed vacantly around, feeling slightly disoriented in these strange quarters until Dahlia's vitality began to rub off on her. The octoroon's flashing eyes and broad smile told Fancy she was glad to be getting back to Natchez. Soon Fancy leaped out of the bunk to gulp down the hot chocolate Dahlia had brought on a tray. But she couldn't eat a bit of the warm croissant on the saucer.

"You don't want this?" Dahlia asked. Fancy replied that she couldn't eat it but she told Dahlia to do so if she wanted it. Dahlia did and they both started to giggle with lighthearted gaiety.

As Dahlia helped Fancy into a pale green gown, the girls chattered away, and then Fancy's heart raced with excitement as she sat for Dahlia to brush her hair. "It's like brown velvet, Miss Fancy, this pretty hair of yours." Dahlia stroked the tresses almost lovingly. All this care and attention had never been showered on Fancy before. She liked it!

Dahlia was used to seeing that Alita Dumaine left nothing behind and she cautioned Fancy accordingly. "Now, don't forget your bonnet over there, eh?"

At about that time Alita stuck her head through the door and smiled, "Oh, Dahlia, I need you desperately to help me with this darned gown. And Fancy dear, I have something for you to take to that nice Captain Benton. Here, dear." Madame Dumaine seemed to be all aflutter this morning as she handed Fancy the envelope. Maybe she was glad to be back too, Fancy thought.

As Dahlia took charge of the back of Alita's gown, Fancy rushed out of the cabin to attend to her first assignment for her new employer. It made her feel most important to be playing this new role. She held her head high and walked spryly across the deck. Her rustling, swishing silk gown swayed to and fro. She'd not taken the time to put on her bonnet so her hair blew wildly around her lovely oval face, as if keeping time with the swaying of her skirt.

By the time she walked out of the door of the captain's quarters, her mission done, she smiled, feeling quite smug that this new job with Madame was going to be like play instead of work. It suddenly dawned on her that the steamboat was idling. Suddenly an explosion of passengers milled around her.

Ahead, pitched on high, impressive bluffs, was the city of Natchez, and she stood at the railing to absorb the view. The docks and wharf were just before them in the distance, yet the boat was hardly moving in the water. Fancy started along the rail at a slow pace, still ogling the sight ahead. The true reality that she was no longer at Willow Bend hit her. This was Natchez . . . her new home!

Nicholas Dubose wasted no time leaping upon the gangplank the moment it was lowered. He intended to take instant charge of that young hellion cousin of his. There would be no repeat of the Memphis escapade here in Natchez. God, as if he didn't have enough on his hands keeping his two younger sisters in line while his parents traveled in the East. Now, this young pup had been foisted on him. His whole idea in leaving New Orleans and coming to Natchez had been to enjoy a well-deserved holiday and to see the new horses his Uncle

André would be racing this autumn.

His long strides were fast paced as he made his way around the deck toward Claude's cabin.

A blur of green rammed into him so hard that the jolt flung that person backward. When Nick's eyes beheld a lovely miss sitting flat on her bottom there on the deck, a strange, shocked expression on her face, he could not suppress the broad smile that came to his face.

Indignation fired her black eyes and her half-opened lips gasped. Fancy's buttocks had taken a mighty slam on the deck when she'd rammed into this giant of a man. Now she was embarrassed and shattered, just when she'd been feeling so grand in her newfound confidence.

"Grin, you fool!" she snapped, and rubbing her hip, she glared at him. Nick swore he'd never seen such a fetching little vixen as the one sitting before him.

He extended his hand to her, but when she made no move to take it, he swept her up from the floor, his strong hands grasping her tiny waist. He realized how petite she was when the top of her head barely came to his chin. The front of him pressed against the back of her and his deep voice whispered an apology in her ear. She whirled around to face him, and when she did the strangest sensation swept over her like a floodtide. Those eyes of emerald green and those flashing white teeth, even the deep dimple in one tanned cheek, belonged to a face etched long ago on her mind. She gasped as though she'd suddenly recognized an old acquaintance. In the next minute she noted the amused look on his face and felt instantly embarrassed. Her long dark lashes fluttered nervously as they always did when she was excited and she bit her lower lip slightly.

Nicholas Dubose remarked, "What is it, *ma petite*? Do you know me?"

Her eyes darted down to the deck and she busily shook the skirt of her gown to keep from looking directly into his questioning green eyes. "Lord, no," she snapped.

"I thought perhaps we might have met," he said, letting his eyes dance slowly over her. Finding the buckle of her slipper caught on her skirt added to her embarrassment and she emitted a disgruntled moan and then heaved a deep sigh. Everything was going wrong.

"Please, *mademoiselle*, allow me." Nick bent down and released the buckle with ease, but he let his hand linger on her dainty ankle. Sheepishly, he gazed up at her and said, "There, it is free."

"Thank you," she muttered, very aware of the heat of his large hand and the strange sensation it stirred. Her sweet innocence did not know what was causing her heart to beat so fast, but the worldly Nick Dubose knew what this breathtakingly beautiful girl was doing to him.

For one brief moment, they were spellbound — man and woman — and the force generating between them was as old as time.

Before he realized it or could stop her, she turned and dashed away before he could learn her name. He stood there as the other passengers moved around him, and only then was he reminded of another face and another time. He shrugged his shoulders, tossing aside the idea. That girl was just a tiny child, but that little face had been the loveliest he'd ever seen and so was this one.

A half hour later when he accompanied his cousin, Claude, across the deck of the boat to disembark he saw the beautiful girl leaving in the company of a woman he knew to be Alita Dumaine. He was elated for he had plans to pay a visit to Madame Dumaine while he was staying here in Natchez.

Who was she, this little black-eyed vixen? Perhaps, a niece of Madame Dumaine's or a young daughter of one of the lady's friends. He intended to find out very soon.

At the same moment Nick was having his private thoughts about her, Claude caught sight of Fancy and exclaimed, "See her, Nick. See that gorgeous girl going along the wharf! God, did you ever see anything so lovely!" He hastened to tell Nick about the night before.

"I think you had better cool your amorous nature for a while," Nick sternly admonished Claude. Claude frowned. Natchez probably wasn't going to be any picnic. Nick could be a cool bastard. Claude tried to match his older cousin's long strides, and his eyes kept darting back to Nicholas. Nick's face was like granite as he turned to give Claude a menacing look and raised his black eyebrows. He seems to be warning me, Claude concluded.

Nick had never been known for his patience and something about Claude had already irritated him. He didn't like his remark about the pretty girl. Girls had already gotten Claude into plenty of trouble. Besides, Nick was laying claim to that charming little creature, and he let nothing—absolutely nothing—stand in his way when he wanted something.

As Fancy followed Madame Dumaine and Dahlia to the waiting carriage, something urged her to look back over her shoulder. Even before she turned she knew the man's eyes were upon her. She could have sworn she felt the green fire of them burning into her.

As she suspected he stood staring at her, a grin on his tanned face. Gallantly, he tipped his hat in a gesture of farewell. He was so handsome he fairly took her breath away, and the overpowering effect he had on her made her weak. She knew this was not goodbye, but the beginning. They would meet again, Fancy knew.

Chapter Four

The high-stepping bays trotted along a city street lined with shade trees on either side. Fancy's eyes danced to one side and then the other, taking in all the new sights. City living was certainly going to be different from living out in the country. There were so many people milling around, and the houses seemed so close. Children played within the confines of fenced yards. Everything seemed so alive and busy to Fancy.

Alita watched the girl's dancing eyes as they rode along, and she exchanged smiles with Dahlia. Both were aware of the girl's excitement when they finally made the turn into the driveway that would take them to the front entrance of Madame Dumaine's home.

As they approached it, Alita knew her decision to make this her permanent home and to sell Dubonnet had been the right one. She prided herself on being a practical woman. This smaller house with its Old World charm fit her needs so perfectly. Now, with Fancy as her companion, and with her staff of devoted servants, her life took on a brighter glow. "Ah, we're home, Fancy! This is it. How do you like it?"

Awestruck and wide-eyed, Fancy exclaimed, "Oh, it's so lovely, Madame Dumaine. So very lovely!" She surveyed the ornamental iron fencing that enclosed the grounds. The two-story house was not on the grand scale of the one at Willow Bend—there were no huge white columns and large verandas—but Fancy found the small over-hanging balconies with the elaborate grillwork far more inviting.

"My Henri had this built when we were first married and patterned it after the Old World influence flourishing in his beloved New Orleans. We'll go there sometime, Fancy. Henri and I spent much of our time there," Alita told her. The matronly lady was already conjuring up many pleasant adventures she and little Fancy would share.

The front door opened and a short, elderly black man greeted the entourage. Behind him stood a tall, willow black woman, smiling. Alita introduced them to Fancy, "My devoted Jasper, Fancy dear, and Claudine. I'd be utterly helpless without these two."

The pair privately measured the young miss standing beside their beloved mistress. Dahlia had already entered the house, and Fancy now followed Alita, who ordered coffee to be brought to her sitting room.

They entered a room that was cozy and inviting. Bright colors dominated the decor with floral patterns predominating in the upholstery of the chairs and settee. Pots of blooming anemones and begonias thrived in the sunny windows and a huge palm enveloped one corner.

Alita casually removed her bonnet and invited Fancy to sit down. She pointed to her kidney shaped desk. "You will work there for me, Fancy. Believe me, dear, I'm not a hard taskmaster. I don't exactly live by strict rules or hours as my sister does. Besides, Fancy, I want you to enjoy your life here."

For the next hour, they sat together and Alita described the various duties she wanted Fancy to take over, those that her niece, Cindy, had attended to before she'd left. It pleased Alita that the girl seemed relaxed and at ease with her. She wanted no stiff formality to exist.

Finally, Madame Dumaine summoned Dahlia and instructed the mulatto girl to show Fancy to her room and get her settled in. "I will see you at dinner, Fancy," she said and then she jested about the mountain of messages she wanted to go through, adding, "By that time I know I shall be ready to take a nap."

When Fancy prepared to leave the room, she gave Alita a backward glance and was rewarded by a reassuring smile. Fancy did feel welcome in this house, and it was a good feeling for an orphan girl like her. Since Fleur's death she had longed to be loved. Chris Kensington had seemed to care, and of course, old Raoul and Chessie had adored her. But no one had filled Fleur's void.

It took Dahlia only a moment to unpack the meager belongings in Fancy's valise. The octoroon said nothing to Fancy, but she knew the mistress would be replacing those soon. She hummed as she worked, wondering if the girl roaming aimlessly around the room realized how lucky she was. Lord Almighty, she'd fallen onto a miracle, having caught the attention of Madame's eye. Dahlia's doelike eyes turned to see Fancy standing by the closed French doors opening out to the small balcony.

"Open them, if you wish, Miss Fancy. I just haven't had a chance to yet," Dahlia told her. The girl wasn't gentry like Madame Dumaine, but she was certainly above Dahlia's station as a servant. "Ah, that's a fine breeze comin' in. You might just want to take yourself a nap until I prepare a bath for you before the dinner hour."

Fancy didn't answer for a second because she was so absorbed in every piece of furniture in the room and in the snowy white curtains. So very pretty it all was! A fresh bouquet of long-stemmed gladioli sat in a tall, cut-crystal vase. In shades of yellow and coral, they matched the colors dominating the room.

She took a few steps out onto the small railed

balcony and her dark head whirled at the magic of it all. To have such a lovely room—all her own— and this quaint little balcony was so perfect. She could imagine glorious nights, listening to the calls of night birds or just looking up at the moon and stars so high up there in a night sky.

"Anything I can get you before I leave, Miss Fancy?" Dahlia called to her.

"Not a thing, Dahlia. Thank you," Fancy said hesitantly. Dahlia smiled, knowing how overwhelmed she was by her new surroundings. She turned to leave Fancy alone for a while to rest before the dinner hour, but she rather doubted the pretty little miss would shut her eyes in sleep.

"Well, you just get yourself all settled in your room, and I'll prepare your bath later before you dine downstairs with the mistress, eh?"

"Yes, Dahlia. Yes, that will be just fine." Fancy was flushed with the glow of utter enchantment and wonder. Oh, if Raoul and Chessie could just see all this, how happy they'd be for her, she thought, whirling around the room as if she were dancing at some grand ball. Why she could be a princess with all this luxury bestowed on her!

With her colorful imagination, she felt as though she'd walked right into one of those fairy tales from the books Fleur used to read to her. Yes, Fleur would be happy for her, Fancy knew it!

Dahlia informed her mistress that she had Fancy settled comfortably in her room. "I think

Miss Fancy sorta struck blind by her pretty room and all," the servant reported.

Amusement played on Alita's face as she nodded her head and dismissed Dahlia. The mountain of messages and letters had melted down to a small pile. One message held her interest. That was the one from the local banker, Aaron Barker. His offer to buy Dubonnet puzzled her for she'd specifically warned young Jason Carew, her lawyer, that she did not want her decision to sell circulated around Natchez just yet. He was absolutely the only one she'd notified about the property being for sale in the near future.

Money was not the most important consideration to Alita. Sentiment played a great part. Dubonnet must go to a very special individual. She would insist on it. She would not consider that weasel of a banker for one minute. She would have a talk with young Jason, she promised herself.

However, tomorrow she had other plans for herself and Fancy. The girl must have some decent clothes. They would go to Madame Charlotte's exclusive dress shop.

Over at Magnolia, the Dubose plantation owned by André Dubose, Nicholas's arrival was anticipated by his uncle. Selfishly, he planned to thrust the responsibility for watching over the place on Nicholas's powerful shoulders while he made a short trip to look over some new horses. He had complete faith that Nicholas would take charge of everything, including his feisty imp of a daughter, Yvonne. His son Daniel certainly couldn't control her and she'd taxed André sorely on more than one occasion. If only Daniel were more like his nephew, André would have been so pleased and proud.

Yvonne eagerly awaited both of her handsome cousins. Her spirits were high and explosive due to their impending arrival. Things should certainly liven up around Magnolia with both those reckless rascals around, she mused delightedly.

As she bounced down the stairway to watch for their carriage, lascivious thoughts about Nick brought a twinkle to her green eyes. She chose the perfect gown to compliment her auburn hair for she wanted to look just right to impress both young men. No one had ever stirred her like her Cousin Nick and she was determined to try to get him into her bed during his visit—by any means she could.

Cousin Claude would certainly add spice to the atmosphere, she thought as she sat on the cushioned window seat in the sitting room off the long veranda they must pass to go toward the carriage house. Suddenly through the lines of poplar trees she saw them, and she rushed to announce their arrival to Daniel, who was sequestered with his oils and canvas.

Dear Lord, the smell of the paints was obnoxious to her. She stood in the open doorway, calling, "They're here, Daniel! Come on!" She hurried away as Daniel turned around to see her fleeting figure. Then he directed his attention back to his landscape. He felt no urgency to say hello to Claude since his cousin would be visiting for a month. Uncle Albert's randy son held no interest for the serious-minded Daniel. Claude's loud mouth and crude remarks made Daniel shrink from him. Of all his cousins, Daniel found Nicholas more interesting to talk with during the evenings, for they could talk for hours about the countrysides of Spain, France, and Italy. Nick's masterful use of words painted a pictures for Daniel — the green hills of Ireland or the foggy, rainy days in England — and through his artist's eyes Daniel could envision them. He looked forward to seeing these places someday with his own eyes.

Daniel knew his presence would not be missed by the arrivals, for he knew his sister, Yvonne, would perform the role of hostess.

Yvonne made her entrance like an actress, one so brilliant and sparkling that Claude almost gasped at her beauty. Gad, she was a knockout! Cousin or not, she affected him when he kissed her on the cheek. Nick stood watching the little minx and breathed a sigh of relief that she'd quit being such a pest where he was concerned. While he could appreciate her vivacious beauty, he had no desire for that kind of headache.

As they chattered away, he sauntered over to his Uncle André's exquisite liquor chest. "A toast, cousins?"

"Oh yes, Nick. That's a wonderful idea,"

Yvonne answered. "A sherry for me. And you, Claude?"

"Same as you, Nick," Claude replied.

Nick picked through the bottles lined up. Most were special imports secured on a buying spree he and his father had gone on the year before. The rums had come from the West Indies, the wines and brandies from Spain and France. As he picked up his favorite Kentucky whiskey, he smiled at the gin they'd purchased from Holland. It had not sold as well as the English version, for it seemed the American taste couldn't accept it a year ago.

"Here you go," he said, distributing their glasses. Lazily he strolled to a chair across the room, allowing Claude and Yvonne the closeness of the settee. Their chatter was unimportant to him so he took two large gulps of the deep amber liquor. Thoughts of Dubonnet and of the black-eyed girl back in Natchez occupied him. His concentration was so deep he was not aware of the serious frown on his tanned face until Yvonne teased, "My, Nick, that's a fierce look you have. Are you mad at someone?"

"No, my pet. Just a business matter on my mind." He gave her a quick smile and went over to the chest to refill his glass.

Yvonne was in a playful mood, pointing out to Claude, "Poor Nicholas, I fear he sometimes finds being the oldest of all us cousins a miserable misfortune."

Nick said nothing, only smiled that devastating

smile of his, which always produced a dimple, and gazed across the room at her with those piercing eyes. She wondered what he was thinking. Did he think she was beautiful, and did he find her appealing? She hoped so. Oh, how she hoped so, for she had every intention of finding out before he returned to New Orleans. However, as reckless and daring as Nicholas Dubose was where women were concerned, the fact that she was André's daughter, and his cousin, destroyed any appeal she might have had for him. His comment that he would not be having dinner at Magnolia didn't please Yvonne. She pouted, trying to control her temper when she addressed him. "I'd told cook to prepare one of your favorite dishes tonight."

A pretty, teasing pout it was, Nicholas had to admit, but it did not faze him. Womanly wiles had been tried on him by lovelies all over the world, and Yvonne was a babe in the woods. He strided over to Claude and gave him a comradely slap on the shoulder. "You are a fortunate young man this evening for you may enjoy the dinner and our beautiful cousin all alone." He turned to Yvonne and remarked, "Business will not wait, my pet." Bending down he planted a quick kiss on her cheek and left the room and a fuming Yvonne. She was certain he was a most unpredictable devil. His booted heels clicking against the highly polished tiled floor, he dashed up to his room before leaving Magnolia.

Only later, as he rode down the drive of Magnolia, did he question the wisdom of leaving Claude in the clutches of the devious Yvonne. He could not forever be the keeper of his Dubose cousins. He had his own life to live, and he intended to do just that. While his Uncle André was his favorite uncle — at times he felt a deeper bond with him than with his father, Alain — he had no intention of taking on the handful of trouble his auburn-haired cousin could prove to be!

Darkness gathered as he rode along a country road lined with a multitude of cottonwood trees, its fields now emptied of fieldhands. The sunset was lovely. Nicholas felt that an artist had swept a brush of magnificent purples and bright rose hues across the whole horizon. He thought of his artist sister, Doreen and how she would admit the beauty of it all. What a shame Doreen and Daniel couldn't have been brother and sister!

Tonight, he planned to enjoy the evening with his friend, Jason Carew for he intended to learn all he could about a certain Madame Dumaine who owned Dubonnet. Before the week was over he intended to pay a call on her. It didn't bother him to scheme and calculate to get what he wanted.

But the vision of that beautiful girl gnawed at him with voracious persistence. He had to find out who she was. She was the most gorgeous female he'd ever seen. Unbelievable as it might seem to those who knew him, Nick had always felt he would know it the minute he looked on the face of the woman who would capture his heart. Perhaps, he was a romantic, but this was a thing he'd always felt. Maybe it explained why his elusive heart had never been won, even though he'd certainly had more than his share of lovelies all over the world.

Something about that little black-eyed girl had him fascinated!

Chapter Five

Seen through the eyes of sixteen-year-old Fancy, it was a fairyland. All the beautiful colors and magnificent finery made her eyes dance with excitement and wonder. She ambled closer, unsure of herself even though she stood beside Alita Dumaine. She found herself trying to hold her head high and to walk in that same confident manner as the lovely lady she was coming to admire more and more. In Fancy's mind, Madame Dumaine was everything a lady should be.

"Ah, *chérie*, so good to see you," a woman called out, coming from the back of the elegant dress shop. She came pushing toward them, her eyes darting in Fancy's direction. In the next moment the woman and Alita were embracing. A few minutes later, Fancy was introduced to Madame Charlotte, owner of the shop, and she learned that the purpose of their visit was to buy gowns and clothing for her. Dear Lord, she felt giddy from this miracle that was happening to her, but she remembered old Raoul telling her that someday good things would come her way. She had not expected something of this magnitude, but never had Raoul lied to her.

Fancy stood there, dazzled by all the attention being given her as Madame Charlotte turned her first one way and then the other. The woman studied Fancy's figure and face with care, a slow smile finally coming as though she approved of what she'd surveyed. "Ah, yes . . . charming! Gorgeous hair and the eyes. *Magnifique!* Almost every shade would be flattering on Mademoiselle Fancy, Madame Dumaine. The daffodil yellow or the greens would be excellent and that new begonia pink and violet would be glorious. This young lady can wear anything."

Alita shared that opinion. If a woman had one outstanding feature such as Fancy's glossy dark brown hair, she was fortunate, but Fancy had also been blessed with a smooth, tawny golden complexion and thick, long black lashes that framed her dark, dreamy-looking eyes. More amazing to Alita, Fancy's was a natural beauty. She had not pampered herself or spent hours on beauty concoctions.

Even the girl's hands were lovely. Her long, slender fingers moved with such grace. Soon all the ugly redness from cleaning and scrubbing would go away. Alita knew how her sister, Alicia, must have resented this girl when she compared her with her own daughter, Roberta.

A thunderbolt hit Madame Charlotte and she exclaimed, "Come with me, *chérie*. I have a gown made up and I think it will fit you, except for that tiny, tiny waistline. While we get Hélène to help you try it on, Madame and I will look at material and patterns for your other frocks, eh?"

Fancy nodded her consent and followed Madame Charlotte like a little puppy. They entered a small room and the shopowner called out orders. Fancy had lost sight of Alita Dumaine whose eye had spied some exquisite lacy undergarments which she was already selecting for Fancy.

Madame Charlotte's expert eye was accurate, for when Fancy donned the yellow gown and draped it over her petticoats, it fit perfectly across the bodice, needing only an inch taken up on either side of the waistline. Hélène said this small job could be accomplished before they left the shop.

Madame Charlotte's soft-slippered feet moved with a lively bounce for she knew this would be a most profitable day. Madame Dumaine was now in her private office choosing materials and designs for three more gowns, the yellow one was sold, and a mountain of other accessories were being boxed. And who was now coming through her door but the wealthy young Yvonne Dubose! Ah, life was wonderful!

Nicholas had dropped his cousin off while he

went on to the tobacco shop and then to the coffee house to chat with some of the businessmen.

Yvonne noticed the two women leaving as she stood in front of the cheval mirror to allow Madame Charlotte to pin one of the fashionable black-plumed aigrettes to the side of her hair. She continued to ogle the pair as a mountain of packages was loaded into their carriage. She had disliked the vivacious Dumaine matron ever since she'd noticed her father's admiring eye on the widow.

As young as she was, Yvonne had taken on the role of mistress of the fine estate of Magnolia and she was determined to remain in charge. Still, her father was a devilishly handsome man even at fifty, and she'd anticipated many ladies would be trying to get his eye. None bothered her except Alita.

Since she'd been aware of his attraction to Madame Dumaine, Yvonne had done everything in her power to promote as little social contact as possible between the two.

In a snobbish, haughty manner, Yvonne inquired of Madame Charlotte, "Well, who is Madame Dumaine's new little waif?"

While Charlotte gladly welcomed the Dubose money which flowed generously to her shop, this girl irritated her at times. Yvonne never let anyone forget just who she was and the power she commanded.

"Waif, *mademoiselle?*" Madame Charlotte played dumb, restraining her hand from jabbing a long pin into the flesh of Yvonne's curved hips. Acid-tongued little bitch, she thought to herself.

"Yes, the girl with Madame Dumaine!" There was an edge of irritation to Yvonne's tone.

"Oh, Mademoiselle Fourney, you mean? Utterly breathtaking, isn't she? She is Madame Dumaine's new secretary-companion I understand. Charming young lady!"

"Another niece she's brought in from the countryside?" Yvonne fidgeted. Something about that girl ignited her instant dislike.

"No, Mademoiselle Dubose, no relative at all."

Yvonne's pert nose rose contemptuously. "Well, beautiful clothes can make any woman attractive, even white trash."

Under her breath, Charlotte Bourget said many things to the haughty young girl standing there. Aloud, she purred softly, "Beautiful clothes can never make a lady though."

"You are absolutely right, Madame Charlotte!" Yvonne smugly agreed, assuming the seamstress agreed with her, although that was hardly Charlotte's meaning.

"Lovely clothing and beautiful ladies are my life, *mademoiselle*, so I can always spot them for what they are." If she was any judge of either, Charlotte knew Fancy Fourney was pretty of face and figure as well as lovely in heart. That was the most exquisite beauty of all.

That kind of beauty would never belong to Yvonne Dubose despite her family's money and powerful name.

A couple of rainy days dampened Natchez after their visit to the dress shop. Alita remained inside but the time passed swiftly with Fancy for company. The girl was bright and clever. Chris and Chad's tutor had done a magnificent job of teaching her and she had obviously been a quick learner. More important to Madame Dumaine, her decision had been a sound one. Fancy was proving to be a rare jewel in many little ways. Time spent around the young girl was a pleasure.

In the evening after dinner they often played games and sipped sherry. Sometimes they talked and laughed like two schoolgirls. It was obvious to Dahlia and the other servants that Fancy was the best medicine for their mistress's lonely life now that her beloved husband was dead.

Dahlia knew of Monsieur Dubose's interest in Alita, and she would swear he'd believe her mistress looked ten years younger the next time he came to call. The truth was she did! If those two someday got together, they would have Dahlia's approval. The owner of Magnolia struck the octoroon maidservant as a very nice man and that was more than she could say for most gentlemen.

Young as she was, Dahlia had had her share of men—black and white—but she knew some man would soon be taking a shine to Miss Fancy.

Alita was realistic enough to face the fact that she would not keep Fancy too long. After all, she remembered all too vividly her nephew's venomous outburst when he'd learned she was taking Fancy from Willow Bend — and him. Fancy's rare beauty would stir the deepest emotions in men. Alita would be foolish to think otherwise. Although, she found herself adoring the young girl more and more each day, she knew their companionship would not last. For a brief moment, she would have the "daughter" she and Henri had never had. Sadly, she accepted the reality that nothing remained the same.

Since summer would soon be fading into autumn and she hadn't been there for many weeks, Alita decided that it might be nice to spend the weekend at Dubonnet. Fancy would enjoy the woods surrounding the property. The girl had told her about the strolls she and Raoul had taken in the woods. She had mentioned that she loved the creatures living there and the wildflowers. Why she could even go horseback riding if she wished.

Later when Fancy joined Alita on the small terrace she listened to her plans with delight. Dubonnet sounded like an enchanting place.

"Good, it's settled then. I think we shall take Claudine, too. Dahlia goes, of course, for I would not be allowed out the door otherwise," Alita laughed lightheartedly.

She was joking, Fancy realized, however, she did not doubt the deep devotion between the two — mistress and servant.

Claudine appeared in the doorway. "You have a

guest, ma'am. Shall I show him out here? A Mister Nicholas Dubose."

Alita slowly set her cup of coffee down, wondering to which branch of the well-known family he belonged and why he should be calling upon her. He was not one of André's immediate family. She knew all of them and had for years.

"Yes, Claudine. Show him out here and bring another cup." Curious, Alita played with her coffee cup.

Claudine had barely walked away before the imposing tall figure of Nicholas graced the doorway. Fancy gasped, realizing who he was. A twinkle sparked in his eyes as he darted a glance her way before turning his full attention to Alita Dumaine. "Madame." He gave her a slight bow as he emerged onto the terrace and approached their table.

Alita motioned him to sit and introduced Fancy as her secretary. "Will you join us in a cup of coffee, Mister Dubose?" Her eyes surveyed him appreciatively. She could not help being impressed by his overpowering personality. He cut a striking figure in his cream-colored pants and deep green coat. These garments exhibited his muscular male body in a flattering way. She noticed a strong resemblance to his uncle, André.

"Yes, I'd like a cup of coffee . . . thank you. I appreciate your seeing me, and I would not have presumed on you so early in the day but for the fact that I may be returning home shortly. I live in New Orleans."

"I see. So you belong to the New Orleans branch of the Dubose family?" She offered him a steaming cup of coffee which he accepted, and they exchanged conversation about his uncle and his family.

Fancy sat quietly, finding his presence very disconcerting. She dared not lift her cup to her lips for her hand was so tremulous, and she knew her lashes were fluttering! When Madame Dumaine had introduced her and those green eyes had pierced through her, she had merely nodded. Words would have caught in her throat. She envied Alita's poise and self-assured manner. Someday she would be able to handle herself that way, she vowed.

A light breeze wafted across the terrace, and she welcomed it, feeling that her face was flushed. She wondered if he could tell how he stirred her. Dear Lord, she hoped not. But why did he make her feel so unsure of herself?

Nicholas was very much aware of her. The sweet fragrance of her nearness greeted his nose. Those jet-black curling lashes reminded him of butterflies' wings. The shape of her mouth and the softness of her lips urged him to kiss her. Honey would not taste sweeter, he'd wager. The very essence of her swept over him. How effortless it would be to lean over and touch her lips with his! God, how he'd like to taste them — savor them! Someday, my sweet Fancy, I shall, he promised himself. Someday soon!

71

Alita Dumaine called his attention back to her, and Fancy heaved a deep sigh of relief when his eyes left her. Giddy from the intoxicating effect of Nicholas Dubose, she heard their conversation as though she were in a foggy bog. He was talking about Dubonnet.

Alita's voice seemed edged with irritation. "I see. I find this interesting, Mister Dubose, in that I had assumed Mister Carew would keep my confidence. It seems you know, and another gentlemen has been privy to the fact that Dubonnet might be for sale." Her eyes flashed angrily.

Now it was Nick who was in a quandary, for he, too, had assumed Jason Carew had told no one but him. "I do not know of any other man Jason told. I know he is aware of my great love for the place, and that might have influenced him to tell me of the possibility of it being for sale. No place around here compares to Dubonnet."

Nick could not have picked more perfect words to soothe Alita's ruffled feathers and to put himself in her favor. "Why how nice of you to say that. You see, Dubonnet is very dear to me. Do you plan to make Natchez your permanent home, Mister Dubose?"

"Part of the year, especially in the spring and autumn during the racing season. You see, Madame Dumaine, I happen to share Uncle André's love for thoroughbreds." His busy eyes danced over to Fancy and gleamed unusually brightly, Alita noticed. She was immediately struck by a whim. "My secretary and I will be staying at Dubonnet this weekend. Perhaps you would like to ride over and look at the property?"

Nick was delighted to hear this encouraging news and he immediately accepted her invitation. After a few more minutes of conversation, he graciously took his leave for he intended to pay a visit to his friend, Carew. The information Madame Dumaine had revealed had not set well with him.

As quickly as his mount, Domino, could gallop there, Nick arrived at the young lawyer's office. Without waiting to be announced he burst through the office door and marched up to Carew's desk. Jason looked up from a stack of papers, startled. Nick seemed very angry.

"What the hell are you trying to pull, Carew?" he demanded to know. "You assured me I was the only one you'd told of the Dubonnet sale!"

"Hold it! You hotheaded Frenchman, what are you talking about? Tell me so I'll know why you're so damned mad, eh?"

"I've just come from Alita Dumaine's townhouse and she informed me she's been approached by someone else."

"Goddammit, that's impossible. You are the only one I've told, Nick old boy. I swear to it! Suppose we were drunker that night than we knew?" A twinkle broke out in the pleasant eyes of the lawyer.

Nick cooled down and reflected on the night they'd spent at Belle's. He couldn't swear that they weren't talking loudly. The crowd had been huge that night. That possibility could not be ruled out. He had no reason to disbelieve Jason.

"Well, I'm going out there this weekend. Madame Dumaine and her secretary are going to be there." Nick slumped down in the seat by Jason's desk.

"Secretary? Alita? She doesn't have a secretary."

"Hell she doesn't, and a sweeter-looking creature you've never laid eyes on. Young too."

"Hmmm, I didn't know that. She's new then. I spoke to her just before she left for Willow Bend and she was speaking about missing Cindy very much. Cindy was her niece and had lived with her for the last few years. A secretary? Well, well, well." Jason straightened up in his comfortable chair. His buddy, Nick seemed very impressed and he was a damned good judge of women and horses. He had whetted Jason's curiosity. Perhaps, he should plan to pay a visit to the Dumaine residence in the next day or two.

Being a man about town and one of the most sought-after bachelors in the city of Natchez, he was always intrigued when a beautiful young maiden came upon the scene. Indeed it was his pursuit of the ladies that had linked him with the randy Nicholas Dubose from New Orleans a couple of years ago.

Like Nicholas Dubose, women found him most attractive, and like Nicholas, he had managed to play the elusive bachelor. But this young lady must be something, judging by the gleam in his friend's eyes when he spoke of her. Jason was tremendously intrigued.

Tomorrow, he would see for himself!

Chapter Six

Dubonnet had to be the most beautiful place in the whole world, Fancy decided after she'd toured the spacious two-story house. The lavish opulence of the ballroom and the elegant parlor left her speechless. But there were also small rooms, so inviting and cozy that they caught Fancy's eye. She was certain Madame Dumaine and her beloved Henri had enjoyed many hours of pleasure within the walls of the study and the library. She could envision the many nights they must have curled up in the matching chairs next to the fireplace to read the books they'd selected from the many leather-bound volumes lining the shelves. Some of the dark wood shelves held pewter mugs, as well as a collection of small books bound in soft Morocco tooled in gold. Bright Turkish carpeting covered the floor bringing color to the dark paneled walls and the dark furnishings. Crossed sabers hung above the mantel.

It was just beginning to dawn on Fancy that her mistress must be very wealthy to have not one but two fine homes to live in when she chose. Yet, she wasn't pretentious, not a snob like her sister, Alicia.

Strange as it might seem, Fancy had stepped into this new world so effortlessly. It was as if she'd been used to luxury all her life. Receiving the admiring attention of two young men like Nicholas Dubose and Jason Carew during her first week in Natchez had made her realize she certainly wasn't ugly and that was exhilarating. Madame Dumaine was very aware of Fancy's effect on the gentlemen. She would teach this sweet innocent girl about the overwhelming charms of men like Jason Carew and Nicholas Dubose, she told herself. Fancy had no inkling about such things, Alita was certain.

When she arrived at Dubonnet and roamed the woods, Fancy felt a tinge of loneliness. She recalled the past and the people she'd left back in Memphis and Willow Bend. She became absorbed in her memories as she strolled about in a pair of pants and a faded shirt Madame Dubose had borrowed from her young stableboy so that Fancy might wear them to go horseback riding. Without a fancy gown on, she was carried back to her past. Madame Charlotte had been unable to complete her riding ensemble before they'd left. That mattered little to Fancy. The loose-fitting shirt allowed her to bend with ease to pluck the wild, blooming verbenas and the pretty yellow buttercups scattered over the floor of the forest amidst the wild ferns that grew out from the rocks where the ground was moist and shaded from the sun.

One particular spot was so beautiful she wanted to linger awhile, and she sat down. A huge fallen tree trunk provided a comfortable back rest. She smiled, thinking about old Raoul. He'd call this spot a fairy's circle because of its magic. Dear Raoul and his wonderful tales! She'd always adore him and the magic he'd brought to her life no matter how far apart they were. She wondered if he thought of her often. Of course he did, she told herself.

There could be no expensive perfume sweeter than the odor of jasmine that wafted to her nose, she thought, leaning her head against the bark of the tree trunk. A marvelous serenity enveloped her, and she closed her eyes to give way to the languor washing over her.

No such serenity engulfed Nicholas Dubose as he roughly disentangled himself from the grasping clutches of his cousin, Yvonne. If she'd taken notice of the green fire in his eyes and his determined "No," she would have realized the futility of her effort to make him stay at Magnolia instead of galloping off on his horse.

It mattered not to him that Daniel could overhear them. He was beyond the point of being gracious. This foolish young girl's games were ludicrous. Perhaps, she could impress someone like Claude or the young dandies of Natchez, but not her older cousin Nick.

"Remove your hands, Yvonne. I'm going," he snapped.

"Where are you off to this time?" Her own eyes flashed fury as she rubbed her wrists, now angry looking and red.

"That's none of your business, my bratty cousin," he smirked, a crooked grin on his face which Yvonne would have enjoyed slapping off. She dared not for she couldn't help being a little in awe of him. He was just rascal enough to slap her back. She had no desire to test him.

"Oh, you are rude, Nicholas and you are certainly not a gentleman."

Nicholas exploded with laughter as he sauntered down the hall. "It's good you've finally realized that, pet. Best you don't forget it."

He went to the stable and saw that the roan Claude had been using was gone. He guessed his cousin was out too. Perhaps Yvonne was already smothering him too. Uncle André had better get his young filly married before a family scandal jarred the Natchez countryside. With a family the size of theirs there were a few skeletons in closets already.

The fine jet-black thoroughbred he mounted was a gift from André Dubose who knew his appreciation for fine horses, and it was a gift that had pleased Nick more than any he'd ever received before. He'd left the horse here in Natchez for his pleasure when he visited. He knew the expert care the horses received at his uncle's stables. No one who neglected André's fine horses lasted long in his stable. He'd named the animal "Domino" because of its color and because of the many games of dominoes he and André had played together when he was just a young lad.

As he took the shortcut lane which would take him to the edge of Dubonnet, he welcomed the sweet solitude of the summer afternoon, enjoying the quiet countryside in Domino's company. Yvonne was a nuisance.

He reined the horse over to the edge of the lane and cut across a field, heading into the woods that would bring him out by the grounds of Dubonnet. Those woods extended from Dubose land into the Dumaine property. Here his Uncle André had introduced him to hunting squirrel and rabbit at the age of fifteen in this flourishing forest of oak trees. He paced Domino to a slow walk, weaving in and around the trees.

His cousin Claude had ridden his roan mare up this way about twenty minutes before him. Like Nick, he'd found the woods so pleasant he'd dismounted and led the roan along. But he'd not anticipated just how pleasant a sight the woods would provide until he'd come to a clearing and spotted a vision of loveliness leaning against an old log, asleep. Under his breath, he gasped. Surely it was his lucky day to have stumbled on the beautiful girl he'd wanted so much to meet on the paddlewheeler several days ago.

Even though her fine traveling outfit had been replaced by an old faded blue shirt and baggy pants, Claude was not mistaken about that lovely face and hair. A more enchanting little creature he'd never seen.

Branches broke under the pressure of his high, polished black boots. The sounds awakened Fancy.

Claude greeted her. "Hello, my pretty one. Please, don't be frightened". Then, hoping to soothe away the startled look on her face, he hastily told her who he was and mentioned that his uncle's property, Magnolia, adjoined Dubonnet. From most people the name of Magnolia won instant respect.

What big doelike dark eyes she has, Claude thought as he sauntered over to where she sat, still saying nothing to him. Seeing that he seemed like a clean-cut young gentleman, she finally remarked, "I'm . . . I'm visiting at Dubonnet."

"And your name, pretty one?" He sat beside her, closer than he should have Fancy decided.

"Fancy Fourney." She felt his arm swing up onto the fallen tree trunk to brush her shoulder. His other hand went to the hand in which she held the cluster of wildflowers she'd picked. He smiled most charmingly at her. "Pretty. Almost as pretty as you."

She gave him a nervous smile. "I . . . I love

them." Everything about her naïve innocence and untarnished beauty fired Claude, and he could not control his wild desires.

When his hands covered hers and she turned to look at him, he muttered huskily, "You are the most beautiful thing I've ever laid eyes on, Fancy Fourney." Before she could think or act, Claude's muscular arms pulled her roughly against his chest, and his lips pressed against hers, preventing her from uttering a sound. But she could squirm and she moan her protest while her lips remained clenched and unrelenting.

She fought like a wildcat so Claude released her just enough to plead his case. "Just a little kiss, sweetheart. Just one little kiss." He didn't give her time to answer before once again capturing her lips, but in the frenzy of his desire to kiss her again, he'd forgotten her free hand. Fancy clenched her small fist and swung it with all her might against the side of his face.

The shock of the blow took Claude by surprise and he broke from her suddenly, only to be stunned by the sound of deep laughter coming from the edge of the clearing. He turned to see his cousin's smirking face devouring him.

Before he could rise, Claude was staring up into the eyes of his older cousin who had a menacing look on his tanned face. Fancy still sat in the same spot, unaware that a couple of buttons had been popped off her faded blue shirt in the scuffle.

The bewitching sight of Fancy's exposed cleavage caught Nick's attention and held him spell-bound, causing his fury at Claude to subside somewhat. His blood boiled and he swelled with desire for her.

However, when Nick again turned his angry eyes on Claude, there was no question of the fury there. Nick extended his hand to Fancy and said, "I assume you got the lady's message." Claude remained silent, not daring to say anything that might rile Nick.

Nick's nimble fingers closed the flap of Fancy's faded shirt. "You're exposed, *mademoiselle*, and that's cruel punishment for any man!" A crooked smile was on his face.

Fancy stood, flushing with embarrassment. His fingers had brushed her flesh, causing strange sensations to shoot through her body. His strong hand held hers and he took control as though he owned her. "I'll escort you back to Dubonnet, little one, and as for you, Claude—I'll see you back at Magnolia later."

Nicholas's face was stern and solemn as though he were making a vow, and Claude had no doubt that this was not the end of this little fiasco. Actually, he and Yvonne both believed that the name of Dubose allowed them unrestrained liberties. This belief combined with his immature thinking had ignited the explosive situation in Memphis. Nicholas had warned him to behave in Natchez. But, trouble followed him, it seemed.

Fancy felt herself hoisted up on Nick's fine steed.

It had been done so easily she might have been a feather. Then Nick leaped up to sit behind her, his muscled arm touching her sides as he held the reins. She could feel his overpowering presence, so strong and masterful. She could not help thinking that if he had been the one trying to kiss and hug her, there would have been no getting away from him.

He always seemed to find her in a predicament, and she suddenly resented that. Who'd asked for his help anyway? Did he think she was a child? He seemed to think it was all right for him to devour her with his lusty eyes. Lord, if eyes could undress a person, his had surely done that! The sensation of being nude before him was so real.

As the huge horse trotted along the trail through the trees, Fancy could have sworn Nicholas's lips were almost brushing against her cheek. Darn him, he made her nervous! She broke the silence between them. "I . . . I didn't need your help back there, you know." Her unsure voice belied her words.

"It looked as though you did to me, *mademoiselle*," Nick said, a grin coming to his face as he tried to keep from breaking into a laugh. She lifted her pretty head arrogantly and her chin rose. She tossed her long hair to the side. It swept across his face and smelled as fresh as the wildflowers she clutched tightly in her dainty hand. Throughout the entire struggle with his cousin Claude she had held the flowers. What a divine little marvel she was! He could not restrain the amused laughter that broke through when he thought of that.

"And what is so funny?" she asked insistently, turning so sharply to face him that her soft lips almost touched his. He kissed the tip of her pert, turned-up nose instead of her rosebud lips and told her, "You, little Fancy! You still have your flowers."

Looking down at her hand, she broke into laughter too, and glanced back up at him. His face was so breathtakingly handsome when he laughed like that. Her mood had suddenly become so light-hearted and gay that she made no protest when his arms tightened around her waist. The truth was she liked the pleasant coziness of his arms around her as they rode toward Dubonnet. She was completely innocent of the hellish torment her proximity was stirring in Nicholas.

Damned, if he didn't want the fetching little vixen as eagerly and lustily as Claude had. His self-righteous act moments earlier had been a purely selfish one.

Had Domino not been carrying them out of the secluded wooded area and into the clearing where Dubonnet sat, he doubted just how noble he would be in another few minutes.

Desire was mounting and his willpower was crumbling.

Chapter Seven

She watched the striking young couple as they rode up the driveway through the manicured grounds of Dubonnet. She watched the radiant look on Fancy's face and noted that Nicholas Dubose appeared to be completely captivated by the girl's charms. What a magnificent pair they made, she thought!

Alita mumbled, as she did often when she was alone and in need of her dear Henri's counsel, "Could it be, Henri? Could it just be?" As she continued to watch them she decided it was very possible that the sophisticated, dashing Nicholas might find such an unworldly, unpampered girl like Fancy a delight — especially since she was so lovely.

When they entered her sitting room, Madame Dumaine's mind was churning with all kinds of ideas. "Mister Dubose, so nice to see you again." She turned to Fancy and smiled, "And you, dear, look so glowing after your stroll in the woods. Nothing like the clean, fresh country air, eh, Mister Dubose?"

"Nothing like it at all!" he readily agreed. His eyes darted over to Fancy who was holding the front of her blouse. When she made an excuse to leave, he knew why.

As she dashed off like a gazelle, Madame Dumaine called after her to join them later when she'd changed out of the pants. Alita could understand Fancy's embarrassment at being caught in such drab attire by this handsome young man. However, it was obvious that her attire had not dampened his ardor or interest. To Nicholas, she remarked, "A dear girl and extremely smart, too." Nicholas took a seat as she urged him to do, quite relieved that Madame Dumaine had not noticed Fancy's shirt and gotten the wrong impression. Alita sighed as she sat down, "She's a gem!"

"I'm sure she's priceless," he replied, privately musing on the possibility that Fancy could bring a world of joy to his life. The truth was Nicholas had decided as they'd ridden Domino out of the woods that Fancy would be his.

For a brief spell he and Madame Dumaine indulged in casual conversation and then Alita brought up the subject of Dubonnet. "So you like Dubonnet, Mister Dubose?"

"I do — always have. I'm prepared to make you a generous offer, Madame Dumaine." Now he turned into a serious businessman. Yet, his brand of charm affected men as well as women.

"May I be frank, Mister Dubose?"

"Please do, and please just call me Nicholas or Nick?"

Alita laughed softly. "All right, Nick. Dubonnet is very special to me so the money is not the major consideration in my decision about who becomes the new owner. So indulge an old lady's whim and tell me something about yourself. You see, I know your uncle very well but that tells me nothing about you."

Nick liked this candid, very direct lady and he sought to tease her a little. He appreciated her way of thinking and understood her feeling of sentiment about the estate which held cherished memories for her. There had been enduring love in this house and he felt it.

A boyish gleam of mischief was in his eyes as he inquired of her, "Just how far back shall I start?" His remark elicited a chuckle from Alita who found him delightfully interesting and charming. She parried in return. "I'll leave that up to you, Nick."

He told her of his earliest boyhood memories, of visiting his uncle at Magnolia, and he confessed his love of race horses surpassed his interest in his father's shipping business or the import-export trade. He told her about his vast travels with his parents on the Continent. Before he realized it, he'd even spoken of Angelique Rocheleau whom he considered his "second mother" due to the fact that his own had accompanied his father when he traveled. When his two sisters had come along he had become, in a sense, their guardian and substitute parent.

The other Dubose interests in banking and lumber did not interest him at all, he confessed. "I smother in an office or beneath mountains of paperwork. I'm a restless breed of man, I guess. I like my days to be different, not molded by the same regular routine."

"Amen to that!" Alita rose from the settee. "Join me in something to drink, Nick? My Henri had a special brandy which he thought superb. May I serve you some?" She found herself liking this handsome young man more and more.

Nick gave her a winning smile and accepted her offer. "Madame, you are a lady after my heart. Nothing compares to good brandy."

"Then you and Henri would have gotten along splendidly. Those were his sentiments about liquor." She served them and they sipped the brandy. Alita set her glass down for a moment and gave way to an impulse. "Would you like me to have my secretary accompany you while you look over the estate? I fear my days on horseback are at an end. I could accompany you in the carriage though."

Nick was feeling exhilarated. Why else would she suggest that he look over the land? She was a wily one, though, and he dare not make her suddenly change her opinion of him. He knew he had her on his side at this moment. "Would that not put you out, ma'am? The heat of the day is here now."

Alita measured him carefully. She reacted as though that realization had come to her like a bolt of lightning. "How thoughtful of you, Nick. Besides the morning hours would be far more comfortable. If it will fit into your schedule, shall we say ten in the morning and then we can return here for lunch?"

Nick rose and took her hand. "It will be my pleasure. I shall be here at ten in the morning, ma'am." He was soaring. She had to be considering him favorably since she'd offered to show him the property. He'd accomplish no more here today, so he knew it was time to take his leave.

After he departed, Alita was more than pleased with herself. Her matchmaking with Cindy had not been so successful, but then Nicholas Dubose would not have been impressed by her niece.

She had no intentions of accompanying the two young people. A drastic headache would be plaguing her, she decided, a gleam of mischief in her eyes. She'd point out to them the perfect spot for a picnic down by the pond where the little ducks swam. The abundant shade of the weeping willows would shelter them from the summer sun. Yes, that was what she would do, and she'd have Claudine pack a delicious picnic basket. She sank into one of the floral-covered chairs, and there was a soft, serene look on her face for she was recalling the sweetest of memories. She'd reached the lofty heights of rapture with Henri. Neither time nor age had dimmed her ardor. She almost envied the young girl who was just getting ready to emerge.

A simple, sprigged muslin with short puffed sleeves was the frock Fancy chose for the carriage ride around Dubonnet, and she felt the leghorn straw, wide-brimmed hat that was trimmed with a rich green velvet band would certainly be in order for the open carriage.

Dahlia had combed her hair, leaving it loose. She'd pulled the sides back and up, but tiny wisps seemed determined to curl around the girl's face. They created a most flattering effect, Dahlia thought. She was a pretty little thing and the green velvet lacings of the narrow ribbon up the front of her bodice seemed to cinch in her waistline making her waist look even smaller.

With Dahlia's nod of approval and a dab of cologne behind her ear, Fancy bounced spritely out of the room and down the stairs as the grandfather clock was chiming ten.

Halfway down she stopped abruptly as she saw Nicholas Dubose being ushered down the hallway. He was dressed quite casually and was coatless. His white shirt was open at the neck and he wore deep brown pants and highly polished brown boots. The heels of the boots made a sharp clicking sound as he strode down the hall. Suddenly he stopped when he saw Fancy perched on the stairs looking down on him. She looked like a girl about to go on a picnic.

"Good morning," he drawled, a slow easy smile creasing his face, and his eyes moved over the simple lines of her gown.

"Good morning, Mister Dubose," she replied, moving down the steps. He noted the way she swayed from side to side coming down the steps, and he found her movements disturbingly sensual. Yet, her motion was natural, as were most things about Fancy Fourney, he was beginning to think. He could not imagine her putting on the false airs of his cousin Yvonne or his sister Denise.

The straw hat in her hand held his eyes and he was overwhelmed by a sensation of déjà vu, remembering a darling black-eyed child rushing into his arms to rescue her straw hat. By some strange quirk of fate could Fancy have been that child? Could four years make such drastic changes?

He had to will himself out of the maze he'd wandered through for a moment. "Hope I'm not late but things around Magnolia got out of hand for a while." His thoughts were still on that lovely child of the past.

"That's a lovely name," Fancy remarked as they walked side by side to join Alita on the veranda.

"It would please my Uncle André to hear you say that. The grounds have so many big magnolia trees I guess that was what inspired him to call it Magnolia."

"I love those huge white blossoms."

"I rather got the idea you liked flowers," he teased her, recalling how she'd clutched the wildflowers throughout her struggle with Claude.

She gave him a smile that made him yearn to take her into his arms and kiss her on those soft lips. Instead, he said, "Perhaps, you should have been called Fleur. However, Fancy seems right somehow." He noticed she looked rather stunned for a moment before she began to speak. "My mother's name *was* Fleur!"

"French?"

"Yes and so very, very pretty," Fancy sighed, a look of sadness coming to her face.

"Ah, I already knew that," he said giving her a sly smile.

Cocking her head to the side and arching her dark brown eyebrows, she asked, "Now how did you know that?"

"Why just looking at you, my pretty one."

Through the open door of the sitting room Alita was privy to their conversation. Oh, yes, Nicholas Dubose was taken with her young companion. Now, she had no doubt of that. So when they joined her she played her little game, dismissing them, with the wicker basket, for their picnic.

The one-horse buggy rolled down the lane running adjacent to the main road that passed the Dumaine estate. The day was bright with sunshine but the air was still pleasant and mild. The row of cottonwood trees broke up the rays of the sun as they drove along the edge of the fields filled with some of the hands.

As they gaily talked, Nicholas found the girl an amazing conversationalist for one so young and unworldly. He was also impressed by the fact that she seemed interested in what he was saying. Indeed, she was a rare exception, unlike the addle-brained females he'd encountered at the fancy soireés and balls in Natchez and New Orleans.

He was amazed when he realized how freely he was talking to this strange, enchanting girl he'd just met. It was not his nature to be so open. Usually he was close-mouthed about his plans for the future or his dreams. Fancy Fourney had a strange effect on him.

In an excited voice she called for his attention, "Look, Nick! Over there! Oh, how beautiful!" She pointed to the pond Alita had told them about. A couple of ducks swam in the water and weeping willows dotted the edge.

His eyes were on her instead of the pond as he declared, "Glorious! Absolutely divine!" He could not help being affected by her exuberance.

He halted the buggy at a spot close to the willows and leaped down to rush around it and help Fancy down. Her petite body lightly brushing against the front of his, tantalized him, and his strong arms clasped her tightly against him while his lips sought the sweet nectar of hers. He forced himself to be gentle for he knew instinctively that she was innocent. Ah, he'd teach her to kiss — and many other things too, he thought, letting his lips linger on the softness of hers.

Fancy had been taken completely by surprise when his muscled arms had tightened like a vise around her waist and his head had bent down to her face. With one hand he'd cradled her head as if to guide it so he might place his lips on hers. She'd yielded to his masterful handling, and the sensations his sensuous lips stirred in her made her respond with an eagerness she'd never known before. She wanted him to continue to hold her close to his broad chest. It was a strange wonderful feeling.

When he did finally release her she found herself breathless and weak. Her hands came down to rest on his chest and she realized they'd encircled his neck. He said nothing but his eyes moved over each feature of her upturned face.

"Why . . . why did you do that, Nick?" she stammered questioning the strange, solemn look on his face.

"Because I thought I'd die if I didn't," he confessed. "God, since the moment I first laid eyes on you I've wanted to."

His eyes looked at her reflecting the heat of his passion. While she'd never known a man's passion she knew what she saw in his eyes. Could he see the fright in hers, she wondered? Could he feel the trembling of her body pressed so close to his? Surely he could for her legs were so weak she felt as if they were going right out from under her.

Staring up at his handsome face during that moment of silence, she realized that he towered over her and that she'd have to rise on tiptoe to plant a kiss on his tanned cheek. Secretly, she yearned to do just that. As if he could read her thoughts, he bent his head to allow their lips to meet. It was a long, lingering kiss. When his tongue prodded her lips for entry she resisted a bit until the pleasing effect overpowered her.

At the same time his sensuous mouth was searing her lips, one of his hands created other exciting sensations as it cupped her pulsing breast and fondled a hardened tip. The tantalizing effect made her moan softly. The overwhelming strangeness of what was happening to her provoked a weak protest, but Nick gentled her almost as he would have done with one of the highstrung thoroughbreds over at Magnolia. "No, no, darling! Let me love you."

"But, Nick . . ." she tried to protest.

"I won't hurt you, Fancy. Trust me, little one. I'll teach you," he pleaded huskily. "God, I want you so much, Fancy. You feel this thing between us. I know it!"

He knew she wanted him too and he was almost at the point where no amount of resistance would stop him. But he was also aware of her fear and tried to control the frenzy of his passion. God, he didn't want to scare her.

With a sudden move that took him by surprise she broke from his strong arms and stood away from him, panting as though she'd been running fast. "I'm . . . I'm not that kind of girl, Nick! You shouldn't have taken so many liberties!" She turned her back to him so she wouldn't have to look into those eyes of his.

"I was making love to you, Fancy. I was kissing you because you have the most kissable lips I've ever kissed and now that I've tasted the honey there I want more," he told her in a deep, serious tone. She didn't have to see his face to know the determination etched there.

"Please, Nick, you . . . you make me so nervous," she admitted candidly. Her remark brought a smile to his face and he thought to himself, I know, little Fancy, and I know why. Aloud, he soothed her, "This time it will be your way. Next time I may not be such a noble gentleman." He picked up the wicker basket and started to walk to the spot where they would enjoy their picnic. Fancy stood, frozen to the spot pondering what he'd just said.

"Well, am I going to eat all of this by myself?" Nick called back to her, a grin on his face. She could not resist his teasing grin, so she scampered down the knoll to catch up, her curls bobbing up and down her shoulders. Again Nick thought she looked like that lovely child he'd caught in his arms that day back in Memphis.

Once the white cloth was spread on the ground and the aroma of the fresh-baked meat pies Claudine had prepared came to Nick's nose he was more than ready to eat. There were a couple of apples, a clump of cheese, and a bottle of wine. Like a connoisseur, he took the bottle of white wine out and sampled it. "Very good! Madame Dumaine has good taste."

"And Claudine bakes the best meat pies!" Fancy chimed in.

They ate with relish. Finally having satisfied his hunger, Nick lay back on the ground. The smile on his face was due to intoxication caused by happiness rather than wine. Fancy sat beside him, her arms clasped around her knees, and they talked idly of this and that. Now she did not feel ill at ease about being so near him. It was a glorious day.

Suddenly a fly lit on the tip of her pert little nose. When her eyes crossed, he exploded with laughter.

Rising, he pulled her playfully into his arms and chuckled, "You're bewitching even cross-eyed!" She joined him in laughter. She couldn't remember having had such an enchanting day in her whole life.

With his arms around her and their bodies touching, their laughter subsided. Fancy looked up to search his face. Was he, too, feeling the funny, tingling sensation that ran through her like liquid fire?

He was, indeed, feeling a hellish torment which he had not meant to inflict upon himself, and now he had a devilish ache in his groin. He burned for her with an agonizing yearning.

Her cheek rested against him and the sweet fragrance of her hair tickled his nose. His arms felt the exciting curves of her young body burning into his, and when she moved back just enough to look at him with those dark eyes and her lips were only a couple of inches from his, he was lost.

"Kiss me, Nick," she whispered softly. "I want you to kiss me." She was serious, not playing a parlor game.

Dear God, she could not know what she was asking!

"Oh, my sweet innocent Fancy," he murmured huskily and let his lips meet with hers. As his lips took her, he swore he'd never make her regret asking for that kiss. He was only a mortal man and he knew this could not end with just a kiss. He was not that much of a gentleman.

He found her willing to let his lips linger and his hands touch. Their ecstasy mounted as he sensed the fire he stirred in her. His hands moved to cup her firm rounded hips and to press them closer against him as his mouth moved to her throat. When his long slender fingers effortlessly freed first one satiny breast and then the other, his touch brought a soft moan from Fancy and she called out his name.

"Want you, little one! Dear God, I want you." His lips and tongue caressed a rosy tip slowly and sensuously. She arched and undulated instinctively, almost as if she'd known love before. Yet, Nick knew she had not. He could not take the act of deflowering her lightly as he had with others, but he couldn't stop himself now!

His hand found her velvet moisture. "I am the

first, aren't I, Fancy? You trust me, don't you?"

She nodded.

"Please do. I'll be gentle, darling," he said, pausing to remove his pants with frantic yanks, not wanting anything to calm the torrid storm of their passions. He moved between her silken thighs and kissed her until her flushed body swayed and pleaded to be taken. He used his lips and hands to arouse a savage yearning in her and then he thrust himself into her, his lips muffling the sudden gasp she emitted. Then he moved with slow, gentle strokes to allow her to accustom herself to his male body.

The second she was feeling pleasure once again, he sensed it and his rhythm began to mount. Fancy found herself being carried along with him. Higher and higher they seemed to soar until finally she felt Nick's muscled body give a mighty shudder and collapse on her. They lay exhausted, encased in one another's arms, and Nick gave her lazy, light kisses on her moist cheek.

His deep voice was weak but warm with love when he whispered in her ear, "My sweet, sweet Fancy!" Fancy smiled, filled with the essence of this man and the strange feeling of rapture she still didn't completely understand. She was content to lie in Nick's arms for he was not ready to release her. The feel of him against her was good.

It took a sudden shower to break in on their lovers' paradise. For a moment they let the raindrops pelt their flushed nude bodies and then, laughing like two children, they scampered to gather up their discarded clothing and get dressed. Slamming their picnic gear in the basket, they ran to the carriage. With one arm Nick encircled her waist while on the other he carried the basket.

As Nick flicked the horse with the reins, he told Fancy, "I wish this day never had to end. Tell me you feel the same, Fancy."

One of his hands held hers tightly. "I do feel that way, Nick. It was the most wonderful day of my life."

His eyes sparkled a brilliant green, and a crooked smile brought out the deep dimple in his cheek. "Why, by God, you really mean it, don't you little one?"

"Of course! I wouldn't say it if I didn't," she told him.

Recalling Alita's comment that Fancy was a rare gem, he pulled her closer to him and planted a light kiss on her damp cheek. "You are a rare, exquisite jewel, Fancy Fourney and I worship you. Do you know that?"

She laughed lightly. "I do now, Nick."

Neither minded that the rain fell on them.

Neither noticed the rider across the way on the other side of the pond in the grove of trees.

Chapter Eight

Across the way astride a fine dappled gray thoroughbred, Yvonne Dubose sat stiff and irate, jealous fury blazing within her. For the last few minutes she'd watched the intimate little scene over by the pond. The most exquisite emerald gem never flashed with brighter fire than her eyes did as she watched Nick's magnificent male body and envied the girl beneath it. God, she hated her for enjoying pleasure she, Yvonne, should be enjoying.

Only a heavy shower of rain drove her to touch the quirt to her horse's rump. Her touch was sharp and harsh, giving vent to her anger.

Any young dude in Adams County would be delighted to share her bed. All she'd ever had to do was crook her little finger, bat an eyelash, or sway a curvy hip to have the young gentlemen panting for her. Claude had cornered her and sought to exploit his male virility within the first twenty-four hours of his arrival at Magnolia.

Yvonne could not believe Nick was so principled he'd deny himself just because she was his first cousin. Dear Lord, first cousins married all the time!

She'd heard enough to know he was a hot-blooded man so why did he always treat her with that cool aloofness? Yet, he often called her "my pet" or used other little terms of endearment, and he could be very gallant and charming. At times, his expert eyes had ogled her sensuous curves.

As she rode toward Magnolia her teardrops mingled with the raindrops. She'd show him, she vowed. Oh, how she'd show him before she was through! That little white-trash bitch would pay the price for her folly as well. How could he possibly desire her more?

The sky seemed to explode over them, and the buggy provided no covering as they rolled down the lane. It was as dark as night, a deluge of rain coming down around them. Within five minutes both of them were drenched, and the wheels of the buggy were splashing muddy water from the ruts of the dirt road.

"Damn! I'm going to take cover here, Fancy. It's an old shed but it beats the hell out of this."

He guided the bay into a path off the lane. Fancy hunched over, not caring where they were headed as long as their destination was dry.

Nick pulled the buggy as close to the shed as he

could, and then they made a dash for the rickety half-open door. Except for an old wooden bench there was nothing else in the shed, but it was a place where they could sit and huddle together. Nick's arm snaked around her to give her his warming body heat. Fancy allowed him to hold her, but Nick was aware of her quiet mood. He wondered if she was having regrets about their intimacy and his usual self-assured armor was dented by frustration. He let his lips brush the side of her damp cheek.

"I adore you, little one. I want you to believe that." He wanted to assure her, to erase any doubts she might have.

Her black eyes turned to him, so trusting and so innocent Nick felt like a cur. Had he heartlessly taken advantage of her naïveté? Her beautiful eyes staring so openly at him made him feel so damned guilty. This was something no woman had ever done before.

"I do believe you, Nick. Had I not, I would never let you have your way with me." She spoke simply and honestly. Her words hurt him.

"And you don't regret what . . . what we did?" The sophisticated Nicholas Dubose found himself stammering.

"I don't regret anything, Nick." She offered him her lips, and he took them as though they were a treasure. Holding her and kissing her, he knew she had cast a spell on him. Sitting there snuggled up together, he swelled with longing for her again but he would not take her in a filthy place like this. He could not explain that even to himself, but it revealed the depth of his feeling for this sweet enchantress who'd stolen his reckless heart. This was a strange new feeling for Nicholas Dubose.

The heavens seemed to abet his decision to be gallant; the rains ceased. He looked out the door to see just a few light drops coming down. "I think we could be on our way now. Shall we try it?"

Fancy got up, swished her wet skirt and gave him a nod. The disgruntled look on her face was caused by the miserable feeling of wet clinging clothes, and he knew just how she was feeling for he shared the same discomfort.

"Come on, my little drenched kitten, and I will get you home," he said, extending his hand to her. She reminded him at that moment of his mother's white fluff-ball kitten when it had been drenched by a heavy downpour back in New Orleans. The appealing creature had finally come inside to shake each paw in utter disgust and dismay at being so wet.

As they rolled down the lane toward Dubonnet, Nick realized he had actually seen little of the estate. However, Madame Dumaine need not know that.

Some hours later as Nick rode back to Magnolia the dark skies were lit up by millions of stars and a bright moon shone down upon him and Domino. His mood was light and gay. He had not known such a feeling of well-being for a long, long time.

After Fancy and he had returned, Madame Dumaine had insisted that he remove his wet clothes and use one of Henri's robes while his own clothes dried. While Nick's trim hips fit into Henri's pants, his broad chest could not begin to fit into Henri's fine linen shirts. So wearing Henri's pants and robe, he'd enjoyed some warming brandy and later joined the ladies for dinner.

It was past ten when he left the company of Alita Dumaine and Fancy. The only difficulty he'd faced that evening arose from being close to the beautiful Fancy but not able to put his hands on her. In the glowing candlelight as they'd dined, she was a vision to behold. Wisps of hair curled around her face due to the soaking it had taken earlier. She looked breathtakingly lovely, he thought.

Her cream-colored gown made her appear to be nude as she sat across from him. It molded itself to the perfection of her body. He knew those curves now and they fired him with flames of desire.

He could have sworn that the all-knowing, perceptive Madame Dumaine could read his thoughts when he saw her looking at him a couple of times during the meal.

Once when he and Fancy had exchanged smiles that spoke of their newfound intimacy, he had found himself feeling self-conscious and a bit guilty. His practical business sense cautioned him that Madame Dumaine could sour quickly on him if she thought he was just dallying with her secretary.

Crazy as it might seem to anyone who knew of his past and of his many conquests, the deflowering of Fancy was not just another conquest. When he'd left Dubonnet and was cantering toward Magnolia, he thought about that very thing. God, he'd never wanted to conquer any woman as he had Fancy, but something would not allow him to consider her in such a frivolous way.

Perhaps, it was the way her big black eyes looked so trustingly at him. Maybe, it was that she gave her sweet yielding body to him so willingly — the most precious gift of all. Once taken, he could not give back her virginal innocence.

He arrived at Magnolia as enthralled as he'd been when as a much younger man he'd possessed his first lady love. The worldly, experienced Nicholas had never expected to capture that feeling again.

Like a thief in the night, he crept through the dark downstairs rooms of his uncle's house, making his way to the sprial stairway. Slowly, he mounted the steps and moved across the carpeted hallway toward his room at the end of the long upstairs hallway. No light was showing under the doors of the rooms occupied by Daniel, Yvonne, or Claude.

He entered his room, closing the door quietly. Moonlight guided him to the overstuffed chair, and he sat down to take off his boots. It had been such a gratifying day in all ways that he felt pleasantly weary and ready to stretch out his long body on the comfortable bed across the room and sleep. He felt assured that Dubonnet would be his — and Fancy Fourney too.

Flinging aside his shirt and stepping out of his pants, he moved over to the big bed. But he'd no sooner collapsed, naked, on the cool sheets than he lunged forward to sit up straight in bed. "Good goddamn! Wha . . . what the hell?" He flung aside the coverlet to see who occupied the other side of his bed.

Yvonne's naked body stretched lazily, and she stared up at him with sleepy, rather dazed-looking eyes. " 'Bout time you got here," she drawled.

Restraining an urge to shout at her, Nick hissed through clenched teeth, "What in the devil are you trying to pull, Yvonne?"

She flung a hip across the sheet and raised her arms up above her fanned-out auburn hair. Her full voluptuous breasts exhibited themselves for Nick's appraisal. She arched her back so that her breasts invited Nick to take them between his lips. She also raised her hips, wanting him to straddle them and thrust his manhood into her. This invitation was more than a man could resist. Had Nick not still felt the flush of his rapturous love-making with Fancy, the temptation would have been too much for him.

When he bent down to take hold of her bare shoulders, he smelled the liquor on her breath. Yvonne thought he was bending down to kiss her and already her lips were parting to take his. Instead, she was hoisted up and out of the bed and placed firmly on the floor. Nick's towering figure stood over her. She watched stunned as he hastily picked up his robe from the foot of the bed. Quickly he put it on and tied the fringed belt.

A menacing look was on his face as he turned to her. "Don't play the tramp, Yvonne. Uncle André doesn't deserve that and I won't defile his house!"

His words stabbed her and hurt painfully. In turn she wanted desperately to hurt him. She stood before him, not caring that her naked body was gloriously displayed in the light of the moon. Tossing her thick mane of auburn hair to the side and clasping her hands, she taunted, "But you don't mind defiling the Dumaine house, do you Nicholas? And of all things with cheap white trash!" She dashed out the door so he would not see the mist forming in her eyes.

He was so stunned that he froze in his tracks. It was probably a good thing, he realized, for he would have struck her otherwise. Knowing what a vindictive little bitch she could be, it didn't set well with him that she had obviously witnessed him with Fancy by the pond this afternoon. For himself, it didn't matter. For Fancy's sake, he did care.

As the fiery Yvonne slammed out of Nick's room and stomped down the hallway, Claude peeked through the door of his room. The noise had whetted his curiosity, and in investigating it he'd seen her exit from their cousin's room.

His mouth turned up at one corner in a smirking smile, although he was neither shocked nor surprised. His cousin, Yvonne had an insatiable sexual appetite. She should have been born a male, Claude mused.

Obviously, he had to conclude that Nicholas had not accommodated her as she'd expected. Claude found that amusing. Yvonne could be wearing on a man. After Claude crawled back to bed, he broke into a gale of laughter.

Nicholas locked his door to insure his privacy for the rest of the night and then went to bed. His sleep was deep and full of pleasant dreams of the black-eyed girl at Dubonnet. Yvonne had been quickly dismissed from his thoughts.

Thoughts of the same black-eyed girl made sleep impossible for Yvonne Dubose and she paced her boudoir floor like a predatory panther. Her green eyes flashed fiercely. She swore to find some way to seek revenge against Madame Dumaine's new companion, Fancy Fourney, who slept peacefully, unaware of the furious hatred for her brewing miles away at the neighboring plantation, Magnolia. Fancy had never harbored such a hatred in her heart. Such pain and agony had been spared her. Nor did she have any knowledge of the torment of jealousy. For only today had she first sipped the ambrosia of passion and sensual desire. The taste was sweet and heady!

Chapter Nine

Nicholas greeted André's return to Magnolia
with the utmost delight, hoping the promiscuous
Yvonne would behave herself now that her father
had returned. Her antics were more than Nick
cared to tolerate and his patience was at an end.
Kin or not, Yvonne was a little tramp with the
morals of an alley cat.

Although he'd heard that André was considered
the black sheep of the Dubose family, he'd never
found his uncle to be such a rascal. If his uncle had
taken a mistress since his wife's death, Nicholas
had heard nothing of it.

André's horses consumed his time, it seemed to
Nick. This particular morning André's spirits
soared as he took Nick to the stables to view his
new prize — a fine young filly from the line of
Sarah Bladen. He boasted to Nick, "Sarah Bladen
won both the races at Natchez and later at New

Orleans that year, Nicholas. Look at the great legs on that filly. But I want to keep it a secret for a while." André's eyes gleamed as he watched his nephew scrutinize the fine lines of the filly and admire its magnificent black satiny coat, dark as a raven's wing.

Finally, Nick passed judgment. "God, she's a beauty, Uncle André!" André was pleased by Nick's statement and responded with a hearty nod. It was at times like this that André wished he could share these special moments with Daniel. But he knew that would never be.

"So what shall we call her, Nick?" André asked Nick.

"Ah, it has to be something special, don't you think?" Without hesitation, he spoke up, "How about Fancy's Folly?"

André considered the suggestion carefully and a broad smile came on his face. "Fancy's Folly! Yes . . . yes, indeed! I like that very much." His hand caressed the filly's black velvet mane lovingly. "Well, young lady, there you have it. You are Fancy's Folly from this day forward."

At that moment Nick smelled the familiar odor of her perfume and even before he turned around he knew Yvonne was standing behind him.

André was just saying that this little filly was going to win at the Turfman's Race Course in New Orleans for him when Nick's eyes locked into Yvonne's bold, reproachful ones. By the time André took notice of his daughter there was a sweet, adorable smile on her face. She squeezed him around the waist, exclaiming, "Oh, Papa, it's so good to have you back home." She whirled playfully around and told André of the small intimate dinner party she'd planned for that night, adding that she'd invited Alita Dumaine.

That statement captured André's full attention. "Alita's back at Dubonnet now?"

"Yes, Papa and her *new* secretary," she said, masking the distaste she felt at his obvious delight. Her eyes darted over to Nick. "I'm also including the Minors and their two daughters. Is that all right?"

"Sure, honey. That's just fine. Now, tell me what you think about Papa's new prize?"

"Beautiful, Papa," she replied. She knew it was what he wanted to hear. Actually she and Daniel did share one thing. She cared no more for thoroughbreds than he. The racing season excited her for other reasons, but certainly not the horses.

"Well, meet Fancy, Yvonne. We've just named her Fancy's Folly," André declared proudly. He took no notice of the sudden sparks in her green eyes.

"Now I just bet Nicholas thought that up, didn't you, Cousin Nicholas?"

Nick felt the urge to give her feisty bottom a swat, but instead he bowed and declared, "I take credit for it, cousin Yvonne."

She turned sharply, swishing her flowing skirt around with a furious jerk. Oh, she hated him for that! Damned if she wouldn't make him pay! If it was the last thing she ever did she'd have her revenge against him and Fancy Fourney. And she might just get it tonight.

The fury churning within her made Yvonne impatient for the appointed hour when her guests would arrive. She paced the floor of her bedroom instead of resting as she would have normally done before an evening dinner party.

She was not aware of the urgent message brought to Nicholas by a boatman from the docks. Nick and André had been in the midst of a mid-afternoon discussion in the course of which Nick was telling his uncle about his plans to buy the Dumaine estate when the messenger had been ushered into André's study. Thirty minutes later, Nick was accompanying the man to a flat-bedded wagon. He loaded his luggage into it, and sped away from Magnolia toward the *River Queen* which was preparing to go downriver to New Orleans.

Mother was ill, the message had said. Since Monique Dubose was never sick, it sounded urgent. Nick had no time to send word to Fancy or see her. He did urge his Uncle André to give her his regards and to explain his absence, and he'd hastily requested André to tell Madame Dumaine that he would be in touch with her about Dubonnet. Then he was gone. By the time Yvonne sauntered smugly down the stairway in her most attractive gown of emerald green taffeta Nick was miles away aboard the *River Queen.* Nick would not be attending her dinner party.

The Minor family were the first to arrive. When Alita arrived with Fancy by her side, André could not help staring at the beautiful young girl for he, too, experienced a spell of déjù vu. She reminded him so much of another young girl from his past, his first love.

Dahlia's musings about Monsieur André Dubose had been right. He'd never seen the vivacious Alita look more enchanting or desirable. He did desire her very much, and privately he vowed to ask her to marry him once again.

When Fancy was introduced to André she noticed a startling resemblance to Nick except for André's mass of graying hair. He was tall and trim like his nephew and just as charming. He smiled at her warmly when he extended Nick's apologies and then told Alita, "He wants you to know he's most interested in discussing the sale of Dubonnet again with you. To have Nicholas owning the adjoining property to mine pleases me. The young man rather surprises me."

For Alita's ear only he bent close and whispered, "For you to share Magnolia with me would please me more." Alita turned and smiled at the debonair gentleman holding her arm. Yvonne and Fancy trailed a few feet behind them, observing the couple. Fancy thought they made a most attractive pair, but Yvonne was annoyed and thought André was making a fool of himself.

However, the evening was just beginning and Yvonne had plenty of time to settle her scores with both of the women she detested. Before Alita Dumaine said good night she'd know there was no room at Magnolia for two mistresses and that Yvonne was the perfect hostess. It was a role she had no intentions of giving up to anyone — not just yet!

The finest Madeira was being served and she'd had the cook prepare a special chicken recipe. It was cooked in red wine with mushrooms and onions. A delectable custard dessert served in individual crocks was to be the final course. It was a favorite passed down through generations of the Duboses.

Yvonne sat at the long dining-room table, feeling quite proud and smug as she observed the guests enjoying the courses and the wines she had chosen. Alita was pleased, too, pleased and proud of her little secretary for Fancy seemed to have captured the attentions of the two daughters of Donald Minor. They chattered away like two magpies with her. Amazingly, Alita noticed the shy Daniel's eyes appraising the girl and she knew his artist's eye was absorbing the perfection of her features. It would not surprise her at all if he asked Fancy to sit for him.

The compliments of her guests pleased Yvonne. Perhaps now, Madame Dumaine would see that there was already an established mistress at Magnolia and she would only be superfluous. With a smug look on her pretty face she glanced down the long dining-room table to lock eyes with Alita.

The shrew Alita was unimpressed by the childish games she'd already suspected Yvonne of playing. She'd reached that point in her life where she did as she pleased. She was not concerned with impressing anyone, except those who truly mattered in her life. Yvonne was just like her mother, and Alita had not cared for André's wife. When she caught the young lady staring at her, she sensed the thoughts running through her auburn head. Yvonne would be petrified if she accepted André's proposal.

Later, though, when she noticed Yvonne had Fancy all to herself in a secluded corner away from the other guests, she was disturbed. She would put nothing past the devious Yvonne, and Fancy was so naïve. She watched them.

Yvonne had waited for this particular moment all evening, and realizing her act of syrupy sweetness was being accepted by Fancy as genuine, she offered her a glass of wine and sat down beside her. In her most angelic voice, Yvonne declared, "Such a pretty name. I may call you Fancy? Why, we're about the same age, I think."

"Why I'd feel funny if you called me anything else," Fancy declared.

"Oh, good. I want us to be friends, Fancy. It's such an awful shame Nicholas was called home to New Orleans and couldn't be here tonight. I hear you two have met." She gestured and sighed, "But then that philandering cousin of mine seems to find every new pretty girl around Natchez."

Fancy did not reply, but Yvonne chattered on, thoroughly enjoying herself. "The devil is a charmer. Even I, his cousin, will have to admit to that. But I tell you, Fancy, he is a rascal where the ladies are concerned. You know what I mean?"

"Y-es. Yes, I know," the guileless Fancy told her.

"Good! I'm glad you aren't like the rest of these silly ninnies who believe that silver tongue of his. Oh, I'll tell you if they could see him laughing about them afterward."

"You mean he comes and tells you about these . . . these women afterward?" She found it impossible to imagine that Nick would do such a thing.

"Oh, honey, he tells me everything. You see, we've been around one another all our lives — practically like brother and sister you might say." Yvonne was amused by the shocked look on Fancy's face.

As though they were intimate friends, Yvonne continued to chatter away, "Every time he comes to see us in Natchez he breaks some young thing's heart. Honestly, I could just kill him. Being his cousin, I know him like a book. I tell you, Fancy, I've never seen a man so irresistible where the ladies are concerned. It's a sin." She watched Fancy's face pale turn a ghostly white.

Fancy prayed her guilt wasn't visible to Yvonne Dubose's green eyes. Well, she'd certainly been his "plaything" on this trip, she realized from what his cousin had just said. She should have known such a man could have his pick of the ladies. He wouldn't choose to give his heart to someone from her lowly station.

She'd believed him! Dear Lord, she'd truly trusted him so completely that she'd yielded to him. Foolish, foolish Fancy! She'd probably never see him again. How she had shamed herself!

Yvonne was talking again, but only part of her conversation was absorbed by Fancy who suddenly became aware that Yvonne was repeating something to her. She apologized, "What did you say, Yvonne? I'm sorry."

Yvonne laughed softly. "Oh, I was just teasing really, Fancy. I know you're too clever to be taken in by any of Nick's shenanigans. Knowing how badly he wants Dubonnet I wouldn't have put it past him to try to play up to you so he might win his way with Alita. He is so cunning, I swear to you. Please don't think I'm awful to talk about my cousin this way, Fancy. The truth of it is I love him dearly but I know he is a rascal."

"Oh, no. I don't think you're awful at all, Yvonne," Fancy stammered. Her anger was targeted at someone else. How could he have used her so sorely? But then, she'd not thought about herself being used where Dubonnet and Alita Dumaine were concerned. Not until now, she hadn't!

The rest of the evening was a blur to Fancy, and later she could not recall the drive back to Dubon-

119

net or her conversation with Alita. Finally, alone in her room, she let her tears flow into the soft feather pillow.

Preparing for bed, Alita pondered what had occurred between the two young ladies. Although Fancy had given Alita no hint about what bothered her and had declared she'd had a lovely time, Madame Dumaine knew she was preoccupied about something.

Mingling with her concern for Fancy, thoughts of André Dubose haunted her empty room. Could she be so lucky in one lifetime as to have two remarkable men, Henri and now André, in love with her? André had sworn tonight that he was, and he'd suggested she give some serious thought to becoming his wife.

Chapter Ten

Claude Dubose lurked in the dark alcove, waiting for Yvonne to pass by on her way to her room. He was damned well drunk and he knew it. Still, he wasn't so drunk that he had dared to make a play for the ravishingly beautiful Fancy. After the episode in the woods, he had taken seriously Nicholas's order to keep his hands off this miss. He'd picked the blue-eyed, gardenia-skinned Beverly with her crown of golden curls, as the object of his attentions during the evening.

Since he had happened upon the spot where Yvonne and Fancy had sat talking and had lingered to listen, he knew what Yvonne's game was. Now, he had a terrible ache in his groin, and he felt no qualm of conscience about using Yvonne to satisfy that need.

He heard her coming and reached out to grab her. "You despicable bitch, come here!" Against

Yvonne's face, his breath reeked of liquor, and she wriggled to free herself, without success. She hissed at him, "Damn you, Claude. Let me go."

"Nope. Don't wanna."

"You're drunk, Claude." She pushed at his chest with all her might, but to no avail.

"Sure am, Cousin Yvonne. So I just thought I'd have a little of what you give so freely to Cousin Nicholas," he laughed huskily.

"Shut your mouth, you fool. Besides, that is a lie. I've never done anything with Nick."

"Yvonne, don't take me for a fool. Besides, I heard all those lies you were spouting to Fancy Fourney. You are so damned jealous you could spit. Now, I've got something to take care of your ache too, eh?" He rubbed against the front of her leaving no doubt about the urgency of his own need.

His hand massaged the front of her bodice and for a moment Yvonne quit struggling. Claude laughed. He knew after a week at Magnolia that even though Yvonne was born of the gentry, she had the heart and body of a whore.

"Damn you Claude! Damn you to hell!" She moaned with pleasure, for his touch was igniting a yearning in her.

"Hell's probably where we're both going to end up, Yvonne so we might as well enjoy ourselves while we've got the chance." His mouth captured her lips roughly, and his tongue prodded her mouth, entwining with hers. There was no gentleness in him as his hands grasped her buttocks pressing her to him. His pants already bulged with the savage desire blazing in him. "See, honey!" He gave out a chuckle. "I can give you anything old Nick can and maybe a little better."

The feel of his maleness ignited a hunger that Nicholas had not quenched when he'd dismissed her from his bed. Gradually, she quit striving to be released and began to let her lips respond, along with her burning body.

"See, Yvonne. It feels pretty good, doesn't it? I'm only whetting your appetite." He moved his hand down the front of her gown to release her breast and take its hardening tip between his lips. He let his tongue tease and taunt her rosy orb, knowing the pleasure he was creating in her from Yvonne's soft moans.

"God, Claude!" she gasped! Then she was as eager as he was to enter his room or hers. He swung her up into his arms and kicked open the door of the nearest room — Nicholas's chamber.

Hastily disrobing, they rushed over to the soft bed and Claude plunged himself between her thighs. Like two lusty young animals they sated themselves. Neither felt anything except physical release and pleasure, nor did either have a qualm that they were first cousins.

As they lay gasping, still in one another's arms, their damp bodies pressed against each other, Claude fondled her full breast and whispered, "Still say you're a bitch, Yvonne, to pull that devious trick on Fancy tonight."

She turned, shifting sensuously and rubbing her breast against his chest. "You are a bastard, Claude! I really could not care what I have to do to get what I want. Right now, I want some more of what you can give me." She giggled and swung her satiny thigh across his hips, slithering over him like a snake.

"Aw, hell, Yvonne . . . I don't think . . ."

She moaned and moved atop him, undulating like an exotic bellydancer. Purring like a kitten, she soothed him, "Oh, sure you can, my big, strong cousin."

"Holy Christ, Yvonne!" Her flesh became flame licking at him, searing and burning him. "You are something else." Never had Claude known such a woman as Yvonne. Her ways were those of a man in the boudoir, and he could not deny that he'd never been more stimulated. Her hands were as busy as the rest of her.

"See, cousin." She laughed softly. "Never doubt what little Yvonne tells you. Ah, how fine and strong he is." She positioned herself just as she wanted and descended on him. "Ah, yes! Magnificent!"

This time Claude managed to satisfy his cousin to the point that sleep consumed her. Utterly exhausted and weak-kneed, he left her there in Nicholas's room to seek out his own chamber. When he fell, exhausted, across his bed his last thoughts were of his home in Memphis. He realized he must

124

return there before too long. A woman like Yvonne could kill a man in a short time!

His small cabin seemed like a prison cell to Nicholas Dubose. Usually he found the rhythmic flapping of the paddle wheel a soothing sound, one that was conducive to sleep. His mother's illness had come at a most unfortunate time. Nick was a clever businessman, and he knew that a deal might slip away if it wasn't completed at the right time.

Damn it! Alita Dumaine would have agreed in another day or two. He felt that strongly. Then there was Fancy! That thought really made his gut twist. Because of the very social Natchez scene many invitations would be arriving at the Dumaine residence, and soon all the young dandies in the city would be courting her. He was hardly a fool, nor was he stupid enough to think his long friendship with Jason Carew would stop that man's roving eye.

Moonlight streamed in through the small porthole as he got up from his bunk to gaze out at the darkness.

Natchez lay back in the distance and that was where he wanted to be. A part of him remained behind with a black-eyed girl named Fancy. He admitted that there in the private confines of the small cabin. The beautiful vision of her oval face and her trusting doelike eyes haunted him, as did his gnawing feeling of guilt because he felt he had wronged her. Why? he'd asked himself a dozen times this evening.

He took another drink of brandy. Hell, he was a sophisticated man of the world and he'd taken dozens of ladies to bed so why did this one haunt him so? Haunt—hell! She'd even managed to humble him and this perplexed him.

Guilt engulfed him again because he resented having to go home because his mother was ill. A son should not feel that way. That Monique was sick also puzzled him, for she was just never ill. Now, if his father had been ailing, he could more readily have accepted that.

A voice prodded him to be honest and to confess that he really looked upon his mother's dearest friend, Angelique Rocheleau, as his mother. The beautiful Monique had been gone so much during his childhood that she had seemed more like his aunt.

When he finally lay down on the bunk and the brandy induced sleep, he couldn't remember feeling so lonely.

The same moon that shone through the porthole of Nick's small cabin gleamed through the sheer drapes of Fancy's bedroom. Her tears had ceased to flow, and she lay quietly staring at the shadows upon the wall.

Well, she had played the dumb country bumpkin for Nicholas Dubose, judging by what she'd learned from his cousin tonight. There was nothing she could do about what had already happened, but she vowed to herself that it would never happen again.

A voice in the night chided her mercilessly. You weren't too smart, were you Fancy girl? it silently taunted her. Such a dashing, handsome man who has all ladies fawning over him couldn't help being a philanderer. A man like Nicholas obviously thought all he had to do was crook his finger and women would come running.

The beauty of her romantic and whimsical fantasy was shattered, and for the first time in her life she knew bitterness. No longer were her thoughts or her heart loving or pure. She muttered to the darkness that she could thank Nicholas for that.

But how could a man's eyes adore one so, or his lips be so sweet when they kissed you? His caress had been so very tender with love—she had thought. His man's body had given her such glorious pleasure when it had joined with hers as though it had been meant to do so.

Disillusioned, Fancy now knew her fairy-tale beliefs didn't apply to everyone . . . certainly not to Nick. She was merely another conquest on his long list. But never again, Nicholas Dubose, she vowed. No man would hold her heart in his hands to toss aside at his whim. She'd pray he didn't get Dubonnet.

A chilly aloofness took root in Fancy that night as she lay in her bed. Although her attitude did not change toward Alita or the house servants, her behavior with Jason Carew, who came to the house

WANDA OWEN

to pay a call, was quite different. His aristocratic handsomeness didn't impress her.

Alita noticed Fancy's cool poise. Her little secretary's offhanded manner only seemed to whet Jason's interest. Madame Dumaine found this rather amusing since she knew most of the wealthy planters' daughters considered Jason quite a catch.

After he'd left, Alita casually commented to Fancy, "There was a time when I thought he and Yvonne would be paired." Taking up her needlepoint again, she teased, "He certainly seemed taken with you, Fancy dear."

"He is a very charming young man," Fancy idly remarked, obviously not that excited by him.

"Well, I consider Jason made a wise decision in never getting serious about Yvonne."

"Oh, may I ask why, Madame Dumaine?" Fancy was mildly curious.

"Because, my dear, I've found Jason to be a hardworking, serious-minded young lawyer, and Yvonne is an empty-headed, spoiled brat."

"She seemed so nice to me," Fancy said, sipping at the glass of sherry she was having. At this time of the day she and Alita usually sat and talked and sipped sherry. Fancy found this a most pleasant hour. She had never had even one full glass of wine before coming to Madame Dumaine's.

"Oh, she can be sweet as syrup if she wishes, Fancy. You haven't been here long, but the Dubose charm is legendary." Madame Dumaine sipped some sherry. "Fancy, my sweet child, you are so

128

good but you will find that there are times the world can be cruel."

Fancy said nothing but privately she thought to herself that she had, indeed, experienced the Dubose charm much to her regret. She was realizing just how cruel and ugly the world could be.

She finished her sherry in one swallow and her second glass had a swift effect and loosened her tongue. "Oh, but I am learning, Madame Dumaine. As far as the Dubose charm, I rather suspect that it doesn't take living in Natchez long to be exposed to it." Her statement caused Alita's finely arched brow to rise. She wondered what the young girl was really saying. Was Fancy slightly drunk by the wine they'd consumed or was she trying to say something in a disguised way?

Alita felt what Fancy was saying was connected to Yvonne Dubose and the night out at Magnolia. What had that daughter of André's said and done to Fancy? Alita was a very intuitive woman. Henri had always told her that, and she was aware of a change in this lovely girl. She pinpointed it to the night of the party at Magnolia.

Long after they'd parted company and she was alone in her room Fancy remained on her mind. Perhaps, it was because this was always the loneliest time for Alita. At this hour she felt the loss of Henri most severely. Suddenly she had the strangest idea.

"Dear God, do you suppose Henri? . . ." she mumbled almost in a whisper. "I hadn't thought of that until now."

To be alone in the woods with a man like Nicholas Dubose would be a tantalizing temptation for any woman. One as innocent as Fancy would be a lamb led to the slaughter with ease. Besides, she recalled that young man's face devouring the beautiful Fancy. He wanted her. Of that, there was no doubt in Alita's mind.

Immediately she decided that Dubonnet would never fall into his hands if he'd used Fancy badly.

Chapter Eleven

The spacious garden courtyard of the Dubose townhouse was ablaze with bright colors. Purple and red bougainvillaea blossoms and sweet smelling cream-colored gardenias perfumed the cobbled stone area. The brilliantly feathered cockatoo sat in his ornate cage, demanding attention. But nobody paid any notice to the noisy Argo.

There was nothing bright and cheery about the two men sitting at the small wrought-iron table. Even the misty spray being blown across Nicholas Dubose's face failed to cool his anger. His father, Alain, understood and tried to soothe his son's ruffled feathers. But what could he say really?

"I'm . . . so sorry, son. Neither Monique nor I had any inkling that the little imp had done it. She's too old now to spank." The elder Dubose sighed dejectively.

"Damned if she's too old for me to spank and I

may just do it yet," Nicholas snapped, his strong hands itching to fasten themselves around his sister Denise's neck. "If her objective was to use me as an escort for her friend who is visiting New Orleans, she's got a big surprise in store for her. I must request that you or mother do not start to plead her cause. I will not do it."

"I promise you I will not, Nick. I'm sorry this interfered with your plans to buy Dubonnet. I ask only that you don't take your fury out on the innocent Chantelle. It is Denise and strictly Denise who concocted this little scheme. *Mon dieu*, if she could only have been more like Doreen!"

"That's the damned truth. Oh, don't worry, Papa, I won't be rude. I know the Charbeau account is important to you, but I will not let my little sister get by with this and play along."

Alain Dubose had never seen his son so irate, but the Frenchman was more disturbed by his daughter's irresponsible sense of humor. To get her way she obviously was willing to go to any lengths. On that point Denise and Nicholas were very much alike, and Alain was tempted to remind his son of that fact.

Since Nick had learned that the frantic message delivered to him in Natchez by one of his father's men was not from his father at all but had been conjured up and taken to the dock for delivery by his sister, he had also found out that it had been a ploy to get him to return home because she hoped to pair him with her very best friend, Chantelle

Charbeau. The Charbeau and Dubose families were lifelong friends, and Denise had thought matching Nick up with Chantelle was a perfect idea. So without considering Nick or his plans, she'd played her devious trick. Although she was always domineering toward her younger sister Doreen, she'd never tried to manipulate Nicholas before this. He was hardly the angel Doreen was, and he vowed to teach his self-centered sister a lesson.

Alain left his son to fume alone since there was nothing more to be said. He had to agree that Denise had gone too far this time; she should have known better.

Argo's annoying chatter irritated Nick and he barked at the brightly colored parrot, "Shut your damned mouth, Argo. I'm in no mood for your noisy talk." Between the parrot's prattle and the trilling sharp calls of the vendors selling their wares outside the walled garden he found no peace.

He bolted from the chair to make his way inside to his father's place of refuge—his study. There he sought the well-stocked liquor chest and helped himself to a sample of the new brandy from France.

It was a superior cognac and its taste mellowed Nick. His father was right. This was the best he'd ever tasted. After refilling his glass, he went over to the massive mahogany desk to write a letter which he intended to send on the first boat to Natchez.

When the letter was finished he dashed out of the house and across the courtyard toward the iron entrance gate. He paid no attention to the feminine voice beckoning to him. Although he recognized his sister's voice he did not yet trust himself to deal with her directly. He marched toward the gate with long strides.

Shrugging her dainty shoulders, Denise turned to her guest, Chantelle Charbeau, and snapped. "Oh, I know he heard me!"

"That is not so unusual for an older brother, Denise. Don't you know that by now?" Chantelle laughed softly, thinking of her own older brother. She observed Nicholas with an appreciative eye for he presented a striking figure as he strode across the flagstone path. Chantelle did not condone nor had she encouraged the horrible trickery of her impish friend. She knew why Denise had sent the message and that knowledge embarrassed Chantelle.

"But, Chantelle, that party is tomorrow night and I wanted to be sure he would be your escort. It's you I'm thinking about. Marcus is escorting me. His friend will escort you if Nicholas proves to be hateful."

Chantelle patted her arm and assured her, "Marcus's friend will be fine. It's not the end of the world, Denise." Chantelle wasn't as concerned about suitors or marriage as Denise.

The two girls had such completely different natures it was amazing that their friendship had flourished and endured. It would have been impossible for the flitting Denise to have sat for two or three hours reading. Yet, Chantelle thoroughly enjoyed books. Denise disliked horses, as did her cousin Yvonne, and she cared nothing for horseback riding which was one of Chantelle's favorite pastimes.

Even their looks posed a startling contrast. Chantelle was as fair as Denise was dark. Denise, like all the Duboses, possessed strikingly dark good looks, while Chantelle's blond loveliness suited her serene personality.

The next morning when Nick happened upon Chantelle sitting alone in the courtyard while his sister slept, he begrudgingly admitted to himself that she was very nice and not the empty-headed idiot he assumed a friend of Denise's would be.

He joined her while he had a cup of coffee and a croissant. "How in the world did you two become friends?" he was urged to ask.

Chantelle threw back her head and laughed lightly. "You sound just like my brother, Nicholas. I suppose that is just a typical reaction of older brothers."

Nick did not consider her a ravishing beauty but there was a quality about her he found interesting. Because she was not trying to make a play for him or to impress, he lingered longer than he'd intended.

As they continued to talk, she told him quite frankly, "I do want you to know one thing while we

135

have this moment of privacy, and that is that I did not have any part in Denise's little plot to bring you back to New Orleans. I truly don't think she stopped to think things out before she did it. It was just an impulsive act."

Nick gave her a crooked smile, "As most things are with Denise, I'm afraid. After meeting you, Chantelle, I rather figured you didn't have anything to do with it."

Chantelle had a sweet face, Nick thought as he sat across from her. Denise observed them from her bedroom window which gave a perfect view of the courtyard. Her older brother seemed to be enjoying himself so she decided not to intrude. Instead she requested Mattie to serve her breakfast in her room.

When Chantelle went upstairs later, she casually informed Denise that she had her escort to the Monteils' soirée that night. Nicholas had suggested he take her. Denise was more than delighted for she had gotten her way—or so she thought.

But that was not true as far as Nicholas was concerned. He genuinely liked Chantelle and felt she shouldn't be punished for Denise's mischief.

Subconsciously, Fancy Fourney punished Jason Carew in the weeks that followed Nicholas's departure and Yvonne's revelations. Jason's friendship with Nicholas didn't deter him from pursuing the beauteous Fancy. When she accepted his invitation to go for a Sunday afternoon drive, he was elated, and he proudly drove his brand-new gig to the entrance of Madame Dumaine's townhouse to pick her up.

For the next three weeks, this attractive couple attended many social events and they were seen at the finest restaurants in the city. Jason flaunted his gorgeous date, knowing he was envied by the men who ogled her when they went to the theater or to the home of one of his friends' for a dinner party. Fancy was also very aware of the irate glares she received from some of the young ladies at the various places she went with Jason. She remembered Alita telling her that Jason was the most sought-after young bachelor in Natchez and that he was gaining prominence as a shrewd lawyer in Natchez and Adams County.

She could not help feeling somewhat smug. Jason loved everything about Fancy, including her light, lilting laughter. He found her a good conversationalist. She fit into his arms when they danced as though she'd been made especially for him. He'd never have guessed that Fancy's dancing ability had come naturally and without instruction. Neither would he have believed that she had not attended a school for young ladies as the daughters of wealthy planters and businessmen did. She had charming manners and a poise rare in one so young.

Still it was a cruel punishment for Jason to be allowed only one kiss when he wanted to devour Fancy with his lips. He always had to leave her with his cravings unsatisfied, so he became even more determined to have her. His desire for her mounted until thoughts of Fancy obsessed him even when he was in his office.

Born of the gentry or not, Jason could see no reason why being married to Fancy would be anything but sheer bliss. When his snobbish aunt quizzed him about Fancy's background and heritage, he quickly chided her for her prying remarks.

Fancy's sweet, tantalizing lips promised such rapture to come that Jason took it upon himself to purchase a magnificent diamond ring and a bracelet which he intended to present to her at the end of the week when they went to see the great Swedish soprano, Jenny Lind. The city of Natchez had been buzzing for weeks about the renowned singer who was coming to their city to perform, and Jason had been one of the first people to buy choice seats. After the performance he had planned a private dinner at the City Hotel during which he intended to ask Fancy to marry him.

Jason didn't fool himself about the magnetic effect of one Nicholas Dubose. After all, he'd witnessed Nick's charm with other women, but Nicholas was gone now so he was not wasting time. Who could say when the rascal would reappear? If only he could get her to agree!

All Jason's romantic plans went awry when Fancy hastily rushed into his office the day before the concert to exclaim breathlessly, "I'm so sorry, Jason, but we're on our way to board the first boat leaving for

Memphis. Madame Dumaine is downstairs in the buggy waiting for me, so I must be off. I'm so, so sorry, Jason."

"B-but, Fancy . . . when will you be back?" Jason stammered. He felt as though the breath had been knocked out of him, he was so shattered. He damned Alita's relative for choosing to die at this inopportune time.

"Lord, Jason, I'd have no way of knowing that." Fancy was impatient to get back to the buggy not wishing to add to Madame Dumaine's difficulties.

"Good-bye, Jason—I can't linger any longer." She whirled around and left, Jason's voice trailing behind her. Like a gentle breeze wafting over him, she was gone.

Dejectedly, he sank down into the leather seat. Something told him that his moment with Fancy had passed. Deep in the pit of his stomach something stabbed at him like a knife. He knew as sure as he breathed that the blissful interlude he'd enjoyed with Fancy was over. Oh, dear God, not that he wanted it to be!

He recalled his old mentor's words of wisdom as he slumped in his chair. Old Henry Rollins had said, "You always strike when the iron is hot, boy." Well, Jason told himself, he'd intended to, but fate had blocked the way. He'd lost her, he knew.

So now Fancy traveled downriver back to the places she'd left just a few months ago. Back to Memphis and Willow Bend—their destination on this sorrowful mission. Charles Kensington had died after a fall from his horse. So sudden and so tragic! Like Alita, Alicia Kensington was now a widow.

It wasn't until the paddle wheeler plowed northward through the muddy waters of the Mississippi that Fancy realized she would be seeing Chris again. However, the circumstances didn't gladden her heart. Mister Kensington had been nice to her. He and Chris were the only members of the Kensington family who had shown her any kindness. Chris was the only one for whom she felt compassion now. For the first time she pondered the new coldness that had become a part of her. What about Willow Bend, now that Mister Kensington would no longer be around to take charge? Would Chris become the head of the family and run the estate?

As the two elegantly dressed ladies strolled silently around the passenger deck, they both thought of the immediate future. Alita was already contemplating Alicia's pleas that she remain at Willow Bend for she knew the utter helplessness her sister would be feeling. Nonetheless, Alicia would have to find her own way, just as Alita had.

Two weeks were all she could give Alicia, Madame Dumaine decided. Only two weeks!

Madame Dumaine did not doubt that these would be the longest two weeks she'd ever experienced. Already, she was feeling sorry for Chris. She knew how Alicia could drain a person. Two weeks and she would return to Natchez, she vowed determinedly.

Part Two
Fancy's Foolish Folly

Chapter Twelve

Was it just the season of summer that had passed or a whole lifetime? young Kensington wondered. Nothing seemed the same now at Willow Bend. Not even Fancy Fourney seemed the same to him when he was around her. The change in her was almost as hard to accept as the death of his father. Charles Kensington had been the family's Rock of Gibraltar, and Chris was jolted by the tremendous burden that fate had placed on his back.

Roberta was as helpless as their mother. However, Chris admired his Aunt Alita even more this last week, even though she'd told him in very definite terms that she and Fancy had to return to Natchez in another week. The past seven days had been taxing ones for Alita.

Actually, he'd found precious little time to be alone with Fancy since he'd arrived. There had been the funeral and the conferences with the family lawyer. At least, Chris had been greeted by the welcome news that his father had been a shrewd, exact businessman and that his records were in good order.

Alita Dumaine had had her hands full with her weeping sister, and Chris had found that Roberta was no help in consoling Alicia. Selfishly, Roberta was upset because her wedding to Wendall Ames would have to be postponed. That bothered her more than the loss of her father. She was her mother's daughter. She and her father had never been close.

During the first ten days at Willow Bend Fancy sought out old Raoul's company. Nothing could have pleased Raoul more for he had missed her very badly. Good things had finally happened for his pretty "Miss Fancy," and she'd never looked more beautiful. He'd told Chessie that first night in their quarters, "Why, she's a lady—lady of quality—for sure. See how high she carries that pretty head of hers, Chessie. Notice how she walks. No bare feet now. No, sir!"

"She sure does look fine, Raoul," Chessie responded, a broad smile of pride on her face. Fancy would always seem a part of them . . . their little girl.

What Alita had no time to see and Raoul didn't notice was the concerned look that appeared on Fancy's face more frequently as her stay lengthened. By the end of the two weeks' stay, Fancy was experiencing sleepless nights and confining herself to her room more and more except when she took her meals with the family.

As each day passed since her arrival at Willow Bend, Fancy became more upset. She tried to recall just how many weeks it had been since she'd had her last monthly flow. She'd never been one to record the dates, but she remembered it had happened at about the time she'd landed in Natchez. So it had to be at least six, maybe seven weeks now. Shortly afterward was when she and Nicholas Dubose . . .

Dear God, she prayed, don't punish me so for that one and only time! Somehow, though, she knew instinctively that she was going to pay the price.

Twice now it had happened when she'd been walking. It had lasted but a second—that spell of whirling blackness. Raoul had not even noticed, but she wasn't one to have the vapors. Why she'd never fainted in her life as she'd seen Roberta do. But she had not really felt faint, just giddy.

She had no one to confide in but Chessie, yet even to her she couldn't confess her shame. So one morning she conceived a plan and that afternoon she joined the black woman in the kitchen at Willow Bend.

Cleverly Fancy chattered away to Chessie about one thing and another, deliberately weaving the conversation so that she might learn what she needed to know.

She sipped on the delicious cup of hot chocolate

Chessie had served her as she sat at the square oak table. Finally she laughed softly declaring, "Poor Roberta, the way she's throwing up her food and having her vapors you'd think she's five months' pregnant."

The black woman turned around and exploded into laughter, "Oh, lordly, Miss Fancy! Watch your mouth, child. Miss Roberta would have your hide for that. 'Sides, that's long over with at five months. Hasn't you ever been told anything, Miss Fancy?"

"What are you talking about, Chessie?" Fancy looked wide-eyed and innocent. Two months ago she wouldn't have had to act.

"Babies and stuff. Some don't even have those things. Others do. First thing's goin' to be no bleedin'. I didn't need no spell or upset belly to tell me. If I didn't see nothin' after four weeks then I knew it was a baby. Happened every time . . . all four times."

Well, she'd found out what she wanted to know. She hardly heard Chessie's other comments. The black woman kept prattling on. "No, sir, by the five months' time you got other discomforts hounding you."

"I . . . I've got to go, Chessie. Nice talking to you," Fancy called back over her shoulder as she hastily rose from the table. She wanted to get away before the tears began to flow.

Dashing down the long hallway, she made for the door. Crossing the veranda and descending the steps, she rushed across the green lawn. She stumbled as she darted across the thick, still-verdant carpet of grass, knowing exactly where she would seek refuge and cry until she could cry no more.

Like a drum it beat in her ear—the name she detested more than anything. Nick—Nick—Nick! Damn him and his winning ways to hell and back! Flinging herself there on the bank of the river's edge she thought of jumping in. With all the petticoats she had on she'd surely, sink and that would take care of all of her problems. She could see Nick's handsome dark face, his brilliant green eyes alive with mischief. No doubt, from what Yvonne had said, he had laughed about his easy conquest of her.

Was that what Yvonne was trying to tell her that night in an offhanded way? Lord, she wondered how she'd face her when she returned to Natchez. Worse than that how would she ever confess to Alita Dumaine the wanton woman she'd been? After all the things this dear lady had done, Fancy had ruined her golden opportunity through poor judgment and stupidity.

She sat up suddenly, and taking the hem of her muslin gown, she wiped both eyes. Using her long slender fingers as a comb she ran them through her rumpled, loose hair.

She had to think of something. There had to be some solution. At least, she mused, she could just run away up the river somewhere.

This was the wistful, thoughtful girl Chris came

upon as she sat there, so still, with her eyes cast down the river. He smiled, remembering her as a girl given to wanderlust and daydreams. Where was she off to in her fantasy now? His dear, sweet Fancy! A part of her hadn't changed he was happy to see.

"May I join you?" he called out before walking on down the slight incline. She had changed so, it seemed to him.

"Oh, Chris," she drawled, hoping her greeting had not sounded reluctant.

Lines of weariness etched his good-looking face, but he managed a smile for her. His blue eyes gazed at her searchingly as he sat down beside her. "Do you realize we've had no time alone in all the time we've both been here at Willow Bend?"

When he took her hand in his, she didn't seek to free it. "We've had no choice, Chris, with the many things you've had to face." A lock of his blond wavy hair fell over one side of his forehead and so she reached her other hand upward to brush it away from his face. It was the first time she'd felt warmth for any male since the incident with Nick.

"I'm not going back East, Fancy. I can't. My plans have to wait. Mother is utterly helpless around here, and Aunt Alita is not going to change her whole life for her. Hell, I don't blame her at all. All of Mother's tears and ravings aren't going to change a thing."

Fancy patted his cheek. "Oh, Chris, I'm sorry."

He grabbed her and captured her lips with his.

It was a hungry kiss which Fancy returned. Her response surprised her as it did Chris. When his lips lingered and his tongue prodded for entry she allowed it. Her own tongue entwined with his. She felt a mutual need as their bodies pressed together. Her fierce hunger startled her though.

Chris released her and gasped huskily. "Oh, God, Fancy—how I need you!" As they both stared at each other both involved in secret thoughts, Fancy was shocked to realize how easily she'd responded to Chris's kiss. Nicholas Dubose had been an expert teacher in his one brief lesson on making love. Chris was thinking that Fancy had certainly improved since that first stolen kiss. He wondered briefly how seven or eight weeks could so change a young lady like Fancy.

"Marry me, Fancy. It's no sudden idea—not really. Long ago, I yearned to ask you. Even when you left to go with Aunt Alita I talked to her about you and my feelings."

"Chris, you know how your family feels about me," she replied, aware that his arms still enclosed her.

"I'm my own boss now, Fancy darling. I don't have to wait until my schooling is behind me to get my parents to agree to anything and that includes marriage to you if you'll agree to it."

Her head was whirling with wild, crazy thoughts. What he said was true. She did care for Chris and always had. Had Nicholas Dubose not entered her world and changed it, she might have thought her feeling for Chris was love. Now, she knew the love she felt for Chris was the sweet love one feels for a dear brother.

Chris assumed her silence to be caused by the stupendous joy a young maiden feels when a suitor asks for her hand in marriage. Actually Fancy did not respond because she was doing some practical thinking. After all she was a young lady with a tremendous problem — one she must face in a short time. She asked herself if she'd be selfish to marry Chris, loving him the way she did, for Fancy knew this was not the all-consuming love a woman could share with a man. It was not like the ecstasy she'd known with Nick. Then she remembered the hurt and pain of that love.

When she was about to speak, Chris kissed her again. For the first time since she'd arrived, she saw a look other than sadness reflected on his face. "At holiday time, Fancy. Damned if I'll wait any longer. Father would happy about us. Fancy. I know it. He was always fond of you anyway, and if he could see you now, Fancy . . ." He was so exuberant he did not notice the look on Fancy's face as he held her in his arms.

"Holiday time?" she questioned softly. "You mean during the Christmas season?" Desolation washed over her at the thought, and then bitter humor took its place. That was over four months away. By that time her belly would be swollen to miserable proportions. What a sight of a bride she'd make then!

"Sure, darling. It would be a marvelous time to start our life together and it would give me time to set things in order around here, Fancy." He said this would also allow her time to assemble a trousseau and to have a wedding gown made.

Fancy could only give him a sweet smile. His plan would be perfect but for one thing. She wanted desperately to cry out to him. Since she probably carried Nick's child within her, she knew she had to change his mind, to get him to advance the wedding date.

As did many a young girl faced with Fancy's dilemma she dwelt on the fading hope that what she suspected might not be so, and she let Chris assume that she was agreeable to his plans. "Let's say nothing, Chris dear — not now."

He agreed and they strolled back to the house together.

As Alita watched the two young people returning, she noticed her nephew's delighted expression. Fancy even seemed in a lighter mood than she'd been lately. Alita hoped so. Willow Bend and its shroud of gloom was telling on her, and she was more than ready to put this all behind her. Her home called to her urgently and she wanted to return.

She might seem cold and unfeeling to her weeping, mourning sister, but the sooner she left the sooner Alicia would realize how things were now. Reality must be faced. Alita knew that wasn't easy, but then Alicia hadn't rushed to hold her hand or dry her tears in Natchez. She would leave at the end of the week, she decided.

She called out to Dahlia, "Order the carriage brought around."

She would go into Memphis this very day, book their passage for Natchez, and pick up a few items she needed. More than anything else, she wished to be away from this gloomy place for a few hours. For some reason she didn't exactly understand she wanted to be alone.

Except for Dahlia, no one knew Madame Dumaine's reason for being absent from Willow Bend the entire afternoon.

Chapter Thirteen

If ever a man looked guilty Jason Carew did as he sat behind his highly polished desk, his eyes constantly darting down to a stack of papers so he might avoid the steady piercing green eyes of Nicholas Dubose. Sensing Jason's discomfort Dubose derived a devious pleasure from making him squirm. Yvonne had wasted no time in telling Nick that Jason had squired Fancy around Natchez after he'd left, so Nicholas wasn't feeling exactly cordial toward his friend. He had tried to keep in mind that his cousin Yvonne was treacherous, but one visit to his regular coffee house in Natchez had confirmed Yvonne's statement.

A couple of his acquaintances had sat around their regular table at the City Hotel early that morning as they habitually did before starting the business day and Nick had joined them there. It had been the white-headed old Doctor Byfield who'd inquired of Nick, "Have you seen your friend Carew since you've come back, Nicholas?"

"No, I haven't, Doc. I'm going by though, as soon as I leave Madame Dumaine's place. I just wanted to drop in here to say hello to you and Donald. Felt the need for another cup of coffee after the ride in from Magnolia."

"Well, you can forget about stopping at the Dumaine house. No one's there but the servants. Alita's sister lost her husband a few weeks ago and she and that new secretary of hers left for Memphis I heard."

That was something else Nick hadn't counted on. He grimaced and finished his coffee. Doctor Byfield noted the disgruntled look on the young man's face. "Guess I didn't brighten your morning, but I can tell you something that will give you a laugh, son. That little filly Alita's got with her now sure had your friend Carew howling at the moon. Talk about a lovesick calf. He sure was one before old Alita swished the girl off with her. I think Jason was just about to end his bachelor days, from the way my wife was talking and the gossip that was going around Natchez. Lord, women's tongues are a busy lot."

The doctor roared with laughter, so amused that he didn't note the awesome quiet of Nicholas Dubose. Nick wanted to smash the old doctor in the mouth.

Instead, he marched out of the hotel, cursing the doctor and Jason Carew. This news had put Nicholas in the blackest of moods. He walked swiftly in the direction of the building housing Jason's law office.

Not waiting for the prim Miss Parnell to announce him, he plowed through the door with such gusto that Jason wouldn't have given two cents for his life. Nick looked like a menacing pirate come to plunder and kill, as he stood there, his tall, muscular body churning with fury and fire.

"God damn you, Jason. I ought to kill you."

"For God's sakes, Nick, what burr's in your hide? Guess I got a right to know, and then we can talk like reasonable men. This is the 1850s and we are civilized, I hope." The eloquent, debonair lawyer tried to soothe his irate friend with the courtroom manners that had contributed to his success.

"Our friendship didn't stop you the minute my back was turned when I was called back to New Orleans, did it?" Nick moved in front of the desk and leaned over to press the palms of his strong hands on its surface. Emerald fire shot from his eyes.

Jason knew, if he hadn't before, just how deep Nick's feelings for Fancy were, but he couldn't admit that to his friend. He had to play dumb if he wanted to salvage his handsome face and he knew it. He was no match for Nicholas Dubose. This angry fool would beat him to a pulp if he didn't choose his next words carefully.

"God, Nick . . . tell me what you mean 'cause damned if I know how I've wronged you in anything."

For a second Nick studied Jason's face. Could it be he hadn't known his feelings for Fancy. "Fancy, Jason. Fancy Fourney is what I'm talking about and the attentions you paid her!"

"You and Fancy, Nick? Christ, you never mentioned a word to me about her. Damn, man! I'm not a mind reader. All I can say is I'm sorry or had I known . . ."

Nick sank slowly into the chair, his explosive temper slowly mellowing and his eyes carefully measuring his friend as he tried to make up his mind whether to believe him or not.

He took a cheroot out and lit it. "You know now, Jason. I trust you will never forget it!" As slowly as he'd sat down, Nick rose from the chair.

Jason's throat felt dry, and he had to admit he'd never felt the sort of fear Nicholas had stirred in those very brief moments. He felt as if he'd looked death in the face even though Nicholas had no weapon.

"Sorry about this misunderstanding, Nick," Jason mumbled in a choked voice.

Nicholas, having already turned to go, said as he sauntered out of the office, "Yes, so am I." At that moment Carew knew his friendship with Dubose no longer existed.

He thought he'd known Nicholas pretty well, but he'd never figured any woman would make him so addled. Actually, he realized, he'd not known Nicholas Dubose at all! Probably no one did.

Jason leaned back in the overstuffed chair and took a flask from his desk drawer. As he swallowed a generous slug of fine bourbon, he shuddered to think what would have happened if he'd carried out his plan to ask Fancy to marry him. Had Alita Dumaine not left Natchez with Fancy to go to her sister's home in Memphis, he would have. Perhaps, fate had done him a favor. He didn't want to be killed for any woman, not even the ravishing Fancy!

Nick walked with long strides, paying no mind to the people passing him. Holy Christ, he would have killed Jason Carew if the man had uttered one wrong word. Even now, his hands were damp with sweat but his heart was no longer pounding so fiercely.

As if his fine leather boots had a will of their own, he found himself going through the doors of the Golden Ram. The bartender, Harvey, called out to him as he sought a corner table instead of marching directly up to the bar. He wanted to be alone for a while to sort out his troubled thoughts.

A bartender sees all kinds of men in a tavern and he listens to their woes. On this late afternoon Nicholas Dubose was a brooding man, Harvey decided. This was no time to try to cajole him or make lighthearted conversation as he might ordinarily have done. He served the drinks and left Dubose alone.

A couple of Harvey's regular patrons entered the tavern and he joined them in conversation, letting his eyes occasionally dart in the direction where André Dubose's nephew sat drinking. The liquor wasn't lightening Nick's mood as far as Harvey could see. Six shots of his Kentucky's finest seemingly had little effect on the young man.

When Nick finally left the Golden Ram it was dark. He walked down by the levee. Time was of no concern to Nicholas Dubose.

Returning to Magnolia did not appeal to him and so he went to the livery where he'd left Domino and then made straight for Belle's.

The carrot-topped, blue-eyed Belle herself greeted Nicholas as he came through the door of the well-known brothel. It was Natchez's classiest, the one visited by gentlemen planters and businessmen. Nicholas Dubose had been there on numerous occasions.

The hour was too early for business and Belle had just happened to be going upstairs after making her nightly inspection.

She had to be nearing forty, Nick thought, but she was a lot of woman with that sensuous body of hers. He could well imagine the striking figure she'd cut as a younger woman. Dressed as she was now in a sheer lavender wrapper over a satin gown of the same color, every curve of her body was defined.

Her luscious, full breasts were partially exposed for his eyes to see, and her peaches and cream complexion seemed as soft as satin. Her blue eyes danced over Nick, silently asking why he'd arrived on her doorstep so early. Although she could smell the whiskey on his breath, he was not drunk or out of control. In fact, he was the same impressive man he'd always been when he'd paid a visit to her establishment.

"Well, my friend Nicholas — what can I do for you? A drink — a girl — or perhaps, some intelligent conversation or a game, eh?"

His arm snaked around her waist and he pulled her closer. "Belle, my darling — before the night is over I may indulge in all of the things you mentioned. For the moment, I'd like a drink and some of your delightful conversation."

She threw back her head and laughed at this towering giant by her side. "Then why don't you just come upstairs with me. We'll share a light snack and bottle of wine before I have to dress, eh?" Should he seek more than that, she'd be happy to oblige him. He was one of the rare ones — Belle could number them on one hand — out of the multitude of gents who paraded through the door. She had all kinds nightly at her gaming tables and in her girls' boudoirs, but in the last ten years only two had been welcomed in her canopied bed. During the last six years there had been only one man, but three weeks ago that affair had ended.

Nicholas Dubose was a decade younger than she was, but she would not hesitate to take him into her bed. Every night some old coot paid to take one of her girls twenty years younger to bed. What fool had set up such one-sided practices anyway? Why was it considered ridiculous if the situation was reversed? she wondered? It would have to be some man who'd made it that way, she thought to herself.

As the pair climbed the stairs and walked down the hallway, Belle's girls darted in and out of their rooms stopping short to admire the handsome gent who was invading their quarters — and envying their boss lady who obviously had him monopolized. Bold, appraising looks came his way.

Nick responded with a brief, flashing smile, which made the little French girl heave a dramatic sigh and turn to her companion to comment, *"Mon dieu,* how would you like to have that one engage you for the whole night?"

Nick heard the remark and he turned around to wink at Babette, the one who'd said it. She winked back. Her big black eyes were framed with thick curling lashes that reminded him of Fancy's. Hastily, he turned his eyes back to Belle. He didn't need that reminder tonight.

They had no sooner entered Belle's quarters than a servant brought Belle's dinner and the madam ordered another serving for Nicholas. As she poured the wine, she inquired of André. "Magnolia must be keeping him busy. He hasn't been here in months now."

"Guess it's the preparation time for the racing season, Belle," Nick told her.

160

"It has amazed me that he's remained unmarried so long. Such a handsome man! In fact, you look very much like your uncle to me. All you have to do is look at your uncle and you'll know how you'll look at his age."

Nick laughed and took the refill she offered. Then his food was served and he found himself quite hungry. When he finished eating, he became quite serious and then he said, "Promise me something, Belle."

"Sure, honey — what?" Belle was finishing off the last bit of the herbed, juicy chicken.

"See that I get on the *Nellie Dee* tonight before she leaves Natchez for Memphis. I've already made my arrangements with Captain Bolton and I've told him I'd board late tonight for the morning departure. But if I should drink too much . . . Well, you know what I mean?"

Belle leaned over and gave him a kiss. "I know exactly what you mean, honey." She poured more wine into his glass and as she leaned over her voluptuous breasts were bared. Her blue eyes teased Nick brazenly. His nostrils caught the exotic fragrance she had on. Everything about this woman bespoke her sensuousness.

"Now, Nick . . . what can we do to please you? A card game, maybe?" She rose from the chair in a lazy, unhurried fashion as if to exhibit each curve of her body for his scrutiny. And the male in him responded. She took a couple of steps toward the hand-painted silk screen behind which she would change into a fancy evening gown. "A girl, maybe?" she purred in a sexy, low voice.

Nick rose from the chair. "I never take a girl, Belle when I can have a woman. Tonight, I need a woman," he told her in a husky voice.

In the brief minute she'd stood behind the screen she had slipped out of her wrapper and gown, and had released the coil of her flaming red hair, allowing it to stream down around her back and shoulders as she emerged stark naked, an inviting smile on her face. "Well, will I do?"

"Damnation — yes!" The sight of her was breathtaking. He felt the bulge in his pants and laughed, "Damn, my need is greater than I realized, Belle honey." He also realized he was drunker than he'd thought.

"I see what you mean, Nicholas," she laughed as their arms encircled each other and he bent to take her lips.

He had a sensuous mouth and it stirred her when his lips teased her without mercy, trailing down her neck to the pulsing tip of a breast. As his tongue teased and tantalized the hardened tip of first one and then the other breast, she found herself gasping with a delight she hadn't experienced for a long, long, time. "Oh, God, Nick. Come on! I can't wait any longer!"

She helped him rid himself of his clothing and without further ceremony they sought the bed. Both were hungry for the pleasures they could enjoy as their bodies meshed, seeking release — taking and giving. Neither Nicholas Dubose nor Belle thought of anything beyond the ultimate delight and rapture of the moment.

Once their needs were fulfilled and Nicholas lay by her side, the fleeting thought came to him that he was glad he had been with Belle and not the dark-eyed Babette who reminded him of Fancy. Belle remained in bed when he leaped up to dress.

"I must get to the boat, Belle." Without further ado, he bid her good night and bolted out the door. He was bound for Memphis, Tennessee.

Belle stretched her flushed, sated body serenely and lazily. There in her dimly lit boudoir she thought about the marvelous interlude she'd just had with the randy young Dubose. Maybe there was something to be said about older women bedding younger men for she couldn't remember feeling this good since she'd been eighteen.

Chapter Fourteen

It was a milling, busy crowd on the wharf as passengers prepared to board the boat for the journey down the Mississippi to Natchez. On the passenger list was a young doctor and his bride who were coming from Saint Louis to establish a practice in Natchez. Madame Dumaine appeared with Fancy, and Dahlia trailed behind them. A couple with two noisy children followed close behind Alita and she wondered why the father didn't quiet them down.

Chris stood on the dock, watching Fancy and Alita approach the rail. Alita had insisted that he not see them to their quarters so that he might return more rapidly to Alicia, because Alita's departure was throwing her into a depressed state. Indeed Alita had forced herself to ignore Alicia's dramatic playacting at the last minute when she had urged Alita to remain at Willow Bend.

Fancy turned to give Chris a sweet smile and a final goodbye wave of her white-gloved hand. Then in the sea of faces below her, she thought she saw a familiar pair of eyes. She quickly whirled around to follow Alita and Dahlia, shrugging off the eyes she'd glimpsed. It couldn't be, for he was miles away in New Orleans.

Dear God, now she was haunted by him, seeing his face in a crowd! Fancy Fourney, you are a fool, she privately chided herself. Forget him.

Shrugging her shoulders she strolled the passenger deck with an independent air. So what if that had been Nicholas Dubose? That was over. After what Yvonne had told her about the rogue, he meant nothing to her anyway. To him she had just been a passing fancy. She must forget him. How easily the words came, but how hard it was to put him from her mind.

Except for saying a last goodbye to Chessie and Raoul, Fancy was more than ready to leave Willow Bend. Last night while lying in her bed and staring at the ceiling she'd been almost glad she hadn't been able to go through with the deceptive trickery on Chris. Lord, she'd tried to make herself do it a couple of times when he'd held her in his arms. She had intended to use womanly wiles to get him to marry her sooner than he'd planned, but when their love-making reached a certain point Fancy always broke it off. Chris—dear, unsuspecting Chris—had taken her reluctance for maidenly innocence, but actually the tormenting, despicable image of Nicholas Dubose had gotten in her way. So Fancy was leaving Willow Bend with no hope of a marriage before Christmas. But she couldn't tell Chris the truth.

Even though they'd agreed to keep their plans a secret for a while, Chris had confided in his Aunt Alita and had cautioned her to take good care of his fiancée.

A few hours after they'd boarded the boat and settled in their adjoining cabins Alita spoke to Fancy about the conversation she'd had with her nephew. "Fancy dear, I got the impression Willow Bend no longer seemed like home to you anymore even though I know you enjoyed seeing your old friends, Raoul and Chessie. Of course, I know Chris was glad to see you even though it was a sad time for him."

"Perhaps, that was what it was, ma'am. It was nice to visit Mama's grave and take her some of the flowers she always loved."

"I'm sure it was. I got to see little of Chris or Roberta for I spent most of my time with Alicia. She will be a problem for Chris and Roberta—especially Chris. Young Chad will not be burdened like the two older ones." Alita hoped to make the point that this was no time for Chris to marry. The responsibility for two women was too much for the inexperienced and unprepared young man.

"Chris told me he saw no reason to postpone Roberta's wedding a full year, and since he's the head of the family now, he agreed to proceed with her plans again." Fancy remarked.

Alita laughed softly. "Well, Chris is smarter than I credited him with being. He's realizing that his mother and Roberta can be a taxing pair. I know poor Charles knew that. So he plans to rid Willow Bend of Roberta—one load off his shoulders." Alita wanted to add that Chris was not the man for Fancy to spend a lifetime with, but she didn't.

She itched to tell Fancy about her plans to bring Raoul and Chessie to Natchez in a few weeks but she decided to let that be a delightful Christmas surprise. They would arrive at Dubonnet before the holidays and Alita could imagine the radiant look of Fancy's lovely face when she realized they were there. When Alicia had told Madame Dumaine that Raoul's days as her gardener were coming to an end because of his age and his leg problems, Alita had offered to take the couple on at Dubonnet.

Usually very assured of herself, Alita now felt hesitant about the other subject she wanted to discuss with Fancy. She was genuinely fond of the girl, more than she would have imagined despite the brief time they'd been together. It was not offensive to her that her nephew wished to marry Fancy, but she did not feel that Chris was the man for her.

The girl had changed since Chris had first voiced the depth of his feelings for her. Somehow she now saw Chris as much younger than Fancy, even though he was actually older. Besides, she remembered Fancy's radiance with Nick.

Sighing heavily, Alita exclaimed. "Oh, Fancy, how good it will be to get back to Natchez and my own sweet home." Somehow, she felt that Fancy might be feeling a little like her. Straightening up, she came to the point and her voice echoed the sincere concern she was feeling. "Fancy dear, do you think you could be happy at Willow Bend even as Chris's wife?"

Candidly, the girl looked Alita Dumaine straight in the eye and replied, "I don't know whether I could or not. Chris has always been very dear to me." Oh, why did she have to be so smart?

Skeptically Alita questioned her as she would have a beloved daughter, "But is that enough for you, Fancy?"

Fancy gave her a wan smile and took a moment before answering her. "Sometimes it has to do when you can't do better." As soon as the words were spoken, she realized how awful they must sound, and she wanted to remove herself as hastily as possible from the prying eyes of Alita Dumaine. "If you'll excuse me, I think I'll go to my quarters, ma'am."

"Certainly, dear. Certainly," Alita replied calmly though doubts washed over her.

Fancy dashed from Alita's cabin to seek the privacy of her own. She was relieved to see that Dahlia wasn't there for she wanted more than anything to be alone. Madame Dumaine was far too observant and perceptive to be fooled, Fancy realized.

It was merely a matter of confirming what he was certain his bloodshot eyes had seen, Nicholas told himself as he pushed through the throng of people mingling on the wharf on this late summer day. He elbowed and plowed his way toward the blond-haired young man leaving the dock area. He recognized him as Christopher Kensington. He'd observed Fancy and Alita Dumaine waving from the passenger deck to this young aristocrat, but he wanted to confirm what he'd seen before doing some wild, crazy thing like boarding the paddle wheeler.

The gypsylike traipsing around he'd been doing lately had begun to wear on him. Having arrived in Memphis less than an hour ago aboard the *Nellie Dee* from Natchez, he felt it would be ludicrous to jump aboard the *Bayou Queen* to go right back down the river unless that really was Fancy Fourney. He'd had only a fleeting glimpse of that lovely face.

The blond young man was stepping into a carriage when Nick's authoritative, deep bass voice stopped him. "Yes?" Chris noted something familiar about this gentleman but he couldn't recall who he was.

"I'm Nicholas Dubose. We only had a brief encounter once before. I knew your father though and I'm very sorry to hear about his death."

"I appreciate that, sir," Chris remarked.

"I . . . I just arrived here from Natchez and I

wished to inquire if that was Madame Dumaine departing on the *Bayou Queen*? You see, I have some business to talk to her about," Nicholas told Chris.

"You possibly did for I just brought her here to return home." Had the young planter said no more Nick's fury would not have been ignited, but Chris's next words made Nick explode like a cannon. "She and my fiancée were on the deck just a minute ago."

Chris stood gaping as Nick's green eyes glared fire and he watched Dubose turn sharply on his booted heels without even saying farewell. Clenched teeth and clenched fists were only two of the reactions Nick experienced as he angrily strode back to the dock and up the gangplank.

Although confused the captain dared not question the scion of the Dubose Steamlines when Nick announced that he'd be a passenger on the departing *Bayou Queen*. Mumbling and stammering, Captain Worth quickly called to the deckhand, Robin, to ready quarters for their new passenger.

"Thank you, Captain Worth. Send a bottle of whiskey to my cabin too. I'll be in the salon until my quarters are ready and could you tell me which cabin Madame Dumaine is occupying on the trip to Natchez?"

Captain Worth hastily glanced down his list and told the angry man what he sought to find out.

As Nicholas gulped the whiskey later in his cabin the words spoken by Chris Kensington echoed over and over in his head like a voodoo drum beating. It couldn't be! He wouldn't let it be! She was his and he'd allow no other man to have her. Nobody took what was his.

Then his anger was turned on Fancy because she had agreed to marry someone else. Had she not felt about him as he had about her? Damned if he could believe she hadn't. He, Nicholas Dubose had bedded enough women to know sweet yielding and passionate response when he felt them.

The combination of little sleep in days, whiskey, and no solid meal had an effect on Nicholas. He fell asleep in his bunk, missing the dinner hour that evening.

When he did slowly open his eyes he was disoriented for it was dark outside the tiny window. Afternoon had faded into night.

Nick's throat was so dry he began to cough and then sat up suddenly in the bed to keep from choking. That movement make him feel as if the top of his head were flying off. A hammer seemed to slam his temples. "Oh, God," he moaned, anguished. He thought to himself what fools men were to deal such punishment to themselves. God knew, he was human, regardless of what others often thought of him!

He sat very still for a second before creeping cautiously over to the edge of the bunk to place his feet on the floor. Assured that his feet were there and that he could stand on them, he rose, only to find his knees were like jelly.

"Christ! My wicked ways must be catching up

with me," he muttered to the emptiness of the cabin.

As he stood there very unsure of himself, it dawned on him that although he had not yet reached thirty he had done a great deal of living. All the reveling, the women and wine might be taking their toll.

Air . . . He wanted fresh air he decided! He staggered out the cabin door to the deserted deck. He took a deep breath, inhaling the night air and the aroma of the night-blooming plants across the way on the bank of the river.

The sky was ablaze with stars as he held his head upward to observe it, thinking how marvelous the breeze off the water felt. It cleared his head and made him aware that he was famished. He moved his head to one side and then the other to ease the stuffed feeling from it.

He experienced a serenity there in the stillness of the night, completely alone. However, when he turned to look down the deck in the opposite direction he realized he was not the only one seeking the solace of the night. A lone figure stood by the railing and looked out over the rippling river current. What was plaguing that passenger, he wondered? Closer scrutiny revealed that a lady was standing there — a very tiny one too. He moved slowly along the railing toward her, for he was almost sure he knew whose petite figure that was. His stomach could wait, he decided, even though he was about to fall flat on his face from hunger.

He moved so quietly Fancy didn't detect the sound of his boots. The noise the boat made, plowing through the water was too overpowering.

As he neared Fancy Nick's powerful body came alive with instant desire, pulsing and pounding. His eyes availed themselves of the sight of her standing by the rail, the soft fabric of her frock molded sensuously to her shapely body. Her thick hair was a wild thing, flowing back from her face and setting off her delicate features. His hunger was forgotten.

While his being churned with blazing passion and desire, his strong hands yearned to shake the hell out of her when he recalled what Chris Kensington had told him.

Like a stalking cat, he moved to stand directly behind her, and his hands and arms snaked around her. When Fancy stiffened ready to scream she found the heated lips of Nicholas Dubose devouring her mouth. Wide-eyed, she stared up at him there in the dark, only the stars witnessing the encounter between them.

At first she thought she was being attacked by some drunken passenger. Alita Dumaine had cautioned her about that when she'd announced she was going out for a stroll before bedtime. Instead, she'd met the devil himself!

She found it impossible to free her arms or hands to pound against his broad chest for release, and so she was rendered helpless against the powerful rogue determined to have his way with her.

She tried weakly to resist his unrelenting mouth but he easily subdued her protest.

When he finally released her lips, he whispered into her ear, "There, damn you! Does that show you you're mine!"

He had a fierce look in his eyes, but aware of what Yvonne had said about his philandering ways, Fancy was determined he'd not use her again. Dear God, how was it he happened to be on this boat?

"It shows me nothing of the kind, Nicholas Dubose," she spat out, wriggling her tiny body in a futile attempt to free herself.

"Then by God, I'll just have to be more convincing, my sweet Fancy. For I assure you, love, that no other man gets what is mine!" He took her lips and his hand claimed one throbbing breast as his. Fancy felt the sweet, tantalizing torment of Nick and she knew she was lost to his devilish charm. "Damn you, Nick!"

Both of them gasped and Nick gave out a deep throaty laugh, "Damn us both, love, if we try to deny this thing between us. To even try is madness. You drive me crazy, Fancy Fourney!"

"Please Nick," she pleaded, "please loosen your arms. I feel as if I might faint. Please?" He looked deeply into her black eyes. She did look as though she might swoon. He obliged her, but his arms still encircled her tiny waist. "Is that better, eh?"

He stood smiling down at her feeling that he'd tamed her now. She even returned his smile, but the thoughts running through her mind were anything but sweet for she was thinking about the sleepless nights she'd endured because of this handsome man holding her.

Like a bolt of lightning the palm of her dainty hand struck his cheek. The move startled and stunned Nick so, he did not react swiftly enough as she pulled away from him and dashed down the passenger deck.

Looking back over her shoulder, she said sarcastically, "You won't add me to your list of women, Nicholas Dubose!" She ran blindly and as fast as she could away from him. The lying little vixen had tricked him!

Suddenly, something stopped her. Fancy's body hit an object with such mighty force that she went tumbling and spinning into the night. Her head took the final blow as she hit the deck, and then she drowned in the blackness that crept over her.

As her scream of anguish pierced the darkness, Nick's chest felt that he had been stabbed. He gasped, "Oh God, no!" Then he rushed forward crying out her name over and over.

Chapter Fifteen

Two men rushed across the deck to get to her limp figure. Anguished, Nick called her name out, and the other man set the pipe in his mouth aside to bend down over the still Fancy. "Took a heck of a tumble, it would seem," he commented. "Know her?" There was a professional tone about his voice.

Later Nick would wonder why he'd answered the way he had for he had not known the lanky young man examining Fancy's pulse was a doctor. "She's my wife."

"Well, I think we'd better get her to your cabin. She might just have a concussion, sir." He wasted no time with extra conversation. They made haste getting Fancy to the comfort of Nick's bunk.

There in the light of the cabin, young Doctor Benjamin Nelson saw the blood on the back of her skirt. "I'm going to have to examine her, Mister

. . . Mister . . ."

"Dubose. Nicholas Dubose." Nick frowned for he saw the blood.

"Do me a favor, Mister Dubose. While I'm checking your wife and tending to her would you go to my cabin to inform my wife as to my whereabouts?" He gave Nicholas the number of his quarters because he was certain the young lady lying there in the bunk was having a miscarriage. He would be busy for a while, he knew.

Nick was seldom numb with concern, but seeing Fancy lying there he was. He nodded to the doctor, and with faltering footsteps he left the cabin. He was aware enough to seek out the cabin of Madame Dumaine after he'd delivered the message to the doctor's wife.

Alita was both astonished and stunned by the news of Fancy and by the sight of Nicholas Dubose there at her cabin door. Nicholas wasted no time trying to assure Alita Fancy was in the capable hands of a doctor. "I don't know Dr. Nelson personally but at least, there was a doctor aboard," he told her.

"Did you say a Doctor Nelson? Why I imagine that's the doctor coming to Natchez. There was an article in the *Free Trader* just about a month ago, I believe. As you said, at least a doctor was available." Alita was practical even though she was upset and nervous because Fancy had been injured. Her curiosity was whetted about why Nick Dubose had happened on the scene, but she was glad to

177

have him near. She was too addled to ask why Fancy had been taken to Nick's cabin. A sleepy-eyed Dahlia listened through the crack of the door and observed the tall, good-looking Monsieur Nicholas Dubose. He sure had a serious look on that handsome face of his, Dahlia noticed, as she struggled into her wrapper. She supposed she might just be going to that cabin to tend to Miss Fancy throughout the night.

But Nicholas now gathered his wits about him and suggested to Madame Dumaine that he go back to his cabin to check with the doctor. "He should have some word for us if it is a concussion."

"You are very kind, Nick. Suppose I let Dahlia go along so she can bring me the news in case the doctor doesn't want Fancy to be moved to her own cabin?"

Nick's eye darted over to the little mulatto peering through the doorway. "All right." He turned to go, paying no attention to the servant girl trailing behind him.

After the doctor's voice had bid them to enter, Nick bent down to give Dahlia an order just before they went into his cabin. "Listen closely to me, girl. I've told the doctor Fancy is my wife. Don't say otherwise — you understand?"

Dahlia frowned. "Why you say that for, Monsieur?" she inquired of the man in an insolent tone.

"Because I chose to. Now, remember!" he told her in a threatening sort of way. Dahlia nodded, her dark eyes flashing with disapproval.

He was a bossy one. After all, that was her Miss Fancy in there.

Dahlia went immediately to the side of the bunk to inspect Fancy. The doctor quickly informed them both that she would sleep throughout the night.

"May I see you outside, sir?" Doctor Nelson rolled down his sleeves and Nick ushered him through the doorway. "A very mild concussion is all the bump on the head caused. A little rest should be enough to mend her on that score.

Having closed the door, the doctor walked over to the rail. "Had your wife said anything about suspecting she was pregnant? The reason I'm asking is I think she had a miscarriage but I can't be certain because if she did, she was . . . maybe just two months along."

"I . . . I didn't know," Nick stammered, feeling like an absolute idiot.

"Well, I didn't question her, but that was what the bleeding was about. Possibly brought on by the tumble she took, I'd say. She couldn't have been very far along I'm certain of that. Probably she didn't even know whether she was late with her monthly or pregnant. Nevertheless, on that score, too, I'm happy to say rest will take care of her. You have a beautiful wife, Mister Dubose. Talking about wives, I'd better get back to mine. Oh, are you getting off at Natchez?"

Nick informed him he was and the doctor suggested he carry his wife to the carriage instead of allowing her to walk down to the wharf. They parted then, the doctor refusing any reward for his services.

"After we arrive in Natchez my fees start," he jested good-naturedly.

As Nick entered the cabin, heavy thoughts bore down on him. He forgot about the mulatto servant sitting by the side of the bunk when he walked over to the washstand to get a drink of whiskey. He jerked around when she spoke in a soft murmur to him. "Think Miss Fancy is resting real good, Monsieur." A pleased smile was on Dahlia's face.

"Yes, she'll be just fine with some rest. You . . . you go on, Dahlia. Go tell Madame Dumaine the report and I'll just sleep over here in the chair tonight, eh?"

"You sure? How you gonna rest in that chair?" Dahlia quizzed him. The servant felt sorry for the man standing there before her. The truth was he looked worse than Miss Fancy who was sleeping so peacefully in the bunk. That man looked like he was ready to drop right there on the cabin floor.

"How long it been since you ate, Monsieur Nick, huh?" she questioned him in her usual bossy way.

"I don't know, but go on, Dahlia. Just get yourself out of here," he mumbled lazily.

Dahlia said no more. She already knew what she was going to do as she went out the door. Nicholas slumped into the chair, but he soon realized he would not get much rest as he shifted first one way and then the other. He was about to slide from the chair to the floor when the cabin door opened and Dahlia came gliding through it. She had two blankets flung over one arm and the other held a tray bearing a carafe of hot coffee and a crock of steaming hot stew.

"Told you that chair wouldn't accommodate that big body of yours, Monsieur Nick," she grinned. He couldn't resist returning the smile of the yellow-skinned servant. "You eat and then see what a bed these will provide, eh." Her deed done, Dahlia left quietly. After Nick obeyed her orders, eating the stew with relish and then drinking the hot coffee, he thought favorably of Dahlia. She was a jewel. Even the pallet on the floor felt like heaven to his tired body, and sleep came swiftly.

Dreams haunted his sleep though. Black eyes taunted and scolded him severely. They weren't Fancy's dark, teasing eyes but those of Angelique Rocheleau. He was remembering a time long ago when he was a small lad and she was tending to him on one of the many occasions when his father and mother were faraway in Europe.

She was pointing her finger at him accusingly and telling him, "Don't try to wiggle out of it, Nicholas. You were, indeed, naughty."

"Me? No, I know nothing about it," he'd declared, innocence reflected in his expressive green eyes.

But Angelique knew him, sometimes better than he knew himself. The hint of a smile had revealed her love for him, but in an unrelenting voice she'd told him, "You will not use that silken, smooth tongue on me. This is Angelique, Nicholas."

Suddenly, there in the maze of his dream was a tiny, wee girl like the one he'd caught in his arms when she'd lost her straw hat—the one with the dark brown hair and the black eyes. In his dream the little girl's face was Fancy's, and she stood close to Angelique, holding her hand.

"Now, you tell her you are sorry, Nicholas, and you give her back her hat," the lovely lady ordered sternly, her eyes piercing him.

"I can't, Tante Angelique. I can't! The wind carried it into the river and it is gone forever with the currents."

"Then, Nicholas Dubose, you must give her something of yours. Something you treasure!"

Nicholas lunged up from his pallet on the cabin floor, damp with sweat and expecting to see his beloved Angelique glaring down at him. The dream had been so real he could not lightly shake it off, so he just sat there for a few minutes. As soft moans came to his ears he realized where he was. He leaped up and rushed to the bunk to find that Fancy's eyes were still closed but she tossed back and forth.

He tested her for fever by gently placing his lips to her cheek and then her forehead, remembering that was what Angelique had done with him. Hands were not always best for detecting a fever, so she'd told him.

Fancy had no fever he was happy to find, so he sank into the chair by the side of the bunk and ran his long fingers through his tousled hair. He stared at the girl before him. Her dark hair was draped out over the pillow. She is hardly more than a child, he thought to himself. An overwhelmingly protective feeling swelled within him as he realized he had taken something away from Fancy Fourney—her innocence. Guiltily, he confessed, "I stole something from you, didn't I, Fancy?"

Now, he must give her something as he'd been told to do in his dream. His elusive state of bachelorhood had to be sacrificed. Christ, he'd already done that last night anyway when he'd declared her his wife.

The complicated dilemma he had created dawned on him. He knew what he must do for Fancy's sake and he knew what he was about to do might destroy his chances of acquiring Dubonnet.

So while Fancy slept, Nicholas dressed, intending to seek a private audience with Alita Dumaine.

That damned dream and Angelique's words haunted him as he slowly sauntered to Alita's door. He was nervous as hell.

In the mist and fog of early morning on the river, he could see Angelique's smiling, approving face and hear her soft voice declaring, "You can give no more than yourself, Nicholas. I'm proud of you."

Why not? The truth of it was, Fancy'd won his

heart the moment his eyes had first seen her.

Nevertheless, the thought of marriage had scared the hell out of him. That was the last thing in the world he'd anticipated for himself.

Chapter Sixteen

It was one of the longest, most gruelling hours Nicholas Dubose had ever experienced in his life. No business deal had ever proved as tedious or wearing on him as that discussion with Alita Dumaine. He had surprised himself once they'd begun talking by candidly telling her the entire, unvarnished truth.

He spared himself nothing and took full blame for everything. Alita's feelings ran the gamut of emotions as this young man was being so astonishingly truthful. By the time he left her quarters she was in agreement with him that this pair must get married immediately, and quite privately to save Fancy's good name in the city of Natchez.

As crazy as it might seem, she knew he was marrying Fancy for more than just duty and honor. He did not have to confess that to her, but he'd sought to do so. Madame Dumaine even agreed to convince Fancy to marry Nicholas should she prove stubborn as Nick had every reason to believe she would after she'd fled from him last night to fall over the wooden bench.

Before Nicholas left Madame Dumaine's quarters, he inquired of her, "So I can count on you to help me convince her of the wisdom of my decision?"

"Yes, you can count on me, Nick."

However, these two had not experienced Fancy's headstrong stubbornness yet. The naïve little girl from the countryside outside Memphis existed no longer as Nick was to discover when he returned to his cabin.

When he opened the door and stepped inside, Fancy was propped up by pillows. She was staring dejectedly down at her hands which rested in her lap. Finding herself alone in strange quarters had ignited a moment of panic which she would not allow to consume her so she'd sat there very quietly trying to piece together just what had happened last night.

She had not succumbed to Nick's charms but she knew instinctively this *was* his room. She'd even wondered if he'd caught her and drugged her to gain his way with her. God knows, her head felt terrible and that was one reason why she'd dared not move out of the bunk.

Just as the massive shadow of Nick filled the doorway, she became aware of something else, and she slowly let her hand trail down the blanket to her thighs to investigate privately.

"Morning, Fancy. Good to see you feeling better," he said moving to the bunk. Almost guiltily, she moved her hand out from under the covers to run her fingers through her hair, brushing it away from her face. She said nothing, just stared up at him. His face didn't look so fierce this morning nor did he ogle her with his salacious green eyes as he had last night on deck.

This Nick made her almost as nervous as the other one had. Seized with concern, she wondered if some awful thing had happened. The Nicholas Dubose confronting her was acting strangely.

"You feel like eating something? Some coffee, perhaps?" he asked.

"Yes—I'd like that," she replied, letting her eyes dance over his face and seek some hint. He left the cabin for only a second and returned to tell her, "It will be here in a minute. After you've got something in your stomach and some coffee to make you alert we've got to talk."

"We? I don't understand. Madame Dumaine—where is she? Does she know where I am?"

"She knows where you are, Fancy, and as a matter of fact, I've just come from her cabin."

Why was he acting so mysterious? she wondered? It was eerie and disconcerting and she didn't like it.

"Was I hurt? Is that what this is all about?"

"You were. In running from me you fell over a wooden bench that had been moved onto the deck.

You hit your head but it wasn't serious."

"Then why was I not taken to my own cabin adjoining Madame's instead of to yours?" The smells of tobacco and leather, and the presence of articles like the silver liquor flask on the stand left no doubt in her mind that this was Nick's cabin.

"My cabin was closer," he lied, wishing not to tell her that he'd told the doctor she was his wife.

"Was it that urgent?"

Nick was spared the necessity of answering by the appearance of the young lad delivering their breakfast tray. He insisted that they have some of the coffee while it was hot. "This will perk you up."

When they had both eagerly eaten every bite and had drunk generously of the coffee, Nick re-opened his conversation with Fancy.

"When all this happened last night there just happened to be a Natchez doctor aboard. He examined you after we brought you in here."

"Lucky for me, I guess," she gave him a soft, easy smile forgetting her anger for a second.

Pale as she was, she looked lovely to Nick. Without thinking, he moved closer. The very essence of Fancy seemed to have that effect on him.

"He thought you might have had a concussion but something more was discovered, Fancy. So I found it necessary to declare myself your husband." He sat there letting his eyes study her for a reaction.

She jerked up straight in the bed, her head instantly cleared. "You what?"

"Under the circumstances I thought it best."

"You thought? What about me, Nicholas Dubose? I didn't know I'd given you charge of my life," she indignantly snapped at him. Under her breath, she muttered that a more conceited man didn't exist!

He loved the fire in her eyes, and he certainly had to confess she was the only girl he knew who seemed displeased about the possibility of becoming his wife. Christ, she was an ornery little vixen.

He could not suppress the grin that came to his face although he knew it would rile her even more. "At the time you were in no shape to take charge so I had to do so, my sweet Fancy."

"Wipe that smile off your face, Nick. You don't have to trouble yourself about me anymore. I . . . I'll be all right. If I hadn't been trying to get away from you in the first place I wouldn't have had an accident."

He pursed his lips and tried his best to project a more serious attitude. "Now all you say is perfectly true, however, I think you've forgotten one very important thing. You were carrying my child. It was my baby you lost."

Oh, the arrogance of the man! She wanted to knock that smug look off his devious, handsome face. She glared at him for a minute before declaring, "Oh, you're so sure? Are you actually so certain I've gone to bed with no other man, Nicholas Dubose? After all, I've not seen you or heard a word from you since the afternoon you had your way with me." A smirk appeared on her pretty face. She wanted to wound that male ego of his.

What is she trying to pull now, Nick wondered? Her words stabbed him with a pain he'd never known. No woman had cut him this way before, and his own temper was at boiling point. He clenched his fist to prevent himself from reaching over to slap her face.

Fancy became even more reckless, provoking him beyond his limit by saying, "I see by your face you aren't so sure . . ." He lunged for her like a panther, his strong arms making her his prisoner. His mouth was cruel and demanding as he took her lips with no hint of gentleness. He would teach her to try such pretenses with him. He knew it had to be his child she'd carried. She was merely trying to hurt him and he couldn't understand why. The male in him forgot that women also have pride.

When he finally freed her lips, he muttered huskily, "Deny it, Fancy. Damn it, I don't want to hear you say it was anyone's child but mine!"

His powerful, overwhelming strength had drained any fight out of her. "Yes, it was yours." She took a deep intake of breath, relieved to see the fury in his eyes easing.

"All right, say you'll marry me now . . . as soon as I can arrange it. Say it, Fancy!"

His arms pressed her closer to his chest until she felt she could hardly breathe. "Nick . . ."

"Say it!" he angrily demanded, daring her to defy him.

"Yes, I'll marry you," she whispered breathlessly.

The savage beast in him was suddenly tamed. But Fancy had had a taste of how cruel Nicholas Dubose could be when provoked beyond his limit.

He continued to hold her close to him but there was a gentleness to his caress now, and his lips whispered softly against her ear, "Damn right you will, my love. No one shall have what's mine and you are mine!"

He didn't have to tell her that for she knew it. But she would not confess it to him.

The minute they disembarked on the wharf in Natchez, Fancy felt some awesome force had taken charge of her life—and that force was Nicholas Dubose. She felt like a zombie, one of the creatures Dahlia had described to her. With no will of her own, she moved around, going through motions.

The world was moving too fast for her and she yearned to halt it, to catch her breath and to stop her head from whirling. Far too much had happened to a simple country girl who had been a servant to the gentry less than six months ago. Suddenly finding herself traveling toward New Orleans as the wife of the aristocratic Nicholas Dubose was overwhelming. Everything seemed unreal.

She had been like a person in a trance during the last three weeks since she'd arrived back in Natchez. Her wedding to Nick had been a small, brief ceremony with only Alita and Dahlia present. The judge who'd married them had given her the oddest looks that had made her feel uncomfortable. Yet, he'd seemed to be a special friend to Nick.

She wore a magnificent diamond and emerald ring which was so exquisite she sighed every time she looked at it. The expensive clothing in her trunk had been purchased by her husband, and the gowns were so gorgeous she couldn't believe they belonged to her.

Now she'd boarded the boat that would carry her and her husband to his home in New Orleans. What awaited her there? How would Nick's aristocratic family treat her? Oh, she was frightened of so many things. Then there was Nick. Husband! Dear God, that seemed strange! Yet, it seemed more right than when she'd tried to envision herself married to Chris just a few days ago at Willow Bend.

An irritating little voice within her seemed to delight in chiding her. "Fancy Fourney, you know you're pleased about it all. He's the only man your heart could ever crave. Every time those emerald green eyes devour you, you go to jelly."

"Shut up, imp!" Fancy muttered, determined to defy the little demon who sorely tried her patience. Now as she waited for her husband to come to their cabin, she was alone, without the protection of Madame Dumaine who was traveling miles away from her and Natchez. She would have no one to turn to, and she was scared as she remembered

Nicholas's fury when he was riled.

A tear rolled lazily down her cheek as she sat on the edge of the bunk as still as a statue. This sight greeted Nicholas as he rushed through the door, a broad smile on his face and his arms encircling a bottle of champagne and a bouquet of roses for his little bride. He was so stunned to see her crying that he was speechless and his smile quickly vanished. He raised a skeptical black brow and moved slowly into the cabin, glaring down at Fancy.

Fancy met his stare and quickly brushed aside the tear from her cheek. She did not know what to do with her hands. They felt as cold as ice.

"Tears, my love?" Nick barked for he felt wounded. He'd done everything he could to make her feel excited and happy about marrying him. Not wanting to let her know how deeply he was wounded, he flippantly remarked, "And I was feeling so festive. See, I brought us champagne to toast ourselves. Here, the roses are a tribute to my beautiful bride."

She took them and her hand touched his. "Thank you, Nick. They're beautiful," she mumbled, knowing her voice was cracking. Actually she felt embarrassed that he'd come upon and found her crying like a baby. What a silly sight she must be!

He turned his back on her and sought a couple of glasses so she couldn't see his disturbed face. "Like you, Fancy." Although his tone seemed gruff to Fancy, he had not intended it to be. He was

more disturbed than he cared to admit. The journey was not starting out on the joyous note he'd
anticipated or desired. Was marriage to him so de-
pressing to her?

Fancy, overcome by the fast-paced course her
life had taken and unsure of the future, assumed
that he was disgusted with her childish behavior.
Her stubborn streak came to the fore. She'd show
him she was no child, and she'd not let him know
that he intimidated her to the point of making her
tremble.

Once she'd determined her course, she set about
carrying it out. As old Raoul had laughingly told
her once when she'd defied one of his gentle admo-
nitions, "You'd do it or die, wouldn't you girl?" And
she would behave now, with the arrogant Nicholas
Dubose.

She moved from the bed in a lazy, unhurried
manner and let her hands run from her tiny waistline over the curve of her hips smoothing the wrin-
kles of her soft silk gown. Once again, she found
herself impressed by the softness and luxury of the
material. Her husband did have magnificent taste
in ladies' fashions as well as in men's attire, she had
to confess.

"Champagne sounds wonderful," she almost
purred.

Nick whirled around to face her and the look on
her face made his eyes flash with delight. It took all
her strength to meet his bold glance.

What was it with this little witch? Now, she was

completely different . . . almost like a cunning, little seductress.

Fancy knew her change of character had him puzzled, and that was somewhat gratifying to her. Flippantly cocking her head to one side, she chattered lightheartedly, "I'd never had champagne until I came to Natchez to live with Madame Dumaine. I found I liked it. But . . . I get a little giddy, more quickly than I do if I just drink a white or red wine."

He found her most desirable as he watched her lashes flutter over those black, black eyes. God, she could not know the sensations she stirred in him at certain times with a particular look. This tiny slip of a girl possessed a sensuousness . . . and someday he'd bring it all out. Oh, yes, he intended to teach her everything—all the magnificent pleasures a woman could know.

She was ecstasy's child and he wanted the flames of that ecstasy to engulf him. A slow smile crept across his handsome face. What better time than the present?

The secluded privacy of their cabin seemed like an ideal romantic setting as they drifted on the smooth currents of the river in the twilight.

Pouring a glass of champagne for each of them, Nick handed one of the glasses to Fancy. A mischievous look was on his face as he searched his young bride's lovely one. "Giddy, eh? Well, my love it matters not what you do when you're with your husband. Here . . . enjoy it."

"I shall," she assured him, remembering that when she and Alita Dumaine had sipped champagne one evening the third glass had caused her head to swim. What she didn't recall, however, was that on this day, she'd eaten nothing but coffee and croissants. She'd had them at eleven this morning and it was now some seven hours later.

The champagne was delicious and she sipped it freely, eager to create an air of bravado. As Nick observed his bride many wild thoughts filled his mind. He commented so sincerely even Fancy couldn't doubt him, "You were born to have a luxurious life, Fancy my love. Champagne, the finest of silks, and the rarest of jewels befit your beauty."

"Why, Nick . . . you can say such pretty things!" She laughed as he filled her glass again, and giving him a teasing smile, she taunted, "You're a romantic, I do believe."

His eyes danced over her, feasting on her charms. Soon, my beauty, he mused, you are going to find out. He intended to romance and love her fully.

How divinely cozy and warm she felt. Her hands no longer trembled, nor were they cold. The truth was she felt very relaxed and comfortable. She found herself telling him about an amusing incident with Dahlia as she was dressing for the wedding, and he laughed deeply and richly. So busy talking and sipping, she didn't realize that Nick had refilled her glass for the third time.

Feeling quite merry, she gave his thigh a pat. When Nick lifted her hand from his thigh to his lips and placed featherlight kisses on her fingers and palm, she allowed him to do so. His lips had a magnificent touch.

His sensuous mouth made her feel good all over. Without any effort, it seemed, he was within inches of her face. His heated breath wafted against her cheek as he let his finger play with the wisp of hair at her temple. When she spoke he could detect a slight slur to her words. "You can be sweet, Nicholas Dubose, and you can be mean."

"I know, my sweet Fancy. I confess to being a mere mortal," he whispered tenderly. By now his lips trailed over the oval of her face and he felt her lean toward him. He surged with delight at her encouraging response. She was a woman of fire, but she didn't know it yet. She did know the force and power of the man so close to her, yet when his arms encircled her and his lips crushed hers, she wanted nothing more than to surrender. As if she'd come to terms with herself, she moaned, "Oh, Nick . . . Nick."

Without interrupting his touches and caresses, he disrobed her. Begrudgingly, he had to separate himself from her to remove his own clothing but not for long. Fancy had become so flushed with the rosy glow of passion she had no intention of denying herself the pleasure he could give her.

He emitted a deep throaty chuckle at the curious look on her lovely face. It reminded him that this was a strange, new world for his darling bride. After all, he would always cherish the fact that he was the first man in her life and he had every intention of being the only one.

He leaned over her. "You are so amazingly beautiful you take my breath away, my love." His voice was deep and low. His control was being sorely taxed for he wanted to possess her but he wanted to draw out these moments.

"Nick . . ." she urged, as his muscled thighs brushed against her and stirred a more urgent yearning within her.

"Oh, yes . . . yes, my darling!" he whispered huskily, wild desire surging and pounding fiercely in him. Knowing he aroused her so excited him even further. Oh, God, he wanted her, but he would also like to make love to her like this forever.

Her kittenlike purrs and sighs told him she was being swept on a tide of ecstasy, and even though he had perfected the art of making love so that a lady could reach the peak of pleasure, he knew his will power was waning.

One more sensuous sway of her flushed body against his and he was unable to stop the explosive inferno smoldering within him.

The current of their passion was so intense that the floodgates broke. Fancy gasped. Nick shuddered fiercely and then collapsed exhausted, saying her name over and over again. As their bodies quieted, he lay by her side, his arms still holding her close to his naked body.

"I think, my love, we've started our honeymoon. Do you wish it to continue?" Nick said tenderly.

Her response was a soft, lazy giggle. She was still glowing from his all-consuming love-making. In her daydreams she'd never imagined such breathtaking, glorious pleasure. She had not envisioned a man who possessed the capacity to make such ardent love.

In a soft, small voice she posed a question that revealed her innocence to her husband. "Nick, will . . . will it always be so . . . so wonderful?"

He couldn't restrain a laugh, although he knew she was quite sincere. He turned her to face him, kissing her first on the tip of her pert little nose and then on the lips before replying, "As long as you want it to be so, my sweet Fancy. It will take me a lifetime to love you in all the ways I want."

She snuggled ever so close to him. Her husband's words had made her happy. Her fulfillment was complete.

He'd even managed to satisfy her curiosity. If what he'd said was true then she'd be delighted to spend the rest of her life with Nicholas Dubose.

Chapter Seventeen

Her aristocratic friends in Natchez would have found the situation in the Dumaine house inconceivable and offensive, but Alita didn't care a whit what they thought. Who shared her loneliness better than her lady's maid, Dahlia? They both labored under a heavy shroud of gloom caused by Fancy's departure that afternoon.

As evening came on, Alita realized just how much she was going to miss the young girl. When Dahlia mentioned the ghostly quiet in the house since Miss Fancy had gone away with her new husband, Alita impulsively asked the little mulatto to share a dinner tray in her cozy sitting room with her. Together they dined and sipped a bottle of Alita's favorite wine. They both shed a few tears and later they laughed together like old friends as the wine eased the pain and gloom in their hearts.

"Madame, this will have to be our little secret.

No one would believe it anyway." Even Dahlia knew this privilege might never be granted to her again.

Alita, feeling the welcoming intoxication of the wine, gave a jolly, lighthearted laugh. "I've shocked one or the other of my friends here in Natchez since the minute Henri and I came here. Besides, I have enjoyed your company more than that of Jessica Waring or Fran Barnes who has a silly laugh."

"Why, thank you, Madame Dumaine," Dahlia exclaimed, swelling with pride. She would remember this night for the rest of her life, and if she were given leave to take unto herself a man and had a child she would take pleasure in boasting of her mistress's high esteem of her as a servant in a grand house.

"I speak the truth, Dahlia." Alita took a sip from the cut-crystal glass and leaned her head back against the lack of the overstuffed chair. "Oh, Dahlia, did I do right by Fancy? Do you think she feels angry with me? Would it have seemed to her that I was pushing her out the door into the arms of Nicholas Dubose?

"Miss Fancy knows you loved her, mistress." Dahlia soothed Alita. While Dahlia had originally disliked the arrogant Monsieur Dubose, her attitude had changed the night when Fancy had miscarried and he'd been so caring and concerned. Dahlia added, "Monsieur Dubose will make her a fine husband."

Dahlia's dark eyes masked more intimate, private thoughts but she kept them to herself. The wine had not relaxed her tongue so much that she would voice those to her mistress. She knew there would be a day that "her" Miss Fancy would learn to appreciate the virile, handsome man the likes of Nicholas Dubose if she hadn't already.

Having enjoyed sexual pleasure herself and having had her first man before she'd reached her thirteenth birthday, Dahlia knew she was right about Nicholas Dubose. He was a "tiger," fierce and mean, but loving and protective of his own. It was obvious to Dahlia that he'd proclaimed Miss Fancy his own. No, she would be all right.

Alita mind was eased by Dahlia's words. Alita, too, was thinking of the life Fancy would share with Nicholas. Oh, she had no illusions about the fights they'd have, but how divine the making up would be. Dear God, she envied the girl those golden ecstatic times!

"He is a handsome devil, isn't he Dahlia?" she voiced aloud.

"Oh, mercy yes, Madame Dumaine," the servant sighed. "He sure is that."

Setting the wine glass down, Alita Dumaine rose from her chair to find herself giving way to a slight giddiness which hardly surprised her. She and Dahlia exchanged amused smiles and Alita declared it was time for her to go upstairs.

"It was a most enjoyable evening, Dahlia. We'll do it again sometime, eh?"

"If you wish it, mistress." Dahlia took her cue and got up. Her head was whirling too, and she had no idea of the hour as the two of them mounted the stairway together.

They said their goodnights and parted company. Dahlia swayed lazily down the steps to go to her quarters at the back of the two-story house. A slow smile came to her face as she pictured Miss Fancy lying in the strong arms of her husband at this moment aboard that paddle wheeler taking them to New Orleans.

That thought brought her a sudden yearning to have a big, fine man awaiting her behind the door of her quarters. But she turned the knob and entered her room, knowing she was going to an empty bed this night. Maybe tomorrow night, she'd ease the ache with that rascal, Corky. Lord knows, he'd been sniffing around and pestering her enough lately.

The wine had not dulled Alita enough to prevent her from yearning for her darling Henri as she lay down at that late night hour. But her last thoughts were of Fancy and she prayed for the girl to be as happy with her husband as she had been with Henri.

She sighed softly, "I'll feel so terrible if I urged her to make the wrong move. So terrible!"

Even the sheet covering her satiny skin made Fancy aware of her nude body as she stretched out her legs and arms in an attempt to rouse herself from a deep sleep. She stared up at the ceiling and smiled impishly. Did she really . . . could she have? . . . Yes, she did. She had loved and been loved by Nick last night in such a wild and wondrous way she flushed just thinking about it. Recalling the touch of his hands, she tingled.

Perhaps, all her foolish fears and fancies were really very childish after all. He'd been so sweet and marvelous last night. A smug little smile on her face, she lay abed and thought that she was, indeed, the wife of Nicholas Dubose. Her name was now Dubose and that was a proud, esteemed name from what Madame Dumaine had led her to believe. Many women would envy her, she knew.

There he lay beside her, his thick, black hair tousled and his eyes closed still in sleep. His thick black eyelashes made a definite outline against his cheek. His impressive good looks were there for her to see, but at that moment she envisioned him as a boy. He certainly looked harmless enough. Yet, she knew he was ten years older than she.

His cheek rested against the upper part of her arm, but a contented languor possessed her. She had no desire to remove herself from her resting place. His warm body felt so good against hers.

Softly she whispered to her sleeping husband even though she knew he did not hear her. "Oh, Nick, I do love you so. If I could know you felt the same I'd be the happiest woman on the face of this earth."

She closed her eyes letting the depth of her love

warm her. Oh, he lusted for her, she knew that. Perhaps, that would have to do for the moment, but she wanted more . . . his eternal love!

Yvonne Dubose refused to believe that love had brought about her cousin's shocking, sudden marriage to Fancy Fourney. No. She suspected the devious Madame Dumaine of connivance. Perhaps she'd dangled the property of Dubonnet under his nose and the deal had included marrying Fancy Fourney. It had to be that.

Yvonne had known Nick all her life. She knew Uncle Alain and Aunt Monique had reared him to become the head of the New Orleans branch of the Dubose family.

For the first time since she, Daniel, and André had heard the news of Nick's wedding, she found something to be amused about. Lying there in her frilly canopy bed, she giggled. That simple, naïve girl would be floundering in a turbulent sea once she landed in New Orleans.

She could just see Monique when Nick marched in with a strange, little bride hanging on his arm. The strait-laced, stern Alain made no one feel at ease. Her own father, André, was nothing like his older brother — Yvonne thanked God for that. Her uncle was an iceberg.

Should she survive that staggering barrier, poor Fancy would never be able to cope with the diabolical antics of Nick's sister, Denise. Only the saintly little Doreen, Nick's youngest sister, would open her arms to Fancy when she arrived in New Orleans.

Yvonne could hardly picture the country girl who had been a mere servant mingling in the elite society to which Nick belonged. All those very chic, sophisticated ladies fawning over him at parties would be more than the simple-minded, unpolished miss could take. Yvonne knew Nick's social circle.

Nicholas would have to see for himself what a wrong choice he'd made for his wife. He'd feel embarrassment and shame when he saw his lifelong friends sniggering on the sidelines. These thoughts comforted Yvonne. She would wait patiently and when the time was right she would strike a mighty blow! Oh, how rich would be the harvest of her revenge!

She never doubted for a minute that she would be revenged — sooner or later. A pretty white-trash girl could woo a gentleman of the gentry into her bed but keeping him as a husband was another story. The only thing that perplexed her was that she'd considered Nicholas smarter. His dallying with Fancy in Natchez she could understand but what insanity had possessed him to take her to New Orleans as his wife? No, the bait could only have been Dubonnet, for he was and always had been a ruthless, ambitious businessman.

Chapter Eighteen

The late September sun was shining brightly as the passengers disembarked in the port of New Orleans. The crowd gathered along the wharf mingled with the departing passengers, as vendors sought to sell their wares to the many people clustered on the pier.

An elderly black man played a lively tune on his banjo as the dancing feet of a young black boy tapped out a jig in time to the strumming. A striking-looking quadroon, her head tied up in a brightly colored kerchief, was selling neatly tied clusters of flowers from a huge wicker basket.

Nicholas found nothing new or strange about the hustle of his hometown, but Fancy's eyes darted in one direction and then the other. Her head was constantly turning and her dainty hand had such a firm grip on his arm that Nick was aware of her excitement though she said not a word as they proceeded down the gangplank and up the wharf to the carriage awaiting them.

As they walked along Fancy sensed her husband's eyes upon her and turned in his direction. He gave her a crooked smile that accentuated the dimple in his cheek, and she was struck by his good looks. That dimple seemed to mellow his ruggedness. She knew for certain she adored him completely.

She looks delicious enough to eat, Nicholas thought, as he gazed into her face which was perfectly framed by her bonnet. Her excitement provoked an unusual sparkle in her eyes, and a feisty sway to her walk. He could feel the movement of her petite body as they made their way down the wharf. His arm was pressed against her side so he had to keep cautioning himself not to take such long strides.

He could not resist teasing her as she turned and looked up at him, "You're a fetching little vixen, Fancy Dubose."

"Am I now?" She taunted him back. He seemed to find it easy to say her new name, and she found herself liking the sound of it more and more.

He bent down to her. "You know damned well you are." He loved the sound of her lilting laugh.

No one observing these two boarding their carriage would have doubted they they were young lovers.

Nicholas Dubose's chest swelled with a new husband's pride as he hoisted Fancy inside the equipage. She was so vital, so alive and so utterly beautiful he couldn't help feeling otherwise. But as they sat in the carriage drawn by the high-stepping bay, neither said a word. Each was occupied by private thoughts. Fancy was suddenly tense at the thought of facing Nick's family. Any minute now she would be meeting them. She doubted that they would accept her.

Suddenly Nick realized the awesome ordeal this might be for the unsophisticated Fancy. Oh, he knew his well-bred parents would be gracious, but there could be a chill that Fancy would sense. If Dorcen was back from Europe, he knew she would greet his wife with open arms. The one he could make no predictions about and the one whose neck he'd wring if she didn't behave was Denise. But he didn't sell Denise short, for her vile little tongue could do damage before he could prevent it.

Then he had no more time for contemplation because the driver had turned the Dubose carriage into a wide driveway and a young black lad had rushed to open the iron gates.

"My home, Fancy." Nick gestured as they circled a cobblestone courtyard in which colorful flowers grew. Instantly Fancy took notice of the quaintness and spaciousness of the house. Nick asked, "Do you like it? A bit of the Old World and my father's great love of France."

"Oh, yes, I do," Fancy exclaimed, letting her eyes take in all the lavish ironwork. Madame Dumaine had said that her home there in Natchez had been patterned after the homes in New Orleans because of Henri's love of that city and of its French and Spanish influences. But that wasn't nearly as grand as the Dubose estate.

The fountain at the south side of the house was impressive, and under the roof of the covered side porch, Fancy noticed a gilded cage that held a brightly colored parrot the likes of which she'd never seen before. Excited as a child, she pointed in its direction, directing Nick's eyes to it.

He laughed, to see that she'd spotted Argo. "Oh, yes that is Argo, my love. He'll either love or hate you. He forms his opinions quickly and never wavers."

"Then I shall try to make a good impression at our first meeting." She giggled.

"You will," he assured her and planted a light kiss on her lips.

She gave him a warm smile, but a frown creased her forehead. Giving a slight tug on his arm, she halted. Her voice trembled slightly as she said, "Will it be so simple with your family, Nick?"

He respected her too much to lie to her, nevertheless, he answered her candidly, "It had better be, *chérie*. It had just better be." She was appeased and appreciated his honesty for his eyes reflected his sincerity.

The heavy oak door opened and a portly short black man greeted Nicholas with a broad smile. "Monsieur Nick." Gleefully, he addressed Fancy's husband, and she knew instinctively that their relationship spanned many years.

"Nat . . . good to see you. My dear, this is Nat and this is my wife, Nat."

With gleaming eyes and a gallant bow, Nat said, "Ma'am, welcome home."

Fancy returned his greeting. Then as Nick urged her on through the door, he teased Nat, "Don't believe anything though he might tell you, Fancy darling. After all, Nat was around when I was an undisciplined youth."

The manservant chuckled and shook his graying head. "I sure was. That's for sure."

Nick gave Nat's shoulder a comradely pat and declared, "I was a rascal, I confess. Are my parents in the parlor, Nat?"

"Yes, sir." The man responded and proceeded to lead the way.

Fancy took no note of the frown on her husband's face, for she was fascinated by old Nat's friendly reception. She liked the man and she felt he liked her. Walking down the highly polished hallway she felt relaxed and at ease. As they passed by a huge gilt mirror she checked to see if her bonnet was set at a proper angle before they entered through the closed double doors of the parlor.

She didn't realize that her husband's mood was anything but relaxed or lighthearted. He was annoyed that his family was being so stiffly formal and that they were treating him like a stranger instead of coming out to greet him and his bride. Their wedding had not been the traditional one and he had not complied with the rules of convention. But he was no young dandy anymore.

Nevertheless, he'd allow no disrespect to be shown Fancy so he entered the parlor ready for battle.

He decided to treat his family with reserved formality as he and his bride approached the gathering. He did not give Monique an affectionate kiss as he usually did when he returned from one of his many trips.

"Mother . . . Father, may I present my wife, Fancy," he said coolly, urging her slightly ahead of him. His eyes were a cool shade of green and they defied his family not to accept her warmly.

Alain moved forward and greeted her with a light kiss on the cheek. "A pleasure, my dear."

Monique followed her husband. "My dear," she greeted Fancy. Nick sensed the stiffness in her usually soft voice. He hoped Fancy didn't.

In a lighter manner, he guided Fancy toward his petite sister, Doreen. "My sister Doreen, Fancy." As he'd suspected he had no worry where Doreen was concerned. She rushed up eagerly to Fancy, hugged her, and declared boldly, "Oh, how very beautiful you are, Fancy. No wonder Nick married you so quickly. And . . . and I am so happy to have you for a sister."

Her exuberance delighted Fancy. "I feel the same, Doreen. You see, I don't have a sister." At once, Fancy felt they were friends and that was encouraging to her.

Nick left Denise for the last introduction. Even before he'd turned Fancy in her direction, his look warned her. "My other sister, Denise. This is my wife Fancy, Denise." He hoped his sister had gotten his unspoken message.

"Dear Fancy, this is such a delightful surprise. Welcome to our home," Denise purred, so sweetly that Nick saw right through the deceptive little imp.

Monique took charge then in her usual grand style, insisting they all have a seat and enjoy some refreshments. "Nat is seeing to your luggage, Nicholas dear. I had so little time to make any changes in your quarters."

He knew exactly what his mother meant and laughed good-naturedly. "No changes are necessary. My wife will be sharing my quarters and my bed."

"Nicholas! You'll embarrass your wife talking so boldly," his mother chided him.

He hugged Fancy close to him thinking that his family might as well get used to his affectionate ways when he was around her. He had a mischievous look on his face as he teased Fancy, "I don't embarrass you, do I, love?"

She played her role to perfection and gave him a loving, warm smile. "Never, Nick." He adored her at that moment. Some innate instinct had urged Fancy to respond as she had. Like the little creatures of the woods she'd roamed so many times in Willow Bend, she smelled something threatening,

213

some danger.

While partaking of the refreshments, she'd felt secure and at ease by her husband's side, but she'd also quietly observed these strangers in the lavishly furnished parlor as they had her. Doreen liked her as much as Denise resented her. That was easy to see. Every time Fancy's dark eyes glanced in her direction there was a smirk on her face. She came to no definite conclusions about Nick's parents, they were a complex pair. It was obvious to her, though, where Nick's arrogant aloofness came from — his father, Alain.

His mother, Monique really puzzled Fancy. The woman was the image of soft, feminine loveliness, and she revealed a genuine warmth when she looked at her son. Her striking beauty was reflected in both her daughters.

Fancy wanted to evaluate Nick's mother fairly. After all, the wedding must have been a shock to the woman since Nick was her oldest child and her only son. She would just have to take her time. Perhaps, Fancy thought, it would be only considerate of her to leave Nick with his family. She could amuse herself and go to their room.

Setting her cup and saucer on the small table by the side of the settee, she turned to Nick. "I think I will go to our room, Nick. I'm a little tired after our trip. Madame Dubose . . . Monsieur . . . I'm sure you will excuse me?"

Monique rose quickly. "Of course, dear. You must be weary. Traveling is tiring. Let me summon Celine and she will assist you with anything you might need to make you comfortable."

Nick made no protest but sat watching Fancy bid his sisters adieu. He felt that Fancy wasn't going to have any problems adjusting to his overpowering family. Many young ladies would have been quaking in their slippers, but she had acted as cool and self-assured as if she'd been born into the lap of luxury. Of course, he knew better. Madame Dumaine had told him about Fancy's background. Still, if she was nervous, she hadn't shown it.

"Get a good rest and I'll see you later, darling," he said, taking her hand and kissing it.

The servant girl named Celine stood waiting in the hall so Fancy left the group gathered in the parlor to follow Celine toward the stairway. She let out a deep sigh as she followed the servant.

"Sho' a wonderful day . . . this one. Sho' is. Monsieur Nicholas bringin' his pretty bride home," Celine declared, giving Fancy a big, bright smile.

"Why, how nice of you . . . Celine, isn't it?"

"Yes, ma'am . . . Celine, that's me." The girl bounced up the steps as Fancy ascended behind her, smiling and thinking that Celine was a feisty little mite.

The upstairs of the house was just as grand and luxurious as the downstairs. At the top of the landing Celine marched down the carpeted hallway, passed a couple of doors, and then pointed out the doorway to Miss Doreen's room and opposite it the one to Miss Denise's.

As she continued down the hall Celine told her where the other doors led: to Madame Dubose's sitting room, to Madame Dubose's boudoir, to Monsieur's upstairs study, and to his chambers. Then they turned a corner to go in another direction. Fancy was pleased that Nick's quarters were somewhat isolated from his family's rooms.

There were no frills and fluffs she noticed as Celine opened wide the two double doors into a rather small but cozy room which had its own fireplace. This room smelled of rich leather and she recognized the pungent aroma of the tobacco Nick used. A desk and comfortable chair, along with a finely carved chest were about the only furnishings. But Fancy's busy eyes did not miss the small miniature painting of a very beautiful lady. It was placed on his desk. Fancy immediately wondered who the lady was.

The woman was somewhat older than Nick but she knew her husband was a most sophisticated, worldly man. She . . . this woman . . . had some special place in his life or else he wouldn't have her picture on his desk.

As she followed Celine into the bedroom she experienced a tinge of jealousy and a pout came to her lips. Celine's prattle called her attention away from the mystery woman for the time being.

"Ma'am, which one?" Celine inquired, meaning which gown would Fancy wear for dinner that evening.

"Oh . . . I'm sorry, Celine. What were you asking me?" Fancy turned to the servant standing by her opened trunk.

"Gown, ma'am. You wish me to press up one? Shall I unpack now or later? If you'd like to rest awhile I can do it later."

After hesitating for a minute, Fancy told Celine to take out the daffodil yellow gown. Nick said that was her most flattering color. The unpacking, she suggested, could be done later. Now, she wanted time alone to absorb this strange new room she'd share with her husband, a stranger too.

Alone, she felt the tremendous impact of Nick's somewhat awesome family. Quietly sitting on her husband's massive bed with the high carved headboard that reached almost to the ceiling, she thought of the family members downstairs. Was it righteous indignation she sensed in Nick's very dignified parents? Why did his sister Denise exhibit such indifference to her on their first meeting? Only Doreen welcomed her wholeheartedly. In the Dubose's butler, Nat, she'd felt warmth, and the maid, Celine, had seemed happy about her arrival.

Flinging herself back on the bed and kicking off her slippers she mumbled, "Well, I have arrived and I am Nick's wife. Like it or not!" No one heard her. Only the four walls of the bedroom looked back at her, but she had given herself the courage to meet whatever challenges might lie ahead.

Chapter Nineteen

The topic of conversation within the walls of the Dubose mansion as the dinner hour approached was the young Madame Dubose. From the servants' quarters to the big, bustling kitchen where the evening meal was being prepared, the talk concerned Fancy. Celine had given a very vivid, detailed account of her to every house servant she'd encountered.

And so it was upstairs with Nicholas's sisters and his parents. Except for a desire to prod her sister, Denise would not have visited Doreen's room as she did this evening, putting on a most casual air as she entered to find Doreen putting the final touches to her toilette.

"Well, I suppose you think she is just divine?" Denise swayed arrogantly up behind her sister and peered into the mirror, her reflection joining her sister's.

Doreen's finely arched brow rose. She could never relate to her sister's attitudes, probably never would. Very positively and directly, she answered, "As a matter of fact, I do. I suppose you don't." Doreen's tone rather took Denise by surprise.

"I think she saw Nicholas as a good catch and worked her wiles on him. After all, our brother is a very wealthy man, Doreen."

"Don't forget he is a very smart one, too. Perhaps you've forgotten, Denise, about Nick's reputation with the ladies? He isn't exactly a gullible youth," Doreen shot back at her rather perplexed sister. Never had the meek Doreen spoken to Denise in that way.

Denise swished her taffeta skirt and turned from the mirror. It was obvious this "Fancy" was going to have an ally in Doreen. Let her! She would not sully herself with any little white trash baggage — not even Nicholas's wife.

"You coming down now, Doreen? I heard mother and father go down the hall just now," Denise said to her sister as she opened the door. There was no point in discussing their new sister-in-law any further. To Denise it was bad enough that she was sharing their table this evening.

"Yes, I'm coming," Doreen answered. She followed her older sister, an amused look on her face.

Monique and Alain had also indulged in a

lengthy discussion about their new daughter-in-law when he'd joined his wife in her boudoir. Now that the newlyweds would soon be joining them for dinner, he felt compelled to caution Monique. Giving her a glass of wine and pouring himself one, he joined her on the cream-colored brocade settee. "Don't say any more to rile Nicholas, *ma petite*. He . . . he seems most sensitive and overly protective about his wife. I thought once this afternoon he was going to explode. Remember?"

His regal-looking wife grimaced. "Oh yes, I was very aware of his reaction. I will do my best, *mon cher*." She gave a dejected sigh.

Alain was aware that his own energy and drive were waning. The responsibility for running the Dubose enterprises must soon rest with Nicholas. Alain no longer anticipated his business trips as he once had. Yes. His strong, virile son should be stepping into his shoes.

"Perhaps, we should give the young lady a chance, eh? She is certainly an enchanting little thing and she seems to adore Nicholas," Alain pointed out to his wife.

Monique gave her dignified-looking husband a quizzical look. So even her strait-laced Alain had not been blind to the girl's spellbinding beauty. Keeping this awareness to herself, she remarked, "Alain, I've never known any woman not to adore our Nicholas from the time he was barely sixteen. My word, remember that

Mademoiselle Pernall who visited the Bushaws the summer of Nicholas's sixteenth birthday? *Mon dieu,* she must have been twenty and Nicholas was a lad, but he was so tall even then. I don't mean to sound smug but what woman wouldn't find him fascinating?"

Alain laughed, but he had to agree with her. Any man would be proud to have Nick as his son for he possessed all those qualities a man desired in his offspring. He had power and strength as well as the ability to attract and entrance women.

When Fancy and Nicholas emerged through the double doors of the parlor, even Monique had to admit they were a striking couple. With her hair upswept in a most fashionable style, Fancy looked taller. Even the wispy tendrils that curled around her neck were appealing. The soft clinging material of her gown exhibited the beauty of her sensuous figure, and its daffodil color was perfect with her dark complexion.

Her eyes were like black polished onyx, so sparkling and bright. Monique noticed a unique quality about the girl that hadn't been obvious that afternoon. She possessed a remarkable blend of sweet innocence and sophistication. There was even a hint of a provocative seductress in those dark, sultry eyes as she fluttered her long lashes.

Unaware that she was staring so intensely at

the girl, Monique sipped her wine. She now realized why her son was so enchanted with his bride. Fancy was unique—totally unlike the other women he'd squired around the world. No wonder the sweet, ordinary Chantelle Charbeau had not interested him. She wouldn't attract a man like Nicholas. He had a reckless streak in him.

Fancy prided herself on the gown she'd picked. Nick's reaction to it had assured her that it was the right choice. Celine was responsible for her hairdo. It did do something for her, and she liked the effect it created. Celine had raved about it when she'd pinned the pale yellow velvet cluster of flowers in Fancy's hair. "You look like some fine lady indeed! The prettiest I ever did see. I swear it, Miss Fancy!"

Fancy thanked her with such warmth and gratitude that Celine hardly knew what to say next—a rare situation for her. Nothing about this young bride of Monsieur Nicholas bespoke anything but gentleness and a good heart, the servant girl concluded. She had no waspishness in her like that minx Denise, and yet Celine was certain Fancy possessed more spirit and fire than the shy Doreen.

The evening was turning out to be a pleasant one by the time they left the parlor for the more formal setting of the dining room. The food was delicious and Fancy enjoyed the lighthearted talk during the meal. She was so confident that she found herself feeling she was actually a part of the Dubose family. She was not reluctant to leave Nick and his father to their brandy and cheroots and to join the women after the meal.

Silently, Fancy credited Madame Dumaine with teaching her the poise she'd acquired. She imitated that woman's queenly ways. Never had Fancy seen Alita ill-at-ease. She had learned much from her.

The women settled themselves comfortably, and they all had a glass of sherry, except Doreen. During the last hour Doreen had begun to relax for it seemed that Denise was going to be on her best behavior for a change. She'd wanted Fancy's first evening to be a nice one and was relieved that it had been. How frightening it must be to go amid a houseful of strangers, Doreen thought to herself.

"Your gown is lovely, Fancy. May I ask if you purchased it in Natchez?" Monique inquired for she appreciated fashionable clothes.

"Why thank you and yes, I did — at Madame Charlotte's. She is a magnificent seamstress," Fancy told her.

"Remember, mother? Cousin Yvonne is always raving about Madame Charlotte this and Madame Charlotte that," Denise broke in. "Oh, by chance, Fancy, do you know Yvonne?"

"Yes, I do Denise."

"Oh." Denise suddenly became quiet. She hadn't expected to hear that.

"Have you been out to Magnolia?" Doreen wanted to know.

"Yes and it is lovely. But I must confess that to me no place is as glorious as Madame Dumaine's Dubonnet."

At that particular moment the men entered the parlor and Nick was delighted to hear Fancy's declaration. It pleased him that she shared his love of the fine old estate he felt destined to own someday. His hands reached down to rest on her dainty shoulders, and he bent to plant a kiss on her cheek, not caring that they had an audience. "I agree on that," he said tenderly. The touch of his sensuous lips fired her so that she knew she must be blushing. She heard Doreen's light giggle and had no doubt she was wearing a rosy glow on her face.

Alain cleared his throat for he was not a very demonstrative man. Secretly, Monique had wished Alain had been more expressive, but it seemed Alain's youngest brother was the hot-blooded one in their family. Nicholas was like André in so many, many ways.

In recent years, Monique had found herself realizing this about Nicholas. Even her dearest friend, Angelique had discussed it with her.

Such a shame Angelique could not make it for dinner this evening. Monique would have liked to have known Angelique's opinion of Nicholas's new bride, but Angelique had politely declined Monique's invitation to dinner. That night, she had thought, should be for the immediate family. However, Angelique Rocheleau did seem like one of the family since her friendship with Monique dated from their teenage years.

When the Duboses had received Nicholas's letter from Natchez informing them that he was bringing a bride home to New Orleans, Angelique's eyes had gleamed with happiness. Monique knew how much he meant to her. "It is time he settled down, Monique," Angelique had declared, but when Monique had suggested she come to dinner the night of the newlyweds' arrival, Angelique had smiled that beautiful smile of hers and declined. "Not the first night, dear. After all, a young bride could be very intimidated by so many new faces at once."

If she wasn't there in person, Angelique Rocheleau's spirit was there, and her thoughts were very much on the goings-on at the Dubose home that evening. Whoever the young girl was, she felt her heart go out to her. She had to be very special to have captured that young man's reckless, elusive heart. She'd not deny for a minute that she was anxious to meet her.

On Nick's last visit to Angelique's home, he had acted as though something weighed heavily on his mind. Now, she wondered if he'd been unhappy because he'd left Fancy behind in

Natchez. Perhaps he'd already lost his heart to her.

Oh, Nicholas! She looked upon him with as much pride and joy as Monique and Alain did. She hoped his new bride would like her when they did meet.

She laid her dark head back against the overstuffed chair back and gave way to thoughts of yesteryears. Such bittersweet thoughts! Yet, there had been compensations to treasure and cherish.

If she had known that Nicholas had inquired of her while he and his father had enjoyed their brandy and cheroots together, the knowledge would have made her very happy. A visit to Angelique was one of the first calls Nick planned to make with his bride. Madame Rocheleau's opinion was very important to him, but somehow, he knew what she would think even before she and Fancy met.

It was long past the hour of ten when Nick took his wife up to their quarters, and the pleased look on her face reflected the way she felt. As she walked pridefully upstairs at Nick's side, she thought that it wasn't so hard to become one of the gentry. Being Nicholas Dubose's wife was not going to be as difficult as she'd imagined.

That evening she had been enlightened about

some members of the Dubose family, especially Denise. She knew that she'd been right that afternoon; Nick's older sister didn't like her. Well, Fancy wasn't too fond of Denise either. But she'd just have to prove that she was a little smarter and not let Denise play her for a fool. Fancy also decided something else about the two sisters. If she could and Doreen would allow it, she hoped to inspire some courage in that sweet-natured girl so she would no longer allow Denise to bully her.

The first evening Fancy spent in the Dubose mansion did not change her impressions of her father-in-law and her mother-in-law. But what they thought of her really didn't matter to Fancy, not with Nick's arm around her wasplike waist. She knew in the privacy of their rooms he'd sweep everything from her mind except his powerful presence.

However, she hadn't been prepared for the romantic setting of the two adjoining rooms. Candlelight glowed, casting flickering shadows against the wall, and at the foot of the bed, Celine had laid one of the diaphanous gowns Nick had purchased from Madame Charlotte. This one was pale peach and beside it was a matching peach satin wrapper lavishly edged with ecru lace.

She laughed, lightheartedly and delightedly when she saw the bottle of champagne and the two glasses awaiting them for she knew Nick had thoughtfully ordered these to be provided while they were downstairs. She whirled around, her heart racing wildly. "You *are* a romantic, Nick!"

He grabbed her around the waist and swung her around before setting her feet back down. "Of course I am, my lovely Fancy." His eyes warmed as her body came to rest against his and he lifted her dainty feet inches from the floor. "I'm getting more romantic all the time." His devilish teasing provoked her to laughter for she felt his urgency.

Her lips moved to meet his and to let him know the flames of passion also lapped and consumed her. "I love you, Nicholas Dubose," she confessed in a soft murmur, barely above a whisper.

His strong arms hoisted her with one mighty sweep and he carried her into their bedroom. Setting her down, he proceeded to disrobe her unhurriedly. His hands had a tantalizing effect on her, stirring wild little sensations wherever they touched her flesh.

"Your skin is so soft and silky. I love to touch you, Fancy. You don't mind, do you, my darling?" his voice was deep and husky.

"Mind? Oh, Nick, I love your touch," she sighed as the warmth of his desire swept over her.

So absorbed was she by the intoxicating magic of him, she was not aware that she stood completely nude in front of him. He now stood bare to the waist, and even though her hands played across his broad chest and trailed up through the soft curling black hair scattered on his chest, she had not noticed how easily he'd shed his coat and shirt.

He loved her unabashed honesty with him, for he wanted no barriers between them. Perhaps, he wanted a lady to reign over his parlor, but in his boudoir he wanted a woman.

He urged her back on the bed, positioning himself over her to kiss her. With one swift motion he sought to free himself of his restraining trousers. Fancy did not realize the dilemma he found himself in until he impatiently muttered, "Damned clothes!"

Fancy was amused by his struggle. She chuckled, and so he taunted her, "You'll pay for laughing at me, you little vixen."

She wiggled out of his reach only to be caught and covered completely by his body. His muscled thighs fenced her in as he burrowed between her legs and thrusted himself forward, eager to be encircled by her velvet warmth. The pleasure he knew as their bodies fused made him moan with ecstasy. Fancy's own soft sigh blended with his cries.

Together they soared to new heights so rapturous she was astonished when they finally lay breathless in one another's arms. She would not have believed that this night could surpass the last time they'd made passionate love, but it had. Was it limitless, the sensual pleasure this man could give her? She lay, delightfully exhausted, there in the dark feeling that she wanted only to sleep in his powerful arms.

It was important to him to tell Fancy just how much he worshipped her. "I've dreamed of you all my life, my sweet Fancy. No other woman could ever have my heart or my love now that I've had you."

When Fancy didn't answer him, he smiled, knowing his darling wife was already sound asleep. Nuzzling his face in the thick mass of her hair, he felt peacefully content as she nestled in the curve of his big body. Forever, Fancy, this is where I want you, he mused.

His sleeping young bride did not know the elation he felt as he lay quietly beside her. He had so much love to give her, so much pleasure to offer her . . . all in good time. Fires of ecstasy were in her sensuous body and he had only to flame them. Slowly he would do so, and he would savor them with rapturous delight.

This was a strange, new feeling for Nicholas Dubose—to want to spoil a woman so completely with his overpowering love that no other man could touch her heart.

Chapter Twenty

Fancy's first two weeks in New Orleans went by swiftly. Nick seemed to know everyone in the city, judging by the many invitations and affairs they'd attended. Even though a million names seemed to be whirling through her head, she enjoyed every minute. Any apprehensions she'd harbored about her future with Nick had vanished, and in their place she found herself utterly and completely enamored of this handsome man to whom she'd lost her heart on that day she'd traveled to Natchez.

Only one thing gnawed at Fancy. Nick's parents seemed more distant now than when she had arrived. Denise's snubs did not bother her. In fact, she tried to ignore Nick's haughty older sister most of the time, favoring the friendly, little Doreen with her company.

Doreen and Nick had shown her the house and grounds of the fine estate. By the end of her first week, she was familiar with the place and she knew house servants by their names.

Fancy visited the quaint tea rooms and shops of the city, and she went for rides in the glorious countryside. It seemed that summer planned to linger forever in New Orleans. By now in Memphis, at Willow Bend, the brisk chill of autumn would be in the air, while in New Orleans at the end of September flowers still bloomed profusely. A few hundred miles made a difference.

Because of the natural curl to her hair, Fancy found the very moist air a culprit. She and Doreen shared that mutual complaint for Doreen's hair was naturally curly too, whereas Denise had the fine, silky hair of her mother. However, Fancy shared more with Doreen than the texture of her hair. Like Fancy, Doreen loved strolling in the countryside, and she was interested in the small animals of the woods. When she displayed her paintings to Fancy, those interests were reflected in the subjects she enjoyed painting on her canvases. She had depicted the birds and squirrels, the colorful wildflowers in the fields, and a view of the river that showed the boats traveling downstream.

On the days Nick spent in his father's office Fancy and Doreen had sought out each other's company. It seemed to Fancy that she only half existed until Nick returned to the house late in the afternoon. Still, she floated in a sea of bliss, deliriously in love with the man she'd married, and she had written a long, detailed letter to Alita Dumaine expressing how happy she was in New Orleans.

Nick left the house one morning secretly promising himself that he was going to return early so that he and Fancy could arrange to pay a visit to Madame Rocheleau. That visit had been delayed because business affairs at the shipping lines had required his attention. The origin of a fire in the hold of one of their ships had seemed suspicious.

That same morning Fancy was surprised by Denise's sudden change of attitude, but she accepted it as an encouraging sign and delightedly accepted an invitation to accompany Denise on a shopping tour.

Gleefully Denise left Fancy in the dining room calling back over her shoulder, "Can you be ready to leave about one?"

"Of course, Denise," Fancy replied, feeling elated at this turn of events. After all she wanted the good will of her husband's family.

"Then I'll send word to Dudley to bring the carriage around at one. All right?"

"Fine. See you then, Denise." Fancy finished her last sip of coffee and rushed up to dress.

As Fancy attended to her toilette she would not have been so lighthearted if she could have seen the smug, pleased look on her sister-in-law's lovely face. Her invitation had nothing to do with a friendly overture toward Fancy. Quite the opposite.

She had every intention of showing Fancy up for

what she was. As Denise put the final touches to her hair, she eagerly anticipated the hostile game she intended to play on Fancy. Then she dabbed cologne behind her ears and descended the stairs, hoping there she would not encounter Doreen. Doreen would know exactly why she'd invited Fancy to attend this popular, quaint little shop. It was a gathering place for Denise's snobbish friends and the perfect spot for her to encounter one or more of Nicholas's feminine acquaintances.

Like a lamb being led to slaughter, Fancy joined Denise in the carriage. Dudley reined the bay into action and headed for the shop Mademoiselle Dubose had specified. If the young mademoiselle lingered as long as she usually did, Dudley looked forward to enjoying a nice nap while he waited.

When Dudley halted the carriage and leaped down to assist the two pretty young ladies to alight, his nose picked up the smell of fresh roasted peanuts that wafted over to him from the vendor's cart. He decided to indulge himself with some. His mouth was watering for their magnificent taste as he helped Mademoiselle Dubose and the little Madame Dubose, as he'd dubbed Fancy, down from the carriage.

Denise chattered away as they walked into the shop. Anyone observing the two young women would have had the impression that Denise liked her companion. Certainly the matronly owner of the hat shop, Esther Babcock, thought so as she watched them enter. Her daughter Liza stood just behind her mother and she, too, watched the two young ladies. One, she knew, but she wondered who the other beautiful stranger might be.

Esther Babcock was a widow. By means of her small shop she had managed to support Liza and herself after her husband, Bill, had died from yellow fever. Good fortune had been hers when she'd managed to lure many of the wealthy French Creoles and the plantation owners' wives and daughters with her exquisite hats and gloves, as well as her lacy shawls. Lately, the soft, light woollen imported scarves and shawls had been selling so well that she'd already ordered more.

Her success had been amazing, for the French citizens usually shunned the American shop owners, preferring to give their business to the old established places. Esther had realized she was lucky when word had spread from one pleased customer to another.

For some reason Esther didn't understand herself, the young ladies enjoyed using her shop as a gathering place where they browsed and caught up on the latest tidbits of gossip. Inevitably Esther sold some items during these gatherings. Indeed, the sum total she had made at the end of the day often amazed her.

Now she smiled brightly as she went to greet the young ladies who had just entered. "Mademoiselle Dubose . . . so nice to see you today."

Denise nodded slightly. Her eyes searched the two alcoves of the shop to see if Abigail or Myra had arrived, and even more anxiously, she sought Samantha, knowing that Nick had squired her around the city in the past.

Denise Dubose's companion intrigued Esther. She supposed her to be a new arrival in the city. Obviously this was a young lady of quality but the shop owner knew she'd recall her had she made a previous visit. Such beauty made an impact that was remembered. The young lady gave Esther a sweet smile. She didn't appear to be snobbish like the Mademoiselle Dubose and her friends. At times, the shop owner was tempted to take her broom and shoo all of them out. Their tongues could be so cutting and cruel. Even her daughter, Liza, had been subjected to their abuse, and Esther had had to bite her tongue or lose money.

Esther blessed her sweet, little Liza for understanding the situation. With a wisdom far beyond that of her years, Liza had shrugged her mother's concern aside and had told her, "I think they are bored, Mama. If they had to work their hands more, they'd work their mouths less."

Now Esther turned her attention to Fancy and inquired, "May I help you with anything, *mademoiselle*? I don't believe you're acquainted with my little shop?" But before Fancy could reply to the lady, Denise took charge. "This is the new Madame Dubose, Esther. Fancy, you will find that Esther Babcock's bonnets are the rage of New Orleans."

"It is a pleasure to meet you, Mrs. Babcock,"

Fancy said. The way she addressed Esther impressed the shop owner who rather enjoyed being shown respect by the younger generation for a change.

"My pleasure, Madame Dubose. It will be a delight for me and my daughter, Liza, to serve you. No bonnet I could ever make would be elegant enough to frame that pretty face of yours, ma'am."

Mrs. Babcock's compliments ruffled Denise, so she flippantly chided the woman, "*My*, I never had such a tribute paid to me, Fancy." She swished over to the counter to pick up a pair of gloves made of lovely lace. Having taken Denise's comment as a lighthearted jest, Fancy was completely oblivious to the seething anger beginning to boil in Denise. When Denise turned back again, she became even more riled at seeing Esther Babcock taking Fancy on a tour of her shop while the two talked away like old friends. This afternoon jaunt was not going according to Denise's plans.

While Denise paced the shop picking up various articles and then tossing them back down, much to the chagrin of the observant Liza, Fancy purchased one of the light woolen shawls in a pale cream color. When Denise saw her sister-in-law admiring a very elegant lace shawl displayed with matching black lace gloves and reticule, she rushed across the shop. Good Lord, a girl like Fancy could not possibly know what those three items would cost. Nicholas had probably purchased every nice item in her wardrobe.

"Hhmm, Fancy, dear, you aren't going to buy that, too, are you?" Denise laughed. "I'll just have to bill anything I pick out to Father and I imagine you are probably in the same fix."

Fancy patted her sister-in-law's arm and retorted gaily, "So will I, for that is what Nick told me to do anytime I wished. Mrs. Babcock and I have already worked that out, Denise dear, haven't we, Mrs. Babcock?"

"We certainly have, dear. The wife of Nicholas Dubose has unlimited credit at this shop." Esther began to dismount the shawl and to box it for Fancy.

After a full hour passed without one of her friends appearing, Denise vowed to settle this score with Abigail Kingsley and Myra Reynolds. Just as she suggested to Fancy that they stop by one of the tearooms before returning home, Denise saw a familiar young woman alighting from a carriage. However, the young lady preparing to pay a visit to the shop was not one of Denise's best friends, so with a brief swift introduction to Linda Delacroix, Denise urged Fancy on to their carriage.

Pleased with her purchases and having enjoyed their afternoon jaunt, Fancy gaily chattered away, unaware that Denise was too preoccupied to listen to anything she was saying.

Young Madame Dubose's face was as radiant as the sunshine, Dudley observed, as he crawled back onto his perch to drive to the next stop, the little tearoom.

Midafternoon shoppers and their carriages filled the streets, and Dudley had to halt the carriage and wait to make the turn into the side street where the tearoom was located.

The scene that met Fancy's startled eyes during that moment's delay completely clouded her delightful afternoon.

Dudley's pause seemed like an eternity to Fancy, for across the way, leaping into a carriage occupied by a lady, whose beauty was so breathtaking Fancy could not help admiring her, was her husband. His face, never more handsome, was creased by a devastating smile. He couldn't wait to clutch the woman into the strong vise of his arms and hold her to him. Her beautiful smiling face told Fancy that this was an act not new to either of them.

Oh, God, she wanted to die. Thank goodness, Denise was looking out the other window and paying no attention to her or to this side of the narrow street. Fancy wanted to scream at Dudley to move the carriage on just as fast as he could. She had to get away from this hellishly tormenting scene.

She wanted to cry but she dared not let the tears flow. Then she felt as if she were going to retch, for her stomach was in knots and her hands trembled with rage and fury. God forbid, sitting in a tearoom and making idle chatter were the last things she wanted to do now.

Willing herself to sound casual, she suggested to Denise, "If you don't mind, could we just get on home. I've a horrible headache."

Nick's sister was preoccupied with her own thoughts. "Wha . . . what did you say? Go on home? Certainly, I wasn't really too eager to go to the tearoom." She informed Dudley of their change of plans and then glanced over at her sister-in-law. Fancy did look pale. Obviously, she was feeling ill.

A surge of sympathy for her sister-in-law seized Denise. Fancy looked so distraught and pained. Denise wasn't completely heartless, just a typical young miss who was self-centered and who had always been too pampered. Devilment had been her intention when they'd started out this afternoon, but as she looked over at Fancy now she felt a touch of warmth.

"You don't feel well, do you, Fancy?" she inquired.

"No, I don't," Fancy replied. Her dark eyes turned toward Denise. There was pain reflected in them but it was the pain of an aching heart. She did not know if there was a cure for it.

By the time the carriage had reached the Dubose residence and the young women had alit, Fancy had swept any thought of tears aside. No tears for her over Nicholas Dubose . . . not anymore! But no fetching siren would be waiting for him this night either. Instead, Nick would find an angry vixen!

Chapter Twenty-one

Problems certainly had arisen at the steamboat line during Nick's sojourn away from the city. Alain Dubose had probably discovered the identity of the culprit who had created the series of accidents at the wharf and aboard his boats in the last eight weeks. For over an hour Nick and Alain had sat in the office discussing this problem. When they had decided on a definite plan of action, their meeting ended.

No upstart steamboat line was going to be allowed to ruin their business. Nick wondered why Jake Rafferty was trying to fight so underhandedly with the powerful Dubose empire. Was he rash or just crazy? Whichever, he would soon find out just what he was up against. So would all his Irish hooligans!

As he left his father and sauntered down the long wharf he realized the shipping line was more important to him than he'd thought. Feeling the need to stretch his long legs after sitting so long at his father's desk, he walked briskly down the street enjoying the magnificent day and the bright sunshine.

His firm, long strides seemed to announce to the world that he was a self-assured man who knew exactly where he was going. He held his head high, and there was a pleased look on his face. He was heading home and hoping his early arrival would please Fancy.

This was the young man who marched up the street toward Angelique's advancing carriage. She instructed her driver to halt and watched him intensely as he came closer. Then she called out to him and he rushed into her waiting arms exactly as he had done so many times. Angelique and Nick hugged one another with genuine warmth and affection.

Having no knowledge of the long-established bond between these two or of who Angelique was, it was natural for Fancy to assume she was witnessing a clandestine meeting. Angelique Rocheleau was unusually youthful looking for her forty-three years and her blue-black hair was free of any gray.

There was nothing matronly about Madame Rocheleau's figure. She was slender and petite, which made her appear much younger too. She patted Nick's broad shoulder and chided him for not coming by to see her. "I know, Angelique. Forgive me, eh?" His brilliant green eyes haven't changed a bit, she mused.

"Of course, you rascal."

"I'm so anxious for you and Fancy to meet. I think the two of you will like one another." His strong arms still encircling Angelique, he laughed, "She's no bigger than a mite . . . just like you."

"Ah, so does she make you behave, you big oaf?" Angelique teased him.

"She does and she's bossy," he chuckled.

"Good. She sounds delightful. Now, just when am I going to meet her, eh?"

"How about the end of the week? Perhaps, this Friday?"

"Perfect. Dinner at my house?"

"We'd love to, Angelique." He gave her another bear hug declaring how good it was to see her and prepared to leave her to be on his way. Smiling broadly, he dismissed her offer of a ride to his house. "I need to walk, Angelique. A honeymoon can make a man lazy."

"Nicholas, I cannot imagine you being lazy and certainly not on your honeymoon," she laughed. "Remember, young man. . . . you are talking to Angelique." She pointed a finger at him accusingly as though to jar his memory and he knew exactly what she meant.

He was in the highest spirits as he walked on for seeing Angelique had made him feel he was really home. That dear woman always had represented an anchor, a security he found nowhere else and with no other person. He didn't try to question that feeling . . . not anymore. It was just a secret thing he kept buried deep within himself for most would find it strange. Even his darling, beloved Fancy would find it hard to fathom these feelings so he hadn't spoke to her of Angelique Rocheleau yet.

Without any mercy or gentleness, Fancy brushed her hair as she stared into the mirror. Her dark eyes flashed, black as burning coals. If only she could brush away the scene she'd seen an hour ago. She'd had no inkling until today what a fierce emotion jealousy could be. It was like a horrible monster that took sharp, slow bites out of her. Then the pain would ease a little, only to start all over again.

She'd come directly to her room, strip off her gown, and don a light robe over her undergarments. Her head pounded so that she instantly freed it from any restraints and brushed her hair. Her frustration and fury were expressed in each stroke.

How could he do what he had done? How could he be such a lover only last night and then rush into another woman's arms this afternoon? Had she been so naïve about men that she'd thought Nick was different? Some of Dahlia's comments about men came to her mind. Perhaps Nick was like most men. After all he was in New Orleans where he'd lived and wooed many a fair lady.

Dahlia had once told Fancy that the fine gentlemen of Natchez had mistresses across town. "Then there's Belle's. That's where all the wealthy gents go to pleasure themselves, Miss Fancy," Dahlia had told her.

Fancy recalled that she'd asked, "But why not with their wives?"

"Honey, you are one sweet one. So innocent it hurts," Dahlia declared. "These ladies — some of them — sweet child, would be mortified if their husbands tried to make love to them the way they'd dearly love to. Some ladies of the gentry are so prim and proper that the act of love is revolting to them and they're relieved when their husbands do take a mistress. You see, child, these women are only interested in a name and a position. They preside in the fancy parlors. The boudoirs are the whores' domains. You see what I mean?"

"I guess so, Dahlia," Fancy had mumbled, not too sure she understood at all.

Now, sitting at her dressing table she longed for the sight of Dahlia. To the empty room she muttered venomously, "This is one lady who won't share her husband with another woman! If he takes another, he won't have any part of me. Not so much as a kiss will you have, Nicholas Dubose!"

As Fancy yanked the brush through her hair determinedly, Nick bounded through the bedroom door to see her sitting on the velvet-cushioned stool, her breasts swelling over the lacy edging of her undergarment. At that moment Nick wanted exactly what she was planning to deny him. . . a kiss. Fancy stared at her husband, no warmth in her dark eyes, no sweet smile on her half-opened lips. Suddenly feeling awkward, Nick tried to cool the yearning that consumed him.

He made a gallant gesture, a bow, and greeted her in a far different manner than he'd planned. "Good afternoon, my love."

"Hello, Nick." Fancy turned her back to him and returned to brushing her hair. "Did you have a busy day with your father?"

Nick slowly sauntered over to the bed and flopped down on it. "I did." His eyes burned a hole in her back and his brow rose questioningly. What had occurred since this morning's sweet passionate kiss? Now she was an iceberg. "And you . . . what did you do today?"

"Oh, I went shopping with Denise during the afternoon," she told him trying to control her voice. She wanted to add that she wished she'd stayed home so she hadn't seen him with another woman, although she knew that would have been pointless. It wouldn't have changed what he'd done. But was it better to know the truth and hurt so?

"And did you find a pretty for yourself?" Nick yanked angrily at his boot while anxious thoughts rushed through his mind. What had Denise done or said to Fancy that had brought forth this cold attitude in his wife? She bloody well hadn't been like this when he'd left her.

"I did. In fact, I was probably very extravagant, but then, after all, I'm Nicholas Dubose's wife. So I guess I have the right."

There was such sarcasm in her voice Nick knew something was wrong. He leaped up from the bed and grabbed her roughly off the stool, his eyes blazed furiously. Fancy did not realize that he was more hurt than angry. "Enough of this, Fancy! I won't take it!"

Her arms and shoulders hurt from his viselike hold. She wanted to hurt him back. "I won't take *this*. Let me go, Nick. You're hurting me!"

The hatred in her eyes shattered him and his hands released her. She saw the frown on his face and watched as he took a couple of hesitant steps away from her.

"I . . . I didn't mean to hurt you." He turned, running his long fingers through his rumpled hair.

Fancy was tempted to blurt out that this hurt wasn't nearly as painful as what she'd felt when she'd seen him hug another woman that afternoon. But she didn't and so she doomed them both to a miserable evening and some unhappy days and nights.

If she had followed her instincts and rushed after him as he left the room, nothing would have pleased Nick more. But she did not. So he left her alone and did not return until the early morning hours. He sought refuge in his father's study instead of in a house of pleasure.

Damned if he'd beg any woman or plead to know what was bothering her — not even Fancy. If she didn't trust him enough to come to him with whatever had upset her, then to hell with it. Already he'd given Fancy more than he'd ever expected to give any woman—his name and his heart.

Part Three

Flames of Passion's Desire
and
Fury's Deception

Chapter Twenty-two

It was a long, long night for Nick Dubose. He searched his mind for an explanation of this drastic, sudden change in his young bride. Was the Dubose family just too overwhelming for a simple, uncomplicated girl like Fancy? Christ, he'd been thinking she'd handled herself so well. In fact, he'd been very proud of her that first evening when he'd introduced her to his family.

He had tried to ease any feelings of discomfort she might secretly harbor by spending those first few days with her.

No, his shrewd, sharp mind could not accept that reason. The trouble had started today, when she had gone shopping alone with that imp Denise. Had that little brat taken her into the hornet's nest of her snobbish friends? He knew that the Babcock Boutique was their gathering place for he'd taken his sisters there numerous times. He could easily envision the delight his devious sister would take in exposing Fancy to her haughty friends. Damn! He'd wring Denise's neck if this was true.

After a sleepless night, Nick sought out his sister and played the same game of deception with her that she used so often with others. When he took his leave, he was satisfied that, for once, Denise was not guilty.

Fancy went through the motions of a normal day, but her thoughts were on her husband. When he returned home late in the afternoon, they maintained a very polite, distant manner toward each other. During the evening meal with the family, the pressure on the newlyweds was tremendous. Oh, he called her dear and darling, but Fancy felt no warmth in his deep voice. His hand didn't reach over to clasp hers, and she missed this closeness more than she'd imagined.

Nick was so miserable that he excused himself after dinner to have a cheroot and stroll alone in the moonlit courtyard. Fancy's face had been like stone when she'd looked his way during dinner.

Fancy ached to rush out into the night after him, but she could not have stood it if he'd dismissed her and told her he wished to be alone. To hear him say aloud that he didn't want her anymore would be like dying, she thought sadly.

For the second night in a row, Nick didn't enter their boudoir until he thought Fancy was asleep.

He now knew the torment of crawling into bed to be tantalized by the closeness of Fancy's warm body and her inviting fragrance when he was not able to take her in his arms as he ached to do.

Tonight, he was tempted to put his arms around her anyway, but he did not because if she rebuked him he didn't know how he'd react. Was he a fool to allow this little minx to make him so cowardly? Who could imagine the arrogant Nick Dubose acting in such a way? Hell, he didn't believe what he was doing himself!

Did he imagine it or were her eyes a little less harsh tonight? Did he really see a hint of softness there?

When Fancy dozed off her sleep was not sound and once she roused, slightly dazed, and swore she'd felt his soft caress on her arm. She lay still for the longest time until she finally concluded she had imagined that sensation. How she missed his strong arms holding her and his sensuous mouth kissing her. Most of all she wanted his body fused with hers.

At the dawn of the new day, Nick slipped out of the bed. This insanity had gone on long enough, he decided. Besides he'd accepted Angelique's invitation to dinner this evening. He wondered if Fancy would flatly refuse to go with him. Well, before he left this room he intended to find out.

Fancy wasn't asleep. Indeed, she was very aware of his towering presence by the bed. For a moment she prolonged opening her eyes, fearful that she would see a menacing look on his tanned face. She wondered if there would be some remnant of the tender love she remembered. As old Raoul had always told her, "You can't run from trouble. You gotta face up to it."

She wasn't exactly pleased with herself the last two days. Old Raoul would probably have asked her where her gumption had gone.

She opened her eyes and they met with Nick's. She loved the way his gaze danced over her, so alive and vital. But she could not miss the weary look on his face.

"Morning, Fancy," he said.

"Morning, Nick," she murmured. Nick was encouraged by the mellow tone in her voice. It had been missing for the last two days. Then Fancy could not resist adding, "You look tired."

"I am. I . . . we . . . we have an engagement tonight, Fancy. Thought I should let you know before I leave for the office. A dinner at Madame Rocheleau's."

Fancy rose slowly. Unintentionally her breasts were exposed to Nick's eyes. He stared wide-eyed and instantly became aroused. Feeling as foolish as an awkward schoolboy because he was so obviously affected by the sight of his sensuous wife, he turned to leave. She almost uttered his name but she stopped herself.

After he left, Fancy snuggled down into the warmth of the silk coverlet, a broad smile on her face. Nick's reaction pleased her and did wonders for her morale. The sight of her breasts had aroused him.

Her improved state of mind was obvious. Doreen and Denise remarked about it when she encountered them at breakfast. While they were eating she learned that their engagement that evening did not include the Dubose family, just Nick and her.

It didn't take long for Fancy to discover that Denise was back to being obnoxious this morning. Sighing disapprovingly, she smirked. "Oh, the saintly Madame Rocheleau, eh? I'm surprised Nicholas has not rushed you over there already, Fancy."

"Denise!" Doreen gave her sister a disgusted look. "Pay no attention to Denise, Fancy. She is a lovely lady and I'll bet you'll like her." She turned her eyes on Denise and chided her older sister. "Nicholas has every right to feel the way he does about her, Denise. She took care of him more than Mother did when he was little."

A new bold streak was showing up in Doreen more and more lately, and Denise found herself dumbfounded and perplexed. She reared up from her chair, not caring to listen to any more of Doreen's praise of Madame Rocheleau.

"If you two will excuse me I have to get ready to go with Abigail. Will you please tell Mother I've gone to Meadowbrook with the Kingsleys to go riding this afternoon?" Denise interrupted her sister's conversation.

Doreen responded with an offhanded mumble and turned her attention back to Fancy and the subject of Madame Rocheleau.

By the time Fancy went her way and Doreen departed to sequester herself in her studio to paint, the dark cloud of gloom that had surrounded Fancy seemed to be fading. She felt she could breathe again and she could not wait for Nicholas to come home. She was going to face him and tell him why she had been so angry. She was going to ask him to explain the scene she'd witnessed. After all, she was his wife.

However, her plans went awry, for Nicholas arrived late from the office and had to rush upstairs to bathe and change his clothes while Fancy awaited him in the parlor.

Breathlessly, he rushed downstairs a short time later, wearing an elegantly tailored coat and cream-colored trousers. The outfit so enhanced his dark good looks that Fancy wanted to embrace him. But knowing Dudley was already at the front entrance with the carriage, Nick gave her a hasty smile and suggested they be on their way.

"Sorry, I'm late," he said, sighing heavily as he rushed her through the door.

Only when they were seated in the carriage did he have a chance to lean back in his seat and catch his breath. Then he allowed himself to absorb the full image of his wife. "You're unusually lovely tonight. Your new shawl and gloves?"

"Yes," she said in a weak voice. She wondered if her decision to wear them tonight was wise. Somehow, the black lace shawl and gloves were associated with a day she didn't want to remember.

He reached over and took her lace-gloved hand in his, bringing it to his lips. His eyes sparkled, as fiery as the emerald Fancy wore on her finger. "No man could be as proud as I am, Fancy, to have you for my wife." His deep voice rang out sincerely.

She stared at him for a moment and then she smiled sweetly, "Thank you, Nick." She was about to say something else, but the carriage was pulled into Madame Rocheleau's drive. Before this night ended Fancy was determined to find out if Nick loved her enough to have no other woman in his life for she knew she could not share him with anyone.

Suddenly, she found herself being ushered into the hallway of their hostess's home. It was not palatial like the Dubose residence but more like Alita Dumaine's town house in Natchez. But even before the sound of swishing taffeta alerted her that the lady of the manor was hurrying out into the hall to greet them, Fancy sensed great warmth in this house even though she knew nothing about its owner except what Doreen had told her.

A blur of deep rich gold emerged into the hall. The curvaceous lady who had appeared was none other than Madame Rocheleau. With a dramatic gesture she held out her hands to Nick and called his name. He, in turn, encased her in his arms and planted a kiss on her cheek.

A case of *déjà vu* flooded Fancy and she stood as if in a trance. This scene had been played for her before and she knew when. Dear Lord, it was the same woman she'd seen him hugging in the carriage. This was the lady who had created the horrible monster in her. He'd never forgive her if he knew how stupid and foolish she'd been. How unjustly she'd punished them both!

"Angelique, may I present my wife, Fancy. Fancy, this is a lady very close to my heart. I hope you don't mind," his voice was etched with feeling. Fancy flinched, wondering if he could read her mind. Lord, she hoped not!

She stepped forward to take the hand the woman offered her. "Madame Rocheleau, it is a pleasure to meet you."

Angelique embraced Fancy and clasped her hand in hers. "Angelique . . . please, eh? Fancy, I am so happy to finally meet you." She broke their embrace and then smiled at Nick. Her face glowed with such loveliness that Fancy could not help admiring her. There was a spontaneous warmth about the woman that reminded Fancy of her own beloved Fleur.

"She is beautiful, Nicholas. But then I knew she would be. Come, my children . . . let us have some wine. I have a million questions to ask. As Nicholas will tell you, Fancy, I am very nosy."

Now, in this lovely lady's presence, Fancy realized just how needless her worries had been. Her face masked the secret thoughts whirling around in her pretty head as she vowed never to act so foolishly again.

Nick was elated for the two women he most cared for seemed to be getting along marvelously.

"This little miss sitting beside me has a curiosity to match yours, Angelique," he said, a broad smile on his face.

The mercurial moodiness of his young bride still puzzled him, but tonight she gave no hint of the shrew she'd been the last two days. Whatever had ignited her firebrand manner seemed to have been swept aside. He realized he had much to learn about this girl named Fancy whom he loved beyond all reason.

Throughout Angelique's simple, but delicious dinner, he allowed the two women to dominate the conversation and sat back observing them.

Once Angelique took notice of his thoughtful manner, saying, "I hope you don't mind, Nicholas, that I'm so busy getting acquainted with your bride. It was not my intention to neglect you."

By the time Fancy and her husband were returning to the Dubose house, she had to confess she liked the woman she had been prepared to hate. The heartwarming camaraderie between Angelique and Nick surpassed the bonds he felt for Alain or Monique Dubose, and Fancy questioned how that could be. No other woman could have taken Fleur's place in her heart.

Because Fancy was quiet, Nick assumed she was sleepy, and she did not resist when he put his arm around her and pulled her to his side.

She'd missed the closeness of their bodies. Now

it felt good and right as they rolled along the deserted New Orleans streets so late at night. The city seemed to be sleeping.

She had many things to learn about this strange, fascinating man who was her husband. One thing she did know though. As long as he held her, the world seemed right and she felt whole.

It was all a matter of trust, Fancy realized, so hard to give completely. Her heart and her body had yielded eagerly but trust did not come so easily. The evil seeds of doubt planted by Yvonne Dubose had sprouted up so easily, Fancy had to admit to herself. The interlude she'd witnessed between Angelique and her husband was completely innocent. She had been the one to misconstrue it.

An overwhelming wave of guilt washed over her. Nick must never know how foolish she'd been. It would be her own little secret. Now she knew that loving a man like Nick was like a two-edged sword, for this was the second time loving him had brought her hurt and pain.

Fancy girl, she thought, you've much to learn! And she would, she promised herself. Tonight though, she intended to make up for the hurt she'd caused Nick, and for the loveless nights they'd both endured needlessly.

Chapter Twenty-three

Fancy would never have imagined herself as being so completely abandoned, but Nick's ardent love-making — his magic touch — had made her so. Never had she anticipated such sensations, so wild and wonderful.

Many miles away, another man lay on his bed, alone, with only his memories to warm him. As it had been when he and Fancy were children, he intended to seek old Raoul's counsel the first thing in the morning. Chris Kensington's last wish before sleep came was that time would turn back and that he and Fancy would be children sitting by old Raoul down on the fishing pier.

The next morning Raoul spotted the lean, lanky Chris coming toward the smithy shop. Raoul's chest swelled with pride for the young master of Willow Bend. He'd done a good job of taking over since Mister Charles's death. Even though he'd gotten Miss Roberta out of his hair, there was still the demanding, nagging Alicia Kensington to endure. Actually, the transition from Mister Charles's control to Chris's had not stirred much ado.

Raoul blessed the consideration Chris had shown him. Now, he puttered around the plantation only when his aging legs would allow. As for Chessie, she still managed to get around the kitchen. One good woman he had in his "Chessie."

He was curious about the man who'd won Miss Fancy's heart. Madame Dumaine had written to Chris about the girl's sudden marriage and about her going to live in New Orleans, a long, long way down that river she loved so much. He recalled the many times he'd seen her look so wistfully up and down that wide stream of muddy, rushing water. He knew how she'd daydreamed about the places along the Mississippi.

Well, it would seem her wanderlust was being satisfied and he prayed she was happy. Poor Chris had been shattered by his aunt's letter, Raoul recalled. So shattered that he had ridden into Memphis on that red roan mare of his and gotten roaring drunk. He hadn't come back from Memphis for four days.

Since then though, he seemed to have washed Fancy out of his blood and turned his thoughts and energies to Willow Bend. Raoul had seen the fruits of Chris's labor reflected in the plantation. His choice of a new overseer was proving sound. Garth

Anderson was a hardworking man, and in his spare time he had patched up and repaired the old shack where Fleur and Fancy had lived. A bachelor, he lived there alone.

After observing the lanky, rawboned Anderson for the last three weeks, Raoul decided he was a very likable sort.

This October day as he and Chris sat under the massive oak, leaning back against the trunk and talking, Chris confessed, "Raoul, I feel a need to get away from Willow Bend. I . . . I want to go back East and finish what I'd started before Dad died. Is that selfish, Raoul? Am I wrong?" A conscientious look was on the young man's face.

Raoul whittled on a stick. "Can't see how, Chris. You got a right to seek your own life whether it be here at Willow Bend or wherever."

"Anderson seems quite capable and he doesn't seem like the drifter. He acts like he wants to settle in one spot for a while."

Raoul nodded his graying head. " 'Pears that way to me too. Hardworking man like him won't stay a bachelor too long I figure."

Chris remained silent for a moment as though he was studying the old black man's face before revealing any more of his plans for the future. "You know, Raoul, I'm thinking of going to Natchez for a visit."

"Sorta' thought that might be what you had in mind." Raoul gave him a sly smile.

"Yeah, I guess Mom will hit the ceiling, but Roberta and Wendall are back and settled in their home now. There is nothing to stop her from going into Memphis to visit them for a few days."

"Not that I can see, Mister Chris," Raoul agreed. Not a thing in the world except her own orneriness, he mused. Alicia Kensington had never been a pleasant lady, and he had never understood how Chessie had coped so well all these years up there in the main house. Chessie was a saint or she couldn't have.

At first when Chessie had told him that Alicia had called her into her sitting room to tell her about Madame Dumaine's offer, Raoul was shocked. Willow Bend was home and the thought of leaving it had never entered his mind. To live and die right here on Willow Bend was how he'd figured his life to run its course. But lately, the idea of living on Madame Dumaine's country estate was not so unthinkable. Miss Fancy had made it sound like a marvelous place. That was another thing which made Willow Bend less enchanting— the absence of little Fancy. Lord, how he had missed that girl.

Chris's next words made the old man jerk to attention. The young man could have been right inside his mind. "Think you and Chessie could be ready by the end of the week?"

"Sir?" Had he heard Chris right?

"Ready to leave for Natchez and Aunt Alita's. I had in mind that we'd travel together, Raoul. I feel I'd like to see you and Chessie settled. I don't have to tell you how much you two mean to me. Why, you and Chessie have been as much a part of me and my life as my family."

Old Raoul's eyes misted. That was a fine thing for Chris to say . . . a cherished memory he'd hold on to always. There was a tremor in his voice when he replied, "Yes sir, we've been around a long, long time . . . me and Chessie."

Chris had given this matter a lot of thought. He wanted the best home possible for Raoul and Chessie should his own life take him a long way from Willow Bend. Somehow, it seemed more secure to think of them at Dubonnet than Willow Bend.

The mulatto, Eula Mae, was now able to take over Chessie's kitchen duties and her husband, Abel, was a big, husky man. The smithy shop could be his responsibility. Chris knew this would be best for Raoul and Chessie even though thinking of their departure from Willow Bend made him sad.

After the two men parted company that day they did not speak until three days later on the morning the trio boarded the *Bayou Queen* to leave Memphis and travel down the river to Natchez. Raoul did not allow any of his own tears to flow for Chessie was weeping enough for both of them.

He consoled his sobbing wife, trying to reassure her and convince himself at the same time. "Cheer up, Chessie. Why I'll bet living in Natchez at this Madame Dumaine's we gonna' be seein' our sweet

Fancy girl more." Chessie's dark eyes darted over to him. Her sobs continued, but they were not so hard and they came less often. He could tell by the look on her ebony face that she was weighing what he'd said.

"You really think so, Raoul?"

"I do . . . else I wouldn't say so, sugar."

"Oh, to see that child once in a while would make a difference." God only knew the main house at Willow Bend had become a dismal place with Fancy gone. Even the disagreeable Roberta had given it a little life and she was gone too. Miss Alicia had become impossible to please, taxing even the patient, good-hearted Chessie beyond her limits. But Chessie had kept telling herself to endure and to try to show the woman some compassion.

Chris had left the two of them by the railing while he attended to some arrangements for their trip. They watched the movement of the steamboat churning up the muddy waters. Both contemplated what awaited them many miles up the river.

Raoul's arm brought Chessie closer and he gave her a sharp hug. "Life's kinda like this old river here, Chessie. It just keeps moving on and on, don't it? Sometimes, it move fast and sometimes it creeps along but it don't stop."

"Guess you right, Raoul." Her face actually had a pleasant smile on it. Raoul chuckled. "Yes, sir . . . we're goin' to be jus' fine. Believe me."

Chessie gave her husband's wrinkled cheek a light kiss. "I've always believed you, Raoul. Don't you know that?"

Anyone taking notice of the black couple by the railing would have thought they were on a pleasure jaunt. In a way they were, now that they'd convinced themselves everything was going to be just fine.

With every turn of the paddle wheel Chris's mood lightened. The heavy weight he had borne for months was gone. Now he stood alone by the rail looking out over the muddy river and inhaling the light breeze on which odors were wafted from the banks of the river.

Crazy as it might seem, Chris felt no remorse or sadness over leaving Willow Bend, and as for his widowed mother, his sister lived nearby and the plantation would operate just fine in the overseer's hands. With his two beloved servants at Dubonnet under his aunt's protection, he was free to pursue his own life. Dear Lord, that was a good feeling!

Still, one question gnawed at him persistently. He had to answer it before he went so far away, had to assure himself that Fancy was happy. Since he'd accepted the fact that she would never be his, he was ready to go ahead with his own life, but he'd never love anyone the way he'd loved her.

He would probably marry some girl who would probably be a tiny little thing that he could swing up in the air. She would have black hair and laughing eyes, and secretly he'd pretend she was his own sweet Fancy. Maybe, that way he could satisfy himself. At least, he'd try.

After spending a couple of days with his aunt
and seeing that Raoul and Chessie were settled in
their new home, Chris left Natchez for New Orleans. Fancy's address was written on a piece of paper tucked away in his waistcoat pocket. He'd
pretended to Alita that he was going to write to
Fancy and had not mentioned his plans to go to
New Orleans. Before he left, he and Alita traveled
out to Dubonnet so that he might bid farewell to
Chessie and Raoul, and when he left the pair he
was satisfied that they were going to be content in
their new home.

On his last evening in Natchez, he asked his
aunt about Fancy and the man she'd married.
"This Nicholas Dubose—you approved of him,
Aunt Alita?"

"I did, Chris. They seem very happy, judging by
the letters I've received from Fancy," she replied.
Perhaps, her nephew would have preferred a lie,
for she suspected Chris's feeling for Fancy was still
very much alive.

"I wish it could have been me," he lamented,
sadness etched on his good-looking face.

"I know, Chris dear." She thought he seemed so
young in comparison to Nick Dubose. She knew
he could never have held a woman like Fancy.

The next morning, as she watched her nephew
depart in the carriage, the strangest chill washed
over her.

"Something wrong, mistress?" Dahlia asked as she observed Alita.

"I don't know, Dahlia. Just a funny feeling I had, watching him drive away." Alita said hesitantly. There was not a hint of chill to the golden autumn day.

Dahlia didn't know what was troubling her mistress but she sought to brighten Alita's mood and lift her spirits. In that bossy way so typical of her, she urged Alita into the house, using a gentle touch. "Now you just come on and let Dahlia help you get ready to go with that nice Monsieur André Dubose to the Pharsalia Race Course, eh? It's going to be a magnificent day, madame."

Alita turned from the door, gave the little mulatto a smile, and did as she'd suggested. Shrugging any forebodings aside and trying to convince herself she was just being silly, she followed the feisty Dahlia up the stairs. What would she do without that little quadroon to boss her around, she mused?

Dahlia had made up her mind that if her pretty kindhearted mistress didn't respond to the charms of Monsieur André soon she was going to pay a visit to Mama Renée's cabin in the woods for a love potion. She was stubbornly determined to see the two of them matched. He could make her mistress happy, Dahlia was sure of it. Life was too lonely without a man!

Lord Almighty, *he* needed no potion from what Dahlia had observed when he called on Alita Dumaine the last time. Loving was on that gentle-man's mind, if she was any judge. Now to spark the flame in Madame Dumaine was all she had to do. Dahlia smiled deviously.

Chapter Twenty-four

As the blossoms of wildflowers that grow in rich, fertile soil brighten in color under the brilliant rays of the sun, so Fancy bloomed, glowing radiantly. And like the flowers she loved so well, she flourished in her newfound paradise with Nicholas Dubose. The heat of his love and devotion, like the sun, had made changes in her looks and her manner, changes of which she was not aware.

Her face had become more beautiful. Her petite figure had become flatteringly full. She was more sensuous and alluring than she had been when Nick had first brought her to New Orleans. No one was more aware of this than Nick.

By now, he knew she was no sweet innocent for he had delighted in teaching her the pleasures of making love. Dear God, she pleased him so! He could have sworn that her beautiful, dark almost almond-shaped eyes were the most provocative he'd ever seen. He knew she had no inkling of what a sultry seductress she'd become. But when other men ogled her when they attended various affairs in the city, he knew what the men staring at his wife were thinking. Many times he'd been tempted to march over and punch one of them in the nose.

A woman so breathtakingly beautiful was a joy to see in gorgeous gowns and jewels, and Fancy never reacted casually to his gifts. She was always excited and delighted by them. She was so different from his mother or his sisters who had lived in lavish surroundings all their lives. Her responses were refreshing and gratifying to Nick. He hoped being the wife of a wealthy man would never change her. Always, he wanted her to remain the simple, natural girl he adored.

Although time had passed since she'd arrived in New Orleans, Fancy still found herself intrigued by the city's flamboyance and vitality. It was a city that never seemed to sleep. Even when she and Nick were driven home from some evening social event, the sounds of music and laughter echoed in the streets. People were about at the most ungodly hours, it seemed to Fancy.

But every now and then she thought of the peace and quiet of Dubonnet, and she yearned momentarily to be engulfed by the sweet smells of the woods, the piny aroma and the scent of blooming jasmine. An array of colorful feathered creatures would please her eyes, and their various bird calls would be a most pleasant symphony to her ears.

She felt that nothing was more delicate and lacy than the wild, verdant ferns growing in the shady, moist earth! Oh yes, there were times she wished for the cozy seclusion of Dubonnet faraway from the bustling city.

The elder Duboses, Alain and Monique, had convinced themselves that only the stabilizing influence of his new bride kept Nicholas in New Orleans. By now he would usually have been back in Natchez for the racing season, but he'd mentioned nothing of this to Alain.

Fancy now had Monique's wholehearted approval. Monique no longer spent sleepless nights worrying about whether Nick would come in late or not at all. She had been concerned about her handsome son's involvement with the wife of one of their friends. The scandal could have been terrible. Although Monique had seen the inviting glances some of these ladies had directed at Nick and she was cognizant of their affairs, their dalliances had never concerned Monique until one involved Nicholas. It was also nice to have him under her roof for such a long period, Monique had to admit.

Angelique had been so impressed by Nicholas' bride, Monique knew she must never voice any unfavorable remarks about Fancy to her. She suspected her dearest friend, Angelique, would immediately come to Fancy's defense. Angelique's attitude certainly had influenced the opinion of Fancy's mother-in-law. Monique decided she probably had been looking at the young girl with a too critical eye. Softened by her friend's praise of Fancy, Monique began to see the young woman in a more favorable light.

Denise contemptuously withheld any friendship from her new sister-in-law. In part, she did so because she envied Fancy's beauty and the attention it attracted when the Duboses arrived at the theater or went to soirées as a family.

Denise also blamed Fancy for helping Doreen to become so brave and daring. Shy Doreen had never had any backbone until Fancy had arrived at the Dubose residence.

Actually, Denise found the two dark-haired girls most irksome when they got together as they had on this rainy afternoon in Doreen's secluded studio. Heavens, Doreen would be shooing out anyone else but Fancy so she could get on with her painting. Fancy seemed to be the privileged one.

The girls' laughter echoed down the long hallway, causing Denise to emit a disgruntled sigh. When she heard Celine greeting someone at the front entrance and the caller's voice was male, her curiosity urged her to jump up from the settee and to toss the book she'd been attempting to read aside. Any visitor would be welcome company on this dismal rainy day, she told herself.

She hurried to the door to assess the stranger just being ushered in by Celine. One glance and she was quickly lifted out of her gloom. His fine clothes were wet and his curly blond hair was damp, but he was a very good-looking young man. Denise immediately took charge.

"Celine, please show our guest in here." Denise gestured in a gracious manner, a warm smile upon her face.

"Yes, ma'am, Miss Denise," Celine answered. "This way, Monsieur Kensington."

Celine led Chris Kensington to where Denise stood in the archway. "He wishes to see Miss Fancy. Shall I get her, Miss Denise?"

Annoyed by the servant girl's statement, Denise snapped, "First you can get a hot carafe of coffee. You would welcome something warm, wouldn't you, *Monsieur?*" she inquired of Chris, urging him on into the parlor. She turned back to the still-lingering Celine.

"Yes, ma'am. That sounds good to me." Chris gave Denise a quick flashing smile.

"Celine!" Denise nodded, dismissing her to her chore. As the servant moved away she heard the young gentleman introducing himself to Denise and explaining, as well as apologizing for, his impromptu call.

"I am just passing through New Orleans."

"So you're from Memphis?"

"Yes, mademoiselle," Chris answered, impressed by the fine surroundings. This young miss had to be Nicholas Dubose's sister. She was a beauty and about Fancy's age, he imagined.

Denise told him that she had relatives in Memphis, and she pretended to find it amazing that

Chris knew her uncle and her cousins. "My what a small world it is," she purred softly, fluttering her eyelashes coquettishly. She found Chris Kensington a most engaging young man. Truthfully, he impressed her more than anyone she'd met in a long, long time. He had a magnificent head of spun gold hair.

As Chris drank the cup of steaming coffee he ran his fingers through his damp hair hoping he would look presentable when Fancy came to greet him. Meanwhile, Denise admired his thick golden curls and his brilliant blue eyes. While he was not as ruggedly built as the men in her family, she liked his trim figure and fine attire. Denise realized that he was from a fine family. One could always tell that, she mused smugly.

Darn that Celine! She wasted no time in telling Fancy she had a guest because steps were approaching the parlor. She could have wrung that mulatto's neck! Nothing could be done now but she wanted more time alone with Chris.

Denise envied Fancy when Chris embraced her warmly and kissed her on the cheek after Fancy had rushed into the room and called out his name with surprised delight.

When Fancy finally broke their embrace, Chris declared breathlessly, "Lord, Fancy . . . you . . . look so good." It was the truth. It was obvious she was blissfully happy for such radiant beauty would not be reflected on her face if she wasn't.

"Chris! What a marvelous surprise!" Fancy

laughed, so lightheartedly and gaily that Chris was certain his presence pleased her, and he was glad he'd come to see her.

For a few minutes the two of them forgot the presence of Denise who eyed them reproachfully. Her brother's wife was far too familiar with this young man to Denise's way of thinking. But then Fancy was a lowly individual with different morals. Never would she understand why her brother, Nicholas, had chosen such a girl to be his bride.

Only when the excitement of their reunion calmed and Fancy led Chris over to have a seat on the brocade settee did she notice that Denise had graciously served her guest some refreshments.

"So, I see my sister-in-law has taken very good care of you, Chris." She smiled. Turning to Denise, she said, "Thank you, Denise. I see no need to formally introduce the two of you. I'm sure Chris has told you we are very old and dear friends."

"Yes, Monsieur Kensington told me." The sullen tone of her voice was not noticed by Fancy who was already turning back to Chris. He'd hoped the pretty miss would take her leave when Fancy arrived, but she seemed to have no such intention. Denise sat in the overstuffed chair as if she did not plan to allow them any private time together.

Chris's blue eyes easily picked up Denise's similarity to own snobbish sister, Roberta. He wondered if Fancy was gullible enough to believe that this young woman genuinely liked her. When Denise put forth her most gracious air and invited him to stay for dinner that evening, Chris got the distinct impression that she was seeking to expose Fancy's inadequacy and demonstrate her own good manners.

Politely, he declined the mademoiselle's invitation. Then turning his eyes back to Fancy, he declared, "I'd like to, Fancy, but my schedule won't permit it. You understand, don't you?"

"I wish you could, Chris. I'd like you to meet my husband," she sighed, having no idea that they'd already met on the docks of Memphis on what Chris considered a fateful day. Had Nicholas Dubose not appeared on that particular day when he'd seen his Aunt Alita and Fancy off, perhaps, Fancy would have become his bride instead of Nicholas's wife.

Now that he'd seen her in the surroundings of her new home and new life he ought to tarry no longer. The truth was he wanted to depart just as hastily as he could. The Dubose home seemed to stifle him, or perhaps it was the stark reality that he had lost Fancy forever.

Chris invited Fancy to lunch with him on the following day. Then he placed a light kiss on her cheek and got into the carriage. She stood there in the drive waving a dainty hand as he pulled away. His hand crunched the slip of paper on which he'd written her address. He'd throw it away as soon as he left the grounds of the estate. Just then another carriage turned into the wide drive and passed through the iron gates. He peered at the passengers to see if Nicholas Dubose was among them. However, he was not.

Two elegantly attired ladies ogled the handsome young gentleman curiously. Monique's friend, Muriel, asked, "A friend of your new daughter-in-laws, Monique dear?" because the two women had been privy to the embrace and kiss Chris Kensington had bestowed on Fancy. Monique had no idea who the young man was, so she found herself bristling at the intimate scene she and her friend had witnessed. *Mon dieu*, of all the people in New Orleans who might be accompanying her this afternoon why had she been with the gossipy Muriel Hathaway. As innocent as all this might be, Monique knew Muriel's tongue could be a most vicious one.

When she did reply to Muriel she lied, assuring her the man was a friend. Nicholas's young wife would have to remember that appearances did count and she must for Nicholas's sake caution the naïve girl about her behavior. Of course, she would do it in a most subtle way and with the utmost finesse.

To be subtle was not Denise's intention when she encountered her older brother late in the afternoon as he returned home and eagerly mounted the stairs to join his adorable wife after a long day away from her.

Denise's revelation of Chris Kensington's visit fired an instant spark of jealousy in him. With each step he took he got madder and his tanned face held no hint of the pleasant greeting that Fancy had been anticipating when she heard his heavy footsteps rushing up the stairs.

As he slammed through the carved oak door Fancy stood before him in a gossamer wrapper that was a flattering shade of emerald green. He'd never seen her look more desirable. Her attractiveness made him more irate. His jealousy blazed heatedly.

Fancy's smile faded when she saw the fierce look on his face. His eyes were piercing her with such a menacing look. Dear Lord, what had him so upset, she wondered?

As innocent as a lamb, she swayed up to him, the sheerness of her attire exhibiting every delectable curve of her petite body. Her dark hair fell softly, and tantalizingly over her shoulders. Nick's glaring eyes beheld her. Damn, she was a gorgeous little vixen!

Chapter Twenty-five

No kiss greeted her, and when he spoke she knew what had riled him so. His sensuous lips curled and his tone dripped with acid. "Well, *ma petite*, I hear you had a caller in my absence this afternoon."

His manner stunned her and she realized at that moment that she and Nick would never be able to live happily under this roof. After all, this could never really be her home nor could she be its mistress. This was Monique's home and she was its mistress.

This had to be Denise's doing. Fancy knew that she'd been very foolish to think Nick's sister had accepted her.

What hurt, though, was Nick's attitude. Wounded beyond words, she sought to hurt him in return. "I did!" Her chin held defiantly high, she whirled around turning her back to him. "Is that not permitted, my lord and master?"

Damn her! He cursed under his breath! Just who did she think she was dealing with?

He would bend only so far for any woman — and even Fancy. A year ago had anyone told him that some female would have him in such a frenzy he would have laughed. It would have been unthinkable to Nick Dubose.

"I am neither your lord nor your master, Fancy. However, I *am* your husband in case you're forgotten," he said, his deep voice laced with such authority that Fancy found herself resenting his overbearing air.

She laughed somewhat nervously as she faced him again. Now her black eyes glowed like smoldering coals. "Oh, I haven't forgotten."

By now, they were both beyond reason. One hurt had begotten another until the whole incident had been blown out of proportion by Denise's devious scheme. Unfortunately, Nick and Fancy had allowed this to happen before they realized what was happening.

The last thing in the world Fancy would do now was tell Nick, as she'd planned to do, that she was meeting Chris for lunch before he left New Orleans. Deceptiveness was not a part of Fancy's nature but Nick had forced her to be evasive.

He marched out of the room to get away from the tantalizing sight of her before he lost control and took her into his arms and held her close. He was seething with anger and passion. That was the perplexing thing about his wife. She had the most ungodly effect on him. Even when he was furious at her, he burned with a savage desire to make love to her.

Because of their argument Fancy spent a most unpleasant evening at the long dining table, and she wished desperately for little Doreen's presence. It would have been comforting to look across the table and see her sweet warm smile. Instead, she felt like a stranger surrounded by the overpowering presence of the Duboses.

She had already discovered that Alain Dubose rarely smiled or laughed. Denise glanced her way from time to time, a sly smile on her rosebud lips. She looked much like the sly little puss she was. Fancy swore that she would never allow that little imp an inch unless she'd already taken a mile. She might be dumb, but each day she was learning. Still, she wondered if the Dubose ways could ever really be hers. Tonight, she found herself lonely for Natchez and the sight of Alita Dumaine. Nick's loathsome attitude perplexed her completely.

She also found Monique's quiet manner somewhat disconcerting. Had she heard all the commotion in their suite after Nick came upstairs? Fury had been evident in Nick's deep voice. Was it her imagination or did she see a reproachful look in her mother-in-law's eyes?

By the time the meal was over and she departed with Monique and Denise, Fancy had decided that everyone was aware of the fuss she and Nick had

had, but no one had mentioned Chris Kensington's visit.

With sudden impetuousness, she excused herself. She had an overwhelming need to be alone. Her satin-slippered feet skipped down the hallway and out the door. On the small veranda just off the courtyard Argo's squawks stopped her. He was obviously upset at having been left out in the dark. She sympathized with the brightly colored bird, "I know, fellow, just how you feel. We have a lot in common." She felt that she, too, was in a cage this night. Without further ado, she lifted the parrot's cage and made for the doorway to the sun room where the servant should have deposited Argo for the night.

This seemed to appease the parrot, so Fancy sank down into one of the wicker chairs for the quiet, dimly lit solitude of the sun room suited her mood. This fiasco had made her aware of a more serious problem. While it was true that Nick was acting childish and unreasonable, the situation had made her realize that living under this roof was like being on a stage with his family as the audience. The thought left her with a foul taste in her mouth. She should be the mistress of her own home. She wanted privacy with her husband . . . and her children when they came.

Even this disagreement with Nick could have been resolved if family hadn't been underfoot. More to the point, their dispute would not have occurred in the first place if Nick's sister had tended to her own business.

"I'll not be a bird in a cage like you, Argo. Not even for Nick Dubose," she vowed in a firm, determined voice. Her spirited nature would not allow that.

By the time she ambled out of the sun room and down the hallway she knew she must find a way to persuade Nick that they should have their own place. She could almost hear Monique saying how ridiculous that was when there were so many rooms here. But as old Raoul had often told her, she could be headstrong at times. This had to be one of those times if she hoped to keep the man she loved, and she did love Nick Dubose.

A chilling silence pervaded in the bedroom when Nick and his bride faced each other later that night. The next morning both were still feeling the strain, but pride and stubbornness prevented them from giving in although each was tempted to do. Nick mumbled a half-hearted goodbye and went through the bedroom door.

Exhausted from the sleepless night she'd spent lying next to her husband's still body, Fancy yearned for him to reach out to her and apologize for his ridiculous behavior. He did not, but she could have sworn he was as miserable as she was. He'd tossed and turned well into the early morning hours.

Later the puffiness under her eyes wouldn't fade even after the application of cold cloths. But Celine fixed Fancy's hair in an attractive style that complimented the saucy bonnet she'd picked to wear with her gold-colored frock and olive-colored jacket. She looked so stunning that no one noticed that her eyes were slightly tired looking.

"Oh, I almost forgot to tell you, Miss Fancy, that Madame Dubose told me to tell you she'd like to speak to you this morning." Celine smoothed down the back of Fancy's jacket.

Wishing to defy Nick's mother and to assert that she was her own mistress, Fancy tossed her head jauntily to the side and retorted to Celine, "Well, Celine please inform Madame I will see her later when I return from my appointment. I have no time right now."

Without further explanation, she left the room and the Dubose residence, instructing Dudley to drive her to the Saint Regent to meet Chris Kensington.

As the Dubose carriage rolled to a halt, Chris Kensington stood on the walk at the front of the hotel and bade farewell to an acquaintance. As the dashing-looking man sauntered away from the hotel he chanced to look back to see his friend, Chris, helping a gorgeous young lady out of a carriage. Fancy could not help noticing that he had turned and stopped to stare at her and Chris. He looked like a blond Viking when he smiled at them and threw his hand up to wave. His lion's mane of golden blond hair was blown askew, but his huge frame was molded so perfectly into his finely tailored deep blue coat and light-colored pants that

286

Fancy could not help admiring his manly handsomeness.

"Who is he, Chris?" she asked, taking Chris's arm to go into the hotel dining room where they were to have lunch.

"A pleasant surprise. . . . an old friend from back East. Eric Swenson. Has his own schooner in port here."

They dropped the subject of Eric Swenson and enjoyed a pleasant lunch. Then Dudley drove the pair to the wharf so that Chris might board his boat. When Fancy watched him walk up the gangplank she was engulfed by an eerie sensation similar to the one Alita Dumaine had experienced a few days ago. A sudden chill gripped her and she hugged herself before she hurried back to the carriage.

"Home, little madame?" Dudley asked, taking her hand to assist her into the carriage.

"Yes, Dudley. Take me home." She wondered if her exhausting night was taking its toll on her. She still felt chilled even though the sun was shining down upon her. Folding her shade parasol she absorbed the sun's rays.

Two blue eyes had watched Fancy with utter fascination and whetted interest. Eric Swenson pondered how his old friend, Chris could attract such a woman. Who was she, he wondered? One so lovely should not be allowed out alone for a rake like himself to pounce upon if given the chance. Christ! He wished he had been given the chance.

When he boarded his schooner and entered his cabin, he found his thoughts still dwelling on the raven-haired maiden his eyes had beheld for a moment. Perhaps, he should linger awhile in New Orleans.

The wealthy Eric Swenson lived by no one's rules but his own. Neither the hands of the clock nor the days of the calendar dictated to him. So on impulse he changed his plans.

For the last half-hour Alain Dubose had impatiently drummed on his desk while he awaited his son's return to the office. Reluctant as he was to speak with Nicholas about his new wife, it had to be done. The family name had to be considered. Nicholas had to understand this, Alain rationalized.

Oh, he had come to like the little miss since Nicholas had returned to the city with her as his bride, but her behavior lately had been unconventional, to say the least. Today, it had gone beyond limits that could be ignored.

A young married lady, especially the new bride of the son of Alain Dubose, did not go to a hotel with some gentleman other than her husband. What had proven more embarrassing to the rather prudish Alain was that he had been in the company of the affluent, respectable Alex Dellacorte when his daughter-in-law had entered the Saint Regent with a young man.

It would have been far better for the family if

Nicholas had picked a girl like Chantelle, but there was that streak of André in Nicholas. Like his younger brother, André, Nicholas's blood ran heatedly where the ladies were concerned. Fancy was a ravishingly beautiful young lady, Alain could not deny that.

Seeing Nicholas go past his door, Alain delayed the task before him no longer. Moving around the corner of his desk, he made for his son's office and called out to Nicholas as he went through the doorway.

"Son, I need to talk to you." Alain's voice halted Nick's hasty steps and he motioned to his father to enter his office.

Alain settled his impeccably clad figure comfortably in the huge leather chair at the side of Nick's desk. He noted that his son was not wearing a jacket coat and he thought that Nicholas himself was a bit of a renegade, hardly one to abide by convention as Alain did. Perhaps, he'd merely laugh when approached about Fancy's behavior. Alain was a stern, serious man, and to him marriage was a very sacred thing. He'd never dallied with another woman since his marriage to Monique.

"What's on your mind, Father?" Nick was now in a lighthearted mood. It had replaced his gloomy one when he'd decided he'd acted stupidly.

Alain went into his oration about the honor of the Dubose name and the respect it commanded in the city of New Orleans.

Nick had heard this lecture many times before

when Alain had disapproved of some reckless adventure of Nick's. But he'd been so damned settled lately that it amazed him to hear it now. Those wild bachelor days had been swept away since his marriage to Fancy.

Eager to finish for the day and get home to make amends with his wife, Nick's patience was wearing thin. With a bluntness that should have warned Alain or cautioned him about his approach, Nick snapped, "So what are you trying to get out, father? Out with it!"

"Your wife, son. Your wife's irresponsible behavior."

"What in the hell are you referring to?"

"Now, Nicholas . . . this isn't gossip but what I saw myself. And . . . and it's probably nothing serious. Fancy is young and very innocent about the ways people in our society behave. Our ways, you know . . . and traditions, son." Alain saw the fire and anger already mounting in Nicholas's green eyes so he attempted to soften his comments. Nick's temper had always been explosive even as a lad, and when angered his son could show a streak of cruelty which he didn't inherit from his father.

"What are you saying about my wife?" Nick lunged up and peered with fury at his father who now regretted bringing up the whole distasteful subject.

"I saw her, Nicholas . . . saw her coming out of the Saint Regent Hotel with a young gentleman at noontime. She had obviously come to the hotel for

Dudley had driven her there. I watched them drive away." Alain's voice was strained to the point of cracking. "I felt you must know this. She is your wife."

Nick's hands clenched into fists. His broad chest heaved in a deep sigh, and his heart pounded with a savage beat. If Fancy had been standing there at that moment his rage was such that he would have wrung her pretty neck. Alain looked upon his son's face. It was cruel and menacing. Indeed he looked as evil as the feared pirates who had once ravaged the city of New Orleans.

Yet, when Nick finally spoke his voice was low and calm. "Yes, she is my wife and I will tend to the matter immediately." The determination etched on Nick's face left no doubt in Alain's mind that he would do just that so he still sat in the chair after Nicholas strode out of the office. Alain Dubose did not doubt that Fancy would pay the price of Nicholas's black rage. Alain felt a certain amount of pity for the pretty girl. He almost wished that he had not mentioned the episode to his son. But his firm convictions about the proper decorum for young ladies had won out.

Somehow, the dignified elder Dubose suspected that Fancy would never be the conventional sort. She was one of those rare individuals who fit no mold, and knowing Nicholas as he did, Alain suspected that was the reason Fancy had attracted his attention in the first place.

Chapter Twenty-six

Like a lumbering ox, Nick blindly plowed through the crowd of milling dock workers. His head was whirling with a dozen thoughts and questions. For a man who'd give himself credit for being so smart and shrewd, he might be the biggest damn fool of all. Hell, he'd knocked around the world, bedded his share of lovely ladies and lived his life to suit himself.

The fact that he'd had a wealthy father had not dented his desire to make his own way and his own money. Thus far, he'd seemed to have the Midas touch. As Jason Carew had once told him when they'd had a narrow escape in Natchez, Lady Luck always seemed to ride on Nick's shoulder.

Funny, that he should recall memories of good old Jason. It was because of Fancy that he'd wanted to kill him back in Natchez. Now he knew without being told that the man she'd seen was

Chris Kensington, and he remembered that she had once intended to marry Kensington. Was it too much of a coincidence that she was without guilt? Was her sweet innocent face merely mask for a wanton, little witch? Had she married him only for his wealth and position? After all, Fancy was homeless and poor except for the generous, adoring Alita Dumaine. One thing he could attest to: he had been the first man to bed her. But he could swear to nothing else.

As he weaved through the ocean of faces, he saw only one. The agony of wondering if that lovely face had played him false was almost more than he could bear. Were his own past sins coming back to haunt him through Fancy, the only woman he'd ever loved? Angelique Rocheleau swore such things happened, but he'd never believed that they did. But then, until Fancy had come into his life he'd lived his life for the moment — for pleasure.

"Hey, fellow." A strange voice jarred Nick to attention. He found himself looking directly into the eyes of an arrogant-looking man who towered as tall as he. A shock of thick blond hair fell casually over one side of the stranger's forehead and his amused bright blue eyes twinkled. Nick suddenly realized he'd slammed into this hunk of granite.

Nick was shaking the man's hand from his shoulder and mumbling a disgruntled apology when he heard a familiar voice calling him. "Mister Nick! Mister Nick! You . . . your father wishes you to return to the wharf." Nick turned to see the bandy-legged old man called Scotty frantically beckoning to him, and he turned from the blond giant of a man he'd rammed into.

Eric Swenson watched the pair go scurrying across the wharf. He wondered just what would have happened if the old man hadn't called that fellow away. He'd seemed like a dude just looking for a fight. There was fire in his veins, if Eric was any judge of men. In fact, he figured that was his kind of man. But he was brooding, that black-haired gent with the devil's fire in his eyes.

At the maximum speed a steamboat could safely make, the *Bayou Queen* headed toward its sister ship, the *Memphis Belle*. Shortly after Nick had left Alain had received a report that extensive damage had been done to the *Memphis Belle* and that a fire set in the hold had ruined the cargo. A few people had been injured, and now the panicky passengers awaited rescue on the bank of the river some twenty miles from New Orleans.

Alain had urged Nicholas to accompany the crew of the *Bayou Queen*. He was certain the damage had been planned and executed by Rafferty and his henchmen. Somehow, they'd hired on the *Memphis Belle* or boarded her to do their dirty work. Captain Norwood would need Nicholas's help with what was facing him once they arrived at the spot where the *Memphis Belle* was stuck.

As her husband traveled down the Mississippi aboard the *Bayou Queen*, Fancy tried to shake the gloom that had settled on her like a black shroud since she'd left the dock. But her thoughts had not been dwelling on Nick. Chris occupied her mind.

When, late in the afternoon, the sun disappeared and the tired-looking, gray sky held a promise of rain, Fancy's mood became more depressed.

Time dragged. She kept glancing at the clock. And in addition to the gloom that enveloped her, she was bored. She found herself suddenly wishing to do many things she'd not done in a long, long time. A quiet, comfortable chat with old Raoul would have soothed her, or a barefoot walk on the soft moist sand at the river's edge. An array of flowers flourished in Monique's garden, but Fancy yearned to stroll in the shaded coziness of the woods and to pick wild verbenas — red, pink and purple.

Overwhelming discontent possessed her, and she wondered why. Almost any woman would be delighted to be the wife of a wealthy handsome man who could provide any luxury her heart desired. But what was it her own heart desired? She didn't know, except that she wanted more than she had right now.

Was she not truly in love with Nick? Oh, no. Hardly. She quickly swept that silly thought aside. Yet, her husband was different somehow, here in New Orleans, than he'd been back in Natchez. How . . . She couldn't exactly pinpoint it.

Perhaps, she was just a country girl after all.

Maybe that was why Dubonnet had been such a haven for her. The glitter and glamor of her first few weeks in New Orleans had dimmed. Much of what she did now seemed superficial. So many parties and so many gowns and jewels. Although these seemed to delight Monique and Denise, Fancy was already finding herself less fascinated with them than she'd been when she'd first arrived in this strange new city.

Where else would she put another gown or bonnet? Her past came back to haunt her, and she remembered Fleur striving to save enough good material from one of her frocks to make Fancy a pretty new dress. Here in the Dubose home waste was was common so she could not share these feelings with Nick. After all, he'd always lived lavishly, but could she live the rest of her life this way? Grave doubts seized her, and she fell back on the bed, her eyes misting with tears.

When she awoke the clock told her it was almost the dinner hour. Leaping from the bed, she summoned Celine.

The atmosphere around the dining table was as gloomy as the weather. Monique sat at the opposite end of the long, white-clothed table, her elegant black gown enhanced by one strand of perfectly matched pearls. "Dear Nicholas, going up that river in all this horrible weather. Was it necessary to send him along, Alain?"

In his stern, serious way, Alain assured her. "I

felt so. It was no accident, what happened to the *Memphis Belle*, Monique. Nicholas and I both feel it was a deliberately set fire, and I want him to find out what's going on, to talk to the captain and crew."

Neither Doreen nor Denise were present this evening. Fancy regretted that she had not had her dinner sent up on a tray because the elder Duboses completely igmored her. Now she faced many days and nights without Nicholas. As Nat moved around the long table she asked for a second and then a third glass of the white wine. She was certain she received a reproachful look from Monique when she requested the third glass.

A perverse streak in Fancy urged her to arch her brow skeptically. "Were you about to say something to me, Monique?" she inquired. She would not call Monique "Mother." That honor belonged to Fleur.

"No . . . no, dear," Monique stammered, darting a look at Alain. She felt restrained with her daughter-in-law this evening for Alain had enlightened her about the discussion he'd had with Nicholas before the havoc had broken out that afternoon. Indeed, Monique had already been aflutter when she'd come downstairs.

She was a lady who insisted that the atmosphere in her home be pleasant and serene. She was unable to cope with upsets. Monique insisted on perfection in her home, dress, and surroundings.

However, Monique could not help feeling a certain pang of compassion for Fancy this evening. Her daughter-in-law looked so forlorn, and the candlelight playing across her face lit up the beauty that even Monique could not deny. Perhaps, she was lowly bred, but there was a patrician air to Nicholas's bride.

"Fancy, dear . . . you hardly touched your dinner."

Fancy noticed Monique's mellow tone, but it didn't matter now.

"I just wasn't hungry. If you will excuse me I think I'll go up to my room," Fancy said, forcing a weak smile.

Inside the privacy of her bedroom as Celine assisting her to disrobe, Fancy caught sight of herself in the full-length cheval mirror. A woman's body was reflected there, one with full breasts and curvaceous hips. Only her tiny waistline remained the same. Her woman's body cried out for the touch and caress of the husband who was now so many miles from her. She wanted to feel his mouth on her lips, playing sensuously there until she welcomed his prodding tongue; his warm, exploring hands moving up and down her back and hips. She imagined that his arms pressed her to him and she could almost feel the heat of his body stirring wild desire in her.

As Celine slid a nightgown over her head, Fancy's thoughts still dwelled on Nick. Chris Kensington no longer occupied her thoughts as he had that afternoon.

While Celine's nimble fingers freed the curls atop her head, Fancy fantasized. She imagined Nick's strong hand cupping her breast, and she pulsed and ached for his touch.

Not being privy to her mistress' secret thoughts, Celine saw only Fancy's sultry beauty and was struck by it. She had seen the promise in her young mistress, and that lovely rosebud had blossomed into a glorious rose. With a virile, hot-blooded man like Monsieur Nicholas to love her how could it be otherwise, Celine thought, amusement playing in her dark eyes. She'd seen it happen before. A man could make a woman blossom or wilt. Miss Fancy would never wilt if Celine was any judge of men. Not with Monsieur Nicholas in her bed.

Had the mulatto servant and her mistress been able to read each other's mind, their laughter would have rung out in gay camaraderie.

Instead, Fancy's sudden request rather startled Celine. "Go ask Nat to give you a glass of white wine, Celine. I feel the need of one."

"A glass of white wine, ma'am?"

"Yes, Celine. A glass of white wine." As Fancy turned to watch the puzzled servant leave the room, she smiled to herself. Anything to numb this flushed, hungry body of hers, Fancy thought, when she was alone in the room with an empty bed facing her.

She remembered asking herself earlier if she was in love with Nick. Preposterous! Her depressed state had nothing to do with not loving Nick. Quite the opposite!

Feeling the relaxing effect of the wine, Fancy drifted off to sleep, hugging the spare pillow to her bosom. So obsessed was she by thoughts of her husband that she did not remember that Chris Kensington had boarded the *Memphis Belle* that afternoon.

Chapter Twenty-seven

It had never dawned on Fancy when she'd asked Denise to drop her at Angelique's house that Madame Rocheleau might be out since Fancy was not expected. Indeed only a lull in the rains and the prospect of a long afternoon ahead of her had convinced Fancy to accept Denise's invitation to go the milliner's shop. She had not realized how close it was to the Rocheleau residence, and as they'd passed it, she'd changed her mind and ordered Dudley to stop there.

"You don't mind, do you, Denise? I honestly do not need another bonnet."

Curtly, Denise shrugged, "Why should I?" But after Dudley helped Fancy down and drove off Denise realized how Fancy intended to get home. But she could not trouble herself over that. Country girls walked down dirt lanes without any thought, didn't they? She giggled to herself, thinking of her sister-in-law's predicament. Perhaps Fancy did not know that New Orleans' streets were flooded when rains hit the city.

A few moments later Fancy realized how presumptuous she'd been when the Rocheleau butler informed her that Angelique was away for the afternoon. Fancy grimaced and thought herself stupid as she politely thanked him and turned away. Angelique's butler, Jules, had recognized the lovely young lady and he had presumed that a carriage awaited her just down the drive.

Hoisting her skirt Fancy walked down the drive trying to miss the puddles created by yesterday's showers. Denise had, indeed, been right. Fancy had not known how easily certain parts of the city became flooded. Now she noticed that the sky had become overcast again in the brief time since she'd left with Denise.

As she turned out of Angelique's driveway onto the street, a fancy one-horse carriage moved swiftly by her, splashing muddy water on the bottom of her taffeta skirt. Fancy exploded, letting out a stream of complaints as she shook the burgundy taffeta that was now spattered with ugly brown spots. She had little time to fret about that though, for she now found herself in a worse dilemma. A sudden sharp rumble of thunder exploded as a streak of lightning cut a path across the gray, heavy-laden sky.

"Oh, dear God!" she sighed, knowing she was going to be drenched before she could possibly make it to the Babcock Boutique so she might ride home with Denise.

She decided to cross the street before the rain became heavier. Then she would be on a straight path to the milliner's shop, and the shelter of the large trees there looked inviting.

Stepping into the street she glanced both ways before darting across. A carriage was coming from one direction, but she could outrace it. Pushing the handle of her reticule up on one arm she grabbed the sides of her skirt, and holding it high above her ankles, she started for the other side of the street.

When she was almost across, Fancy moaned with pain as she slipped in the mud and her ankle twisted and then gave, causing her to fall. She landed on her side, like a domino knocked over.

Her head struck the wooden walk at the edge of the street, and Fancy fell into a deep black abyss.

The carriage came to an abrupt stop and a man jumped out. He gathered up the fallen, limp woman and carried her to his hired gig. Water rushed rampantly down the street by now, so only one thing occupied the man's mind. He had to get to higher ground and find shelter from the deluge that showed no sign of letting up.

He turned the gig around and headed for his schooner, the slumped figure of Fancy on the leather seat beside him. Those passing the gig driven by the wild-haired blond man thought him an idiot or a drunk. But Eric had only one thing on his mind and that was to get this beautiful lady to the safety and dry comfort of his cabin. Once there, he could assess how serious her injury was. He'd been startled to see her gorgeous face cradled in the wet black velvet bonnet. She was the enchanting miss who'd haunted his dreams since he'd seen her walking with his old acquaintance, Chris Kensington.

Never had he expected to meet her and certainly not like this. Since Chris had left the city, Eric had had no way to find out this woman's name but he knew she was a lady of quality. He'd known that the first time he'd seen her. But why was she out without her own carriage? That *did* muddle his mind.

The sight of his schooner was a most welcome one for the rains still fell unceasingly.

In the galelike wind Eric exerted his firmly muscled body to the limit to carry Fancy whose dripping wet gown made her quite heavy. His own clothes were as saturated as hers. They clung to his body. Water had managed to invade his black leather boots and he knew when he removed them from his feet a nice little stream would flow out.

As he sped past his first mate, Barney Craig, he barked out an order for some items he wanted brought to his cabin. Barney rushed to carry out his captain's commands, curious about the bedraggled lady he carried in his arms.

Rivulets of water dampened the plank floor as Eric laid Fancy on his bunk and removed her bonnet. Carelessly, Eric tossed the bonnet on the floor and then he soothed the moaning half-conscious Fancy, assuring her that she was safe.

"Eric will take care of you, *mademoiselle.*" He moved away only long enough to grab his deep blue robe so it would be ready to slip on her. "Come on, cause we've got to get this damn stuff all off." He raised her and located the complicated fastenings of her gown. Working as fast as his huge hands could, he tugged the gown downward. She was really a tiny little thing with those yards of silk removed. He heaved a deep breath as his eyes beheld her bare satiny shoulders, and the alluring cleavage of her ripe breasts teased the very essence of his manhood. Without realizing it, he sighed, almost in anguish.

"Holy Christ . . . sheer enchantment, you are, love!"

Fancy didn't know she had such an ardent, admiring audience, for she was slowly coming out of the blackness.

Eric denied himself the delectable sight of her

nakedness after savoring it for a second. He pulled and pushed her arms into his oversized robe. Snuggled tightly in a blanket, her wet hair pulled away from her face, Fancy gave a soft, contented moan and turned on her side. Only then did Eric's thoughts turn to his own drenched state, and by that time, Barney was coming through the cabin door with a pot of coffee and an unopened bottle of brandy, along with a steaming teakettle of hot water.

"Pour me a hefty shot of brandy, would you, mate?" Eric urged, a smile on his face. With a yank he rid himself of his shirt. He eagerly gulped the brandy before stripping off his pants.

Barney stood, curious as a cat about the damsel with his captain. Disheveled as she was, she was some looker, but then Captain Swenson always picked the best-looking ones whenever they pulled into port.

"Pretty little thing," Barney commented, peering toward the oversized bunk. Fancy's dark brown hair was fanned out over the pillow. Amazingly, most of it was dry because her velvet bonnet had shielded her head. Little ringlets had already formed over her forehead, and they gave her a childlike air.

Eric slipped into a pair of dry pants and stood, wiping his broad chest before putting on his shirt. "Prettiest thing I ever saw." His eyes turned to the bunk and then back to Barney, who didn't have to be told that Eric Swenson was smitten by this woman, whoever she was.

"Uh, anything else you need, sir?" Barney felt that he wasn't needed right now. Eric shook his head, which he had draped with a towel, turbanlike, for his blond lion's mane was as wet as if he'd taken a swim in the river.

"Maybe later." Eric mumbled offhandedly as he pulled a dry stocking on a bare foot.

Backing up toward the door, Barney echoed Eric's comment, "Yeah, later." He exited the cabin knowing no more than he had when he'd entered. A little more, perhaps!

Shoeless and shirtless, Eric sat for a moment, reflecting on the strange afternoon as he slowly sipped his brandy. Hell and damnation! Who said there wasn't a fairy godmother! He felt as if he'd been granted his dearest wish by having this woman practically flung into his arms.

He'd check out her ankle and see if she could walk on it later. A dainty ankle it was, too, but it showed no bruising and certainly wasn't broken. Perhaps, a sprain. The slam her head had taken had stunned her for a while, and a small bump had risen on her temple. But that was not serious either.

Kittenish sounds now came from the bunk and the blanket was moving as the woman flung her legs about beneath it. Eric removed the towel from his head and brushed his fingers through his hair as he moved over to check her out now that she appeared to be regaining consciousness.

"What . . . where? . . ." Fancy's stammering voice was almost a whisper. Eric hastily poured a cup of coffee and laced it with brandy. Sitting down on the bunk beside her, his strong arm went around her to support her to a sitting position. "*Mademoiselle* . . . feel better?"

She stared at him for a moment. A blond Greek God could not have been more handsome, yet his Nordic features revealed a friendly warmth.

He smiled broadly and then motioned for her to take a sip, and she did. "*Monsieur* . . . I . . . I . . ." Eric shook his head and forbid her to try to speak. "Ssssh, just sip this right now, eh. I'll do the talking. Eric Swenson, your humble servant, ma'am."

Fancy's dark eyes danced over his face and down to his bare chest. Other than her husband's magnificent body, she'd never admired any other man's, but this man was striking. She'd have to be blind not to see that. How had she ended up with him, here on board some kind of ship? Her eyes were focusing quite well now and she knew she was in a ship's cabin.

Eric noticed the apprehension reflected on her face. "Here . . . can you hold the cup? I need some more brandy. That rain had a chill to it, and the two of us were drowned rats by the time I got us to shelter. You are on board the

Caprice, mademoiselle, and perfectly safe, I assure
you. I am the captain."

"I thank you, Captain, for easing my mind."
She smiled, her eyes twinkling. "I shall now introduce myself. I am Madame Fancy Dubose."

A devious gleam appeared in Eric's blue eyes
even though he felt a deep sense of disappointment at hearing that she was married. "Well,
Madame Dubose, you obviously couldn't have
a more proper name, for a fancy lady you are.
When you were a babe, your mother must have
peered into a crystal ball and seen what a lovely
lady you were going to become to have named
you that." Eric's silver tongue had always been
an asset where the ladies were concerned. The
mere fact that she was married didn't dent his
ardor or deter him from pursuing her now that
he'd met her.

He spent the next hour conversing lightheartedly with Fancy. Eric confessed that he'd
seen her with Chris Kensington in front of the
Saint Regent. Then they shared a light feast of
fish chowder, which Fancy praised as the best
she'd ever had. Generous slices of the cook's
fresh-baked bread accompanied the soup. This
food was as tasty as anything she'd eaten at the
Dubose home. She laughed. "You won't rescue
me again. I must have been famished." A capti-
vating smile was on her face.

"Ah, now . . . that's where you're wrong. I'd
go to the ends of the earth to rescue you, but

there would be one catch . . . I'd never let you go, love." Eric's blue eyes suddenly looked like sapphires. He churned within, aching to kiss the honey-sweet lips that taunted him.

Fancy knew that look now — Nick had taught her well — and she suddenly trembled, realizing the state of her dress. She flushed with embarrassment at the knowledge that he'd surely been the one who'd undressed her. Dear God, how was she ever going to explain this afternoon?

"Captain Swenson, I must get home. My . . . my family will be greatly concerned about me." She had no inkling of the time but certainly a few hours had passed since her accident.

"I think the weather is going to determine that, *mam'selle*. Please excuse me while I go up on deck to see what we're faced with." He grabbed a jacket off the peg on the door and gave her a quick, easy smile. He was not fool enough to escort her home and be met at the door by an irate husband. He knew the name of Dubose and most likely this Nicholas, her husband, was a hot-blooded and hot-tempered Frenchman.

No, my pretty, he thought to himself. A message will be sent, and he can come to my ship to pick you up. Eric always tried to make the odds in his favor.

He sent one of his deckhands, with a message, to the Dubose address before returning below to his cabin where Fancy waited. She found to her displeasure that her undergarments had not been spread out separately and were still damper than her gown. Being quite practical, she chose to toss them out the small window and wear only the drier gown.

She giggled, feeling very wicked because she was not wearing undergarments and was in the cabin of a strange man. Who would know but her? she rationalized. He would be taking her home shortly and that would be the end of it, Fancy told herself.

Her concern over facing the awesome Dubose family was somewhat diminished now. After all, she had done nothing to be ashamed of, for nothing improper had happened. The man had rescued her, and if her welfare was a real consideration, Nick and his family were in debt to this Eric Swenson. She was feeling very confident by the time the good-looking blond captain returned to the cabin.

"Everything is taken care of, Fancy," Eric told her.

"I thank you, Captain Swenson," she replied. She had noticed that he had not addressed her once as Madame Dubose, instead he'd insisted upon calling her Fancy.

She started to rise from the chair, presuming he intended her to prepare to leave the schooner, but noting that he sat staring at her with a piercing, heated look, she wondered if his eyes could see right through her gown. No, that was impossible, not with all those yards of material. "Are you not ready, Captain Swenson?" she pointedly inquired.

A slow grin came to Eric's face. "You must have misunderstand my intentions, ma'am. I sent word to your home and family where you were."

His announcement met with her disapproval and Fancy did not try to mask it. She took a seat, clasping her hands in her lap and trying to control her temper.

God, she was tantalizingly desirable when she was mad, Eric mused. He sought fire in a woman, which he'd found few had. He found himself wanting to rush to where she sat and crush her in his arms. But he knew it was too late for that now. Being a man not used to bridling his desires, he rose to excuse himself, intending to wait upside. At this point, he wasn't so sure of himself.

"I've duties to tend to, Madame Dubose." Hastily, he disappeared through the door.

Fancy grinned slyly. He'd called her Madame Dubose finally. He'd accepted that she was a married lady. Fancy had no doubts about the yearning she'd seen in Eric Swenson's eyes. Oh yes, she was certainly aware that he wanted to make love to her. As a woman, she couldn't help being flattered. Perhaps, men thought themselves the masters, but women weren't exactly without power either. The things she was learning about this world of men and women continually amazed her. Even more astonishing were the things she was finding out about herself.

Fancy Fourney was becoming a stranger, and Fancy Dubose became more real as time went by. She liked this new Fancy, she arrogantly told herself as she waited for the Dubose carriage to arrive.

Chapter Twenty-eight

Once the disgruntled passengers had been transferred aboard the *Bayou Queen* to be carried to Natchez or to Memphis, there was nothing more Nick Dubose could do aboard the *Memphis Belle*. The arsonists had done a thorough job on the hold of his father's boat. The evidence was there to see, and Nick had all the information he needed to confront Rafferty with when he returned to New Orleans. That bastard had hired hoodlums to fire the boat. But there had been one slip-up. One of the ruffians had been a victim of the melee, and just before he'd died he'd confessed to Nick and the captain, and he'd named his boss.

So when the *Nelly Dee* came down the Mississippi from up Natchez way, Nick hitched a ride back to New Orleans. The journey was slow and tedious because of the heavy rainfall, but Nick was not cognizant of the turbulent weather. He was tired and weary, having gone many hours without rest, and once aboard he fell into a deep sleep.

He did not know that a lady by the name of Samantha was a passenger on the *Nelly Dee*, and he failed to hear her calling out to him frantically when they disembarked at the landing later in New Orleans. Nick's thoughts were or Fancy and on how he was going to tell her the sad news about Chris Kensington.

A crushing blow to the head had taken Chris's life. In one of his pockets a folded slip of paper bearing Alita Dumaine's letterhead had been found. Fancy's name and address had been written on it. Nick chided himself about how he had behaved toward Fancy because of his jealousy of this young man. That made it difficult to face her now with these sad tidings.

He should never have doubted her love for him; he knew that now. He was impatient to get home and make amends for his petty behavior. His only excuse was that he loved her so damned much the thought of another man with his wife sent him into a jealous frenzy.

As the carriage carried him homeward, Nick fingered the two pieces of jewelry he'd not had the chance to give Fancy because of his unexpected trip up the river.

He wished he were astride his thoroughbred, Domino, instead of in this carriage. He could go so much faster. Suddenly he was seized with an overwhelming urge for the surroundings of Natchez, a wild gallop across the countryside on Domino, and more private time with Fancy without his family always underfoot.

Fancy's resentment built even more when she was finally alone in her room. She had dismissed Celine because she could not allow the maid-servant to assist in undressing her when she had nothing on under the burgundy gown. The family inquisition had left her in the foulest of moods for she'd seen no concern for her on Monique's or Alain's face. She'd noticed the despicable Denise restraining her laughter. Damn her! Fancy muttered to herself. One day she'd even the score with that wicked little miss!

Why, poor Dudley had been more worried about her. Well, she didn't care what the Duboses thought, Fancy decided as she shed her gown for a wrapper. Then she summoned Celine to order a bath.

Nick entered the front door, but he did not announce his arrival to his family for one thing obsessed him—the sight of Fancy. He had no desire to sit talking about the incident with his father. He wanted to hold his wife in his arms and to kiss the sweet honey of her soft lips. He had a hungry need to feel her body next to his, and his blood boiled as he took the steps two at a time.

Nothing could have stirred such sheer delight in him as the scene that met his eyes when he entered their boudoir to find Fancy in the tub, surrounded by the sweet fragrance of jasmine bath oil. Her dark brown hair was piled high on her head, yet stray tendrils hung around her dainty neck. She did not hear Nick's entrance.

Nick wanted to smother Fancy's satiny shoulders with his kisses. Silently, he motioned to Celine to leave, and she smiled, knowing exactly what Monsieur Nicholas had on his mind. As Celine exited Fancy lay back in the tub, her eyes closed.

He moved like a cat to position himself, and then he bent to take her relaxed, half-open mouth with his. With one hand he turned her head toward him. Fancy's startled eyes opened wide to see Nick's dark head bent against her face. But never did she ponder whose mouth had captured her lips.

Not caring that his shirt got wet, Nick gathered Fancy to him, crushing her breasts forcefully against his chest. His mouth released hers and he huskily confessed, "I want you so, *ma petite Fancy*."

"Oh, Nick! Nick, my darling," she sighed, enflamed already by the torrid heat of his sensuous lips and the feel of his strong body pressing against hers.

"Tell me you missed me, Fancy my love?" he whispered in her ear as he raised her dripping body out of the tub. Her arms encircled his neck and her fingers lovingly caressed his hair. She was oblivious to the water that fell on the expensive carpet.

Her body was so stirred by her husband's magic presence that she breathlessly confessed her need for him and her loneliness when he was gone.

Nothing she could have said would have pleased him more. She was yielding to him as he had dreamed she would. She clung to him as he carried her to the bed, and he found it hard to release her long enough to remove his restraining clothing.

As her dark eyes stared up at him provocatively, her naked body sensuously invited him to join her. Quickly he shed his trousers and sank down by her. He loved the soft little moans of pleasure she emitted as his lips took hers and then trailed down her throat to a rose-tipped breast. Small volcanoes erupted liquid fire within her, and she pressed him closer, unable to get enough of him.

"Oh, God!" he moaned. "What you do to me, woman!" His joy in the feel of her carried him to blazing heights as he burrowed himself between her velvet thighs. He could tarry no longer at those silken portals, but sought to enter eagerly. She greeted him with a wild undulating arch of her body and they moved in perfect harmony, their tempo becoming faster and faster.

His swift, powerful thrusts surged through her like the wild, tempestuous current of a raging river. Fancy was unaware of the soft moans that bespoke her rapturous pleasure, but Nick heard them and they added to his boundless pleasure.

As he reached the ultimate point of ecstasy, he, too, moaned, "Only mine, Fancy. Only mine you can be."

She sighed breathlessly, "Only yours, Nick." They lay, slowly descending from the heights of their passion.

Any doubts that had plagued Nick or Fancy had been swept away by the rapture they'd found in each other's arms.

The sensual bliss they'd enjoyed was still with them at the dawn of the new day. But Nick knew he must now face the unpleasant reality of telling Fancy about Chris Kensington's untimely death aboard the *Memphis Belle*.

In the privacy of their bedroom, he told her, finding no way to soften the blow. He was hardly prepared for her outpouring of tears and grief. At first, he nearly felt helpless, unable to comfort her, but by the time he had finally finished dressing to go downstairs, he was experiencing a wave of resentment that he tried desperately to fight.

Naturally, she was sad about the death of the young man she'd known since childhood, he told himself. So why didn't that satisfy him? Why did it irritate him to see her shed so many tears over Kensington? He didn't like to picture himself as a heartless, unfeeling brute, but neither could he deny the resentment that gnawed at him this morning.

When he returned home in the late afternoon, he didn't have to be told that Fancy had spent the day mourning, for her eyes reflected a day of weeping.

He felt constrained in her presence, not knowing what to say or do. He couldn't cope with his tenseness, so he left her alone hoping that would be easier for both of them. Tomorrow would be better, he told himself.

Fancy felt Chris's death very deeply and she yearned to snuggle in the secure arms of her husband when they retired but she did not feel free to do so. Her feeling seemed ridiculous after the night they'd shared, she supposed, but he'd exhibited a querulous air when he'd returned home and he'd maintained it throughout the evening. He had withdrawn behind an armor she was unable to penetrate. Dear Lord, he didn't seem to realize how hard it was for her to smile, for she kept seeing the image of Chris, so young yet gone forever. Fleur's death had had a startling effect on her, and now she found Chris's untimely passing almost as shocking.

During the afternoon, Fancy sought the privacy of her room for she realized that neither Nick nor anyone in the Dubose family could appreciate how she was feeling. She could not expect them to understand. However, the image of Eric Swenson, the tall blond gentleman who'd rescued her, came to her while she sat alone in her bedroom. He'd known Chris Kensington, and she had no doubt he'd be stunned to know about Chris's death.

She also remembered other things, though, that made her reluctant to go to him with the news of their mutual friend's death. As quick as that foolish impulse came to mind, she dismissed it.

Such was not the case with Eric Swenson for he had not dismissed Fancy Dubose from his thoughts. He did not intend to write off the possibility that he might add this charmer to his list of conquests.

Like Nicholas Dubose, Eric possessed a cunning, irresistible charm that lured lovely ladies to him, and he was also able to ingratiate himself with gentlemen. His blond image spoke of strength and power and made him appealing to both sexes.

Eric had been busy the last two days learning as much as he could about the respected Dubose family from various sources in New Orleans. He'd wandered the wharves and talked to the river boatmen, visited the houses of pleasure and gaming halls. He had favorably impressed the well-known banker, Arthur Merril, and had been invited to his home for dinner. Merril's attractive wife and daughters had been enchanted by the dashing Eric Swenson. This was an old game to Eric, and he played it with finesse.

As he moved around the city and along the busy wharves, he heard the news of Chris's death but he dwelt briefly on it. He allowed nothing to spoil his reckless pleasures—not even his father's threats that he'd disown him if he didn't straighten out his life.

At twenty-four he was full of ginger, and his quests for lovely ladies and his bouts at the gaming tables never ceased to thrill him. Wealthy, married ladies were his prey for they usually delighted in rewarding him generously for his favors. His reputation for prowess in the boudoir and his powers of persuasion rarely failed to get him the lady he desired.

Now he pinpointed Fancy as his next conquest, and with the patience of a cat, he set the scene for her seduction. Her dark, sultry looks and sensuous curves intoxicated him. He was drunk with the desire to get that spirited miss in his bed.

The very fact that she had not eagerly tumbled into his arms that day on his schooner, but had been coolly indifferent, made no difference to him. Eric's conceit didn't allow defeat.

He didn't consider that Fancy just might love her husband too much to dally with him or any other man, nor did he count on a man like Nick whose possessive love would fight the devil himself to hold on to what was his. Eric Swenson's arrogance was monumental.

Being clever, he picked a time of day when he knew Nicholas Dubose was in his office down by the wharf, and then dressed in his finely tailored deep blue coat and cream-colored pants, he paid a visit to the Dubose residence. He smiled sheepishly as he put the black velvet reticule in his pocket.

When he arrived and was ushered into the parlor to await Fancy, he used his blond charm generously on the spellbound Denise who was sitting there. She flirted boldly with him, taking advantage of the moments before Fancy joined them.

"Captain Eric Swenson . . .you said? Well, so the fine schooner, the *Caprice* is yours then?" Swishing her sky blue muslin skirt to the side she took a seat and invited him to join her on the settee.

"At your service, beautiful lady," Eric told her bestowing on her a flash of his white teeth.

"Mercy, my sister-in-law meets the most interesting men. I could envy her, I swear," Denise purred, a teasing smile on her lovely face.

That practiced grin still on his face, Eric remarked, "Women like Madame Dubose can't help whetting the interest of men, *mademoiselle*. Not if they still breathe. But the Dubose family seems to have more than its share of beauties."

Denise was finding it difficult to maintain her flippant air for the man's nearness was affecting her. He stirred her deeply and the results were unsettling. His blue eyes devoured her so boldly that she pondered what she'd do if he actually leaned over to kiss her.

She tried to sound casual as she spoke. "I . . . I can see why Fancy was so late getting home the other day." Despite her efforts there was a slight tremor in her voice.

He measured his next words most carefully for out of the corner of his eye he'd caught a figure in the archway. "I must confess to you, *mademoiselle,* she was very eager to get home, and that is why she left her reticule behind. I am returning it now. She was very concerned about the fact that her family would be worried."

Only then did the figure move through the archway and into the parlor to join them. Unlike the shrewd Swenson, Denise had had no inkling that they were about to be joined by another.

Chapter Twenty-nine

Monique Dubose was a vision of elegance and refinement as she moved gracefully to join her daughter. Displeased by her daughter's outrageous behavior with this young gentleman, she had waited in the entrance, unannounced, to hear the captain's comments on her daughter-in-law before letting her presence be known. His answer having met with her approval, she introduced herself and apologized at the same time for having to take her leave.

"My daughter-in-law will be here shortly, Captain Swenson." Turning a critical eye on Denise, Monique curtly summoned her. "Come, Denise, or we'll be late for our appointment with Madame Montiel. If you will excuse us, Captain Swenson." Monique marched out grandly, a disgruntled Denise following behind her. Denise muttered under her breath. It wasn't fair! It seemed to

Denise that that little piece of white trash had all the luck.

How could a man like Nick put up with a wife who seemed to catch men's eyes so easily? Denise had to flirt and encourage them to get any attention.

Moments later Eric enjoyed seeing Fancy enter the room. She was dressed in an olive-green gown that was trimmed in a russet-colored braid. Its lines were basic, but its simplicity only enhanced the beautiful mold of her body. Her only adornment was a pair of earrings, small jade stones encrusted in gold. Her loose hair flowed over her shoulders.

She smiled when she saw Eric Swenson, for Celine had only told her a gentleman awaited her in the parlor. Something about his face, so openly friendly and warm, was a welcome sight to Fancy.

The foggy maze she'd walked through the last two days had left her desolate. Her only clear experience had occurred the night Nick had walked into their room, lifted her from the tub, and made all-consuming love to her. Oh yes, that had been real and wonderful! But since then she'd walked in a mist as real as the ones shrouding the banks of the river at Willow Bend. Often when she'd stepped outside the shanty there, the billowing fog that floated in from the river was so thick she couldn't see across. She'd felt that way lately.

"This is a surprise, Captain Swenson." She greeted him pleasantly.

"I know how a lady feels when she loses her reticule, and this is such a pretty one, Madame Dubose."

After some minutes of casual chatter they became just "Eric" and "Fancy." He seemed so compassionate and understanding about the death of Chris Kensington, but his tenderness and sympathy were assumed, a web of deception to win Fancy's favor.

By the time he took his leave, Fancy's spirits felt lighter, and she had come to the conclusion that she could not wallow in mourning over Chris. He was gone. Tonight, she would put forth a new face for Nick. No longer would she be the red-eyed, lifeless wife he'd encountered the last two days and nights. After all, a vital man like Nick Dubose could not be left wanting too long. Far too many women would be more than happy to occupy him.

She took special care with her toilette and chose one of her prettiest gowns for the evening. But when no heavy boots bounced up the steps at six or even at seven, Fancy was as perplexed as Alain and Monique. A number of emotions played over her before she excused herself from the family gathering to go to her room. Her worry and concern were coupled with impatience and anger. She tried to hide her embarrassment from Celine when the mulatto helped her out of the pretty lavender gown. Celine felt so sorry for her little mistress who was obviously trying to keep up a brave front.

When the clock chimed eight Nick dashed

through the front door and bounced up the steps paying no heed to Monique who called out to him from the hallway. He shrugged away her inquiry and continued his determined path down the carpeted upstairs hall to his rooms. Celine sidestepped the irate Nick who looked like a raging bull, but his face did not escape her dark eyes. Monsieur Nicholas had been in a fight. His cheek was angry-looking and was becoming discolored. One side of his face was dirty as well.

"Ah, mercy." Celine heaved a deep, dejected sigh. "Wonder what done happened now? Wonder what the other man looks like?" Celine swayed thoughtfully on down the hall, praying silently that he had no more fury left to cast at the little mistress. He still had the look of the devil in those green eyes.

The smile on Fancy's face quickly faded as Nick came through the door. The fire in his eyes burned her flesh, and she remembered once before seeing that cruel, menacing look on his face. Curious as to what had caused his awesome, black mood, and having no idea that it had anything to do with her, she walked up to him innocently. "Nick? What . . ."

He stepped back instantly for he wasn't sure of what he might do at that moment. She stood still, her dark eyes dancing over his face, silently asking how the cuts and bruises had gotten there. Her innocence cried out to him, and her intriguing body tempted him to explore it beneath her gossamer lavender gown. Angry as he was, he wanted her. But he couldn't, not after what he'd found out. Hell, she hadn't even mentioned anything about Eric Swenson and the little fiasco which had put her alone on his fancy schooner for an hour or two. What more was there to tell that Swenson hadn't told him?

His voice was low when he spoke and his tone warned Fancy not to test him. "It's best we do not talk tonight, Fancy. I . . . I don't know where it would all end if we did." He turned from her, running his long fingers through his rumpled dark hair, and he strode over to the doorway. There was anguish in his voice as he muttered, "For your sake and mine, just go to bed."

Instinctively Fancy did as he'd bade her, and she lay very still not knowing what he was doing. Finally, she realized he was attending to his cuts and bruises, and afterwards undressing. She could hardly breathe when he was so close and in that kind of mood. Her quiet presence was as disturbing to him. The essence and fragrance of her wafted to his nose and tantalized him to madness. Still he didn't trust his hands on her silken flesh. He willed himself to stay on his side of the bed until this insanity left him. Never had he exploded as violently as he had a few hours ago, and anger still smoldered within him.

Nick's restless night was nothing compared to the pain endured by Eric Swenson, who had found out he was not the finest cock around by any means. His male ego was as shattered as his face, and his overwhelming vanity was marred beyond repair since witnesses had viewed his defeat at the hands of Nicholas Dubose.

He was afraid that his handsome face might never be the same after the unrelenting beating the Frenchman had given him. Eric never did learn how Nicholas had found out about his interlude with Fancy but it was enough that he had.

Eric's sojourn in New Orleans was over, and he'd issued orders to set sail as soon as he'd come to his senses. He wondered what would have happened if his first mate hadn't pulled the big dark brute off of him. He hurt like the devil, but he was alive.

The harsh lesson Nicholas Dubose had taught him had registered more pointedly and profoundly than any of his father's threats.

Unintentionally, Nick Dubose had accomplished the impossible or so Eric Swenson's father would have thought. The battered man did not realize, as he set sail from New Orleans on that late autumn night, the impact his encounter with Nick would have on his future.

Nick woke up at the crack of dawn and the first sight his sleepy eyes beheld was the glorious vision in lavender nestled beside him. A heaviness engulfed his heart. His future with her lay in the balance, and he knew it. Sometimes, he wished he'd never brought her to New Orleans and this house.

330

A sudden impulse seized him, and without wasting another minute, he prepared to dress. Wise counsel was what he needed, so he decided to seek the sage advice of Angelique Rocheleau.

He dressed with awkward movements, trying not to awaken Fancy. It seemed imperative that he get out of the room before she woke and began to question him.

Christ! He loved her! He didn't want to create a barrier that they could never remove, one that would mar their happiness forever.

He didn't breathe easily until he'd slipped through the door, his leather boots in his hand. Luckily, he was spared any encounter with his family as he left the house and headed straight for Madame Rocheleau's home.

It was a ridiculous hour to intrude on her, and he knew it. Only his dear Angelique would not think him an idiot. He expected to be asked for a full account about his face, but that didn't bother him as much as facing his parents would have.

When Nick arrived at the Rocheleau house, his familiar face did not upset the butler who invited him to enter. A short time later, unceremoniously, he was climbing the stairs to Angelique's boudoir. These two had never complied with the conventions of the people around them.

Nicholas thought no more of entering Angelique's bedroom or of being received by that lovely lady in her gown and wrapper than he would have if she had been Monique Dubose. It had always been that way.

He never ceased to marvel at her astonishingly ageless beauty and at the fact that she'd remained a widow for so many years.

Holding out her hands to him, she greeted him, "Nicholas, what a nice way to start my day." But was it? she silently wondered? Something troubled the young man striding toward her. He wouldn't come so early if this were just a social visit, and the lines around his eyes revealed that he'd spent a restless night. She prayed she could give him the comfort he was surely seeking from her as he had so many times in the past.

As he silently admired her, she, too, pridefully surveyed him as he seated himself beside the bed in which she sat, propped up against the mountain of pillows. "I've ordered a tray. Will you share one with me, Nicholas?"

"Just coffee."

When Angelique inquired about Fancy she noticed that he flinched, and she knew instinctively where his problem lay. His face was something else, however; she knew Fancy was not capable of doing that.

As he saw her eyes dancing over his cuts and bruises, Nicholas began to speak. He left nothing out about the previous day or evening, telling her how he'd stormed aboard the *Caprice* and proceeded to beat Eric Swenson. "I could have killed him, Angelique. I swear it!"

Yes, she believed it for Nick was a man whose

emotions were as strong as his body.

He spoke of his doubts about Fancy . . . those lingering tormenting doubts! Angelique listened intensely, letting him talk. When he finally ceased speaking and accepted another cup of coffee, he seemed very weary.

Angelique could have told him many things. What she longed to tell him she could not, but she was sure of one thing, Fancy loved Nicholas. Now she knew just how deep his love for his wife was.

"Love is so fragile sometimes, Nicholas. Once broken or shattered, it can never be put back together. Gentle handling is necessary, my son. Remember that always." How well she knew how swiftly love could slip away, for it had happened to her.

"That, dear Angelique, is what bothers me so. From the minute I saw Fancy I knew she was the one I'd waited for all my life." He broke into a grin and mischief played in his eyes. "Oh, I know my reputation as a rake and a womanizer started even before my twentieth birthday but they . . . None of them meant anything. Then Fancy came along with those big black eyes of hers and I was doomed."

Angelique laughed softly, "Oh, Nicholas . . . I adore you! Ah, that is a symptom of love I would say."

Dear God, he was glad he'd come to see her, for now he found himself laughing a second time. He stood up and stretched his long legs. "I gather you don't believe Fancy is playing me for a fool then?"

"We are the only ones who make ourselves fools. Usually we do it without help from anyone else. I hardly think Fancy considers you a fool, Nicholas. I saw the look of love on that young lady's face. Such love doesn't come and go with a whim. It endures, Nicholas."

He bent and kissed her cheek. "Thank you, Angelique. Thank you for so much I will never be able to repay you."

Nicholas saw only the sparkle in her eyes, but there was a mist of tears too. Later she'd allow herself the luxury of crying, but they would be tears of joy.

"I must go, Angelique." He turned swiftly on his booted heels about to leave, but then he whirled around and faced her again. "I think my wisest move would be to get Fancy and me our own home. Don't tell anyone I told you that." He grinned and hastily made for the door. Angelique didn't have time to reply but he might as well have been reading her mind, she thought. That was the very thing she'd hesitated to advise him to do. It was far better that he'd come to that conclusion by himself.

Like a lazy cat, she stretched out in the bed, feeling serenely content. He'd come to her a disturbed young man, and he'd left with his spirits lifted. What more could she have wished for him.

Chapter Thirty

For a long time to come Nick had no doubt that he would explode with laughter each time he was reminded of the scene he'd come upon in the hallway of his home that late afternoon.

He'd stood back, leaning against the balustrade, puffing on his cheroot and grinning as he'd listened to that petite firebrand, his wife, tear into his sister Denise. It was priceless and he'd enjoyed every minute of it. Denise had gotten the dressing she so deserved for all the mischief she'd been up to recently.

Now the hour was late, and Fancy lay in his arms, exhausted and spent as he was. The spitfire in her was gone. Indeed, she'd been a purring feline when they'd made love.

He wished he'd heard the whole of her episode with Denise, but when he'd entered the hall Fancy had been telling his sister, "My, you were a busy, little bee, weren't you, Denise. You just couldn't wait to run to Nick and tattle. And tattle what, Denise? Hardly the truth but a lie you hoped would cause trouble. Next time you dare to put your nose into my affairs I might just forget I'm Fancy Dubose. I might just be Fancy Fourney, that little white trash girl you were speaking about this afternoon with your friend, Abigail, and I might pull every hair from your head. I hope you get my message!" Having said that, Fancy had turned sharply and plowed into Nick who was standing behind her, a broad smile on his face.

Her eyes were black as the night, and her face was flushed with a rosy glow. Her half-opened lips gasped as Nick's arms encircled her. His open admiration was obvious to her, and she smiled up at him when he winked at her. "You were truly magnificent, my love." Swinging her up in his arms, he turned back to look at his stupefied sister and said, "If she doesn't tend to you, I will."

Giggling and laughing together, Nick and Fancy disappeared up the steps the tension that had engulfed both of them was suddenly released. They were flooded with lighthearted giddiness. Nick's jubilant air almost caused him to knock over a jardiniere of greenery.

"Whoops! Almost did it," he laughed, steadying the jardiniere with one hand before they went through the door to seek the privacy of their own rooms.

He had much to say to his wife, and more he

wanted to do with her. Impatience played across his handsome face, giving it a boyish look. Fancy's eyes adored the Nick she saw now. She wished he could always be just this way.

Although he yearned to make love to her once they'd entered the room, he exerted his will power so they might talk and thereby remove the barriers tormenting both of them.

Fancy lay snuggled in his arms as he told her about his fight with Eric Swenson. She had sensed that the egotistical arrogance of the captain needed denting, and she was amused and satisfied by what her husband had done.

But it was the last thing Nick said that was an answer to her secret prayers. When he'd declared, "We should have our home, my love, and you should be the mistress. I plan to remedy that soon, Fancy," she'd flung her arms around his neck and drawn his head closer so her lips could meet his. "Oh, Nick!" was all she had said to let him know this was what she desired too. Then no other words were spoken. Their bodies took command, talking and touching.

He found her eager for his love and her touch stirred wild sensations in him. The little vixen was like flame. Her dainty hands and fingers possessed such magic as they played across his back and over his chest that he drew in his breath sharply. Her own soft moans blended with his. She was passion's lady, bold and daring, and he adored her. Her sweet yielding, her satiny body swaying and arching to join his, was sheer ecstasy.

Ah, yes, she was his and he was a fool to think otherwise. Yet, it was this very intoxicating rapture he wanted as his own — to share with no man — that ignited the jealousy that was so hard for him to check and control.

He wanted to remain as assured as he was at that moment. If only he could!

Fancy's mounting desires matched his own as they approached the pinnacle of their passion. Christ, he wanted to stop time and linger in that delicious state, but his firm, muscled body shuddered as Fancy gave an impassioned moan of pleasure and clasped her hands into the flesh of his back. "Nick! Nick!" she breathlessly whispered.

Their moist bodies remained pressed together for the longest time, refusing to be parted. When Nick finally sank down beside his wife, he realized she had gone to sleep. From the look on her lovely face, it was a contented, serene sleep.

He did not mind lying awake while she slept, for he, too, was so completely sated and happy to have her back. His sweet, sweet Fancy! Forever, she would be, he vowed fervently.

Celine bossily ordered the servant girl not to disturb the two lovers sleeping in their suite. In the carpeted hall by Denise's and Doreen's bedrooms, she instructed the new girl, "Go no farther than that corner there, gal . . . not until I tell you. 'Sides this is going to keep you busy for a while."

She left the girl, Sally, to go back downstairs, humming a lively tune as she went for she felt very spritely this bright sunny morning. She didn't know why because on that first day of November she had to start the extensive cleaning and preparations for the busy holidays to come.

After Alain Dubose left the house, Doreen gulped down a cup of hot chocolate and nibbled half a croissant so she could get to her painting and put the final strokes to a picture she'd been working on the last two weeks. Denise followed her mother into the sitting room, for venom had built in her since the day before. She had barely slept the night before because she had been anticipating this talk she would have with her mother when she could get her alone.

Celine recognized Miss Denise's voice as she jauntily walked by the open door of the sitting room.

"This was my home long before *she* came along, wasn't it?" Denise's voice snapped angrily.

"No question about that, my darling," Monique quickly responded.

"Then mother, you or father had better speak to my dear brother about his wife's threats. To think that strumpet would dare to put a hand on me . . . the audacity of her!"

Celine quickly covered her mouth to prevent a giggle from escaping as she strained to listen. Monique's voice inquired, "She said she'd what?"

As Denise repeated Fancy's threat to her, she

watched her mother's face scrutinize her. She did not like Moniques' look — Denise knew her mother's strict code regarding a lady's behavior, that it must be beyond reproach — so she hastily chattered on. "Mother, I felt it my duty to tell Nicholas what I did. It was the Dubose family I was thinking of. Nothing is more important than our good name. That's what father is always preaching, isn't he?"

"That is so true, darling. You, too, should remember that at times, I think."

Denise sighed dramatically. "I know, mother dear. But . . . but Fancy is surely flirting with scandal even if she is innocent." She raised a skeptical brow, as if trying to impress her mother of her own grave doubts.

"We have to remember, Denise, that Fancy is Nicholas's wife whether we approve or not," Monique pointed out to her disgruntled daughter.

"Then she should remember whose house she's living in. I won't take orders from white trash." Denise bounced out of the room, almost colliding with the snooping Celine. Luckily Celine was as agile as a gazelle or she'd have had some explaining to do.

Celine had moved so rapidly that her bright colored kerchief had tilted to one side of her head. She took a deep breath and straightened the cotton headpiece as Miss Denise walked on down the hall as though Celine were not even been standing there. "Lord, there's trouble brewin' in this house.

Sure as God made little green apples there's goin' to be trouble between that little hellcat and Miss Fancy," she mumbled.

But in the days that followed there were no indications of that. The antagonistic feelings Fancy and Denise harbored for one another did not erupt into open hostility, even at the evening meals. Denise had become preoccupied with her new suitor, while Nick had secretly urged Doreen to get Fancy to sit for a portrait.

The idea had delighted Doreen and she'd gleefully told her brother, "It will be my Christmas present to you, Nicholas."

Nick had assured her that nothing would please him more or be more treasured, so Fancy had suddenly found herself sitting daily for Doreen. She enjoyed these sessions for she liked to watch Nick's sister work. The two young women conversed to break the quiet of the bright, sunny room, and Doreen found Fancy to be a perfect model.

". . . to say nothing of your beauty, Fancy," Doreen was now saying. "Your beauty would inspire any artist . . . the bone structure of your face and your coloring. Ah, I'm enjoying this so much." Doreen's eagerness was apparent to Fancy and it made the time pass even more pleasantly.

Celine's foreboding that a storm was brewing seemed to be wrong. From all indications a peaceful calm had settled over the Dubose household. However, Celine would call it the calm before the storm.

341

The peace that had settled around the Dubose home even seemed to extend to the steamboat lines. No more mishaps had occurred on any Dubose boats in several weeks. Alain Dubose had approached his son about the possibility that they could dismiss the armed guards on the runs to Natchez and Memphis.

Nick was not so complacent as his father. He'd dealt with men like Rafferty more than his father had. If he was wagering, he'd say Rafferty's next move would be against their cargo-filled warehouses because the man knew their steamboats were now guarded. Word of the guards had traveled up and down the wharves, Nick knew. The river boatmen who clustered in the taverns were a gossipy lot, as bad as house servants.

The shipping business had never been more prosperous for the Duboses and the full warehouses posed a problem Nick had not yet resolved. Perhaps, there would be no pleasant way to handle it. But now he was waiting until the holidays were over before heading to Natchez on a quest to purchase Dubonnet. This time he'd succeed. He was confident now that he'd get Dubonnet, especially since Alita had written that she planned to marry his Uncle André in the spring.

Fancy had been overjoyed about the news and had excitedly urged, "We will go to the wedding in the spring, won't we Nick?"

He'd laughed. "Wild horses wouldn't keep us away, darling." What he had not told her was that they might be living in Natchez by the time spring came.

Nick couldn't believe how happy they'd been the last few weeks. The endless ecstasy she gave him constantly amazed him for he was never seized by the desire to stray from her side. For a man with his past that was a miracle.

Chapter Thirty-one

The Grand Ball at the palatial home of the Bushaws was an annual event attended by a very select group of New Orleans families. The Dubose family had always been invited. The Bushaw mansion was turned into fairyland setting for the occasion. It blazed with hundreds of candles, and garlands streamed over doors and archways. Delectable food and a wide selection of wines were served, while in the huge ballroom the guests danced until dawn. This was always a night to remember.

Each lady pressed her particular seamstress for an outstanding gown to wear, eagerly anticipating that hers would surely be the prettiest one there. This year, as usual, the Dubose women had all chosen new gowns. Monique's elegant black velvet was gorgeous, its simplicity setting off her jewels. Doreen's love of pastels had urged her to choose a pale pink gown trimmed with tiny rosettes of pink velvet, whereas Denise had picked a gown of robin's egg blue in an off-the-shoulder style.

Madame Montiel had suggested an emerald green gown for Fancy. Such vital beauty like hers should be set off by a more striking color than a pale pastel. Since Fancy was a petite lady the simple lines of this gown suited her, and once Fancy had tried on the lovely creation, she knew Madame Montiel had been right to suggest it.

Madame had envisioned Fancy's dark brown hair piled high atop her head to reveal her exquisite emerald-and-diamond teardrop earrings. Fancy would be a vision of elegance. Enchanting elegance! Madame chose an emerald green cape lined with rich gold-colored sarsnet to complete the ensemble and Fancy had to agree with her. Without a moment's hesitation Fancy had purchased it.

Denise, who stood at the far end of the shop with her friend, Myra, couldn't resist a catty remark on Fancy's choice of a gown.

"Wouldn't you just know it, Myra? She'd pick something bright and gaudy."

Myra looked slightly startled.

That remark made Myra stammer a reply with which she hoped to keep Denise in her good graces although truthfully she thought Fancy's choice one of the most gorgeous gowns in the shop. She found Denise a rather difficult person to be around lately, and she wondered why she seemed to have such an insane dislike for her sister-in-law. When Myra had spent brief moments talking with Fancy Dubose she'd left with the impression that Fancy was a genuinely nice person, so although Denise had been her friend as long as she could remember, she was beginning to think Denise was jealous of her beautiful sister-in-law.

What Myra only suspected, Doreen Dubose knew to be a fact and that made her all the more protective toward her sister-in-law. She never failed to speak up in Fancy's defense in front of Denise's friends or to members of her family. Doreen was no longer intimidated by her strong-willed sister and somehow that change in her had begun when Fancy had come to New Orleans.

When the night arrived for the Bushaw's gala affair the Dubose house sparkled with activity. Nick and his father played host to the two young gentlemen who had arrived to escort Doreen and Denise. It was obvious that the two brothers, Richard and Roger Barbiere, were very nervous and impatient as they awaited their dates in the parlor in the company of the stern-faced Alain and the formidable Nicholas. Something about the girls' brother inspired awe in the two young dandies.

At this same moment in another part of the city in the backroom of a tavern owned by an Irishman named Clancy, Rafferty held court with four of his hooligans.

"I'm holding you four responsible for seeing that

the job is done right this time. No more blunders! The men you've hired better know what the hell they're doing. You are to strike at midnight . . . you understand, Kelly?" Rafferty's face had a threatening look about it.

"Yes, sir, Mister Rafferty. We've gone over it a couple of times just this last week. All the buckos are good lads, sir. Any one of them can hold their own if there should be any trouble. They'll all ship out at dawn after the job's done. Couldn't be a more perfect setup, sir."

"Yeah, I like that idea that they'll be leavin' the city for a few months. Since the Dubose warehouse is bulging at the seams with cargo, we are goin' to play hell with it, eh. They're goin' to have a lot of unhappy people on their hands." Rafferty gave out a raucous laugh.

Hooking his thumbs in the belt of his pants, he stood with his legs spread apart. His potbelly hung over his belt like a sack of grain as he dismissed the group.

"Next time we gather I hope to hear a good report. Here, Kelly," he said, tossing the man a leather pouch so he might pay his ruffians for the devil's work they were to perform that evening.

As for himself, he intended to spend the evening celebrating at Rosie's, enjoying her supple body and some good whiskey. While the arrogant, haughty bunch of Duboses were across town at their hoity-toity party, all of their warehouses along the levee were going to be destroyed along with the valuable cargo and goods stored in them. He laughed loudly just thinking about it.

Fancy had every reason to feel confident about the way she looked this evening. Nick had been more than generous in his praise of her. Now he proudly guided her through the glittering entranceway to greet their host.

Monsieur Bushaw and his charming wife, Laura, were impressed by Nicholas's bride. Laura had heard many comments about the young lady who'd managed to snare the elusive, handsome Frenchman who had a reputation for leaving broken hearts behind him. Some people had raved about her striking loveliness while others had been viciously unkind. Laura had decided to keep an open mind until she met the young woman.

She formed a couple of hasty impressions about Fancy during their brief encounter. Nicholas worshipped her, and Fancy was a very poised young women with grace and charm. Laura was not the sort of woman who derived pleasure from indulging in gossip, so she now imagined envy had created antagonism in some for Fancy Dubose.

Fancy was awestruck by the opulence and beauty of the Bushaw mansion. The setting was everything she'd imagined one for a grand ball should be. She liked Laura Bushaw instantly, and she marveled at her ability to manage such a gala affair. It had to be Laura who'd made it all turn out so wonderfully. The very thought of such an undertaking would petrify her. From the time she'd arrived in New Orleans a silent fear of such social obligations had gnawed at her. At times, the impact of being Nicholas Dubose's wife was tremendous.

Had she but known at that very moment, as Nick paraded her through the crowd, the admiring appraisals she was getting from the various gentlemen present, she would have been more confident.

One man who had known Nick for many years stood across the room, entranced by the enchanting girl at Dubose's side. So like old Nicko, as Sean Sullivan always called him, to snare the prettiest girl at the party. The lean, lanky man was in no hurry to rush over to that side of the room, for he was enjoying the view he had. He ogled Fancy as expertly as he would a fine thoroughbred. To him she was a "high stepper" with life and spirit.

It had been over five years since he and Nicholas had last met, and he wondered if Nicholas would remember him. For Sean it had been no problem to pick out the handsome Frenchman in this vast crowd. Nicko was still the good-looking rascal he'd met in Ireland, a man whose love of fine women equaled his fondness for fine horseflesh.

During the lavish repast Nick never noticed the mischievous blue eyes that darted his way from where Sean sat with the elderly couple he'd accompanied to the ball. The respected Colonel Baylor and his wife had secured Sean's last-minute invitation to the Bushaws' soirée.

Sullivan's Irish sense of humor provided him with a way to make his presence known. He would wait until the music began to play for the dancing, and then he'd cut in on Nicko and his beautiful lady. He smiled roguishly, anticipating the stunned look his old friend would have on his face when he tapped his shoulder. It suited Sullivan's jocose nature to conjure up something like this.

Indeed, when the music began Nick wasted no time inviting Fancy to dance. He could not resist planting an affectionate kiss on her forehead now that they were not surrounded by people. "You're the most beautiful woman here tonight, *ma chérie*. I already anticipate losing you for the rest of the evening, but the first and last dance shall be mine," he declared. Silently, he'd vowed to control his jealousy.

She smiled up at him adoringly. "But I will be without you too. Beautiful ladies will be dancing in your arms."

"None so ravishing as you, my love." His arms held her close. Those watching the two dancers did not doubt the love of this couple. Denise caught a fleeting sight of them and felt embarrassed by their open display of affection. A lady didn't show such ardor on a crowded dance floor, not even with her own husband, she thought. Nick had never acted that way with ladies he'd escorted before either. But now he was so bewitched by this lowly born Fancy Fourney that he acted like some kind of fool. What a blight she was on the Dubose family!

During the next three dances Fancy appeared to be a golden harvest of delight rather than a blight as gentlemen claimed her in turn. Sean Sullivan realized his little trick wasn't going to be so easy to pull off. When Nick finally claimed his bride on the fourth number Sean bolted across the floor to cut in.

Even though Sullivan was considered a tall man, he was a good four inches shorter than Dubose. He was well aware of this difference when he patted Nick's shoulder and remarked, "May I?" An amused grin appeared on his face when Nick turned sharply, frowning with displeasure.

There at his side stood a man with flaming red hair, shining blue eyes, and a broad smile that one found hard to forget. Nick gasped, words refusing to come out for a second. Then his frown turned to a smile as he exclaimed, "Sean . . . can it be?"

Their laughter mingled as they embraced in comradely fashion. Fancy stood by them, feeling a little confused. Her curiosity was shared by the couples dancing nearby. Looking over Sean's shoulder, Nick took note of the stir they were causing and quickly pulled Fancy into their cluster.

"Sean, I want to present my wife, Fancy. Fancy my love, this is Sean Sullivan, the best horse trainer in the world. Come on, we've got some talking to do."

But Sean was not going to be deprived of his dance. Shaking his head, he dismissed Dubose.

"No, no, Nicko. I labored too hard to get a

dance with your beautiful lass. A pleasure to meet you, ma'am and shall we?"

A light gust of laughter came from Fancy as Sean's arms encircled her and he shrugged Nick aside.

"Sorry, old man. I can wait to talk to you, but let it never be said that Sullivan made a lovely lady wait."

He broke into an infectious laugh, and Nick chuckled as he walked away, allowing the Irishman his dance with Fancy. This was the same old Sean, full of blarney.

Sean was as lively a talker as he was a dancer. Fancy could not imagine anyone not liking him for he was so warm and outgoing. He made no effort to keep it a secret that he thought she was a striking young lady.

"Ah, miss . . . you'd have to be mighty special to capture old Nicko. But may I add that Nicko would have to be a fool to have let you slip by him," Sean told her. "Can't get over it . . . Nicko married!"

Fancy giggled, taunting him, "Why, Sean what are you trying to tell me about my husband?" The thought of calling this man anything but Sean never entered her mind even though they'd been strangers up to a few minutes ago. That was his effect on her . . . she liked him instantly.

She was such a tiny, little thing, Sean realized as they whirled around. As light as a feather in his arms, she moved in unison with him even though they'd never danced together before. Sean felt her genuine warmth, and it made him understand why Nicko had probably found her so priceless compared to the other ladies he'd courted.

Amidst the gaiety and music, neither Sean nor Fancy had been aware of the commotion created when the two Dubose men had been summoned to the door by a messenger. Already Alain and Monique had gathered their wraps and were scurrying to their carriage. Nick hurriedly sought out his wife and Sullivan. Finally spotting Sean's red head, he rushed through the dancing couples.

When Sean started to voice a loud protest, thinking that Nick was going to cut in on him, Nick shook his head saying, "No, old friend . . . I just wanted to request you to do me a favor and escort Fancy home. I've been called to the warehouses. There is some trouble."

"Would you like me to come along, Nick?" Sean thrived on a good fight and was looking forward to one.

"No. But I'll explain everything to you later tonight. Just see my lady home. That responsibility I'd not trust to everyone, Sean."

"What is it, Nick? What's happened?" Fancy wanted to know for he looked so tense and riled.

"I'll tell both of you later. Just enjoy yourselves while I run over there and see for myself, eh?" He turned swiftly and hastened out of the ballroom.

Although Sean Sullivan was an engaging, entertaining gentleman Fancy was concerned about the trouble Nick was facing at the warehouse. Sean sensed that her festive air was now clouded, so he suggested he see her home to await Nick's arrival. She heartedly agreed. As they traveled toward the Dubose house a golden glow lit up the sky. Fancy gasped. "Oh, God, Sean! Look . . . look over there! The warehouses lie in that direction. See?" Obviously there was a blazing inferno over there. She knew without being told that the Dubose warehouses were going up in flames. The glowing destruction rose to the heavens, mingling its dappled flares with huge billows of smoke. It was an awesome sight!

Sean noted the blaze and he had no doubt that this was the trouble Nicko had gone to investigate. To soothe her somewhat, he told her, "I'll get you home and go over myself, all right?"

As he guided the horses into the driveway, she replied "Yes, Sean. Yes, I wish you would." Something told her Nick would have need of the spunky Irishman before this night ended. She stood in the doorway of the Dubose mansion watching Sean's carriage tear down the drive as if it were pursued by demons. Slowly, she turned to walk into the house, encountering a worried Monique who rushed out to meet her.

Like Fancy, she knew only that Alain had dropped her off to go down to his warehouses. Monique invited her to join her in a glass of wine.

"Yes, I think I would like that," Fancy mumbled, knowing the wine wouldn't ease her worries but hoping it would numb her a little.

An hour later, two glasses of wine had not lessened Fancy's anxiety. However, the wine had calmed Monique. She moved out of the chair she'd been sitting in and announced, "Fancy, dear, I think we are accomplishing nothing, only exhausting ourselves. I suggested we go to bed."

"You go ahead, Monique. I think I'll stay up awhile longer." The clock in the hallway had just chimed out the midnight hour.

"Suit yourself, dear." Monique's words were slightly slurred. It didn't dawn on Fancy until her mother-in-law had left the room that she'd casually called her Monique. But she shrugged that realization aside, remembering that Madame Rocheleau had insisted she call her Angelique.

Now as she sat alone each minute seemed an hour. She tried to make herself think about anything that would keep her from worrying about Nick. She tried to recall the delightful evening they'd been enjoying before the havoc had started. Among the beautifully gowned ladies and finely attired gentlemen, she'd seen many familiar faces. Why hadn't the charming Angelique Rocheleau been among the bevy of guests at the Bushaws? Was she not included in this particular circle of the Dubose's friends? Angelique's absence seemed strange to Fancy.

Chapter Thirty-two

A dense curtain of smoke still hung over the area, and the collapsed walls of the warehouse still smoldered and would continue to do so until nothing remained but a mountain of ashes. Nick had argued with Alain about sacrificing one wall to stop the fire from spreading. Finally, he'd ignored his father's protest and ordered the crew to tear it down for there had been no time for debate. In the end he had been right.

Along with a dozen men, Nick had fought the crawling snakelike flames with coarse jute gunny bags until his muscled arms were limp and weary, while buckets and barrels of water from the nearby river had been handed up an assembly line of dockmen and volunteers. Although the Duboses suffered a substantial loss, a good part of the cargo was salvaged by a couple of shrewd maneuvers Nick had made in the days that preceded the

Bushaws' soirée. He had had a part of the cargo secretly movèd aboard the docked *Merry Maid*. Somehow, he'd felt that made sense and it certainly had. Another segment of stored items he had had moved to a different section of the warehouse—one seldom used. Nick had handpicked the men who made these shifts. None were newly hired dock hands, but all of them had been with the Dubose Lines for several years. Even Alain had not known of the move.

By the time Sean came upon the scene Nick was struggling to help an injured black man whose head was bleeding profusely where it had been cut by a falling piece of timber. His arms locked under Solomon's armpits, Nick tugged laboriously and groaned with the effort, so he gladly welcomed Sean Sullivan's added strength.

When the three of them finally staggered into Nick's office, Solomon sat in a chair and his mouth broadened into a big grateful smile. "Thank you, Mister Nick. Thank you very much and you too, sir." He turned to smile in Sean's direction.

Already applying a compress to Solomon's wound, Nick urged Sean to get a bottle of whiskey from the cabinet by his desk. "Sean Sullivan, meet Solomon, my father's oldest, most trusted man."

"A pleasure it is, Solomon," Sean told the black man, meanwhile pouring generous amounts of liquor into a glass and then a cup before he put the bottle to his own lips unceremoniously.

Now that he'd had time to see all of Solomon he

knew why Nicko had struggled so. The man was gigantic!

Nick sank into a chair to rest and slugged the whiskey down in one gulp, immediately pouring himself another. His face was smudged with black, and his fancy dress shirt was torn and soiled. His finely tailored cream-colored pants were beyond cleaning. He heaved a deep breath, not intending to tarry long here. Before the dawn broke he would find that son of a bitch Rafferty. The cocky little Irishman was sure to have a few of his ruffians at his side but Sean Sullivan was pretty handy with his fists. Nick recalled a few of their visits to Irish pubs.

He lit up a cheroot and savored the whiskey more slowly now. "I'm going after the bastards that did this, Sean." His green eyes shot sparks of fire. Immediately, Sean's face lit up.

"Fine, Nicko. You just say when," Sean quipped, taking himself another healthy slug of whiskey.

"I go, too," Solomon said, taking a second helping from the bottle Sean held.

"I don't think you're up to a fight, Solomon," Nick pointed out.

"This not stop me," Solomon told him, rising to sit straight in his chair, and as if to boast of his strength, his broad chest expanded. "I have score to settle too, Mister Nick, and nothing stop me," Solomon declared in a deep, determined voice which convinced Nick he couldn't stop him if he wanted to.

"All right, we three will go. One more for the road," Nick told him searching in the drawer for the pistol he kept there.

Solomon wrapped a fresh towel around his head to hold the compress tightly against the wound. Excusing himself from Nick's office for a minute, he returned with a wicked-looking knife for himself and an iron bar which he handed over to Sean.

Sullivan could have sworn the black man had to be seven feet tall for he suddenly felt like a dwarf. "Let's be about it, buckos!"

The three of them set off in an old flat-bedded wagon with Nick at the reins. They headed toward a place where Nick suspected Rafferty and his cohorts might be. It was long past midnight and Nick was counting on the element of surprise to work in their favor.

Nick gave the crafty Rafferty credit. He'd done his homework well. Indeed, his success indicated that some Rafferty men had been planted in the Dubose line. That would be taken care of in due time.

Now the wagon rolled down narrow, unlit streets. Only the bright full moon shone down on the rutted road. A few rundown taverns were open, but Nick drove on by.

He was heading for an old tumble-down two-story house. It was the brothel Rafferty frequented, and it was run by a woman named Rosie.

As the three formidable figures entered it, no one challenged them. Down the darkened hall that ran to the back of the house there was a dim ray of light, and sounds came to their ears. Nick motioned to Solomon to stand at the base of the rickety stairway as he and Sean moved noiselessly down the hall to check on the room's occupants.

The sounds proved to be the sonorous snores of a drunk sleeping beside one of Rosie's whores. Nick and Sean let the sleeping pair be. Perhaps, he had been one of the culprits but the two Nick wanted to get were Rafferty and a bum by the name of Kelly.

The three took to the stairs and the weight of their booted feet made the planks squeak loudly. Suddenly a disheveled figure loomed at the top of the landing. Nick called out to the man whom he recognized as Rafferty.

"Hold it! Hold it right where you are, scum!"

He rushed up the steps ahead of his companions, and his fist met Rafferty's ruddy cheek. As the man's half-clad body slumped to the floor, doors flew open and three naked women ran into the hall, screaming. Behind those same doors, three naked men were scrambling to get into their pants knowing by now that they had a fight on their hands. Kelly had seen Nicholas Dubose, and he knew the big black with him. That man could kill with his monstrous hands and Kelly wanted no part of him. He did not aim to stay around and fight Rafferty's battle. With his pants on and the payoff money stuffed in his pocket, he made for the window.

But as one leg hung out, Kelly felt himself being pulled back in. Teasing blue eyes stabbed through him. "Going somewhere, bucko?"

Kelly never got the chance to answer for he was turned to face the red-haired, cocky stranger, and then a sharp, agonizing blow to his groin made him pass out. As he lay on the floor, Sean left the room to see what he could do next to help his friend, Nicko.

Solomon, meanwhile, had chosen his own victim. His strong hands had a viselike grip on the man's throat as his deep voice stated coldly, "You pay now for what you did to Mister Nick."

Nick's attention had turned to a fleeing man, and he chased him down the steps, leaping over the still figure of Rafferty.

The frizzy-haired Rosie had slipped into her wrapper and she now crawled along the wall to reach Rafferty while Sean and Solomon were occupied. Holding a knife in her hand, she frantically shook her lover. The swiftness of Nick's fist had laid Rafferty low or the burly Irishman would have put up a more fierce battle.

As Rosie's shaking brought him around, her voice was laced with the panic flooding her. "Christ's sakes, Raf, come on before that bastard comes back to finish you off. Here, take this," she whispered in his ear trying to keep her voice as low as possible.

All her girls had already fled down the backstairs, and she would have done the same thing but for her man, Raf. The three invading her premises were like a herd of raging bulls busting up the furnishings and Raf's three friends were beyond helping him. She'd noticed that.

Downstairs Nick had cornered the swift-footed rogue who was trying to make a getaway, and he'd made him confess that Rafferty had ordered the fire. In a shaking voice, the man admitted he didn't even live in the city. He said he was due to ship out at dawn.

Nick admonished the man to stay clear of New Orleans in the future if he cared for his life and was preparing to release him when something hit him in the back. He gasped, more from surprise than pain. Then he turned and saw Rafferty's ugly face and the frizzy-headed bitch standing by his side.

He staggered toward Rafferty cursing and calling the man foul names as the woman urged him to get away. "Them other two are coming down the front way, Raf. Christ's sakes, Raf . . . let's get gone!"

She'd barely gotten the words out when a mighty force swept her aside, flinging her so violently against the wall that she crumpled to the floor. Rafferty again raised the knife he'd plunged into Nick's back. With an almost hypnotic look in his dark eyes, Solomon grabbed Rafferty's wrist in his mammoth hand and determinedly twisted it. He targeted the vital spot where he wanted the knife to enter. Although Rafferty's hand held the weapon, it was Solomon who guided it as it penetrated the Irishman's heaving chest. The execution carried out, Solomon flung the body aside and stepped over it to get to Nick.

Sean came rushing down the hall, but he stopped when he saw Solomon carrying Nicko in his arms. As soon as the black man told him what had happened Sean took charge like a general in battle. His friend needed a doctor and fast!

They placed Nick in the flat-bedded wagon, and then Sean showed the team no mercy with the whip. He was concerned about Nicko. They gave no thought to the carnage they'd left behind— three badly injured man and one dead one. That damage wouldn't even the score if Nick ended up a fatal victim.

Even before the Dubose butler, Nat, opened the door to their frantic rapping he knew in his bones that something was very wrong.

When he saw Monsieur Nick in the giant black man's arms all he could say was, "Oh, no . . . not Monsieur Nick." Sean rushed Solomon on through the entrance and followed him.

As Fancy came dashing down the hall, the sight she beheld made her heart almost stop. She felt she could hardly breathe. She was afraid to ask Sean if Nick was alive because she did not want to be told he was dead. Sensing this, Sean quickly assured her that Nick was alive and that he needed a doctor to attend him immediately.

She screamed for Nat to go fetch the doctor. But Solomon spoke up.

"No I go. I can go faster. Where you wish him, missy?"

"This way." Fancy hastily guided the black man and Sean followed them. When Nick had been placed on the bed, he began to mumble and became partially alert. He knew where he was and he was aware that Solomon had carried him like a baby. Now Fancy was smiling down at him and he wanted to hold her hand. But she urged him to lie still while Sean removed his shirt.

Fancy sent Sean to the kitchen for extra cloths and summoned Celine to heat water. She didn't know what else to do until the doctor got there, except to hold a clean white shirt to the wound until Sean returned. At least this shirt was not filthy like the one they'd removed from him.

It seemed only moments passed before Solomon returned with the doctor. While the physician attended to Nick, Fancy served Solomon and Sean, some brandy, and they filled her in on what had transpired. This was what they were about when Alain came upon them.

Having left the scene of his still smoldering warehouse he'd fallen exhaustedly into bed. Monique was sleeping deeply, so she was unaware that he'd come home. Alain's age had forced him to leave before some of the others, but he'd ordered a dozen of his employees to stay for the rest of the night. However, in the havoc he'd lost track of Nicholas.

At this early morning Fancy took on the role of

mistress of the mansion. She brought her father-in-law up to date, and when he took the two men downstairs for another uplifting shot of brandy, she scurried back to check on her husband.

At that moment Denise peered through her door and came out to inquire, "Lord, who were that trashy pair of hoodlums?" She wore the haughty look Fancy so detested. It was the wrong time and place for Denise to encounter Fancy.

"Just the trash who saved your brother's life tonight," Fancy retorted, marching on into her bedroom and leaving Denise wide-eyed and wondering.

An hour later the doctor left, so Fancy lay down beside her drugged and resting husband. Sean had been quartered in a guest room, and Fancy had insisted that Solomon's head wound be tended by the doctor before he took his leave. The black man was overcome that the little mistress showed concern for him. She was something . . . that one. Then nothing would do but that Nat put him up in the quarters over the carriage house. Solomon was too weary to object. Sean Sullivan was exhausted too. Both Sean and Solomon were closer to falling in their tracks than they'd realized until they'd sat down in Alain's study.

She had stood before the two men, giving orders neither could deny or defy. "You're both exhausted and you will go rest. I insist!" The genuine warmth and concern in her dark eyes endeared her to both men, so they gave her no argument.

The black man said, "Thank you, ma'am. Thank you for everything."

Sean Sullivan quipped, "It has been a long, long night and glory be, I'm tired." As his head hit the pillow a few minutes later one fleeting thought struck him. His old friend, Nicko had picked himself a winner. Ah, to be loved by such a pretty miss like Fancy must be the grandest thing that could happen to a man.

Sean Sullivan was convinced that she was a true thoroughbred. Being a horse trainer and connoisseur of fine horseflesh, he was paying her the grandest tribute possible.

Chapter Thirty-three

Sitting in the cozy warmth of her sitting room on that winter afternoon, Alita Dumaine read Fancy's long letter once again. It was almost uncanny this perception she had about the people dearest to her, Alita thought, for only yesterday Fancy had been on her mind constantly. Today the letter had arrived.

Even now, months after dear Chris's death Alita recalled the strange chill that had swept over her on the day he'd left her house. Had it been a foreboding of his death or just a silly coincidence?

Ah, Fancy seemed so very happy and that pleased her so much. How wonderful it was to hear that Nick's health was almost back to normal after his close call with death! Fancy had written all the details of that horrible night. Indeed, her praise of Sean Sullivan and of the black man, Solomon, had been glowing.

Alita had to admit that the opportunity to see little Fancy had convinced her to accept André's invitation to accompany him to New Orleans. Then, too, carnival time in New Orleans was like no other time, and it reminded her of the rapturous times she'd shared with Henri. That would be hard on her now. Feeling that way made her feel guilty because André deserved more than she was prepared to give . . . perhaps ever. She was afraid to love again.

Although she was not a conceited woman, Alita had never considered herself addlebrained or frivolous. Yet, she wondered now if the gaiety and warmth of the holidays had spurred her into accepting André's last proposal of marriage. She had agreed to wed him in early spring.

Was the ghost of Henri holding on to her, refusing to let her go? This was not something she could discuss with lifelong friends and Dahlia would have thought her insane to mention it. The mulatto was obviously delighted about her forthcoming marriage to André.

Fancy . . . maybe she could talk to Fancy about the gnawing doubts that plagued her.

To unite her life with that of André Dubose seemed ideal. She was physically attracted to him, and they shared mutual interests. Oh, they enjoyed the time they spent together.

André had booked passage on the *Marigold* for the trip downriver to New Orleans. It had not been decided whether Yvonne would accompany

them, but Alita hoped she wouldn't. However,
Madame Dumaine did not concern herself about
Yvonne, not when she thought of her marriage to
André. The girl didn't like her, but Alita wasn't
fond of Yvonne either. Sooner or later, that problem would be solved when Yvonne married some
young man. Daniel was a dear and would never
present a problem.

Alita found Dahlia amusing as the days went by
and she helped her pack for the journey. Dahlia's
excitement seemed to be catching, and suddenly,
Alita found herself lighthearted and gay.

Yet, she felt serene too. That might have been
just another one of those strange feelings she could
not explain to anyone, not even herself. But somehow she knew she was going to find the answer she
sought in New Orleans. One way or the other by
the time she returned she'd know whether it was
right or wrong for her to marry André Dubose.

Since 1838 Mardi Gras had been celebrated in
the city of New Orleans in a most flamboyant
style. Old and young enjoyed that marvelous time
of year, as did the tradespeople, the wealthy and
the poor. Certain traditions were followed to create
the carnival atmosphere of the city. The shops and
stores put up elaborate decorations, and parties
and elegant balls were planned well in advance of
the week before Ash Wednesday. Now, some fifteen years later, the tradition went on. Frolicking,
torchlight processions paraded down the streets,

and people danced and sang in accompaniment to the strolling musicians. Much thought and effort went into the costumes that were worn. For that night at the masked ball everyone could leave reality behind to be a makebelieve character. Perhaps, that magic transformation made this such a festive time.

No one was more excited about the advent of Mardi gras than Fancy for Nick had recovered, except for the occasional stiffness which reminded him of the night Rafferty had stabbed him.

As far as the public knew the fires at the warehouse had started for an unknown reason. The four battered hooligans hired by Rafferty were not seen around the city after that night. The New Orleans *Picayune* had a small article about Rafferty's death. It was attributed to a lover's quarrel because Rosie was found with the knife in her hand. That night Solomon had set the scene that way. A couple of her girls had slipped back to the house and had found her and Rafferty lying on the floor. But Rosie was no fool, so when she recovered consciousness she left before the law was summoned. Nick, Sean, and Solomon exchanged amused smiles when they saw the article.

The weeks Nick had spent recovering had brought a new dimension to his relationship with Fancy. Fancy found it effortlessly easy to shrug aside Denise's attempts to make her feel a stranger in the house. Since the night of Nick's injury Fancy brooked no interference from any of the Dubose family, not even Monique.

She did not mind that the holidays had to be spent quietly and that no social affairs would be attended because Nick was not up to them. They enjoyed those quiet times. Amazingly Nick was strong enough to desire to make love to her after only one week of bed rest.

Fancy had been most secretive about their costumes for the upcoming Mardi Gras. The only thing Nick had insisted upon was a comfortable one with no cumbersome materials to burden his left shoulder. Not even Doreen could pry out of Fancy what she and Nick would be wearing to the masked ball.

Good-naturedly, Fancy teased her sister-in-law, "You'll have to wait and see."

"Oh, come on, Fancy. Tell me. I won't tell a soul," Doreen pleaded.

Fancy giggled girlishly. "Do you know how careful I've been to keep this a secret although I've had Nick's costume and mine to get ready and he has been confined at home? No, Doreen, I'm not going to tell even you." She gave the girl an affectionate kiss on the cheek and smiled at the pout on her lips.

Nick's young sister would have protested more and would have nagged Fancy longer, except for the arrival of their guests. Fancy and Doreen rushed out together to see if André and Alita had arrived.

Celine was just admitting the striking couple.

Neither Alita nor Fancy could resist rushing into each other's embrace. André smilingly walked up to give his niece a hug. As he watched Alita and Fancy he realized just how deep their affection was.

"Oh, I'm so glad to see you again, Madame Dumaine," Fancy declared, her eyes misting.

"And I you, Fancy dear. I must say you seem to have become more beautiful, and I'd have sworn that wasn't possible."

"Talk about beautiful . . . you look younger and lovelier than when I left Natchez," Fancy exclaimed. She turned to André to greet him. "Good to see you again, sir."

"Why thank you, Fancy dear." He gave her a warm smile, and his green eyes danced busily over her face. André's height and coloring matched Alain's, but André's manner was so different, Fancy thought to herself. He was more outgoing and friendly. Nick should have been André's son, Fancy mused.

Doreen quickly informed them that her father was still at the office. "Mother and Denise should be here in a minute. They had last-minute fittings at the seamstress." She asked Nat to see to the luggage and requested that Celine bring refreshments.

"And where is that nephew . . . your husband, Fancy my dear?" André inquired for he was eager to see Nick. Nick had not made his usual visit to Magnolia during the racing season and he had been missed by his uncle who was eager to boast about his young filly, Fancy's Folly. She was going to be a winner, André just knew it.

When Fancy told him Nick was upstairs, André turned without saying another word and dashed up the steps. Alita joked about his hasty exit, "Those two!" Then she turned her attention back to Fancy.

Almost an hour passed before Alita realized that she was weary from her journey. Besides, by this time Monique and Denise had joined their circle. Although Alita liked Nick's younger dark-haired sister she found Denise haughty and snobbish.

Sitting there, she realized that if she married André this would be her family, too. Monique presented an image of dignified elegance, but Alita wondered just how she and Fancy had gotten along under the same roof all these months. It was impossible for two lovely ladies to reign. Had Fancy accepted this?

Obviously, she was not expecting a child yet, for her waist was as tiny as ever. This rather surprised Alita, since the virile Nick was her husband. Had something happened when Fancy had miscarried Nick's baby before they were married? What a shame it would be if these two magnificent people could not share a child of their love.

When she noticed the hands of the clock she excused herself, wanting to rest before the dinner hour. Fancy accompanied her upstairs.

"Nick will be so glad to see you again, Madame

Dumaine."

"Ah, I look forward to seeing him at dinner too. Will he be able to come downstairs, Fancy?"

"Oh, yes. He's hardly confined to his bed now. Have a good rest and I'll see you in a few hours. May I tell you again how good it is to have you here?"

Alita gave a soft little laugh. "You certainly may, my dear. You were the main reason for my coming."

The two parted company then, to meet three hours later in the Dubose parlor. When Fancy entered on Nick's arm the family had already gathered and was enjoying some of Alain's best Madeira. It was an unexpected surprise to see that Angelique Rocheleau had been invited. Her escort, Edmond Bertram, was seated beside her.

Nick had enjoyed his long chat with André, and when he saw how radiant Alita Dumaine's face was this evening, he could easily see why she enchanted his uncle. He had been happy to hear that André was marrying again. Nick had not felt that his uncle's first marriage had been a happy one. Perhaps, this one would be.

He greeted Alita warmly as he did Angelique. Like Fancy, he had not known that she and Bertram had been included for the evening. Appreciating lovely ladies as he did, Nicholas felt that this evening the Dubose parlor most assuredly held the most attractive women in the whole world. Of course, Fancy was the loveliest of all. He was consumed by possessive pride.

Nicholas Dubose had always been aware that he was a complicated man, yet this evening he was experiencing feelings he couldn't understand. He'd been born in these magnificent surroundings, still, he'd never felt that he'd truly belonged here.

None of the people in that fine parlor could have imagined the musings going on in Nicholas's mind, not even Fancy, although in the last few weeks he'd never felt so close to anyone in his life. They'd spent so many loving hours since he'd been confined at home.

Nick drifted back to the afternoon when his Uncle had come to his room. As it had always been with him and his Uncle André, he felt free to confide in him, to tell him his plans for the future. Nick was sure that Fancy was again carrying his child. When he'd spoken of this to André, his uncle had jested.

"I'd be very disappointed in you, Nick, if she wasn't." In a more serious manner, he'd pointed out to his nephew, "Alain is not going to be pleased about this move."

"That can't be helped, sir. Fancy and I have our lives to live. It hasn't been too easy here at times."

His uncle gave an understanding nod of his head. Monique Dubose was the perfect wife for his older brother, Alain, but he would not have wanted such a wife. Nicholas had inherited a part of him, André thought, but he saw no hint of Alain in his nephew.

Nick told André he was delighted about his upcoming marriage to Alita Dumaine, and then André confided to Nick, "Well, it should make your quest for Dubonnet more successful. However, be aware that you're dealing with a very stubborn woman." At this point André had left his nephew's room.

Now that they were all assembled in the parlor, awaiting Nat's announcement that dinner was served, Nick observed Alita and André and he decided his uncle could find the happiness with Alita he'd never found with his first wife.

It was a gala evening. The dinner was delectable, the setting elegant. Monique's fine china and cut crystal adorned a table lit by candlelight. The capable Dubose servants stood ready to serve the diners. The grand setting and the spirited conversation prompted Angelique to remember yesteryears. The overwhelming impact of her memories was almost more than she could endure, even though her face reflected none of the agony. Angelique Rocheleau was not even aware that her dark eyes had locked with André's green ones when she'd glanced across the table. As their glances fused Angelique drifted back some twenty-odd years, to the time when she'd come to New Orleans to visit her newly married friend, Monique. That was a lifetime ago.

It, too, had been carnival time, and she'd journeyed in from Baton Rouge to spend two days.

André, Alain's young randy brother, had also just arrived in New Orleans. In that glorious atmosphere of reveling and merrymaking they'd found rapture and ecstasy that night. For Angelique Rocheleau, it had been an endless ecstasy she could never find again with any other man.

Had André remembered? Was every golden moment as vivid to him as it was to her now as she sat across the table? His eyes seemed to say that he remembered. *Mon dieu,* they seemed as passionate and intense as they had been that night!

Engulfed as they both were, neither realized they were being scrutinized by Alita Dumaine. She, too, was having private thoughts. She was reminded of the day Nicholas Dubose had brought Fancy to the house after they'd encountered one another in the woods at Dubonnet. His eyes had adored her with such passion and such a burning desire that Alita had known the two of them were destined to be together.

This evening she saw the same look in André's eyes when he looked at the gorgeous Angelique Rocheleau. He'd never gazed at her so intensely. Perhaps, this was what had made her hesitate to accept his offer of marriage. Maybe, this was the answer she had come to New Orleans to find. Who can say how the hands of fate work?

Odd though it might seem, she felt no hurt. But she *did* have her answer. Now there was no need to speak to Fancy as she'd planned. In fact, she didn't even plan to say anything to André until they'd returned to Natchez. Then she might just enlighten André about his real feelings. He was in love with Angelique Rocheleau, and perhaps he should do something about that before it was too late.

Actually, Alita felt as if a heavy burden had been lifted from her by the end of the evening. She planned to enjoy herself to the fullest while she was in New Orleans. When she returned to Natchez the first person she planned to visit was Carew. There was a matter she intended to see to immediately — a wedding present for dear, little Fancy!

Chapter Thirty-four

Monique Dubose did not think about the sudden calm that settled in around her palatial home. It was just the usual aftermath of Mardi Gras. The exhilarating activities had exhausted everyone. Their houseguests had boarded the steamboat to travel back upriver to Natchez and she was ready to enjoy the slower paced days and evenings. Alain seemed glad to return to his normal routine again.

Fancy was unable to enjoy the serene calm, however. At first, she'd dubbed the culprit an upset stomach, blaming too much champagne on the night of the masked ball. That, coupled with all the rich, spicy foods she'd eaten seemed the most likely reason for her dilemma.

Nick didn't voice his opinion to her but he and Celine exchanged smiles on a couple of mornings. He swelled with pride at the prospect of Fancy being pregnant.

He'd even overlooked her waspish mood, when he'd teased her about drinking too much champagne at the party and had received a rather puzzling, sharp retort from her. She'd snapped at him harshly.

"What was I supposed to do, Nick, if not drink and make merry like everyone else? I'm sure it would have delighted that . . . that Samantha to no end if I'd stayed home so she could have had you all to herself."

Her comment made no impact on Nick, nor did he dwell on it. He'd decided Fancy was merely giving way to a moment of jealousy.

But the scene with Nick and his former love, Samantha, had not left Fancy's thought. She could not erase what she'd seen and heard. Had Sean Sullivan not caught her in his arms as she was rushing from the ballroom and taken her to the moonlit balcony to calm her, she was not sure how the evening would have ended.

For all of Sullivan's sound logic, she couldn't erase the sight of the curvy Samantha pressed against her husband's muscled body, his lips fused with hers. There was no way she could know that it was Samantha who had pulled Nick's face to hers, or that he'd been surprised by the devious little wanton.

Sean had reasoned with Fancy, but he too had been concerned about what Fancy had told him and his heart had ached at the hurt he'd seen on her face. The last few weeks he'd fought his own overwhelming feelings of love for Fancy. If she had not been Nicko's wife he would not have battled so hard.

Holding her in his arms that night, her sweet face looking up at him and her lips half-opened, it had been agonizing to restrain himself from doing what he yearned to do. Sean knew he'd be lost forever if he even allowed himself to kiss those sweet lips.

Instead, he willed himself to play the gallant, loyal friend to Nicholas Dubose. He assured Fancy that she had no cause to worry.

"Ah, for sure, love . . . I admit he was a libertine before he met you . . . the wildest libertine I know. But that is not true now, Fancy my love."

He seated her on a bench and sat down beside her. She looked childlike and helpless as she sighed dejectedly.

"Oh, Sean . . . perhaps, I'll never be the kind of wife for a man of Nick's stature. I was not born of the gentry." She laughed nervously. "But then I don't have to tell you that, I guess."

"Well, love . . . you sure could have fooled me!" He laughed infectiously. God, did she not know than none of the so-called ladies of gentry held a candle to her!

"Fancy, let me point out something to you. I have known Nicholas Dubose a lot longer than you have, and he is a rebel despite his fine breeding. Nicko doesn't exactly fit into the mold himself. I rather think, love, he'd never want you to change."

Sean was so utterly sincere that Fancy found his declaration easy to believe. It gave her the courage and assurance she needed to return to the festive activities inside, so they'd left the secluded moonlit balcony to join the others. Fancy never guessed the turmoil she'd caused in the good-natured Irishman. But Sean Sullivan was a practical man and he was loyal to people he cared deeply about. There was only one solution for all concerned. He had to leave New Orleans. Nicko would give him a rough go of it but he was good at conjuring up stories, so he'd think up something to convince the Frenchman. Better that than to feel his wrath!

Fancy credited Sean with being smarter and wiser than she when Nick came home the following day and presented her with an exquisite lavaliere; an import from France's finest jewelry house.

It added to his pleasure in giving that she was so thrilled by his gift. He told her with boyish excitement that it had just arrived that morning.

"Do you know how it got the name *lavaliere?*"

He pulled her onto his lap to fasten it around her neck.

"Tell me, Nick?"

"Well, it's said to be called that because it was named after King Louis XIV's mistress, Louise de La Vallière."

How smart he was! She told him so and expressed a wish to know more, adding, "You've been everywhere and seen so much. I feel so ignorant."

He gave a deep throaty laugh, "Ah, my sweet

thing, I didn't marry you for your brain, but I promise you, my love, we've just begun. We'll see the world together. There, does that make you happy?"

She flung her arms around his neck, wondering how she could have doubted his love. His eyes adored her and warmed her whole being.

It was his fervent intention to make love to his wife had Celine not rapped at the door and informed him that a man wished to see him in the parlor. Disgruntled, Nick cursed as he released his hold on Fancy. Then, a devilish grin on his handsome face, he playfully ordered her, "Stay right where you are, *petite amie*. I shall return soon, I promise you."

She laughed softly and then teased him like a coquette, "Then don't be too long, Monsieur Dubose."

Her body was flushed with the flaming sensations he'd ignited, and she lay there, smiling in anticipation of what would happen when he returned.

But as the minutes went by and Nick did not come back, Fancy became impatient. Finally an hour had passed since Nick had gone through their boudoir door.

She jumped from the bed, muttering, *"Mon dieu!"* Without any awareness that she was doing so, she'd used her mother-in-law's expression of disgust. When irked, Monique always sighed, *"Mon dieu."* Fancy was not cognizant that she had absorbed some of the Dubose's ways like their occasional use of the French language around the home. Nick had never spoken words of endearment to her in French back in Natchez but here in New Orleans he often did.

Swishing her skirt and brushing back her tousled hair, she rushed out the door and down the steps.

Celine was moving at an unhurried pace in the hallway.

"Do you know where my husband is, Celine?" she inquired.

"Ah, yes, ma'am. I think he's still in the study."

"Is he alone?"

"Oh, yes, ma'am. That gentleman who came to see him has been gone awhile."

A frown ruffled Fancy's brow as she proceeded toward the study. She did not bother to knock on the heavy carved-oak door, but entered to find Nick quietly sitting in the leather chair by the small stone fireplace. He was so preoccupied that he didn't turn to greet her.

"Nick?" she said hesitantly as she moved over to the chair to face him. "Is something wrong?"

"Sit down, Fancy." He seemed serious and thoughtful. Indeed he felt burdened by the news he'd received from the stranger from Memphis, and for the last half hour he'd pondered what to do. To deny Fancy what was rightfully hers went against his grain, but he did not want to upset her. He did not want to lose this baby.

He had lingered so long after Garth Anderson had left to weigh which way he should go for Fancy's sake.

Now, it seemed that fate had taken the decision out of his hands, for he sat there with the parcel in his lap and a glass of brandy in his hand. Fancy had the curiosity of a cat, so he could hardly conceal the old yellowed journal from her inquisitive dark eyes.

Indeed, at that moment she asked, "What in the world is that, Nick?"

Nick chose not to answer her question and instead asked her, "Fancy, do you remember a man by the name of Garth Anderson who worked at Willow Bend?"

She started to shake her head and say no, but then she did recall that Chris had hired a new overseer. The name had a familiar ring to it. "Yes, I . . . I think that was the overseer there, but why, Nick?"

"Well, he was the man wanting to see me earlier."

"But, wha . . . why did he want to see you, for goodness sakes?"

"Did you know he's been living in the cottage you and your mother once occupied since he's been working for the Kensingtons?"

"No, I didn't," she answered him, puzzled that he would inform her of that. What was the point of all this anyway?

"He has," Nick told her. God, he was taking a

devilishly long way around the subject and he knew he could delay getting to the point no longer.

"This was your mother's diary, Fancy. Garth Anderson discovered it in a hiding place under the plank floor. Naturally he read it, or else he would not have brought it to us here in New Orleans. It seems he's left Willow Bend and Alicia Kensington. He didn't want her to possess the diary, so he was kind enough to bring it here. Damned decent of him too."

He handed her the torn, yellowed pages, adding, "You'll see why after you read it, Fancy. I think, darling, I shall leave you here alone while you do."

Perplexed at his behavior, she mumbled, "All right, Nick."

Her mind whirled crazily as she took the old book. Its pages were loose and seemed ready to fall apart. She'd never known that Fleur had kept a diary. Her mother must have written in it long after she'd gone to bed.

Nick strolled the grounds of the estate after issuing strict orders to Celine that his wife was not to be disturbed in the study.

Some of the pages were so smudged that Fancy was unable to read them, but the ones intact revealed why Nick had been so serious. She appreciated the generosity Garth Anderson had shown in bringing the diary to her and Nick.

Like little dams breaking, a maelstrom of emotions flooded Fancy. First, she shed tears of sorrow and indignation over being Charles Kensington's bastard, instead of Louis Fourney's daughter. The beloved image of her beautiful mother, Fleur, was now smudged and tainted, and Fancy felt disillusioned until she remembered how it was to love a man.

Suddenly, her remorse changed to amusement when she realized that she was as much Charles Kensington's child as the haughty Roberta or the dear sweet Chris.

It was gratifying to know Charles Kensington had sired her instead of the drunken Fourney. She swelled with pride for he was a wonderful man. He'd always been good and kind to her. Yet, according to the old diary he'd never known that she was his child.

Finally, as if she'd been struck by a bolt of lightning she reared up in the leather chair and gasped, "Dear God!" What if Nick had not come back into her life when he had? She would have gone through with the marriage to Chris . . . her half brother. The thought petrified her.

By the time Nick entered the study, Fancy had wiped away her tears. He looked at her calm, serene face and it gladdened his heart. His prayers had been answered.

He rushed to her and knelt down by the chair. "My sweet darling, I'm so happy to see that smile. I hoped this wouldn't be upsetting to you." His green eyes danced so lovingly over her face that she clasped her hands around the back of his neck to pull his head to her bosom, declaring, "I love you so, Nick."

Having his head pressed against her warm firm breasts fired him with desire. He wanted to make love to her.

As if she could read his thoughts, she purred, "Make love to me, Nick. I want you so very much."

He broke from her, a broad grin on his handsome face and emerald fire sparking in his eyes. In a husky voice, he said, "With the greatest of pleasure, *ma petite amie*. With the greatest of pleasure!"

Without a moment's hesitation, he lifted her in his arms and strode jauntily out of the study, and toward the stairway. They were too caught up in their anticipated pleasure to notice Denise observing them with total disgust. However, neither would have cared if the whole Dubose family had been standing there.

After this afternoon, Fancy knew something she had not known before. She was the daughter of the wealthy, respected Charles Kensington and he was gentry!

She, Fancy Fourney Dubose, was as much a lady of the gentry as the haughty Roberta Kensington or Denise Dubose!

Chapter Thirty-five

He watched her undress, savoring the movements of her hands and of her petite body. She was like a dancer, exotic and seductive; yet he knew her movements were not staged. Her grace and charm bewitched him.

She wanted him just as wildly and eagerly as he wanted her. Knowing that stirred Nick's desire. His loins hardened, and he ached to bury himself in her satiny softness.

"You are gorgeous, Fancy Dubose, and you're all mine . . . forever and ever," he vowed as he pulled her into his arms for he could no longer wait to touch and caress her.

"Nick!" she said breathlessly as she felt his manliness pressing urgently against her. His flaming heat intoxicated her, overwhelming her and making her dizzy. As his hands caressed her breasts, she moaned softly with pleasure.

Fancy wondered if other wives acted like this with their husbands, or was she just a wanton little minx. For one brief moment she thought of Fleur and Charles Kensington. But the powerful essence of Nicholas Dubose would not allow her to think of anything long.

He, too, fleetingly thought that a husband was rarely lucky enough to find such sensual pleasure with his own wife. He recalled the boasting and bragging of his gentlemen acquaintances at the houses of pleasure in New Orleans.

Fancy's undulating flushed body quickly made him turn his wandering thoughts back to her, though, for he knew he was reaching that peak of rapture where even he no longer had control. Sweet Jesus, she was a woman of fire and flame! Had he searched the world over he could not have found one more desirable than his sweet Fancy.

"Oh, Nick . . ." She gasped as if in agony, but her pain was tantalizingly sweet. He knew exactly how she was feeling so he thrust in answer to her plea. They moved together as one, faster and faster, soaring higher and higher to climb the pinnacle.

Together they gasped and sighed, expressing a pleasure beyond words, one only true lovers understand when they exchange knowing, intimate smiles after making love.

When they lay spent and sated, their bodies damp and moist, Nick held her ever so close to him and smiled, thinking to himself that if she did not already bear his seed within her she surely did now. He would not have believed he could love a woman as he did the dark-eyed beauty lying beside him. She was his life, his reason for living and he had no doubt that would be so forever.

Celine held the cold cloth to her young mistress's face. "I think you should see a doctor, Miss Fancy. I swear to goodness, I think you goin' to have a baby. All this mornin' pukin' and upset stomach."

All Fancy could do was wave her hand, gesturing Celine to be still. Maybe she was pregnant, but maybe she was furious because her husband had just announced that he must go on a business trip and that she could not accompany him. Men! Why was it that they had the freedom to just take off at a moment's notice? Why could she not go with him?

She had been so angry that she'd thrown one of Monique's prized vases at him. The devil had stood there and laughed his fool head off which had infuriated her even more.

How could she have been so carried away with love that night when only two nights later she resented what she considered his thoughtlessness in leaving her behind. She didn't like feeling that she was a "thing" to be taken out at his whim or put back when he desired. In most expressive terms, she'd told him so. Their parting, when Nick left, had been a chilling one, and now Fancy was miserable.

No, she wanted to scream at Celine. You can thank your dear "Monsieur Nicholas" for my miserable condition. She knew how Celine adored Nick. It would have been futile to try to make the little servant think that Nick was anything but a paragon. From the moment Fancy had arrived in this house she'd seen the admiration in Celine's jet-black eyes.

What Fancy did not realize about Celine was that the little mulatto admired her just as much. Many times her heart had gone out to her little mistress because some of the family looked down their aristrocratic noses at Fancy.

One of the worst of the lot, the Dubose mademoiselle from Natchez, had arrived this morning. Celine detested this young woman wholeheartedly. Bag and baggage, Mademoiselle Yvonne Dubose had entered the portals, haughtily arrogant as usual.

Celine was thankful that Monsieur Nicholas was not here, not with that viper around. At least, Miss Fancy would not have that problem. Gentry or not, Mademoiselle Yvonne was no better than the ladies down on Rampart Street, the ones she turned her regal nose up at, Celine reflected.

But now Celine's attention returned to her mistress, and she inquired of the pretty young woman propped up against the pillows, "You want me to bring you a tray up, miss? Maybe a little coffee help?"

"Yes, please . . . just coffee, Celine. That's all."

Fancy tucked the pale blue wrapper with the matching pale blue lace edging over her bared exposed breasts. She felt weak and slightly chilled.

Celine left the room, but quickly returned with a tray bearing a carafe of coffee and a cup. A commotion downstairs reached Fancy's ears as the servant came through the door, causing Fancy to inquire, "What's the ado downstairs, Celine?"

This was usually a quiet time of the day at the Dubose mansion. Mornings were slowly paced, with the servants going about their duties and chores quietly so as to not disturb Monique.

Setting the tray on the nightstand, Celine said, "We have a newly arrived guest, ma'am. Mademoiselle Yvonne from Natchez. You met her yet, miss?"

"Yes, I know her," Fancy replied, her tone telling Celine that Fancy did not share Denise's liking for Yvonne.

Those two were already huddled together downstairs gossiping like two magpies. Fancy was the topic of their conversation. Yvonne was crestfallen to learn that Nick's charming presence was elsewhere and that he'd left a couple of days ago.

"On some kind of business trip, he told Father," Denise informed her cousin.

Yvonne sighed, "We probably passed each other coming down the river. Well, I must tell you about this utterly charming gentleman I met while I was in Memphis. You'll see what I mean, Denise. He's accompanying Claude here in a day or two on some business matter. I'm sure he'll be staying here, for Aunt Monique will insist on it."

Yvonne expounded on the man's masculine charms. Of course, his wealth and position in the city of Memphis had impressed her even more.

"My word, he sounds gorgeous!" Denise's eyes sparkled with girlish anticipation. This gentleman must be something if Yvonne was so excited. "You must have had a wonderful time in Memphis, but we missed you at carnival time."

Yvonne smirked as she remarked snobbishly, "I did not wish to accompany Father when he brought that . . . that woman."

"You don't like her?"

"I detest her! She is crude and coarse. Why else would she have taken such a shine to a mere servant girl like Fancy? She tried to present her in Natchez as a companion. I'm sorry, dear, and I know she's Nicholas's wife now, but gowns and jewels doesn't change one's breeding."

Denise said nothing, only nodded her head. Yvonne was a year older than she, and Denise had always admired her. She thought Yvonne a ravishing beauty with her flaming auburn hair and emerald green eyes, and Denise knew how all the young dandies in Adams County vied for her favors.

"Honestly, Denise . . . I think dear Nicholas was tricked into that marriage by that foxy, clever Madame Alita Dumaine. He wants Dubonnet very badly, and I think Fancy Fourney was a

means to pry Dubonnet loose from Madame Dumaine."

"Really, Yvonne? Do you suppose? It was so
sudden and unexpected to all of us when he
brought that white trash to New Orleans."

Smug and confident, Yvonne assured her, "Of
course. Why else, when Nicholas could have any
woman he desires?

"Well, she is beautiful, Yvonne. Even you have
to admit that. You wouldn't believe how the men
fawn over her at soirées and parties we've gone to,
and she has won the loyalty of Mother's friend,
Angelique Rocheleau. You remember her. Dear
Lord, Doreen adores her," Denise confessed.

"Well, Doreen is a sweet child, Denise, but she
doesn't have the sophistication you or I have. As I
recall Madame Rocheleau was lowly born and
married into wealth, so that isn't hard to figure.
You see what I mean?"

"Yes . . . yes, I do, Yvonne."

Yvonne sat back, pleased, and sipped her coffee, already anticipating ways she and Denise
could make Fancy miserable. She nibbled on a delicious little ladyfinger. Her aunt always served
those delectable little cakes when she visited New
Orleans.

Yvonne and Fancy had their encounter at
lunch. Yvonne was prepared to meet the young
woman she'd known in Natchez, not this woman
who had been Nicholas's wife for many months.
This new poised, self-assured woman left Yvonne

utterly perplexed. Yvonne thought Fancy's audacious manner absolutely shocking.

Yvonne was livid with rage when Fancy cut her down sharply and mercilessly, making her look like an idiot. Even Monique admired her spunky daughter-in-law in this instance. They had sat down to lunch and Nat was serving the five ladies an enticing, delectable plate of creamed chicken sprinkled with green peas and mushrooms. Fancy's appetite was being whetted by the smell of the fresh baked bread when Yvonne, thinking herself clever, remarked, "Well, Fancy dear . . . I'm happy to see you've adjusted so well to your new home."

Fancy's dark eyes moved slowly and delicately from her plate to Yvonne. She batted her long, thick lashes and smiled sweetly before saying anything. "Adjusted, Yvonne?" She gave a light laugh. "I think Yvonne, you chose the wrong word, for to adjust means to change and I don't think my husband would have wanted me to change. After all, he fell in love with me just as I was in Natchez."

Fancy turned her attention back to her food while Yvonne flushed with fury. Doreen grinned broadly and Denise fidgeted nervously at seeing her cousin's outrage. Monique began to eat her creamed chicken as Fancy was doing.

Yvonne was the only one who picked at her food. Every piece lodged in her throat because she was so angry over being outfoxed by Fancy.

Whether or not she approved of Fancy's manner with her niece, Yvonne, Monique had to admire the young woman. With cool poise, Fancy excused herself from the dining table after finishing the last bite of her creamed chicken and Doreen quickly followed her.

Flying like a gazelle to catch up with Fancy, Doreen exclaimed to her sister-in-law, "Oh, Fancy . . . you were absolutely magnificent!"

"You think so, Doreen?" Fancy smiled at the sweet-faced girl at her side.

"I know so, especially knowing Yvonne as I do. She was fit to be tied and I know Mother was finding it hard to hide her amusement. Nick would have been so proud of you."

Fancy bristled at the mention of her husband's name. "I'm not too happy with my husband at this moment, Doreen."

"You mean because he left on a business trip?" Doreen became serious because she wanted no discord between Nick and Fancy. While she adored her older brother she could understand that his nature would be complicated and perplexing at times. Nick was such an independent man, and he was a stubborn one!

Fancy must be a rare woman, Doreen reflected, to have captivated Nick as she had. Nick had been an elusive bachelor for so many years before she'd come into his life.

Doreen's devoted loyalty to Fancy urged her to caution her sister-in-law about Yvonne and about what she considered Yvonne's unnatural feelings for her cousin, Nicholas. However, all Nicholas's sister could bring herself to say to Fancy before they parted company was, "Yvonne can be terribly vindictive, Fancy. I just wanted you to know that."

Fancy gave her sister-in-law a grateful smile and thanked her. "I'd rather figured that out about her," she added.

In the peaceful solitude of her studio, Doreen's thoughts dwelled on Fancy. Secretly, she vowed to try to be her protector while Nick was away. Fancy would need one. With two wicked little schemers like Yvonne and Denise under the same roof anything was possible. Doreen didn't trust either of them.

Part Four
Forever, My Fancy

Chapter Thirty-six

Sean Sullivan had enjoyed a spot of Irish luck at the faro game, so he strolled cockily back up the embankment of the levee from the busy, crowded pier. Tomorrow, he was leaving New Orleans and the opportunity Nicholas Dubose had offered him behind. Fancy's sweet face had gotten in the way. Hell, he didn't blame her, but neither could he control his roguish heart.

Perhaps, someday when his passions and desires cooled he would return. Then if Nicko realized his dream of owning Dubonnet and raising race horses there, he could be his trainer. Right now, staying was out of the question, for Sean knew that would only bring disaster to the two people he loved.

But he had to see Fancy one more time. That might have to do for a lifetime. So he went to the livery to hire a gig.

Twenty minutes later, he halted the carriage at the impressive entrance of the Duboses' spacious two-story house. Old Nat met him at the front door, a broad smile on his face. Monsieur Sullivan had become a familiar face at the Dubose house the last few months, and the butler knew how much Monsieur Nick thought of the Irishman who had such a buoyant, bouncy way of striding into the house. Sean always greeted Nat flippantly, a devilish gleam in his bright blue eyes.

"Little Madame in, Nat old friend?" he inquired.

"Ah, yes sir. She sure is, and if you'll just come this way, I'll tell her you're here, Monsieur Sullivan."

"Ah, Nat, I'd be much obliged to you." Sean followed old Nat's slow footsteps toward the parlor.

While Sean awaited Fancy, he wondered if he could persuade her to come with him for a pleasant ride in the gig. Somehow, he wanted to say his farewell outside the Dubose home, and it was a pleasant day. The sun shone brightly, warming the cool March air.

Sean's wish was granted, for Fancy gleefully responded to his invitation. "Just let me get my cape or shawl." Hastily she got a wrap and they sped away in the buggy.

Fancy tossed her head back, exclaiming with carefree delight, "Oh, you are a godsend, Sean

Sullivan! I needed to be away from that house in a most desperate way." Her dark eyes sparkled with gratitude as she looked in his direction. "Thank you, Sean . . . thank you for asking me to go."

"A treat for me, Fancy. You see, I'm a very self-ish man really," he jested lightly.

"Tell that to others if you like, Sean. I know better. You can't hide the truth from me." She giggled as she brushed her black hair away from her face.

His smile hid what he was really thinking. He'd bloody well better hide the truth, he thought to himself as they went down the main road before taking the lane that led to the edge of the river.

"Tell me when do you expect our Nicko to return?"

Her pretty mouth tensed, and she sighed disgustedly. "You would probably know as well as I. I had no idea of his plans until the very morning he left."

"I gather you are in a temper, little one?"

"I most assuredly am! I don't like the idea that Nick can suddenly go off and leave me here. The Duboses aren't my family and they're . . . well, they're—"

Sean interrupted, "A big dose of tonic to take, perhaps?"

"How perfectly you understand me, Sean. At times too much!"

403

"Well, I think Nicko feels the same. Give him a little time and things won't remain as they are now, Fancy. Believe me."

She smiled. "I suppose I have to, Sean, for you always prove to be right where Nick is concerned."

The buggy had been halted for several minutes now, and Sean knew he must come to the point, get Fancy back home, and be on his way. To remain too long down by the river lined with weeping willows on such a glorious day, with her sweet fragrance taunting his nose and her radiant loveliness tempting him, was dangerous.

But he'd cherish this moment. Dear God, a million times he'd envision it! He'd recall that the birds never sang a sweeter melody, that flowers would never smell as sweet as the native jasmine blooming there. This would always be a special moment in time.

"Fancy, my sweet . . . I had, as I told you, a very selfish reason for asking you to come for a ride with me. You see, I've a golden opportunity offered to me. I must take it, so I have to leave before Nick returns. In Tennessee . . . got to be there in just a few days. So I wanted to say goodbye to you before I left." He felt that he was a miserable liar. He'd never had that problem before.

"Leaving? Today? Dear Lord, Sean, I can't believe it! Nick will be so surprised to find you've left." She took his hand in hers, adding, "I'm going to miss you, Sean Sullivan."

She never realized just how much her words meant to him. Sean knew she was sincere, for he'd sensed that about Fancy the first moment they'd met. She was an honest young woman, with no desire to play games with people. He admired that trait and respected her candid manner.

"Hey, you and Nick will see me again. I'm not about to quit pestering you." Damn, he had to get this over and get out of her sight! "Fancy, have you got a little kiss for this old bucko for I dare not ask for one in front of the house. Old Alain would challenge me to a duel." He chuckled.

She flung her arms around his neck and kissed him on the cheek with genuine warmth, considering him a dear friend. "Oh, Sean . . . Sean! What can I say?"

He had to keep this light and gay. "Say, you'll name one of your little tads after old Sean, eh?" She couldn't see his pained face, but if she had, Sean Sullivan's feelings would have been obvious and revealing. When he felt her soft body moving out of their embrace, he faked a devious smile. "Promise me that and I'll be forever happy, love."

"Your wish is granted, my dear friend," she said seriously.

Straightening himself up on the leather seat, he prepared to urge the bay into action. As the buggy rolled along the road back into the city, Sean kept up a constant stream of chatter, tossing in samples of his Irish humor to make Fancy break into lighthearted gusts of laughter.

She had no inkling when they finally parted that Sean Sullivan's heart had never been so heavy in his thirty years of reckless, carefree living.

But he had succeeded in turning Fancy's depressed miserable day into a cheery one. She was well fortified to meet the next challenge Yvonne Dubose intended to present to her.

Yvonne had spent the afternoon allowing her evil thoughts to fester, for seeing Fancy leave in the buggy with that very attractive gentleman was all the fuel she'd needed to conjure up her witch's brew.

She could not imagine Nicholas Dubose approving of his wife going for a ride alone with any man, even his trusted friend. She wasted no time inquiring about the gentleman she'd seen Fancy leave with that afternoon, and then she directed an innuendo at her aunt. Surprisingly, Monique did not respond as Yvonne had expected.

Instead, she smiled and remarked quite casually, "Yvonne, dear when you come to know Fancy better you'll understand her. She's different . . . she's . . . let's say a colorful, beautiful butterfly that needs freedom from rules and regulations. Nicholas seems to understand that and indulges her accordingly."

"I find it hard to imagine Nicholas indulging any woman, Aunt Monique, much less his wife," Yvonne retorted, totally devastated that the lowly born Fancy had obviously cast a spell on her sophisticated aunt.

"I know, but its true. You will see what I mean, *chérie,* when you see him around her. At first, it was hard for Alain and me to believe, but now we are convinced of it."

Doreen took a special delight in chiming in. "The truth of it is Nick absolutely worships her . . . thinks the sun rises and sets in her. Lord, I just hope some man feels the same way about me someday. Wouldn't that be wonderful, cousin Yvonne?" Doreen's face was so innocent and sweet no one would have suspected the mischief behind her remarks.

With an ostentatious air, Yvonne retorted, "Dear, dear little Doreen . . . I've had that pleasure. I don't mean to boast, you understand."

With a diplomatic flair Monique took charge of the scene for fear that her precious Doreen was taking on more than she could handle with her more sophisticated, older cousin. "We know Yvonne that you are the belle of Adams County. It is easy to see why, dear, for you get more beautiful all the time." Her praise and soft, smooth voice seemed to soothe Yvonne's ruffled feathers for the moment, as Monique had intended.

To change the subject, Monique inquired of

her niece, "You mentioned that we might expect Claude tomorrow? How wonderful! He will be accompanied by a Monsieur François Martel . . . I believe you said?"

"Yes, Aunt Monique."

"Then I shall see that Celine prepares their rooms." She pondered a moment before continuing. "The name Martel . . . it seems so familiar to me."

"It's well known and respected in Memphis. François said his grandparents had migrated there many years ago from Saint Louis," Yvonne informed her aunt. "You will like him very much, I think. A charming man."

Denise chimed in, "Yvonne makes him sound divine, Mother."

Alain Dubose just sat quietly, a stern look on his face as he listened to the endless chatter of the women. He firmly believed that his brother, André, had not been strict enough with Yvonne, and he didn't relish her visits to his home. Denise didn't need that kind of influence, Alain thought, and he intended to mention this fact to Monique.

When people pointed out that Doreen was more like Alain, it rather pleased and gratified her straitlaced father. Doreen always seemed to be a proper young lady. However, recently Alain had noticed some distinct changes in her, and he privately admitted he was delighted that Doreen was not allowing Denise to run roughshod over her.

He didn't welcome the news that Albert's son Claude, and his friend were coming to visit. Probably this Martel was an irresponsible young dandy like Claude. Albert had not been a hard enough taskmaster to his elder son, Alain thought.

Of all the Dubose dynasty in the various cities of Memphis, Natchez, or New Orleans, the only promising heir was Nicholas, Alain proudly thought. His ruling hand had reared him, and Nicholas was the best of the lot!

Miles up the river in the city of Natchez, André Dubose shared his older brother's sentiments, as he relaxed in the cozy study at Magnolia. That evening he was sampling a good bottle of brandy with his favorite nephew who had just arrived in the city. Nicholas had secured lodgings in the Mansion House Hotel, which he considered a wise move under the circumstances. However, if he'd known Yvonne was out of the city he'd not have made that arrangement.

On this visit to Natchez Nick had one purpose in mind, and he did not intend to put up with the antics of his promiscuous cousin, Yvonne. He knew what that little witch was capable of doing. Yvonne could be dangerous, even to a saintly man, and Nicholas knew he was no saint.

Of course, André was appalled that Nicholas had taken a room at the Mansion House, but

Nick had cleverly conjured up a tale to explain why he'd gone there the first night. Since he'd learned about Yvonne's absence he'd agreed to stay under his uncle's roof.

André was visibly pleased that Nick had agreed to come out to Magnolia the next morning. However, after the two men had settled into a relaxed mood and were savoring sips of brandy and puffing on their cheroots, André stunned his nephew when he announced, "There will be no wedding in the spring, Nick. Alita has changed her mind."

Nick's firmly muscled body reared up out of the overstuffed chair, and he set his glass down on the table. "What the hell happened? Why did she change her mind? Everything seemed to be going so right in New Orleans."

André laughed deeply, "Not one thing went wrong. Let's just say Alita Dumaine is one hell of a smart woman. She perceived something I was too blind to see for years."

"I'm afraid I don't know what you're talking about, Uncle André."

"I can understand that, Nick. Believe me, she stunned me when she first told me what she'd decided and why. Now, I know every word she spoke was true. Would you like to hear an incredible tale, Nick?"

Not understanding what his uncle was saying, Nicholas answered, "I would."

"All right. Somehow, you, of all the people I

know, could understand this. You'll see why as I go along. Years ago, I was as much of a hellion as you've been, according to my family's standards. Albert was already married and Alain had just married your beautiful mama in New Orleans. I happened to land in the city at carnival time and this lovely, gorgeous creature . . . Monique's friend just happened to be there too. I was, at the time, already betrothed to Daniel's and Yvonne's mother. The wedding was to take place a week after I returned from New Orleans. I was having one last fling before becoming an old married man, shall we say."

Nick broke into a broad grin. He could well imagine that his uncle had been quite a ladies' man when he was younger for he still had striking, good looks.

"Now I can't speak for other men, but you, Nick, I think can relate to this. I suspect that you were affected by Fancy the way I was that night when, across the way, my eyes gazed on the most beautiful woman I'd ever beheld. The message that traveled across the space separating us was so overwhelming and powerful that we moved toward each other as if some force pulled us. Even if we had resisted, we could not have helped ourselves."

"She must have been something! It's true, Uncle André, that is exactly the way my little vixen Fancy affected me."

"I thought so and shall I tell you something?

"I thought so and shall I tell you something? This woman I speak about is most beautiful to me, yet until Alita wisely opened my eyes I'd been a stupid old fool who did not understand many things that plagued me. As you know, after my wife died I . . . hell, I never married again or took a woman as a mistress. Now, I think I know why. Always, this woman haunted my thoughts. Didn't know your Uncle André was such a romantic fool, did you?"

He paused long enough to refill his glass and Nick's and then he took a seat. "Life is so strange. You see, Alita saw an obvious display of passion on my face when I was in the same room with this woman."

Nick flinched! Dear God, was it his mother, Monique, that André adored so? What a hellish torment to endure, being in love with one's brother's wife!

"The same message traveled between us, Nick. I saw it on her face although we didn't say a word; and I'm certain she knew what I was thinking and feeling. God, that one night of ecstasy, so rare and wonderful! No man can forget it if he's ever had it, and I had it with my lovely Angelique."

Nick almost choked on the sip of brandy he'd just taken. Stunned, but relieved to know André wasn't in love his mother, he finally managed to request a confirmation of what he thought he'd heard.

412

"Angelique Rocheleau was the woman?"

"Yes, Nick . . . my heart was lost to Angelique over twenty years ago, but I guess it took Alita to make me realize it had remained so all these years. Nevertheless, let me assure you, Nick, Alita and I will always be the dearest of friends."

It was a rare thing for Nick to be speechless, but tonight it took him several minutes to absorb everything André Dubose had revealed. Even his all-consuming thoughts of Dubonnet were pushed aside. Finally, he taunted his uncle by pointing out, "Well, it isn't too late, you know?"

André's green eyes sparkled as he confessed, "I've thought of nothing else for days. I may be traveling back to New Orleans sooner than you think."

With gusto the two joined in laughter!

"Then we shall go together, Uncle André," Nick laughed. "Back to the women we love, eh!"

Chapter Thirty-seven

No one could deny that Francois Martel was a flamboyant, handsome individual. Fancy found him likable and charming. From the moment his dark, exploring eyes met hers and danced lazily over her face and figure, she knew he found her most attractive. She also knew her sister-in-law was churning with excitement over the presence of the good-looking houseguest.

It struck Fancy as amusing that Yvonne and Denise just might become rivals vying for the handsome Frenchman's affections. It was obvious to Fancy that each girl was playing up to him, and she suspected that François was amused by their little parlor games.

Claude Dubose, knowing his friend's reputation with the ladies, gave him a stern, stiff warning about Nicholas and his hot temper. "Don't be stupid enough to try anything with his wife, Francois," he cautioned his friend shortly after their arrival when he'd seen that gleam in his friend's eyes. "You might never leave the city alive. Believe me, I know! They weren't married then, but old Nick had set his cap for her and I damn near lost my head over trying to get just a little kiss from her."

François exploded into laughter over his friend's cautious warning and assured him, "I promise, *mon ami,* I shall be very careful around the young madame. However, you've whetted my curiosity about her. She must be a ravishing dish, *oui?*"

"Absolutely breathtaking! Eyes as black as midnight and her face could tempt the devil himself. If you knew my cousin Nicholas and his reputation with the ladies, then you'd understand why she has to possess some rare allure to hold his interest."

"Hhmmmmm, she must be very desirable," François remarked. Later, after they'd arrived and he'd seen the young lady called Fancy, he had to agree with Claude wholeheartedly. She was utterly divine.

She treated him so casually, making no effort to fawn over him as Mademoiselle Yvonne or Mademoiselle Denise did, that he was challenged to seek her attention. Yet, she was very sweet and gracious when he engaged her in conversation . . . a perfect, well-mannered lady.

François was delighted to find himself in the stimulating environment of the Dubose home. He never felt more alive and vital than he did when his interest was spurred more by some beautiful female.

The other two young women left him cold. Denise Dubose was a silly, annoying child who got on his nerves. As for the lovely, sensuous Yvonne, she was beautiful and her figure was designed to pleasure a man's lusty desires, but she was no challenge to François for her message was too obvious. A romp in bed was there for the taking, but that didn't appeal to François Martel. He liked being in charge . . . the master!

At first, he'd wondered if his good friend, Claude, was trying to play matchmaker for his cousin Yvonne, so he played his cards very carefully and discreetly around her. He quickly learned that she was a clever and conniving minx. On that score, he did enjoy outsmarting her. That was a challenge!

On his second evening at the Dubose home he watched Yvonne try her wiles on her cousin's pretty wife. He knew instinctively what Yvonne intended to do and he felt disgust for the auburn-haired beauty.

Her voice was as sweet as syrup as she remarked, "Fancy is from your part of the country, François. Isn't it remarkable you never met in Memphis?"

"That was my misfortune, I assure you," François curtly replied, his dark eyes piercing Yvonne's across the long dining table. The acid-tongued wench!

With her head high and a lovely smile on her

face, Fancy laughed liltingly. "I hardly moved in François's circle of friends, Yvonne. Surely your memory is quite bad for one so young." The sting of Fancy's scream made its mark on Yvonne.

Once again Fancy had bested her and made her look like a fool in front of a man she was desperately trying to impress. She flushed and clenched her teeth until they felt as though they would crumble. An uncomfortable silence descended on the diners.

François wanted to shout gleefully and to applaud the lovely young woman whose bold eyes defied the haughty Yvonne to say anything.

He could not resist saying, "Never would I forget the vision of your beauty, Madame Dubose. Never in a million years!" He bowed his dark head gallantly and smiled. Fancy thanked him.

From that moment an unspoken understanding existed between Fancy and the handsome François Martel. The compassion and attention he showed her irked her sister-in-law and Yvonne Dubose, but at least, Fancy didn't feel so alone and deserted.

Drastic ideas began to haunt Yvonne, for she was determined to land the very elegant, wealthy Martel as her suitor. Yet, he was as elusive as the colorful butterflies flitting around her aunt's garden. The special care she took with her toilette and in picking the gowns that enhanced her figure seemed to have no impact on François. But when Fancy entered the room, his eyes sparkled. Oh, she hated her.

When she and Claude found themselves alone, she spit out her anger at Nicholas's wife. "What is it about that lowly bitch that seems to bewitch every male in her presence. Don't give me the runaround, Claude! You are just as bad as the others I speak about."

Claude shrugged his shoulders, a grin on his face. He wasn't about to subject himself to one of Yvonne's harangues. He jauntily walked away and quipped, "I couldn't make you understand even if I told you. It's something you can't put into mere words. 'Bye."

Let her fuss and fume all she wanted, Claude thought, for he couldn't make François desire her. He just wasn't attracted to Yvonne. That was not Claude's problem, nor would it affect his friendship with Martel.

He shared François's feelings and felt a touch of pity for Fancy. Aware of the scheming and plotting of his two disgruntled cousins, he determined to keep his nose out of it. Claude wanted no taste of Nick's revenge when he returned from Natchez, and he would be coming home anytime.

Nick could be a heartless, cruel bastard when he wanted to be!

Fancy became enraged and tore to pieces the message delivered by the riverboat captain that late afternoon. "Damn you, Nick! It would serve you right if I boarded a boat and came to Natchez," she muttered angrily, wishing he were present so she could vent her temper on him instead of an empty room.

How dare he leave her here to do constant battle with the two despicable little witches downstairs! She knew they were thoroughly enjoying themselves at her expense. Thank God for her ally, François! Nevertheless, the situation was draining her. She was miserable and lonely.

She realized there was a problem, too, where François was concerned. No longer was Fancy a simple-minded country girl, and she knew that an explosive situation could easily be created by a man of François's devastating charms.

Once she would have been naïve and innocent about a man like François, as she had been with Nick. But not anymore. Now she knew why Yvonne disliked and resented her so. The auburn-haired minx envied her and her position as Nick's wife. Doreen had let her know that Yvonne had been attracted to Nick for years.

Fancy wondered just how long she could keep François at bay. He was a persuasive man with a masterful, dominating personality; he had a winning way about him very much like her beloved Nick. This awareness frightened Fancy.

She was lonely for Nick, for his loving, comforting arms. She needed him with her for many reasons.

Celine could be right about her being pregnant. It had to be at least two months since she'd had her monthly flow. Remembering her previous pregnancy didn't help because it increased her anger at Nick. She recalled her sleepless nights and the worry about how she was going to deal with her situation. Then she hadn't felt too kindly toward Nick Dubose. Neither did she now!

In this huge house dominated by Duboses, to whom could she turn to cry out her feelings? Even Doreen had gone to the country estate of one of her friends. Suddenly, she thought of Angelique Rocheleau.

Without further ado, she summoned Celine to help her dress. An hour later, her attire did not reflect her downcast mood in the least. She looked elegant in her dark forest green ensemble as Dudley drove her in the Dubose carriage toward the Rocheleau house.

François Martel thought that Monique, too, had looked elegant in her berry wine gown. He had stood back in the shadows of the quiet, peaceful courtyard garden and had admired the striking figures of both alluring ladies as they'd left the stately old mansion. The older Madame Dubose had boarded the carriage of a lady friend and had departed several minutes before the Dubose driver had taken the lively little Fancy somewhere. François wondered where she was going and wished he were in the carriage beside her.

But today he must go his way alone. At noon he had a rendezvous to keep. To rid himself of Claude's company, he now invented a lie that would provide him with an excuse to leave the mansion alone. Poor shallow-minded Claude probably thought François had come to New Orleans to socialize, but François had a far more important mission. Actually he was an astute businessman. Power and wealth were the dominating forces in the Frenchman's life. He wanted to profit from the new age this country was entering.

The vast landowners who ruled their holdings like kings must make way for the advent of industry. Steel production had been revolutionized by the Bessemer converter. The railroad now operated between New York and Chicago. A man by the name of Isaac Singer had invented a sewing machine that would replace the many hands stitching ladies' frocks and finely tailored suits for gentlemen. François Martel had visions of a future that staggered his imagination. These aristocratic plantation owners who lived so lavishly were in for a rude awakening in just a few years.

François wanted his finger in many pies, so when an acquaintance told him about some wealthy German gentlemen who were very influential in Europe and who were meeting some other prominent gentlemen from this country in New Orleans, François eagerly accepted an invitation to be a part of this gathering. François was convinced these were men of vision and wisdom. He was honored to be included in their circle.

He was exhilarated as he left for his surreptitious meeting an hour later.

In her own way, Angelique Rocheleau needed Fancy's company on this winter's day every bit as much as the younger lady needed hers. The last few weeks had not been easy ones for Angelique. Old wounds had opened up that she'd thought were healed long ago. What a fool she'd been to think so!

With a lighthearted air, she suggested to Fancy that they should probably indulge themselves in a shopping spree. "I hear it's the tonic recommended for ladies who feel gloomy."

"You, too?"

"I must confess the truth, Fancy. I've been feeling slightly depressed, and I fear my servants have not found me to be too pleasant."

"Oh, Angelique . . . I rather doubt that you've been that harsh," Fancy smiled.

"Never mind me, dear. What has you so downcast? If it's Nicholas, I'll have a good talk with him," she teased.

"You'll have no talk with him unless you travel to Natchez which I've been tempted to do. He's been gone over a week, and just this morning I had the brief message that he's to be gone at least another week. I resent being left here while he goes roaming whenever the mood hits him, Angelique."

Angelique wanted to tell Fancy what she thought Nick was doing, but it was not her place to do that. She suspected he was probably finding the "nesting place" he'd mentioned several weeks ago. When he did return with his mission accomplished, Angelique knew Fancy would be overjoyed. However, that didn't ease her present aggravation.

"Is something else bothering you, dear?" With Nick gone and Fancy left on her own at the Dubose home, Angelique wondered if Denise was being unduly hateful?

Fancy's tears seemed to flow easily lately. Indeed, on several occasions she had found herself crying for no particular reason. Now the kind, caring Angelique Rocheleau seemed to be inviting a tearful confession. Hesitantly, Fancy told her, "Oh, I just didn't know where to turn but to you, Angelique. I've been so miserable without Nick and then Yvonne arrived."

"Yvonne's here?"

"She, her cousin Claude, and a friend of his, François Martel."

"*Mon Dieu*, tell me . . . has something happened to upset you?" Angelique could well imagine the mischief Denise and Yvonne could create when they were under the same roof. "If so, why don't you just come here with me and stay for a few days, eh? I'd love it . . . every minute!"

"Don't tempt me, Angelique!" The idea certainly appealed to Fancy but she did not want to take the cowardly way. She was too stubborn to run from her home. After all, whether his family liked it or not, she was the wife of Nicholas Dubose. What really hurt her was Nick's neglect and his obvious desire to be away from her.

"Be patient, Fancy. When Nick returns you'll see he had a good reason to be away. Never doubt that he loves you. This I know, *ma petite*."

"I hope you're right, Angelique. You see, I think I'm carrying Nick's baby." She hadn't meant to say that.

Nothing could have been sweeter music to Angelique's ears. A son or daughter for Nick! How wonderful!

Such a surge of happiness shot through her it was all she could do to restrain herself from telling Fancy what Nick was doing. Instead, she embraced the dear girl sitting there in her parlor and declared sincerely, "Oh, Fancy if I'd ever been blessed with a daughter I would have yearned for someone just like you. Always . . . always consider me your very good friend, will you, dear?"

Angelique Rocheleau could not have known how much her warm words meant to Fancy that day and in the days to follow.

When Fancy returned home she knew she'd made a wise decision in seeking out Madame Rocheleau. The woman had bolstered her courage.

It still amazed Fancy that it had seemed so natural to tell Angelique her suspicion that she was pregnant. Perhaps, Angelique just inspired confidence. She knew how close Nick felt to this dear, kind woman. Fancy felt that Angelique was a kindred spirit. She didn't quite understand why but she had sensed it at their first meeting.

Chapter Thirty-eight

The trio sitting on the veranda and enjoying the sunny afternoon shared a bond of love for a particular young lady named Fancy: the chubby black woman draped in her favorite shawl; her husband, Raoul; and Nicholas Dubose, who had come to Dubonnet to bid them farewell before he returned to New Orleans.

There was no happier man than Nick now that Dubonnet was his and Fancy's. The elderly couple with him were certain their prayers had been answered and that they had been rewarded in the winter years of their lives. To live out their days on the fine estate of Dubonnet with their precious Fancy was the greatest blessing they could have.

Old Raoul rose, using the magnificent cane presented to him by his new master. "Monsieur Dubose, you done made me and Chessie the two happiest people on this earth. You tell our sweet

Fancy we'll have her new home shining when you two get back here. Won't we, Chessie?"

"Surely will." As Chessie laughed her whole being swelled with joy. She could not believe she and Raoul were so lucky. Such a nice, generous man as Nicholas Dubose married to Fancy! Lord o'mercy, he worshipped her. Such a big, handsome devil! Enough to make any woman go weak in the knees.

Why he'd brought a fine gift for each of them the first time he'd come out to Dubonnet. The shawl had become her favorite, and he'd given Raoul an elegant cane fit for the finest gentry. They'd sat and talked for hours on a couple of occasions. Once, the three of them had eaten lunch in the small dining room — at the same table. Mister Nicholas was a very unusual man to Chessie's way of thinking. Miss Fancy's husband was a prince of a man.

Nicholas slowed his long strides to match Raoul's as the black man walked to the hitching post where Domino stood. He'd already made arrangements for his prized Domino to be stabled at Dubonnet when he boarded the boat to New Orleans.

As he mounted the magnificent beast, he could not resist reminding Raoul, "Now, you tell Chessie to order anything necessary to fix up that little room off the master bedroom, Raoul. I've made arrangements for any funds you'll need."

A broad grin creased Raoul's ebony face. "Yes, sir. It will be all done time you get back. Fittin' for our little prince or princess. Yes, sir!"

"See you, old friend, in a few weeks." Nick threw up his hand as he galloped away on the midnight black stallion. He was a man in a hurry to be on his way down that wide, muddy river to Fancy. Now, he had everything he wanted . . . Fancy and Dubonnet!

The merrymaking Yvonne Dubose had anticipated enjoying in the vital city of New Orleans had not been realized. Her first big letdown was that Nick was away, and François had proven to be a big disappointment during the week she'd stayed at her Aunt Monique's. Her exclusive little circle of friends bored her. She found their afternoon teas depressingly dull. After a week, even Denise's company palled.

A couple of romps in bed with Claude had provided Yvonne with a brief reprieve. However, Claude was not much of a lover. He certainly was not very inventive, and her voracious sexual appetite was unsatisfied.

Her arrogant vanity prohibited her from admitting that François Martel was not attracted to her, just as it had made her refuse to acknowledge Nicholas's disinterest in her at Magnolia. She had to blame someone else for the aloofness of the Memphis gentleman. Fancy became the culprit.

Yet, Yvonne had failed to derive any satisfaction from that thought. As distasteful as it was she had to admit to herself that the girl was sharp. Lowly born or not, Fancy was foxy.

In a strange way, Yvonne could not help admiring Fancy's cleverness. Fancy stood alone against her and Denise, but she was full of fire and spirit. Even Yvonne could see that her beauty would excite men like Nicholas and François. Nonetheless she knew there must be a way to realize the revenge she sought.

An opportunity to do so occurred in a strange, unexpected way. At midafternoon a youth ambled through the iron gates into the courtyard of the Dubose residence. A searching look on his face told Yvonne that the boy had never been on the grounds before. Ordinarily she would not have troubled herself over a mere youth, but something urged her to inquire of the lad, "What do you wish, boy?"

Stammering and nervous, he asked, "Are . . . are you Madame Fancy Dubose? I've . . . I've a message from your husband, ma'am." The young lad was awestruck by the glorious beauty of this shapely woman with emerald green eyes.

"Yes, I am Madame Fancy Dubose," Yvonne lied, taking the message from the boy. "Thank you, young man."

She dismissed the boy and eagerly sought the shadowed privacy of the small patio where Argo's cage stood. The parrot screeched a protest as she invaded his territory to read the message intended for Fancy's eyes only.

"Shut up, you bastard!" Yvonne admonished the bird as she opened Nicholas's message to his wife. Her lips curved into a smirking smile as she read the note. The suave, debonair Nicholas was not reflected in his writings to his wife. He sounded like a moonstruck young boy, anxious to get home to her and hold her in his hungry arms.

Oh, Nicholas, she sighed under her breath. It was hard for her to believe this was that high-stepping, arrogant man who used to visit Magnolia a couple of times each year. Dear God, how he'd changed!

She knew what she must do. Somehow she must get Fancy to go on a weekend jaunt to the country place of François's friend. Nicholas would be annoyed because Fancy was not waiting to rush into his arms when he arrived home. Assuming Fancy had received the message that he was coming on the *Nellie Dee* from Natchez, he would be further irked to find she had traipsed off with the four of them, especially since Monique and Alain were not going to the Van Meters' estate. Yvonne tore the message into shreds.

After a sly devious little laugh, Yvonne mumbled, for only the brightly colored Argo to hear, "Of course, she won't see it, will she Argo?"

Argo barked out a sharp sound that sounded disapproving. The discriminating cockatoo had a personality of his own. He liked some of the people at the mansion and disliked others. Fancy had somehow won his favor during her months in residence.

As Yvonne ambled into the house she pondered just how she and Denise could entice Fancy to accompany them. A sudden burst of sweetness would be too shallow. The girl would see right through that. By the time she mounted the steps to go to her room Yvonne had concluded that François would be the best one to urge Fancy to go to the Van Meters'.

Sequestered later with Denise, she inquired of her cousin, "What do you think?"

"I think it is perfect! Oh, I'd love to see her put in her place. Dear Lord, it's not only Doreen she has eating out of the palm of her hand anymore. Father and Mother seem to have accepted her. That galls me to the core, Yvonne," Denise declared disgustedly.

"Well then, let's do something about it, cousin Denise. Let's fix that little baggage once and for all. I have the most marvelous idea."

"Tell me!" Denise eagerly urged.

"Well, you've told me how terribly jealous Nick is of the little minx, so what if he found her and François in a compromising situation? Can you imagine how he would react?" She laughed wickedly.

"From the expression I've observed on his face when some man was eyeing her at a party, I'd say François could end up with a bloody nose or worse."

"Oooohhh, now wouldn't that be terrible. And

431

what would you think he'd do about Fancy?"

"Nicholas is a very possessive man. He always has been for as long as I can remember. If he really thought something had gone on between the two . . . well, I couldn't venture a guess. He could just hightail it off and leave her," Denise contemplated.

"Well, I think that's all I need to know to start on the next step of our little plan. Wish me luck!" Yvonne tossed her thick auburn curls off her shoulder and winked at Denise before bouncing out of the room.

François! She had to seek out Monsieur Martel. Dealing with him would take subtlety and cunning for Martel was a very perceptive man. Yvonne realized that Françis and Nick were sharp in much the same way, so she must be very cautious if she wished to work things her way.

Rain pelted the window panes as viciously as it had that day many weeks ago when Fancy had become the victim of a cloudburst and the handsome Captain Swenson had rescued her. For one fleeting moment, she thought about that handsome man. She wondered how many damsels in distress he'd rescued.

Then she smoothed a straying wisp of curl into place, dabbed some jasmine water behind each ear, and gave a final shake of the blue-green taffeta skirt of her gown before leaving her boudoir to join the others for dinner.

As she advanced down the long carpeted hall, François was just about to go down the steps. He halted at the top of the landing to wait for her. His dark eyes devoured the lovely sight of her as she moved toward him. She was a divine little creature whose innate sensuousness made her all the more desirable to him.

"Good evening, Madame. May I say how lovely you look on this miserable night. Have you noticed how the rains are coming down?"

"I have. It seems New Orleans always gets more than its share of rain. It didn't seem to rain so much in Natchez as it does here," she remarked casually as she took his arm. He was a magnetic man, Fancy could not deny that. When he leaned close to her as they walked down the long winding stairway and whispered in her ear, his powerful maleness was effective. "I need your help, Fancy," he murmured softly.

"Mine, François?" she inquired, having no idea what he could be talking about.

"Yes, that's why I'm delighted that we have this private moment before joining the others. You see, I want you to accompany me to the Van Meters' this weekend, or else I'm going to end up a most rude, callous cad."

As they halted on the steps, Fancy raised a skeptical brow.

"Let me try to explain, *ma petite*. I do not wish to insult my most gracious hosts here but neither do I wish any . . . entanglements, shall we say, with Mademoiselle Yvonne. Please . . . please do not think I'm a man who talks boldly about ladies, but she isn't so easy to discourage. *Mon dieu*, I pray you don't take what I'm saying the wrong way."

"I think I do understand you, François, but I — "

François hastened to continue his plea before she said no. "You see, I know that you are a happily married lady. You would be safe as my dinner partner and I, too, would be safe." He laughed, a devious gleam in his dark eyes.

The imp in Fancy came out. She found the whole situation very amusing. Why not do it? Yvonne had tried to make her miserable ever since she'd arrived. Perhaps, a couple of days in the country would be just the tonic she needed since Nick would not return for several days.

Patting his hand, she teased him. "All right, François I will play your protector. Besides, I'm a country girl at heart and fresh air sounds good to me. Why, I might just shed my shoes and go barefooted."

His eyes darkened when his vivid imagination pictured her as a barefoot goddess. Desire welled in his chest, and his voice reflected his warmth as he spoke. "I can think of no more wonderful sight than you barefoot in a meadow of wildflowers or sitting on the bank of the little lake behind the Van Meters' house. There are some swans there."

"Really?" Fancy found the idea more appealing as he spoke.

"Yes. You might enjoy yourself, and God knows, you would certainly be doing me a favor for which I would thank you from the bottom of my heart, dear lady. Your husband is a lucky man, indeed!"

"You're very kind, François." She smiled up at him. For one fleeting minute just before they entered the parlor where everyone else had gathered she wondered if she'd regret accepting his invitation.

All eyes were on the couple as they entered the archway, and Monique could not help noticing how radiant Fancy looked this evening. The gown she wore was especially flattering. "You look especially beautiful tonight, my dear," she exclaimed, knowing their houseguest shared her feelings. Something made her wish for her son's hasty return to this city and his home. His young wife was far too attractive to be left alone too long. Never had Monique been more aware of her daughter-in-law's rare loveliness.

François's aristocratic face masked a multitude of emotions. He knew his eyes revealed his admiration for the lady he'd escorted into the Dubose parlor, but when he glanced around the room to lock eyes with Yvonne Dubose she gave him a smile and a secret message.

Everything about Yvonne repulsed him, and he wanted to shout at her, "Stupid bitch!" Did she really think that he had joined in frivolous folly? Not for one minute! Let her think what she would, he had his own game to play and it did not include

Yvonne for one minute.

Fancy Dubose was worth a million Yvonnes. He'd met that sort of woman all over the world during his travels, but a woman like Fancy came along only once in a lifetime, if a man was lucky.

Chapter Thirty-nine

As Herman Van Meter's elegant carriage rolled down the long drive of the Dubose estate, Claude followed it atop the dapple gray mare. Denise, Yvonne, Fancy, and François sat inside the carriage on its lavish red velour seats. High-stepping black horses rapidly drew the equipage through the streets of New Orleans and soon they were in the country.

The day was glorious, with blue skies and bright sunshine. The mild weather made it seem like May instead of March. The entourage was light-hearted and gay, and the carriage resounded with their chatter.

Fancy felt a little smug at the knowledge that her presence might irritate Yvonne. Perhaps this would take some of the wind out of her sails, Fancy mused. So she sat, listening to the others talk and only occasionally joining in on the conversation.

How happy she would be if Nick were by her side instead of François, she thought desperately.

"You're awfully quiet, *ma petite*," François remarked, turning his head in her direction. Fancy smiled, as she replied, "Oh, I was just enjoying the beauty of the day."

"It is a beautiful day, isn't it? I'm so glad you came, Fancy . . . truly." François found it easy to forget the existence of the two ladies across from him. Yvonne gave Denise a nudge and smiled, thinking François was working his charm on Nicholas's wife.

Herman Ven Meter's penchant for surrounding himself with lovely ladies and entertaining gentlemen was gratified when this entourage arrived in his newly acquired carriage. The forty-year-old bachelor was titillated by the sight of the beauties alighting from the carriage. Martel was most assuredly his kind of gentleman, and he must make a point of rewarding their mutual acquaintance for introducing him to François.

With a dramatic gesture, François helped each lady from the carriage and introduced her to their host. As Van Meter greeted each woman, his beady little eyes scrutinized her.

"Mademoiselle Yvonne, Mademoiselle Denise, and Madame Fancy Dubose . . . my great pleasure!"

What a vision and a contrast of loveliness! Black eyes, green eyes, dark brown hair, and gorgeous flame-colored hair. When it came to the womens' figures, to Herman the one called Yvonne was the most voluptuous and full breasted, but he would not say she was the most sensuously provocative. Perhaps that was true of the dainty little miss who was so perfect proportioned. The way her tiny body moved made Herman's blood boil. Yes, he found himself entranced by the one called Fancy.

He had not missed the impressive name of her husband . . . an arrogant, imperious personality. Although he'd never met Nicholas, he'd met Alain Dubose on occasion. The Dubose influence was certainly felt in the city of New Orleans.

After this bevy of loveliness had been ushered up the stairway, he, François, and Claude retired to his magnificent library and he declared that he was delighted to have them as his guests for the weekend. "This is my favorite home I have to admit. New Orleans offers me more than the other residences I occupy during the year."

"You have other houses, Monsieur Van Meter?" Claude asked, awed by the grandeur around him.

"Oh, yes, young man. I have three other places where I hang my hat as you say." He chuckled. "I have a home in my native land. I have a home back east in New York, and I own a townhouse in London which is my sister's residence. So you see, I am a gypsy of sorts. In fact, I leave for the east next week."

Claude was obviously impressed by the wealthy German. All he'd known about him was what François had told him—not much. Yet, it was obvious he had vast holdings. The library where they now sat drinking fine cognac bespoke of his wealth. It was lavishly furnished with many expensive imports. The smell of leather and the aroma of pungent tobacco kept in the silver jar resting on the satinwood table were almost seductive to Claude. The high ceilinged room was paneled in a dark rich wood, and bookshelves lined one wall. The leather-bound books were probably first editions, Claude thought to himself.

The impressive Van Meter family crest hung above the fireplace mantel, and a colorful antique tapestry adorned the opposite wall. The portrait of a severe, stern-faced gentleman hung over Herman's desk. Claude assumed the man was his father for they looked so much alike — the same beady little eyes and cruel mouth. However, Herman sported only a mustache whereas that man was bearded.

After the men had enjoyed a second glass of cognac, Herman suggested they go to the stables while the ladies were resting. "I have a magnificent stallion I've just acquired. I understand that your uncle appreciates fine thoroughbreds, Claude. Maybe I've mixed up the brothers; is it your father?"

"No, it is my Uncle André in Natchez. My father is a banker."

"Most remarkable family from what I've heard. So your father is the banker. Alain, I know, is in the shipping lines; and your Uncle André raises many fine race horses in Natchez. I've been to the Pharsalia. I'm acquainted with the turfman, Colonel Bingaman, so your uncle and I probably share a mutual friendship."

"You just might. I don't know the gentleman but I've enjoyed many good racing seasons in Natchez and stayed at my uncle's plantation just outside the city. Perhaps, you've heard of it . . . Magnolia?"

"Ah, yes. Magnolia. The lovely estate of Dubonnet also comes to my mind."

Claude grinned broadly. "Now you are talking about my cousin's impossible quest. He wants to own Dubonnet. He'd give one arm to get that place. He's as crazy about horses as Uncle André, and he too, has the reputation of being a fine judge of horseflesh."

Herman nodded his head. "I can believe that after meeting his charming wife. You see, a very fine thoroughbred is much like a woman . . . beautiful and enchanting. Both have spirit and fire. Both challenge a person to tame them. Even if a man succeeds, he admires and respects them. Do you agree?"

"There is something to what you say, Herman." François laughed. "Never thought of it that way before."

Fancy fit that description to perfection, and François suddenly realized what he yearned to do more than anything—to possess and conquer any resistance she might offer.

As Van Meter, Claude, and François arrived at

the stable, a magnificent stallion was released from its stall to run in the fenced area beside the stable, François saw exactly what the German meant. There was a look of defiance in the beast's eyes, and it held its head high. This was a proud animal. Its thick black satiny mane gleamed in the sunlight, as did its lustrous black tail. The stallion pranced fiestily around the field.

Perhaps, Fancy wouldn't appreciate the comparison but François was reminded of her breathtaking beauty, her fiesty walk, and the way she held her head as she tossed her dark wavy hair to and fro.

She was a thoroughbred! He wondered if Nicholas Dubose prized her as much as he should.

They were a couple of hot-blooded men, fired with love for the women who held their hearts. Nicholas and his good-looking uncle made an impressive pair as they disembarked from the boat and strode jauntily down the gangplank to the wharf. Both men were churning with a boyish eagerness which swept away the gap in their ages and had their spirits soaring. Both reached the same towering height, and had the same broad shoulders and gleaming green eyes.

André intended to seek rooms at the Saint Regent Hotel instead of staying at his older brother's home. Nick understood this and did not fuss about it. Although he knew Alain or Monique would not understand, Nick had agreed not to reveal his

Uncle André's presence in New Orleans until André wished to announce it. They had worked out this little agreement during the trip from Natchez.

André would remain at the hotel while Nick went on to the Dubose mansion. First, André wanted to pay a call on Angelique Rocheleau. He was praying it was not too late for them to have the life he should have offered her far too many years ago.

As André watched his nephew rush to his wife, he smiled with amusement. He understood too well the young man's impatience. Dear God, he felt as though the years had rolled away for him too! Under his breath, he said a silent "thank you" to Alita Dumaine.

An exuberant Nicholas Dubose greeted old Nat some twenty minutes later. With a hasty hello to the elderly butler, he lunged up the stairs and rushed down the long, carpeted hallway to the rooms he shared with Fancy. It did not occur to him that he would not find her there at this time of the afternoon.

When he did rush through the door calling out her name, he got no response. The room seemed so empty and lifeless. Fancy's sweet fragrance and presence was what brought it to life. It was no longer just his room. She had put her mark on it as she had on his life.

Soft footsteps echoed in the hall and he rushed to the door to see Celine, not Fancy.

Nick called out to her, "Celine, could you tell me where your mistress might be?"

The mulatto turned, surprised to see Monsieur Nicholas standing there. She'd not known he'd be arriving. Miss Fancy would surely be disappointed that she'd left. "Why, *monsieur* . . . how nice to see you back!"

"Thank you, Celine. Now tell me . . . where is your mistress?"

"She's not here, *monsieur.* She went away for the weekend." Having already sensed Nicholas's exasperation at not finding his pretty wife in their room, Celine didn't like the way his eyes flashed and his brow arched.

"Went away?" he barked. "Just where in the hell did she go?"

Lordy, he is riled, Celine mused. "She went with Mademoiselle Denise and Mademoiselle Yvonne, *monsieur.*"

"The family went somewhere? Mother and Father . . . is that what you're saying?" He shifted his body and slapped his muscled thigh dejectedly. Hadn't Fancy received his message? he wondered.

"No sir. Your parents didn't accompany the ladies. Monsieur Claude and that Monsieur François Martel went with the ladies to the Van Meter country place." She spoke hesitantly because Monsieur Nicholas looked like a volcano ready to erupt.

"So Claude and Yvonne are both here, eh, and this François Martel is staying here, too?"

"Yes, sir," Celine replied, knowing that everything she was telling him was aggravating him. He grimaced as though he had a foul taste in his mouth. Then he turned abruptly and without saying another word, he went back to the empty bedroom. A few minutes later, his footsteps heavy, he went back downstairs and left the house.

This was not the homecoming he'd anticipated all the way down the river from Natchez. The news that greeted him had brought forth instant and vehement indignation. Thinking of Claude and Yvonne under the same roof with Fancy when his protective eye was not observing them made him concerned. He didn't trust that pair at all . . . and then there was this stranger, François Martel.

Had his obsession to attain Dubonnet cost him too much? He didn't like the feeling of foreboding that consumed him. It was so strong and overpowering.

As he rode away from the mansion in the late afternoon, Nick knew he hadn't conquered his tormenting jealousy where Fancy was concerned. He recalled that day in the woods when Claude had tried to force himself on Fancy. Before that there had been Jason Carew. Each time his fury had been so great that he could have killed the man had his sanity not returned in time. Nor could he forget the blond giant, Eric Swenson.

His indignation ran amok as his mount carried him along. He had no particular destination. He actually didn't know where he wanted to go. Thoughts of Fancy troubled and tormented him. Why would she go away with that group? She was a married woman, his wife. Indignation swept over him like a raging river overflowing its banks. His skull felt ready to explode.

When he approached the Golden Ram Tavern, he impulsively led the bay up to the hitching post. Every muscle in his body was tense as he leaped down and tied the reins. His green eyes flashed with violent fire and his fine-featured, tanned face announced that he was not to be trifled with.

He strode up the flagstone walk and through the door of the tavern, hellbent on drowning his torment with some of Casey's best whiskey.

Chapter Forty

The last rays of the sun were fading and darkness was engulfing the lovely Louisiana countryside. Fancy stared out of the window enjoying the last moments of twilight. It was a lovely place . . . this country place of Monsieur Van Meter. But it was still not as serene and peaceful as Dubonnet. A sudden urge washed over her. She wanted to be walking in these woods, to inhale the intoxicating smells of the pines, and to feel the graceful branches of the willows draped over her.

Yet, she also wished that she'd not come to this place. Why had she allowed François to talk her into coming? A voice chided her mercilessly, telling her she knew why. She was desperately lonely lately, and filled with uncertainty about Nick's love and devotion. Why had he chosen to be away from her for such a long time? Was it because of a beautiful woman instead of business?

Then the voice provided her with another reason why she'd come. She was enjoying a smug feeling of revenge against Yvonne and Denise, the two who'd sought to make her miserable and to cause trouble between her and Nick since the moment she'd arrived in New Orleans. As she savored the sweet taste of vengeance she remembered the times she'd fought back her tears as their vicious tongues had referred to her as white trash. Well, she'd show them. When the time was right she'd delight in telling Yvonne and Denise just why she'd come this weekend.

Her musings were interrupted by a soft rap at the door. She bid whoever it was to enter and was relieved to see that it was one of the many maids at the Van Meter residence.

"Evening, *mam'selle*," the girl addressed her pleasantly. "May I assist you with your toilette? I'm Colette."

Fancy accepted the offer, letting her thoughts fade and turning her attention to her toilette. She decided that she might as well enjoy the evening ahead. François was pleasant company and she was determined to have a good time. Why shouldn't she, she reasoned? After all, Nick had probably not been sitting by a quiet hearth every night he'd been away from her. Hadn't Yvonne hinted at that more than once?

Nick had introduced her to his sophisticated sphere, and living with him in it had brought an awareness of the world around her that she could not dismiss. She was not the same person she'd been in Natchez. Only one thing hadn't changed and that was her all-consuming love for Nicholas Dubose. He remained a fever in her blood, and this evening she ached to feel his strong arms around her. He'd introduced her to that need too.

She was so distracted by thoughts of Nick that she didn't hear little Colette sighing, "Ah, *mam'selle* . . . you . . . you're absolutely breathtaking. I . . . I hope you like the way I styled your hair."

"What? . . . Oh, yes, Colette. You've done wonders. I thank you so much." Fancy praised the girl's handiwork with the comb and brush as she surveyed the upswept hairstyle she'd effected. The girl's lovely face brightened with delight.

"You really like it, *mam'selle*?"

"I truly do. I'm tempted to whisk you away from Monsieur Van Meter and take you with me." Fancy laughed lightly. Something in the girl's face told her that the idea appealed to Colette. She could well believe that the harsh-faced German might not be the most pleasant man to work for. He reminded her of a fat pig.

"The gown, *mam'selle*?" Colette lifted the magnificent creation up with her hands. Such a beautiful color it was, a rich deep purple which would be so flattering to the dark complexioned lady; and the exquisite amethyst and diamond earrings were perfect on the dainty ears of this lovely lady. Colette wondered if tonight this woman would be the prey of the lecherous Van Meter.

An hour later, Van Meter and his guests gathered around a long dining-room table lavishly set with expensive silver and china. The sparkling cut-crystal glasses were filled with the best wine the Van Meter cellars could provide, but Van Meter needed no wine to intoxicate him. The sight of the three young women decorating his table did that.

Denise was a vision in her peach-colored gown, and the gold-colored gauzy material of Yvonne's dress enhanced her good looks. In the glowing candlelight Yvonne's decolleté neckline invited Herman's eyes to stare at the lovely cleavage of her full breasts. He was delighted by her voluptuousness, and he envisioned the rosy tips of her breasts. His mouth fairly drooled, his hunger and desire were so great.

"A feast to any man's eyes, my dears," he exclaimed aloud. Controlling himself was almost impossible, and his finely tailored cream-colored pants swelled to the limit.

As if this wasn't enough to tax the will of the devil, a masterpiece of divine loveliness sat before him in that rich purple gown. He had no words to describe her ravishingly beautiful face and figure. But she held his attention like a magnet with such tremendous drawing power he felt as if he were in a trance. Damn that François for meeting her first!

François shared Herman's admiration of Fancy. He was impatient to get her away from the others and was deviously plotting to manage that before the evening came to an end. To make love to her, he'd sell his soul, but if that was not possible, he'd gladly chance one sweet kiss for the slap he would probably receive.

There was always the remote possibility that she'd respond to him. Christ, what ecstasy that would be!

The sumptuous repast and the fine wines served made Fancy lax and unresponsive when François suggested a walk in the moonlight after dinner. Still, they left Van Meter and Claude in the parlor to be entertained. Denise was going to play the piano, and then Yvonne would sing. The auburn-haired Yvonne knew exactly how the movements of her body were affecting Herman. She was amused and delighted. The others paid no attention to François and Fancy as they slipped out into the night.

Amused, François winked at her, and she giggled and nodded her head as they quietly shut the doors. It delighted him that she had accepted his invitation to stroll.

"Ah, this is much better, isn't it, *ma petite*?" he remarked, guiding her down the two steps of the terrace to the grounds.

"Much. I need to walk after all that food," she confessed. Her appetite had been ridiculous lately. Of course, Celine had a very sound reason for that. "A baby causes that, Miss Fancy."

The first time Celine had told her that she hadn't been convinced, but lately she knew the little mulatto had probably been right all along.

Even now walking with François, she felt her breasts strain against the bodice of her gown, and the waistline pinched slightly although this outfit was not a month old.

"Monsieur Van Meter has a beautiful place here," she remarked to François. Because for some unexplained reason her thoughts had been on Dubonnet earlier, she found herself chattering away about the fine old estate back in Natchez. Suddenly, she realized how comfortable and easy she felt with François Martel, and she realized that she had told him a good deal about herself.

"Dear Lord, forgive me for bending your ear so. I . . . I have probably bored you to tears, François."

"Hardly, my dear. I find your conversation very interesting. The place you speak about sounds enchanting," he said, urging her toward the wrought-iron bench they approached. They had walked from the sprawling two-story house at a leisurely pace, but now they were far enough from it to avoid prying eyes.

This was the ideal setting for what François had in mind: tonight he would kiss those sweet, sweet lips just once.

The night air was filled with the scent of shrubbery and the moon was bright and full. Over in the nearby woods, an owl screeched, a shrill, sharp call interrupting the ghostly quiet of the night. As François rested his arm on the back of the bench, he felt Fancy tremble slightly. "Are you cool, *ma petite*?"

She smiled. "Oh, no. I don't particularly like to hear an owl calling. It started when I lived with Madame Dumaine in Natchez. Her servant, Dahlia swore an owl's call was bad luck . . . something was going to happen . . . something bad." She turned to face François and added, "I know that's silly."

"Not at all . . . not if you really feel it strongly." His hand clutched her shoulder, pressing it slightly, and Fancy found herself leaning against him. "But I'd never let anything harm you, Fancy. Not if it was within my power to prevent it. You've become very important to me, Fancy Dubose."

She had not intended this to happen, and now her instincts warned her. The look in François's eyes bespoke his desire. Damn Nick! If he'd been where he should have been instead of roaming off like a gypsy, she would never have been placed in such a vulnerable situation.

She could not deny the nearness of this charming man and the intimate moonlight setting were having an effect on her. His strong arms did feel serenely comforting and the closeness of his head to hers told her François intended to kiss her. And she was hungry for the touch of a man's hands, for a man's kiss. Nick had awakened her sensual appetite, and it seemed a long time since she had feasted on those pleasurable, stimulating sensations. Thanks again to her husband's self-imposed absence!

Under her breath, she cursed Nick. What she was about to allow was wicked and wrong, but in this brief fleeting moment she wanted François to kiss her. A part of her tried to justify that craving, and she wondered if François could stir in her the savage abandon that Nick did. That possibility frightened her as François brought his lips closer.

He murmured tender and impassioned words. "Ah, *ma chérie* . . . I've never felt about anyone as I find myself feeling about you." His lips met hers, searing her with the heat of his desire.

Wide-eyed and shaken by what she'd allowed François to do, Fancy pushed against his broad chest and tried to protest.

François was a man whose blood now boiled with purpose. Unrelenting, he held her to him with no hint of gentleness as she pleaded for her release.

"François . . . please!" Fancy begged helplessly, weak from struggling against the steel-like vise of his arms.

"No, I can't let you go, Fancy! I can't! Not now," François said, his voice husky.

Like rumbling thunder, an order roared through the night, "Oh, I think you can, *monsieur*, and I know damned well you'd better!" A menacing giant of a man towered over the couple.

François jerked around to stare up at the fierce figure threatening him, and he recalled Claude's warning that Nicholas Dubose had killed a man once when he'd crossed him. This little romantic interlude was going to cost him a heavy price, François realized. That was his last conscious thought before the furious man struck a mighty blow!

Chapter Forty-one

As the violent winds of a tornado sweep over the countryside with destructive force and then disappear into the sky to leave an awesome quiet behind, so had Nicholas Dubose arrived at and left the Van Meter country estate.

With black rage in his pained eyes, he had beheld the woman he loved in the arms of a loathsome stranger he wanted to kill. He had beaten the bastard's handsome face to a pulp and would have done more if Yvonne had not pulled him back to the edge of sanity.

Fancy had stood there, shocked, too numbed to speak. She still felt numb even though Nick and Yvonne had left and François lay on the ground at her feet. As if he had branded them on her brain, Nick's only words to her were burning deeper and deeper into her mind. Bitch! Bitch! Bitch!

No, he could not have said those horrible words to her. She tried to make herself believe this was a nightmare. It would end and she would wake up. But that was a lie, and the hatred in Nick's piercing green eyes would not fade. He despised her, Fancy realized as she'd stood there watching him leave her behind when he crossed the grounds with Yvonne.

Dejected and wretched, she had sunk to the ground and cried. How could he be so cruel and coldhearted if he loved her? He had forsaken her to go off with his cousin, who must be gratified at the way this evening had turned out. Fancy was too shocked and stunned to notice that Nick had staggered away. His jealous rage, combined with the liquor he'd drunk earlier, had forced him to accept Yvonne's support to get back to his carriage.

By the time they'd traveled back to the city he'd become vexed by Yvonne's solicitude and sympathy.

"For God's sake, Yvonne . . . shut up! No one asked you to come along," he snapped.

Yvonne obliged him and laid her auburn head back against the seat, smiling like a Cheshire cat. Everything had gone just as she'd hoped it would—even better. When she'd seen Nick plowing down the highly polished hall demanding to know where his wife was she couldn't have been happier to learn that Martel and Fancy were taking a walk in the moonlight.

She applauded her shrewdness and poor

François's persuasive powers. Most of all, she congratulated herself because Fancy had played right into her hands and she now had her long-sought revenge. The handsome Nick was by her side, where she wanted him, and the evening wasn't over yet. If Fate was still favoring her, she would be more satisfied before morning arrived.

She knew her handsome cousin had already had his share of liquor. His breath reeked of it.

There was a wildness about Nick as they rolled along in the carriage and it stirred Yvonne more than anything she'd ever felt for any man. It was primitive and savage! Dear Lord, she only hoped that nobody was up when they arrived at the Dubose mansion.

The eerie silence in the carriage was almost frightening to Yvonne, but she dared not speak to him. His face was like granite, hard and cold. When he spoke abruptly, she turned suddenly, surprised. "Was this your idea or was it my precious sister Denise who encouraged my wife to go on this little escapade?"

Yvonne did not have to be told she was with a dangerous man. Trying to sound casual and be calm, she remarked in a straightforward manner, "Actually, neither of us encouraged her. The decision to go was hers, and the invitation was from François, Claude's friend, Nick. Neither Denise nor I can be blamed for it."

"No, I guess not," he muttered reluctantly. It irked him to have to admit that Fancy had gone eagerly and willingly, just as she'd allowed herself to be held and kissed by this François. Damn her!

When they arrived at the entrance of the house, Yvonne wondered what Nick would do. Would he isolate himself in his room and proceed to drink himself into a stupor? Could she manage to entice him into letting her join him for a drink? If so, maybe he'd forget that they were cousins for this one night?

She had no pride where Nicholas was concerned. She'd do things for him that she would do for no other man.

His strong hand took hers as they dismounted from the carriage. Yet after Nat let them through the door, Yvonne made no effort to go toward the winding stairway. Instead, she turned back to Nick and flippantly announced, "I feel the need of a good, stiff drink. How's about joining me, dear cousin?"

"Why not!" He broadly grinned, and there was a mischievous glint in his eye as he added, "Maybe several, eh, cousin?"

She laughed, elated that this night was going to be hers. Anticipation of what might follow titillated her as his arm snaked around her waist and they strolled down the hall together to the library. She thought the long roomy leather couch and the huge fur rug in front of the stone hearth could provide delightful places for Nick to make love to her. Liquid heat was creeping through her from head to toe.

When the carved oak door closed behind them and they stood in the dimly lit library, Nicholas nonchalantly ambled over to the teakwood liquor chest. "What's your pleasure, pet?"

She felt like telling him what her pleasure really would be, but instead she requested some cognac. He concurred. "That does sound good. Yvonne, I'm glad you returned with me." He felt like a drowning man.

Pouring the cognac, he handed her one of the glasses and took a seat beside her, whirling the deep amber liquid in his glass for a second before sipping it. A funny look came over his face as he turned toward his cousin. "A toast, Yvonne. A toast to fools wherever they may be!" He laughed suddenly and explosively. "And to me, the biggest fool of all!"

"You are not a fool, Nick. I will not drink to that. It is your wife who was and is a fool."

"Then let us drink to foolish Fancy, eh?" He took a generous gulp of the cognac, relishing the warming sensation it evoked as he swallowed it.

Yvonne laughed gaily, "Now, that I will drink to. To foolish, foolish Fancy."

Their laughter rang out harmoniously, then stopped abruptly when the door behind them slammed. A familiar voice each recognized instantly screamed out indignantly, "By all means drink to foolish Fancy! She was a fool!"

The agony Fancy felt eclipsed any pain she'd

ever endured before. She had insisted on being brought back to the city. She had to make Nick listen to her. He had to know there was more to consider than their pride. There was a child to think about. Regardless of his feelings for her she carried his child.

When she'd entered the front door old Nat had been reluctant to tell her where she might find her husband. But laughter had echoed down the hallway, and she had only to look at Nat's downcast eyes to know Nick and Yvonne were in the library. "It's all right, Nat. Go to bed," she urged the elderly butler. "The hour is late."

For a moment, she hesitated before opening the door. They were cavorting inside the library, and Fancy was fearful of what she would behold. When she did open the door, the toast was being made and Yvonne's full breasts were overflowing her gold gauzy gown as she pressed them toward Nick's face. He was sprawled on the couch, a glass loosely held in his hand, his green eyes glazed. His state sickened Fancy.

Before she made her exit, she had one final comment to make. "Never call me a bitch again, Nicholas Dubose. The bitch sits by you now. Congratulations, Yvonne. Welcome to him! I don't want him anymore!"

Her eyes were black smoldering coals as she glared at them. Yvonne sat up on the couch, feeling like the warrior who has just won a battle. Nick sobered somewhat as he, too, sat up and gazed upon the tiny woman in purple by the door.

Despite all that had taken place this horrible night when his strong hands had wanted to wring her neck because another man had taken liberties with her, his groin blazed with desire. Never had she looked more provocative and alluring. Never had she bewitched him so! He found he could not take his eyes off her, and a need for her had seized his strong body.

As she whirled around and rushed out the door, he wanted to rush after her, to kiss her honey-sweet mouth until he bruised her lips. Damn it! She was what he wanted, but his arrogant pride said no and held him on the couch, arguing that Nicholas Dubose could not humble himself. Christ, his head felt like a cannon had just been fired inside it.

Yvonne was the first to break the awesome silence. "Well, there you have it, I guess!" she said as she shrugged her bare shoulders. A dramatic mask cloaking her indignation, she declared, "I certainly resent the likes of her calling me a bitch, Nicholas."

Nick removed himself from the couch and Yvonne's side. Slowly, he turned his eyes on his cousin who stared up at him. Fancy's strong words haunted him. His voice was low, but forceful as he tried to gain control of himself. "Something tells me you've been at the bottom of all this, Yvonne. When or if I find out you have, you had better pray I never lay eyes on you. Fancy was right about one thing, you are a bitch!"

Then, as dawn broke, he walked from the room and the house. His broad shoulders slumped. His face was tense and revealed the pain and agony of a man whose whole world has crumbled. He did not know how to try to put it back together again . . . but he knew why he left the house. He'd never find the peace his soul sought there.

Fancy sat by the window in the darkened bedroom for hours after the scene in the library. Tears cascaded down her cheeks until she had no more to shed.

Had she known Nick had left the house alone, her pain would have been eased, but she did not and when Nick didn't come to their boudoir that night, she could only conclude that he was with Yvonne. For that, she hated Nicholas Dubose!

The next day she sequestered herself in their room, eating what little she could swallow from trays brought by Celine. The servant's heart went out to her pathetic little missy. A second night and day passed with no sight of Nick at the Dubose mansion. When the third morning arrived and Celine brought the breakfast tray, the servant was pleased to see her mistress eat as if she were famished.

"Oh, missy . . . I've been so worried about

you. Just no call for you to do yourself in. There is the baby to consider."

"That's the conclusion I came to last night, Celine. As soon as I finish this, I want you to help me get dressed. I have an errand to run." Fancy's manner had changed so that Celine wondered just what she was up to. Her mistress had such an assured air now, almost a cold, calculated aloofness.

When Fancy had dressed and Celine had completed the final touches to her hair, she walked over to pick up her reticule. Turning to the servant, she said in an unwavering voice, "I've put a list on my dressing table, Celine. After you've gone down to inform Dudley that I need him to drive me, I'd appreciate your seeing to the things I've written down. I'll be leaving New Orleans in the morning."

Celine stood, shocked beyond belief. Finally, she stammered, "Missy . . . You—"

Fancy stopped her, "Please, Celine! Please don't say a word to anyone and please say nothing to me in protest. I must leave." Indeed she could do nothing else now.

Celine reluctantly moved through the door to carry out her orders to fetch Dudley. Something about Fancy's lovely face told Celine it would be futile to try to change her mind. If only she could think of a way to do so.

Such sadness swept over Celine that she could not stop tears from gathering in her eyes.

What had gone so horribly wrong between Monsieur Nick and his beautiful lady? There had been such love between them.

She stood at the window and looked down as Fancy boarded the carriage. Celine could not recall when she'd felt such heaviness in her heart. It would not be the same with Miss Fancy gone. With great reluctance, she picked up the list and noted how few gowns her mistress wanted packed. No jewels listed. She was leaving almost everything behind in New Orleans — and Nicholas Dubose.

Chapter Forty-Two

If Angelique Rocheleau had gazed into a mirror she would have seen the radiance reflected on her face. She could have been a woman of twenty-five instead of forty-three. Love must do that to a woman regardless of age.

How glad she was that she had not denied André and herself the endless ecstasy they'd just enjoyed. They weren't married yet, but they would be — and soon. Her most impossible dream had come true. Forever, she'd remember the night they'd just spent together, lying in one another's arms. *Mon dieu*, her rapture was just as overwhelming and ecstatic as it had been at sixteen!

His magnificent male body and his stirring touch had worked a long-remembered magic, firing her passion anew — a passion she had thought was dead. Desire she had considered no longer possible. *Mon dieu*, it was though!

With the first light of dawn, she lay beside him, enjoying the sight of his rumpled mane of graying hair and the fine features of his handsome face at rest.

The appealing essence of the man was still there. The years had not changed a thing about André Dubose. She wondered if he felt the same way about her. His eyes told her he did.

Dear God, she agonized, should she gamble on this wonderful love recaptured? How could she do otherwise if they were to join their lives? She could not be completely happy as long as she harbored her long-closeted secret. Yet, did she dare chance losing his love forever? Was telling him worth that?

She knew the answer, but fear churned within her at the thought of rejection showing in his eyes.

Fancy's unexpected arrival seemed like a welcoming reprieve to Angelique. When her maid gently knocked on her bedroom door, she quietly slipped into her robe and left the sleeping André. It was obvious that his sleep was deep and contented.

She smiled as she remembered their night of love-making. Drawing her sheer robe about her, she moved down the stairs to the sitting room where Fancy awaited her. She couldn't help being curious about what had prompted this visit so early in the day. Usually, Fancy's visits had been made in the early afternoon. And she knew Nicholas had returned to New Orleans with André.

Angelique had come to know Fancy quite well since she'd arrived as Nicholas's bride, so she had only to enter the cozy little sitting room and see the lovely girl's face to know something was wrong. Angelique's perceptive eyes immediately observed Fancy's pain.

"Fancy, my dear . . . what a nice surprise," she said, moving to sit beside her.

"Angelique, I'm sorry to come by so early but I had to."

"You are always a welcome sight, Fancy. You know that, I'm sure."

From the first, Angelique Rocheleau had opened her arms and her heart to this young woman, and she was one of the people Fancy really trusted here in New Orleans. It wasn't going to be easy to say what she must, Fancy suddenly realized. She knew but one way to do it, and that was just to tell the truth.

Without tears, she told Angelique what had happened and what she was planning to do. Madame Rocheleau sat, stupefied.

"Oh, Fancy . . . do you think leaving is going to solve anything? The two of you need to talk," Angelique pointed out to her.

"I can't talk to a man who doesn't wish to even come home or to be under the same roof with me."

Angelique could not argue with that. "Nicholas can be a headstrong devil, I know. I think he must be somewhere nursing his hurt masculine pride. That is a fierce thing, as we both know." She gave Fancy a knowing smile. What a fool Nick was, she sadly mused!

"Well, I have a little pride left, too, Angelique. I won't crawl either. That is why I must leave, even though I'll love Nick forever. But he hurt me, Angelique. He said such cruel things . . . things I didn't deserve."

Angelique moved over to the girl she'd become so fond of, a well of compassion swelling within her as she embraced and comforted Fancy. She knew how it hurt to love a man so.

"Dear, dear little Fancy. I wish I knew what to do to ease your turmoil," she sighed. "I just hate to see you leave though. It's like saying the future is hopeless for you and Nicholas."

"I must, Angelique. I must go back to Natchez to find the answer. This isn't, nor has it ever seemed like, my home. Not even my deep love for Nick made it so. Don't you understand what I'm trying to say?"

Angelique released Fancy and surveyed the girl's face. She did see. She understood what Fancy was saying, so she'd not try to change her mind. Perhaps, the answer did lie in the city where their love had begun. Madame Rocheleau knew what she must do to help these two young lovers avoid the fatal mistake she and André had made so many years ago.

She asked one last question before the girl took her leave. "You are carrying Nicholas's child aren't you Fancy?"

"Yes . . . well, I'm almost as sure as a woman can be without a doctor's confirmation. Yes, Angelique, I think I am about two months along."

"I thought so. Does he know?"

"I didn't have a chance to tell him. I couldn't tell him anything he was in such a fury."

Fancy rose, knowing she had one last stop to make before the afternoon was over. The two embraced, and Fancy took her leave.

As Angelique watched the carriage roll down the drive, depression descended on her. She had no choice left now. She must reveal the secret she'd kept hidden so many years. A solemn vow had to be broken, and if she lost André she'd just have to bear that.

In his rich, brown silk robe André stood at the top of the landing, watching Angelique. He'd seen Fancy departing just as he'd started to come downstairs and he'd halted until she'd left.

It would hardly have been conventional to march downstairs in his state of attire and greet his nephew's wife. However, after the front door had closed and Angelique still stood frozen in the same spot, he knew instinctively something was wrong. Something about her shoulders and her bowed head told him she was crestfallen, so he moved slowly down the steps wondering how to approach her.

He had awakened to find Angelique gone and had leaped out of bed to seek the lady he loved. God, after the night they'd shared, he never wanted to be far from her side again.

Noticing her attire, he assumed Fancy's call had

been unexpected. Such an early visit made no sense at all.

"Angelique, my darling?"

His deep inquiring voice made her whirl around. She said nothing, just rushed to his outstretched arms. As he held her close, she sighed. "Oh, André! André! Just hold me for a moment."

And he did for a long, long moment.

The hour Angelique spent postponing the revelation she knew she had to make was a painful one. She delayed until he'd dressed and eaten his breakfast. She'd been unable to eat, but she forced herself to drink some coffee.

"Shall we go into the sitting room, André?"

Angelique smiled wanly for she was actually trembling with fear. He might react violently to the shock she was going to give him. She could understand that. Did she dare to hope he would be so elated that what she must tell him wouldn't matter? Would that be asking the impossible?

With lazy, contented movements, he pushed back his chair and told her, "A man could easily get spoiled by such royal treatment."

She laughed softly and replied, "I'm trying to do just that. I . . . I never want you to leave me." She wanted to murmur that she was afraid he would do just that.

When they were seated, André prevented any further delay. "Angelique, something is wrong.

I've known it since I saw you when I first got up. Tell me, my darling, for I'm such a happy man I feel I could conquer the world if I had to."

"I'm very upset, André. You saw Fancy leave earlier. She'd come to tell me farewell. She is leaving Nicholas and returning to Natchez." She told him in detail what had transpired between the two since Nicholas's return to New Orleans.

When she finished speaking, André looked angry. His brow rose in a frown. He, of all people, knew how Nick had labored all those weeks in Natchez to prepare Dubonnet for the time when he'd return with Fancy and present her new home to her. What had that all been for if he wasn't going to fight for her? Christ, he loved the young lady with all his heart and soul. To this, André would swear.

"And Fancy told you the rascal hasn't been home?"

"That is what she told me. Oh, André, we've got to do something."

"And we will! I can't understand the young fool though. Damned if I can! How could he let the woman he loves slip away from him?"

Words poured out before she realized she was speaking. Her impulsive words surprised her. "The same way you did, André, when you were a young, handsome rascal like Nick." She took a deep breath before going on. "Nick is his father's son. I'm surprised that you never questioned the startling similarity, the closeness you two always

472

shared from the time he was a mere tot."

André's face froze as he stared at her, disbelief etched on his features. He stammered and his voice cracked with emotion, "What in the hell are you saying, woman? I've never known you to be a prankster!"

A puzzling calm washed over Angelique now that she'd revealed the secret she'd kept hidden so long. "Sit down, André. I've much to tell you. I speak the truth. Nick is your son, not Alain's, and I am his mother, not Monique. One glorious night of love, like the one we shared last night, created this love child of ours, Nicholas."

"Holy Christ!" he moaned, sinking down beside her. He felt that he'd been dealt a might blow in the pit of the stomach.

"You remember the sixteen-year-old girl you met so long ago as Monique's friend from Baton Rouge? I had lived at my wealthy aunt and uncle's plantation. Monique and I had grown up together and been friends, regardless of the fact that Monique was the little princess, while I was . . . a relative. When Monique married your brother she was very lonely here in New Orleans and so I'd visit her every now and then."

André confessed, "I'll never forget the first time I saw you. I thought you were the most beautiful thing I'd ever laid eyes on. I still do, Angelique."

"It was that way for us both, André. Like a bolt of lightning striking! That night during carnival when we . . . Well, you know what happened that night. But you returned to Natchez to marry the girl you were engaged to, and I returned to Baton Rouge. I realized too late that I carried your child . . . Nicholas. When I confessed my dilemma to Monique, we plotted what has been our secret for all these years. Oh, Alain knew. He helped."

Dear God, how the years rolled back. André recalled, as if it were yesterday, coming to New Orleans for one last bachelor's folly before marrying Yvonne's and Daniel's mother. Alain, his older brother, had married the beautiful Monique two years earlier, and he remembered teasing him about the fact that he'd not got his wife pregnant after two years. Now, Angelique was telling him that Alain had been in on this charade. He had a son he'd not known was his all these years.

"We were all so young, but our plan worked so well. I was almost three months pregnant when they took me back to Baton Rouge to stay while Monique and Alain made their tour of the Continent and the East. When Nicholas was born I assumed the name of Dubose, as far as the doctor was concerned. When Alain and Monique finally came back to New Orleans, they were the parents of a month-old son. Their parentage was never questioned by anyone. A year after Nicholas's birth I married Philippe Rocheleau here in New Orleans. He was a friend of Alain's and much older than I."

Angelique searched André's face for some hint

of what he was feeling, but it revealed nothing. So she continued to reveal the facts from the past. "Our marriage was brief. Philippe's untimely death made me a widow after two years. He had a bad heart and we had no children. Monique allowed me all the time I wanted with my son. In fact, she continued to travel extensively with Alain and she was glad that I took charge of Nicholas. That arrangement formed a bond between Nicholas and me, one that has endured throughout the years. You can see why I've always considered myself a very lucky woman."

André's green eyes danced over her lovely face, and his voice was mellow when he asked, "And you never married again, did you?"

"No, André. I shared a part of Nicholas's life, and he was so like you, André. As I said before, I wondered many times if you had suspected the truth."

Still flooded with overwhelming amazement, André shook his head. In almost a whisper, he muttered, "I find it so hard to conceive that Alain would have a part in all this."

"Alain was protecting the great Dubose name from the slightest scent of scandal. You should know that, André. The family name is everything to Alain; it was even when he was the young businessman. And he was so enamored with his new bride he would have done anything to please her. One other thing which Monique confided in me influenced him. When Monique was not with

475

child after their first year of marriage, Alain was alarmed that they might never have any children. To have Nicholas, a son, filled a need for Alain."

Her tale told, Angelique sat back. Now, she would find out whether she had destroyed her chance for happiness. André was so silent an eerie chill shot through her body, but she sat proudly, determined to face whatever might happen. She offered no excuses for what she and Monique had done nor did she regret having done it. Nicholas had made it worthwhile.

Andrés tanned hand reached across to take hers. Slowly their eyes locked. A moment passed before he spoke. "*Ma petite amie*, you should hate me for what I've done to you, but I know you don't. Instead, you've given me the most wonderful gift of all . . . your devoted love that's stood the test of time and the finest son a man could ever want." There was a mist in his green eyes as he continued. "If you could but know how many times I've wished that Nicholas were mine and how I envied Alain. Dear God, Angelique . . . I'm so damned happy I'm scared!" He clasped her in his arms and kissed her tenderly. Their laughter mingled with tears of joy, and when they finally broke their embrace, he teased her, a glint of mischief in his eyes. "We've got to get married at once or history will repeat itself."

Angelique gave a delighted laugh. "Oh, André, I wouldn't mind at all, but what would our children think?"

"I couldn't care less, my darling! Right now, I feel twenty again." He took her in his arms again and made ardent love to her.

Nicholas was his son!

Chapter Forty-three

Her will power and strength were ebbing by the time Fancy boarded the *Bayou Queen*. The final act of bidding farewell to New Orleans and Nick Dubose had not been something she could prepare herself for, so by the time she secluded herself in her cabin, she felt weary and drained in body and spirit. She had no desire to stand by the rail of the side-wheeler and survey the sights as she traveled up the Mississippi River to Natchez.

Disenchantment consumed her. Was it only last autumn that she'd traveled southward with the man she loved more than life itself? How golden was that day! What a child she'd been then! Now she realized just how naïve she'd been when Nick married her. She'd always cherish the memory of those autumn days, regardless of what the future held for her.

Now, spring was emerging, and with spring

came new life. Within her, there was a new life, the child of the love she and Nick had shared. Knowing she must face life without Nick, especially since the child existed within her, was devastating. She flung herself across the bunk and gave way to tears. Dear God, what had possessed her to scream out that she didn't want him anymore that night in the library? She wanted him more than anything in the world.

How foolish she'd been to allow herself to be swept into Yvonne's conniving hands that night. Now, it was too late for regret and remorse. She had left New Orleans and Nick.

She urged herself to get a grip on herself and to think about what awaited her up that muddy, wide river. Perhaps, there she'd find a solution. At Dubonnet perhaps she'd find the strength to put her life together after the overwhelming impact Nicholas Dubose had had on it.

Slowly she rose from the bunk and dried the tears on her cheeks. She smelled the familiar, sweet fragrance that wafted from the banks of the river. Night-blooming jasmine grew wild along the water's edge, and its scent permeated the cabin. She crossed to the porthole which stood ajar.

Through the darkness of the night she could see a small flicker of light, probably some shanty back in the swampy bayou. Something urged her to go out on deck, and she moved thoughtfully through the cabin door. She was still very preoccupied as she strolled to the rail and lingered there.

She'd known love in a shanty and a mansion. She knew it didn't matter where one lived. Wealth and riches did not assure one of happiness.

She seemed to be the only person strolling the deck, and that was just as well as far as Fancy was concerned. The night was quiet and pleasant. The air was still. Fancy heard only the sounds the boat made as it moved through the water, and she did not notice a figure moving slowly toward her.

Uncertainty prodded him. Was that Fancy standing there? When the moonlight focused on her he knew it had to be Fancy because he saw her rich velvet brown hair. Never had he seen a more gorgeous mane of thick, glossy brown hair on a woman.

He'd lost his heart to this girl many months ago, and the ring he'd intended to give her remained unworn. He found it inconceivable that the hot-headed, jealous Frenchman was allowing her to travel alone. Remembering his last encounter with Nicholas, he approached her carefully.

"Fancy . . . Fancy Dubose," he said as he walked up behind her. She whirled swiftly, surprised to hear her name.

"Jason? Dear Lord, it is you," she exclaimed. His familiar, smiling face was a welcome sight at this particular moment. She reached out her hands and he took them in his and reached forward to kiss her cheek.

Christ, she was more beautiful than ever! He had to confess that marriage to Nick had brought her a sophisticated beauty that fairly took his breath away.

"Nick in the cabin? I find it hard to believe that he'd let you out of his sight," Jason remarked, still holding her gloved hand and admiring her stunning new beauty .

"Nick isn't with me, Jason."

"I see. You going to Natchez?" he drawled, wondering why she was traveling alone. He didn't believe Nick would allow Fancy to do that. However, he sensed her assurance and self-reliance.

"Yes, I am, and I must assume that you are going home from New Orleans?"

"That's right. I went there to settle some business for a client. New Orleans is nice for a day or two, but Natchez is always a welcome sight to me." He laughed lightly.

Her soft voice had a serious tone when she openly confessed, "Well, it will be to me too." His lawyer's instincts told Jason that something had gone awry between Nick and her. "You going to Alita's?"

"Yes, I am."

"Well, she'll be thrilled to see you. I don't have to tell you how glad I am to see you again, Fancy. In fact I invite you to dine with me for old times' sake."

"For old times' sake, I accept." She smiled at him. For the moment she forgot about Nick and enjoyed the pleasant company of Jason Carew.

* * *

Captain Bronson raised a skeptical brow at the sight of Nicholas Dubose's wife in the company of the flashy, good-looking Natchez lawyer at dinner. But he couldn't say anything. Mister Carew had traveled on the line before and the captain had heard that he was quite a womanizer. He felt a certain loyalty toward the Dubose family and so he did not like to see Madame Dubose in Carew's company. While Fancy and Jason dined he handed her an unexpected surprise about Alita. "You did not know? Well, I just assumed that she'd written you, Fancy."

"No, not a word! I wonder what changed her mind. Everything was set for the spring when she and André visited New Orleans a few weeks ago."

"I can't say, but I can tell you she's not crestfallen about it. So I'd say she was the one who called it off." He could say no more for he was bound to keep the rest of what he knew confidential. Alita Dumaine would have to tell it to her.

By the time Jason escorted her to her cabin he had learned nothing more about her and Nick. She had given him no hint as to why she was making this trip alone. But, encouraged nonetheless, he told her good night and remarked, "I hope we'll be seeing each other while you're in Natchez."

"Of course we will, Jason. I thank you for a most enjoyable dinner. Good night," she said, and suddenly she was gone.

André Dubose bore no malice toward his

brother Alain for keeping from him the startling fact that Nicholas was his son, nor did he feel ill will toward Monique. As for Angelique Rocheleau, he loved her even more for revealing the truth to him. Dear God, if he blamed anyone it must be himself for being so irresponsible and for being such a reckless rogue in his youth.

However, now that he knew the truth, he had no intention of going on with the lie. Whether or not his decision sat well with his brother and his sister-in-law, he must do what he could to right the wrong he'd committed so many years ago.

The first thing on his agenda was marriage to his beloved Angelique. Nothing was going to delay that any longer. This time when he left New Orleans Angelique would accompany him to Magnolia. Dear Lord, if only he'd taken her with him years ago Nicholas would have been born at Magnolia. André regretted the loveless years he'd spent with the woman he'd married. Misery had been their lot from the very beginning. What a terrible waste it had been for both of them!

Three days after Fancy's visit to Angelique's home, Madame Rocheleau found her life changing so fast that she was giddy. She'd never realized what a dynamo André could be when he set his mind on something. Yet, something marred the newfound happiness in her own life.

Finally, she confessed to André that they could not leave New Orleans without finding their son. "We must, André! If we have to search every corner of the city. I know he's here somewhere. We've got to help those two save what they're about to throw away. We can't let that happen."

"I know, Angelique. I was thinking the same thing when I spoke to Alain today and he could give me no hint of Nick's whereabouts. I'll find that young rascal though. I promise you that. At dawn's first light I shall start out, and I won't return until I have him in tow. All right?" He pulled her to him and kissed her tenderly. This was a vow he was determined to keep.

As the couple ascended the winding stairway a short time later, another woman invaded his thoughts. Secretly, he sang the praises of Alita Dumaine, and he wondered if he should confess her part in all this to Angelique?

He'd ponder that course later, he told himself, for at the moment he had more pressing matters on his mind. They hardly included Alita.

It was a bittersweet occasion for Alita Dùmaine when Fancy arrived in the escort of her lawyer, Jason Carew. Although utterly surprised and confused, the very sight of Fancy delighted her and the excited, dumbfounded Dahlia, but knowing Nick's plans, Alita was aware that Fancy's sudden appearance in Natchez did not blend with them.

That first evening should have been a joyous reunion for the two women, but the image of Nicholas Dubose clouded it. By the time they'd said their good nights and each had retired to her bedroom,

Alita was feeling quite frustrated. How could she help these two people so dear to her heart? There had to be some answer, for she knew the love they felt for each other — a love so rare it could not be dismissed.

Long after she'd gone to bed her thoughts lingered on Fancy and Nick. It was obvious that something had prevented them from discussing Dubonnet. Fancy did not even know that André had returned to New Orleans with Nick.

Nick had been in such high spirits when he'd left to return to her, yet obviously this horrible misunderstanding must have taken place as soon as he'd arrived. How sad!

Alita had felt this wasn't the time to discuss Dubonnet, but she had explained her reason for not marrying André. "Perhaps, Fancy my dear, you can find the answer you seek here as I did in New Orleans. I only had to see the two of them together to know that it was Angelique, not me, André loved."

Fancy had never thought about that possibility, so Alita explained that they'd known one another years before. "When we came back I told him of my decision not to marry him and why I wouldn't. A friendship remains where André and I are concerned, but marriage would have been a horrible, horrible mistake. I know now that was what caused my apprehension. You see, dear, if it had been right there would have been no hesitation on my part. Something was trying to warn me." She laughed flippantly. "Maybe, my darling Henri from up above, eh?"

Although she said this in jest, Fancy knew Alita was quite serious. She recalled the evenings when Alita had told her about her beloved Henri.

As Fancy laid her head on the soft silk pillow that night, in the same room she'd occupied before Nick Dubose had taken her away from Natchez as his new bride, she knew that as much as it had pained her to leave Nick and New Orleans she had had to do it.

Softly, she moaned out his name. "Come to me, Nick. Come to Natchez." To her, that could be their only salvation.

As one day drifted into a second and then a third, Fancy began to realize that the proud, arrogant Nicholas Dubose would not be coming to Natchez — and her. When the end of her first week in Natchez yielded no sight of him, Fancy became receptive to Jason Carew's visits and invitations although her decision met with Alita Dumaine's disapproval.

The feisty little Dahlia had observed Fancy being driven off in Monsieur Carew's fine new carriage. She, like her mistress, did not want to see Fancy become involved with Jason Carew. She remarked to Alita with obvious aversion, "That man ain't goin' to let any grass grow under his feet. No sir!"

With a scheming look on her face, Alita replied. "Well, Dahlia . . . we've just got to do something about this." She winked deviously at Dahlia.

Dahlia's face broke into a broad, approving smile. "Yes, *mam'selle*. We sure will have to do something." Turning around to attend to some chores, she swished her curvy hips provocatively as she went down the hall. "You just let me know what," she called back over her shoulder, a mischievous grin lighting up her own face.

"Oh, I will, Dahlia," Alita assured her cohort. She cared too much for Fancy to sit idly by and not make some kind of effort to help this stubborn, hardheaded couple. Dubonnet was the answer!

Chapter Forty-four

Alita felt no qualms over meddling in Fancy's affairs when she conspired with Dahlia while Fancy rested. Alita had seen a new boldness in Jason Carew when he'd escorted Fancy back to the house. It was urgent that she get her out to Dubonnet, away from the city and Jason Carew if she hoped to prevent a disaster before Nicholas Dubose could get here. After all, Fancy was a very sensuous woman, and anyone might yield to temptation at certain times.

She handed the message to Dahlia, saying, "Tell Jasper that he is to give this to Captain Branston who is going back to New Orleans on the *Bayou Queen*. Be sure he gives it to no one else, Dahlia."

"Yes, mam'selle . . . I'll caution him," Dahlia assured her.

At dinner, Alita found it easy to whet Fancy's desire to go out to Dubonnet the following morning, especially with the delightful reward of seeing her beloved Raoul and Chessie. The irony was that Dubonnet was now Fancy's and if she but knew the tedious effort Nick had put into perfecting every foot of the house during his weeks in Natchez she would know he loved her with all his heart. This terrible thing that had happened between them could only have been the result of the volatile tempers of two spirited, independent people like Nicholas Dubose and Fancy.

Guileless and unsuspecting, Fancy chattered away about her afternoon with Jason Carew. It was obvious to Alita that her spirits had been lifted by Jason's company. The two women dined by candlelight in the intimate coziness of the smaller dining area. The food was delicious. Claudine had prepared beef medallions surrounded with mushrooms and peas, and the fine red wine served with their dinner definitely relaxed Fancy.

Alita listened as Fancy told her about the wonderful afternoon she'd had and about Jason's understanding and comforting words. What a conniving rascal he is, Alita thought.

"I guess there was a side to Nick I never saw, from what Jason confessed to me this afternoon," Fancy sighed.

"Oh?" Alita raised a skeptical brow. She saw right through Jason's scheme.

"Do you know Nick raged into Jason's office one day and was ready to beat him up?"

"Well, did Jason also tell you what Nick was so

irate about? I can recall my dear Henri's hot French temper exploding many times." Alita laughed and shrugged her shoulders in an off-handed manner.

"But Jason was his best friend here in Natchez at the time." Fancy frowned.

"*Ma petite*, Friendships . . . the very best . . . do not grant unlimited privileges. Do you see what I mean?"

In a hesitating voice, Fancy stammered, "I . . . I guess so."

Alita hastily announced her plans to depart for Dubonnet, and Fancy's exuberance over seeing Raoul and Chessie more than pleased Alita. They would leave very early in the morning, Alita decided.

There were hints of spring everywhere as they rolled along the country road. At every bend as familiar landscapes came into view, Fancy felt her excitement mount. She was experiencing the overwhelming exhilaration of coming "home." Every mile that brought them closer to Dubonnet confirmed it. She turned to Alita and exclaimed, "I still say this is the most beautiful place I know!"

Madame Dumaine had never seen a face more radiantly beautiful than Fancy's was that bright sunshiny morning. More than ever, she knew her decision about Dubonnet was right. It should be Fancy's home to cherish throughout the years. She envisioned the children of Fancy and Nick running and playing on those spacious manicured grounds.

"I'm glad you feel this way about Dubonnet. I guess you've felt that way since we first came out here after you'd come to live with me. Isn't that so?"

"It was instant love, Madame Dumaine," Fancy replied, a bright smile gleaming on her face. She suddenly realized she could easily have been speaking about her feeling for Nick, too. The moment she'd gazed up at his tanned handsome face and his devastatingly, flashing green eyes, it had been instant love. Alita noticed that Fancy suddenly sank into quiet thoughtfulness, but it did not last. As soon as she spotted the gray-haired Raoul sitting on a bench Fancy sat up, as excited as if she were a child again. "There's Raoul! Oh, God love him!"

Alita smiled, pleased at Fancy's joy in being reunited with the black man who'd been so dear to her.

Sometimes it is not possible to give peace and serenity to those you love, Alita mused, but perhaps she had been able to give them to Fancy Dubose. Here in this place the girl had always loved she'd find it.

Oh, the sweet haven of Dubonnet! The warmth of it already embraced Fancy. As soon as the carriage halted, Fancy raced to Raoul who was struggling to rise from a wooden bench.

A broad grin appeared on the black man's face

as he mumbled, "My sweet child! That's my sweet Fancy! Prettier than any rose ever I seen."

By the time he'd managed to get to a standing position with the support of his cane, Fancy's arms were clasping his shoulders. "Oh, Raoul! My dear Raoul!" she cried, tears cascading down her cheeks.

His weathered, wrinkled hands patted her shoulders—he was too overcome with emotion to speak—and tears ran down his face. His chest had swelled with pride at the sight of her as she'd rushed toward him. Such a beautiful young lady! No wonder that fine Monsieur Dubose had lost his heart to her. Yes, sir, Fancy had done herself proud. She had herself one fine husband.

Fancy's reunion with Chessie was an emotional one too, and tears were shed anew. These were tears of joy, unlike the ones she'd shed over Nick.

There was one thing she had not considered when she'd anticipated coming to Dubonnet and that was the overwhelming essence of Nicholas Dubose that permeated the place. It was so strong she felt giddy when she gazed toward the woods.

That evening in the dining room she envisioned him sitting across the table from her as he had that night when he'd dined with her and Alita.

Later as she lay awake for hours staring out the window at the quiet blackness, she remembered the picnic by the small pond. Her life had been changed that day when she'd succumbed to the forceful charms of Nicholas Dubose. Now she relived every vivid minute of the afternoon when she'd yielded herself to him so willingly and eagerly. The memory of his strong, muscled arms holding her made her yearn for him to be beside her. She knew the touch and feel of his body so intimately.

Her hands traced the slight roundness of her stomach, reminding her that a part of him was with her. She might have left him in New Orleans but she could not rid herself of him, even here. She held her hands as if she were cuddling the child within her. That seemed to comfort her. She relaxed and sleep came.

In the bright morning light of the new day, Fancy noticed new additions to the bedroom she'd paid not attention to the night before. The changes were recent too. A new armoire had been added, and a small dressing table and bench had been replaced by a more elaborate table and a beautifully upholstered chair. The soft rich velvet on the back and seat of the chair was a robin's-egg blue.

"Why that dear, sweet lady," Fancy sighed, noticing that her favorite perfumes now stood atop the dressing table in exquisite cut-crystal bottles. Near them lay a silver brush and comb, obviously for her use. Beside these was a jewelry chest with mother-of-pearl inlay on the lid. How tastefully Alita had redecorated the room. Fancy would have to compliment her on these changes when she went downstairs.

Curious now, Fancy ambled across the room to

the door that led into the little sitting room adjoining the bedroom. What wonders had her friend created in that little room, she wondered? It had been so cozy when she'd stayed here before.

Surprisingly, the door was securely locked.

Shocked by the lateness of the hour Fancy dressed and went downstairs to join Alita for a late breakfast. Perhaps her inability to sleep for such a long time after she'd retired or perhaps the fresh country air had made her sleep so late.

When she entered the small, informal dining room of the house, there was no one around. She was about to summon one of the servants when Raoul came limping into the room.

"Good mornin', Miss Fancy. You sleep good?" he asked. Chessie trailed behind him carrying a tray bearing steaming hot coffee.

"Too well obviously." She smiled. "Good morning, Chessie." She took a seat while Chessie poured her a cup of the coffee. "You look like you rested just fine," Chessie remarked, adoring the girl with her eyes as she moved around the table.

"Madame Dumaine . . . where is she? Has she already had her breakfast?" Unless she had changed her routine, Alita Dumaine was a late riser.

"Oh, miss . . . she ate over an hour ago," Chessie responded. "Said to tell you just to enjoy yourself and she'd get back out here day after tomorrow."

Puzzled and confused, Fancy mumbled, "She

mentioned nothing about going back to Natchez to me." Chessie and Raoul exchanged glances behind Fancy's back. Chessie gave Raoul a warning sign and a shake of her head.

Shrugging Fancy's remark off with a casual air, Raoul replied, "Well, you in good hands and Madame Dumaine knows that." A warm smile creased his face.

Fancy returned his smile. "Of course, I am . . . the very best." She gave no more thought to why Madame Dumaine had left. Instead, she joined Raoul in a slow stroll around the grounds after she finished breakfast.

It was a glorious day. The azure sky was splattered with white fluffy clouds that looked like giant cotton bolls.

"Oh, look, Raoul . . . a crocus blooming already," Fancy exclaimed, pointing to a spot of purple a few feet away.

"Sure is. There's another one right over there too."

Raoul directed her eyes to another purple blossom jutting up through the grass. Sweet memories returned of the strolls she and Raoul had taken when she was just a small child. She remembered him pointing out the wonders of nature in the woods. Then because his ailing leg demanded it, Raoul suggested they sit down on a nearby bench.

"Those little purple flowers match the little ones on your frock, Miss Fancy."

He plucked one and tucked it in her hair and

they both laughed. He was right, Fancy noted, looking down at the sprigged muslin gown with little purple flowers scattered over the cream-colored background.

"God been so good to us, Miss Fancy. Look at that beautiful blue sky and those pretty white clouds. There's all this green, green grass and the sweet-smelling flowers to enjoy. Hear that mocking bird across the way? Mercy, it's a pretty day, and here I got you sittin' by my side again after all this time." He chuckled.

Fancy's heart swelled with loving warmth for the old gray-haired black man. Her arm went around his bent shoulders and she hugged him.

"I love you, Raoul. What a shame everyone couldn't be like you!"

"There you go with all that fancy talkin'. No wonder your mom named you Fancy." He tried to make a light-hearted jest to stop the tears that were about to flow. "Well, missy, there's a lot of good people around. You jest gotta' look for the good instead of the bad. See this high-tone cane here. Your good husband gave me that."

Fancy surveyed the expensive cane he proudly exhibited for her appraisal. "Nick? Nick gave you that?"

"He did. He's one fine gentleman. You are a lucky woman to have such a fine man, Miss Fancy."

She stiffened, knowing he had no knowledge that she'd left Nick. But then how could he know?

In an effort to change the subject, she quickly declared, "This is the most beautiful place I've ever been."

"It surely is that," Raoul remarked. She didn't fool him for a minute . . . the little minx! She didn't want to hear him singing the praises of Monsieur Nick but she was going to.

"Well, it is your — It is a peaceful place," Raoul stammered. Lord, he'd almost put his foot in his mouth. He could almost hear Chessie chiding him in that particular way of hers, saying, "Old man, you just about did it!" He'd almost said Dubonnet was Fancy's now . . thanks to Monsieur Nick. He and Chessie had been informed that morning that Fancy had left her husband, and it had been a tremendous acting job for them to hide the sadness in their hearts about this development. This was the reason he'd wanted to stroll with Fancy. Like Alita Dumaine, Raoul intended to make Fancy see the big mistake she was making if she let Monsieur Nick slip away. No sir, he'd not let that happen!

Shortly, Fancy was to find that out.

Chapter Forty-five

Fog obscured the view from her window as Angelique peered out at the street in front of her house, but the light misting rain had stopped. The dark, dismal day had been endless. As she awaited André's return, she had to keep reminding herself that he'd not said when he'd come back.

He'd vowed to find Nicholas and bring him back. That was the day before yesterday when he'd set out on his quest. Obviously he was finding it no simple undertaking, Angelique concluded after a day and a night had gone by.

Many questions had been answered during this time. The news of the marriage to André had stunned Alain and Monique, but once the shock had subsided, they'd offered their congratulations and best wishes. Today, Monique had paid a visit, and Angelique had told her about the revelation she'd made to André before they'd married.

"He is most serious about telling Nicholas the truth, Monique," she'd confessed to her lifelong friend, apprehensive about her reaction.

Cool and calm, Monique surprised Angelique when she remarked casually, "I knew it when I came today. André told Alain the other day what he was going to do. What could either of us say? Perhaps, it is long overdue. How many friendships have stood the test of time like ours, eh?"

They then collapsed into one another's arms, and Angelique was filled with gladness that Monique understood how she and André felt.

The grandfather clock chimed seven when Angelique noticed two men riding up the drive. When they entered she saw a bedraggled, weary-looking pair. Each gentleman's green eyes were bloodshot and each gave her a wan smile. André's eyes were mellow and warm, sending her the message that everything was all right. As worn and bone-tired as he was, Nick embraced her and whispered in her ear, "I should have known. Later, we have much to talk about, but I must find a bed or fall to the floor, my beloved Angelique . . . mother."

Angelique did not press for more, but André told her later as they lay in bed where he'd finally found their son. Stubborn determination had sent him to practically every tavern, inn, and gambling hall in the city of New Orleans, yet he'd found no clue to Nick's whereabouts.

As Angelique lay by her new husband listening

intensely to his tale, she realized the invisible bond that had existed between André and Nick throughout the years. Then suddenly he straightened up in bed and pushed the pillows behind his back.

"Tell me something, Angelique . . . have you ever had an idea strike you like a bolt of lightning?"

"I have . . . many times," she answered him.

"Well, so it was with me when I grew tired of sleuthing around this city. I recalled Nick telling me about a place down by the swamps where he'd gone as a youth of sixteen when he was mad at Alain. With all that had happened between him and Fancy I figured he had to be mad at the world so I rode out there. There he was, sure enough, unshaven and nursing a magnificent hangover he'd gotten from drowning his sorrows with whiskey. So I spent the night with him in the shanty, and we had our father and son talk. I hope you don't mind that I sought to do this alone."

"I think I understand, André. You feared how he would react?" She knew he wished to spare her any hurt.

"I did, after I saw the state he was already in. If he was going to explode I wanted to be the one to receive the brunt of it. I am the one who deserved that . . . not you, my darling."

His words were most precious to her, and Angelique's hand went to her husband's cheek as she sought to soothe him. "We were both so young, André. So very, very young."

He kissed her tenderly. "Thank you, *ma petite amie*. I'm proud to say, though, we have a fine son. The night in that old swamp shack will always be a part of me. We bared our souls as few fathers and sons ever do. When Nick is rested and the two of you talk, you will see for yourself what a wonderful young man we've created. I am proud to call him my son."

So it was on the next day, when Nick finally roused from his almost drugged sleep, that he and his mother had their talk. Angelique could not help noticing the lines around his eyes or the weight he'd lost during this self-imposed exile at the shack. Like Fancy, Nick had paid a painful price, but there was one more thing she felt compelled to talk to Nick about. She hesitated no longer. "Nicholas, Fancy carries your child. Perhaps you didn't know that, my son."

"She didn't tell me, but I was certain of that even before I left for Natchez to make a deal on Dubonnet. More than ever I wanted that place for us."

"Then, my son, you'd better not waste any more time. Nothing is worse than a lost love. You now know the terrible ache it leaves you with. But finding love is ecstasy . . . endless ecstasy. Go find yours, my son. It waits for you in Natchez with Fancy. Don't let it slip away from you. You might not be as lucky as André and I were."

His familiar broad grin appeared, and his eyes flashed a brilliant green.

"I have no intention of letting her get away from

me." As he bent over to kiss Angelique, he declared. "I love you, Mother, but then I always have."

Then her son was gone, and Angelique's heart swelled with joy for she knew everything was going to be just fine. As she'd watched him stride out of the room, she had realized nothing would prevent him from getting what he wanted.

When Nicholas left Angelique's house, he was a man driven by urgency. His destination was Natchez—and his darling Fancy. However, he had to make one detour, and that, too, was for a very definite purpose. He was leaving New Orleans for good, going home to Dubonnet. Sure of himself and his aim, he would not allow Fancy to deny him or their future together.

When he rushed through the front door of the Dubose mansion and instructed old Nat to accompany him upstairs, the butler followed obediently although he wondered why the young man had requested him to do so.

Nat's silent question was answered when Nicholas started tossing clothes into a piece of luggage and hastily ordered him to pack certain items in the room. Old Nat frowned and scratched his head in confusion.

"You leaving this house, Monsieur Nicholas?"

"That I am, Nat. I'm going to be living in Natchez. I am relying on you to see that my clothes and the things I've asked you to pack are shipped on the next boat after I leave this afternoon."

Shuffling around the room at his slow pace, Nat shook his head and mumbled, "Sure gonna' miss you, Monsieur Nicholas. Sure am."

Nick laughed, "Oh, you aren't going to be rid of me forever, Nat. I'll visit from time to time, but Natchez will be our home."

This seemed to appease the butler who'd known Nicholas so many years. "Well, it will be nice when you and your fine lady come to visit." Nat stood for a moment staring up at the portrait of Fancy painted by Doreen back in December. "I'll see that this is packed most carefully, *monsieur*."

Nick turned to see what Nat was talking about. "By all means, Nat. I have a special place where I intend to put it at Dubonnet."

When he'd changed his clothes and snapped his bag shut, he did not linger in the room. He bade Nat goodbye and rushed down the stairs. As he started across the walled courtyard, he felt no inclination to look back, but a sharp cry stopped him. He broke into a deep, throaty laugh and turned around.

"What the hell! Come on, old boy . . . off you go, eh?" He picked up the cage holding Argo and marched through the iron gate into the street. The parrot was quiet and content as Nick carried it down the street toward the wharf.

The sight of Nicholas Dubose walking along the wharf with a bag in one hand and a parrot's cage in the other resulted in a few raised eyebrows.

The departure time of the *Memphis Belle* was less

than an hour away as Nick arrived at the loading wharf. Passengers were already boarding the boat. Captain Barton caught sight of Nick and knew he'd have to quarter him in one of the cabins. Fortunately this trip was not solidly booked. The captain was greatly relieved that he wouldn't have to make some fast changes in accommodations.

As Nick weaved and swerved by the last stack of cargo piled on the pier for loading, a soft hissing sound stopped him. "Psssst, Monsieur Dubose . . . over here." Nick turned, searching the wall of wooden crates and jute sacks. A tiny slip of a girl peered around them. Nick raised his brow in a frown for her strange bruised face was not known to him.

"Me? You speaking to me?" He moved back amid the crates, for the very sight of her provoked pity in him. It was obvious the girl had been beaten.

"Oh, please, monsieur . . . I know no other soul in this city to turn to but you, or maybe your sweet wife."

"I beg your pardon, *mademoiselle*, but I've never laid eyes on you before in my life. As for my wife, I can't imagine how you know her," he curtly retorted.

"Please, I know how this must sound to you. It was I who saw you, but you did not see me that night at Herman Van Meter's. I was a maid and I tended to your beautiful wife. I delighted in seeing you beat that Monsieur Martel so deservedly.

504

Your . . . your wife was so very nice during the brief time I served her. I . . . I know I am assuming a lot, but I felt she could and would help me." Tears were dampening the ugly blue and purple bruises on her face. Nick knew instinctively the girl was in a situation that had made her desperate.

"What do you need, *mademoiselle*? Money, perhaps?"

"I . . . I was hoping your wife could use my services as a maid or that she would help get me away from New Orleans . . . away from that horrible maniac, Van Meter. Oh, please, *monsieur*!"

Nick was silent for a minute, and then he asked, "Maid, eh? Van Meter beat you like that?"

"*Oui, Monsieur Dubose.* He is a terrible beast. That night I feared he might pick your beautiful wife for his prey, but thank God, that did not happen. I saw many terrible things in that house, I can tell you. I saw the results of your beating the gentleman . . . his friend, Martel, and oh, how I delighted at the sight of him. I . . . I tried to see to your wife, but they said she was gone."

Nick grinned, "What is your name, girl?"

"Colette, *monsieur.* Colette Barbeau."

"Well, Colette Barbeau how would you like to be my wife's personal maid and go with me now to Natchez?"

"Oh, please, *monsieur* . . . please do not tease me if it isn't true. My life is in jeopardy if Monsieur Van Meter catches me."

"You have nothing to fear, *mademoiselle*, from

Monsieur Van Meter. Come . . . we go to catch a boat for Natchez, eh?" He gestured for her to accompany him, and with an eager nod of her head, she followed like a dutiful child, excited and eager.

It was a strange entourage that went up the gangplank of the *Memphis Belle*. Nicholas Dubose was now followed by the tiny, limping girl who carried the parrot's cage. The captain, spying this new addition sighed and wondered where Dubose had picked up such a little ragamuffin.

Chapter Forty-six

Nick sauntered along the deck of the *Memphis Belle* which seemed to be deserted except for him. He'd just left Captain Barton's quarters where the two men had shared a few shots of whiskey and a couple of laughs. He was amused by the thoughts that had run through the old captain's mind when he'd come aboard with the girl. It must have been a comical scene, but Nick had easily explained to the captain how it had come about.

This was another of the many times in his life when impulse and instinct ruled him, he guessed. Until now, he'd given no thought to how this situation was going to look when he arrived at Dubonnet. But he'd be damned if he could have left that poor, pleading girl on the wharf at the mercy of a brute like Van Meter. One fleeting glance at Van Meter that night he'd marched into his house in search of Fancy had aroused instant dislike in

507

Nick. Not for a minute did he doubt the tale little Colette had told him. Whatever obstacle she might present at Dubonnet he would work out, he told himself.

As he walked by the cabin where the girl was quartered he heard Argo squawk, and he stopped in his tracks. He could not believe what his ears heard and his eyes saw. That old cantankerous parrot was taking crumbs from the gentle girl as though she were an old friend. In a soft voice she prompted him to say, "*Merci*." Acting as docile as he could, Argo mimicked his new friend saying, "*Merr . . . ci!*"

Nick shook his head in disbelief and quietly walked away, wishing not to disturb their play. Obviously Argo was favorably impressed with little Colette, and the old parrot's instinct for people was uncanny. He recalled Fancy's first encounter with the bird. Argo's reaction to her had been instantaneous as it was now with little Colette.

He headed for his own quarters, knowing sleep would escape him on this night. Like a child anticipating Christmas morning, he churned with excitement over what tomorrow would bring his way.

For Nick, the *Memphis Belle* moved through the muddy waters at a snail's pace, and the familiar bluffs of Natchez seemed to be just beyond every bend of the wide river. He fumed with impatience.

When that final turn of the river was made and he caught sight of the high cliffs rising straight ahead, he heaved a deep sigh and grinned.

He was not aware that Colette had come up behind him until she said, "That is Natchez, Monsieur Dubose?"

"Yes, Colette," he said taking notice of the girl's appearance. Her bruises were still there to see, but she'd obviously found some way to mend the torn part of her simple muslin frock and her hair was neatly combed. Nick still looked upon her as a pathetic little thing.

"You are most anxious to get there. I can see it in your eyes. I know your beautiful wife must be as anxious to see you. She was such a nice lady . . . much nicer than the other two that night. I attended all of them."

"I'd agree on that, Colette. You see one is my sister and the other is my cousin." He laughed.

A startled look came on the girl's face when she realized her faux pas. "Oh, forgive me, *monsieur!*"

"Ah, but, *mademoiselle*, you speak the truth. We are in agreement." The broad friendly grin on his handsome face helped Colette to relax, but his smile quickly faded and he turned from her. It had not dawned on him until now, but the new turn in his life had made Yvonne his half sister. Denise and Doreen were not his sisters at all, but his cousins. That was going to take awhile to get used to.

Nevermore would he worry about the mysteries that had plagued him all his life. The shadows were gone now, and Nick knew that was better. So many things seemed simple now. He knew why he felt a closeness to the gentle Daniel although they were very different men. Daniel was, in fact, his half brother. Dear God, these changes still boggled his mind!

For all her womanly wiles and her attempts to entice him, Yvonne's charms had never whetted his appetite. That was hardly usual for the reckless, randy Nick he'd been before his marriage. He had wondered about that reluctance himself, for Yvonne had always been a very alluring girl, but something had always deterred him from seeking her favors. Abhorrence consumed him now as he thought about what he'd have done if he'd taken her to his bed . . . his own half sister!

The same little caravan that had attracted curious stares when it boarded the *Memphis Belle* now drew the attention of the people on the wharf when it disembarked at Natchez. Once again, the girl who wasn't five feet tall trailed the tall, towering Nicholas Dubose. She had taken full charge of the colorful Argo and was carrying his cage. His brilliant plumage—green, blue, red, and yellow—made him a rarity to those who'd never seen such a bird.

Perhaps no one was more curious than a fair-haired gentleman who happened to catch sight of the entourage. He spouted a stream of curse words as he realized he should have known all along that Nicholas Dubose would show up sooner or later. That arrogant Frenchman never allowed anything or anyone to stand in the way of what he wanted.

Jason Carew jerked the reins of the bay pulling his gig. A warning voice buzzed in his ear, telling him to forget Fancy now that Dubose was back in Natchez. It was futile to think that Fancy could ever be his. The last two weeks there had been a glimmer of hope that she might, and he'd even gotten the ring out of its resting place a couple of times. Again, he was at the point of offering it to her.

Now he tarried no longer, nor did he seek to greet his old friend, Nicholas. Instead, he sped on his way to see his new client, a prosperous Natchez planter. Fancy Dubose had to be forgotten — forever. He was finally convinced of that after seeing Nick.

The ride out to Dubonnet seemed as endless as the boat ride to Nick. Colette was the excited one now, and her eyes busily took in the strange countryside as they rolled along the dirt road. She was relieved to be a long, long way from the grasping paws of Herman Van Meter. For the present, that was enough for the girl. She gave no thought to what the future offered. At the moment just being safe was enough.

Dubonnet looked like paradise to Colette as they turned into the long graded drive. Indeed she had enjoyed the tranquil atmosphere that had prevailed as soon as they'd rolled past the outskirts of the busy port city. The wharves were a beehive of activity and the city streets were noisy and alive with the flow of people. Out here, it was different.

Cotton fields stretched away on either side of the road. She noticed a few laborers working in them as the carriage passed. Now that they'd slowed down to go up the drive, Colette viewed the fine brick two-story house for the first time. A few feet behind the main house was a small two-story building. The two structures were connected by a covered walkway. That had to be the servants' quarters, Colette figured.

The grounds boasted a generous array of shrubs, and tall oak trees provided shade.

It almost seemed unfair, Colette thought to herself, for a woman like Fancy Dubose to have such a magnificent home and such a dashing, handsome husband. Oh, to be in her shoes, Colette mused!

When the carriage came to a halt, Monsieur Dubose eagerly leaped down, forgetting about her completely. At the door he was met by a plum-dark black woman whose head was covered in a bright colored kerchief. They embraced like old friends, instead of master and servant. For a moment they whispered in hushed tones before Nick motioned Colette to come forward. She knew she was being explained to the black woman he'd embraced and she felt ill at ease as she joined them.

"This is Chessie, Colette. She has charge of everything here at Dubonnet, so I will let the two of you get acquainted. I have another matter to attend to." He turned, but did not enter the house.

"Come with me, child," the motherly Chessie said, nudging Colette through the door. Like

Nick, Chessie felt instant compassion for the frail-looking girl with the big black eyes and sad little face.

"The parrot, too?" Colette wanted to know.

"Lord a' mercy, I guess," Chessie muttered, puzzled as to what she was to do with that creature until she talked to Monsieur Nick. Somehow, she figured that might be a long time from now. The first thing he'd wanted to know was where Fancy was. Chessie just hoped that this one time Raoul wasn't at her side. As she waddled under the covered walkway with the new girl in tow, she was glad to see Raoul asleep under the umbrellalike branches of the weeping willow. She smiled, glad to know he was behaving himself for a change and staying off that bad leg of his.

Nick, too, had seen the sleeping Raoul, as he went to the barn to saddle up Domino. He didn't know the direction Fancy had chosen for her walk, and Chessie could not direct him. All she'd been able to say was that she'd seen Fancy leave the house with her wide-brimmed straw hat in her hands.

On horseback he figured he could cover the grounds much faster than if he set out walking, and he intended to be speedily reunited with his wife. Enough time had been wasted on petty arguments and misunderstandings — enough to last him a lifetime.

Once before, after an argument, Fancy had run away and they had lost their child. He would not risk letting this happen again. He led the horse out of the stable, mounted, and followed the lane across to the woods. If he knew Fancy she would make for the wooded area where a small creek angled off from the river. As he urged the horse into a trot his green eyes surveyed the landscape for any sight of her.

Fancy had no inkling that the man dominating her thoughts was so nearby as she lay resting by the edge of the creek. All she knew when she'd left the house was that she wanted to be alone. Even though she loved Raoul with all her heart, she did not want to be with him.

Her mind had been in turmoil the last two days and Dubonnet wasn't giving her the peace she wanted because Nick's haunting presence was with her day and night. Everywhere she turned she saw his mischievous handsome face smirking at her as if to say she'd never be rid of him no matter how far she traveled.

As she strolled down the path to the spot she sought, she swung her straw hat back and forth in a lackadaisical manner. Its long streamers caught on the tall grass so she halted her lazy pace, grumbled, and gave the hat a sharp yank.

Was everything and everyone against her? Somehow, it seemed so. Raoul's loyalty seemed to lie with Nicholas Dubose. Chessie gave her funny looks when she thought Fancy wasn't looking. Oh, she'd seen them, even though the dear old woman thought she was being very sly! Then there was

Alita's strange disappearance from Dubonnet. What was going on, she wondered? Well, she didn't know, but she did know she felt like an outcast.

When she came to the cozy spot at the edge of the woods and the familiar old fallen tree trunk still lay where it had many months ago, a pleasant feeling of contentment came over her. A little squirrel scampered out of one hollow end of the trunk, and she smiled, watching him rush away.

Wild ferns and violets were already sprouting on the grassy floor of the woods, so she sat down to pick some of the tiny purple violets. She recalled the day Claude Dubose had come upon her sleeping peacefully in this very same spot. She had been leaning against this same tree trunk. When Nick Dubose had come upon the scene of her struggle with Claude. He'd been her knight in shining armor. They'd even ridden away on his black charger, just as lovers did in fairy tales. She remembered vividly how her young virginal body had come alive with wild, wonderful sensations that had made her tingle.

His strong, powerful arms had encircled her waist as he'd held the reins of the horse, and their swaying bodies had brushed against each other as the huge beast trotted along the path. She could remember the heat of his lips so close to her cheek but not quite touching it. She had yearned for them to caress her. Dear God, how she'd wanted that! She'd known his very sensuous mouth could tease and delight her senses.

She moved back now to lean against the log, for all these sweet memories had suddenly calmed her. She shut her eyes and thought about that day. As they'd ridden along she had felt his broad chest against her back.

She sighed deeply as if his forceful presence was with her now. A rustling breeze suddenly seemed to invade the little clearing, sweeping her straw hat from her side and sending it scurrying across the ground. She watched the hat be swept by the gust of wind until something stopped it. Then her heart pounded wildly. She gasped, "Nick!"

He stood like some menacing giant, his black hair blowing over one side of his forehead, and his eyes danced with a wicked glint as they seared her, moving slowly form her head to her toes. He said nothing for a moment, just held her hat in one of his tanned hands. She did not speak either, but her eyes traveled the length of his firm, muscled body. His white shirt was partly open, revealing a small cluster of curly hair on his chest and his pants were molded to his hips and thighs. Excitement stirred in her. His overwhelming maleness and virility taunted her relentlessly. Did her face reveal her desire? she wondered.

In a deep, demanding voice Nick murmured, hardly moving his lips, "Come to me, Fancy. Come to me as you did a long, long time ago. As a child, so sweet and innocent." His face was solemn and expressionless.

She stood, with half-parted lips, and a mist gathered in her black eyes. He had known she was that twelve-year-old wide-eyed waif all along, she realized, recalling how she'd run into his waiting arms outside the warehouse in Memphis when she'd traveled with Raoul into the city. That had happened years ago and yet it seemed like yesterday.

She rushed to him, almost lunging into his waiting arms. "Oh, Nick . . . I guess I've loved you since that day you saved my old straw hat," she confessed, just before their lips met in a kiss. His hands and arms encircled her body, pressing her close to him and telling her of his urgent yearning and hunger. How good it felt to hold her again.

He released her lips long enough to whisper huskily in her ear, "From that day, Fancy, you've always been with me. I fell in love with a little girl whose face was the most beautiful I'd ever seen." Suddenly, she felt herself being swept into his arms and carried to the secluded bower behind the log. He, too, remembered this beautiful spot in the woods. "I'm going to do what I ached to do right here a long time, ago."

She smiled and reached up to kiss his tanned cheek. Her whole being ached with a desire as intense as his, a desire enflamed by the his touch. She moaned impatiently as he laid her down on the soft carpet of leaves.

"Oh, Fancy, my precious love . . . I need you so!" he groaned as his lips trailed down her throat to take the tips of a pulsing breast between his lips. Flames shot through her body, making her undulate and arch upward as he hovered over her.

Never had she looked more beautiful than she did lying there with her dark brown hair fanned out against the ground and her eyes full of passion, eyes as black and gleaming as onyx. Her sensuous lips parted to taunt him so wickedly that he cautioned himself to let this moment of rapture linger as long as possible. But that was not possible when he gazed upon her full ripe breasts and hardened nipples. The swaying provocative body beneath him demanded fulfillment, so he burrowed himself between her satiny legs evoking a moan of pleasure from her.

"Oh, dear God, Fancy!" He sighed, almost in protest for his will power was being sorely tested.

"Oh, yes, Nick. Yes, now . . . Yes!" She gasped, delighting in feeling his searing flesh pressing into her and carrying her on a raging current down an endless stream. She was drowning in the rising tide of Nick's love.

Nick realized that his mother had spoken the truth. For him endless ecstasy could only be found in Fancy's sweet arms and sensuous body. Greedily, he took her, savoring her velvet softness. The fires of their passion had never glowed so vividly.

When their hunger had been temporarily satisfied, his arms still enclosed her. He laughed mischievously and teased her. "Ah, Fancy, *ma chérie* . . . you must promise never to leave me again.

You're making an old man out of me — all this running up and down that damned river."

She responded fervently and quickly, convincing him that she was forever his and his alone. After all, it had been here on Dubonnet's grassy earth that she'd given herself to him so completely a long time ago. She was merely confirming what she'd known that day, but now her love for Nick was much stronger, was all-consuming.

Epilogue

It was the opening day of the fall racing season in Natchez and an extraordinarily large crowd was expected to attend. The opening was quite a gala occasion in the city of Natchez, and no one was more excited then Nick Dubose or his beautiful wife, Fancy. Nick's racing stables were now known throughout the Lower Mississippi Valley. Of his six horses, three had won in the New Orleans races in the spring. On the racing circuits Nick Dubose was now known as the King of the Turf, and always at his side was his "queen," the lovely brown-haired Fancy.

In Adams County and the surrounding countryside the striking young couple were viewed as royalty. Fancy's breathtaking beauty was envied by the women and admired by the gentlemen, while the ladies found Nick attractive and the men had great regard for his abilities as a horseman and a judge of horseflesh.

All this adoration and attention had not turned Fancy's head, but she did have to pinch herself from time to time. In the last few years life at Dubonnet had surpassed her wildest dreams of happiness.

This evening was no exception. They were preparing to go to Magnolia for André and Angelique's traditional ball to herald the racing season. Members of the Natchez Jockey Club were invited as were their wives, but Fancy was perplexed as to why her mother-in-law had insisted they allow the twins to accompany them. Nick was as much in the dark about his mother's request as Fancy.

"Whatever mother's reason might be, I can assure you that our children are elated." He laughed lightheartedly. Like Fancy, he was puzzled. This was not an affair the young attended, especially not his spirited three-year-old imps!

Each time he looked at them he swelled with boundless pride and his love for Fancy mounted. He always swore she'd planned it that way, to surprise him with two instead of just one. The conniving little vixen! She would always fascinate him.

Each time he looked at his black-eyed Angelina he saw Fancy when she was the little girl who ran into his arms. Raoul swore she was the "spittin' " image of her mama. As for little André, according to Angelique he looked just like Nick had at that age, and that didn't wound Nick's ego at all. Fancy teased him constantly, saying that he preened like a peacock when he walked his son around the estate or rode over the Natchez countryside with little André before him in the saddle. Nick just gave her a broad grin, never trying to deny it. The doting grandparents, Angelique and André, openly displayed their affections for the youngsters, and if this wasn't enough to spoil the Dubose twins, old Raoul and Chessie, still at Dubonnet, lavished love and attention on them.

Aunt Yvonne and Uncle Daniel had not seen their nephew and niece yet. Daniel had felt that England would be the perfect place to pursue his painting and when he'd gone abroad a few years ago, Yvonne had accompanied him. While there he'd bought a little shop which required his attention. Yvonne had not returned home either, for she'd married a wealthy English lord.

Denise, too, had married. She had wed the dashing young scion of one of New Orleans' prominent families and much to Alain's delight Denise's husband had taken over the helm of the Dubose shipping line, filling the gap Nick had left when he'd settled at Dubonnet. So it seemed everyone had found a "nesting place" except Doreen. The last they'd heard she was visiting friends in Tennessee and was still not married.

That evening as twilight fell over the Mississippi countryside and Nick's carriage rolled along the road from Dubonnet to Magnolia, he was filled with contentment and pride as he gazed at his family. Fancy was gorgeous in her ball gown. Her upswept hairdo made her look like a queen, and the low cut of her emerald green, watered silk gown revealed a teasing hint of her full rounded breasts. As Nick looked at her, desire stirred in him.

The dressed-up twins were excited. Their eyes sparkled and they were giggling. He didn't have the heart to dampen their exuberance by insisting that they stop squirming. He loved them and he knew how much they were anticipating going to the grown-up affair at Grandmama's house.

When they arrived at Magnolia and dismounted from their fine carriage, a pair of bright blue eyes observed them as they came up the walk. Fancy would always hold a special place in his heart; he'd never deny that. But he'd found his own little black-eyed darling, and he adored her. He couldn't wait to see his old friend's face when he told him that he and Doreen were married. With Irish logic, he swore fate had arranged it, for they were the most unlikely pair to end up married.

It had happened, though, like a bolt of lightning striking. They had blended wonderfully. His love of the outdoors and horses had been understood by the sweet-natured Doreen, while he, in turn, appreciated her intense need to put beauty on canvas and he realized that her painting could not be ruled by the hands of a clock. So they were not a conventional couple, nor did they wish to be. Doreen loved "her crazy Irish man," as she called him, and Sean could ask for no more.

Oh, it had not been easy at first to forget the

beautiful Fancy. She'd haunted many of his nights after he'd gone to Tennessee, but perhaps that was the reason he'd thrown himself into his work. That, too, had paid off for Sean. He now had the fine reputation of being the best horse trainer in Tennessee and Kentucky. It was as if Fate had placed Doreen at that summer barbecue at Willow Bend. He'd seen Doreen on the manicured lawn of the fine old plantation and lost his heart to her at that moment. Doreen had confessed that she'd felt the same.

No ghost of Fancy plagued him now nor did any fear of facing his old friend, Nicko, and being flooded with guilt. He loved Doreen, and no man could have been happier when she'd agreed to become his wife.

Both of them had decided it would be great fun to come to Natchez and surprise Nick with their news. Doreen eagerly anticipated seeing Nick, Fancy, and the twins. Angelique had helped them plot their surprise by suggesting that they arrive earlier than the rest of the invited guests so their reunion would be a private one.

As soon as Angelique had greeted her son and his family, she directed them to go to the sitting room, saying that she would join them shortly. Mischief danced in her dark eyes, for she was finding it hard to play Sean's little game. She could not resist winking at Fancy as she walked away.

When Nick opened the door to the sitting room, he stopped suddenly, making Fancy, who was following him with the twins, slam right into him.

"Holy Christ! Sean? Doreen? Wha . . . what the hell? . . ."

"So it is, Nicko! In the flesh!" Sean roared with laughter as he rushed to give Nick a hearty embrace, and Fancy and Doreen hugged one another, laughing too, as the two puzzled tots watched the grownups.

When they finally sat down, Sean told Nick about his marriage to Doreen. Now more than ever he knew his instincts had been right about leaving when he had. What misery he'd saved all three of them: he, Fancy, and Nick. There had to be some advantage to his Irish sense of foreboding.

As they lifted their glasses of wine in a toast to their happy reunion, Sean could not resist chiding Fancy, "I'm crestfallen, love. You promised that a boy would be named after me." Now, he could come to terms with the knowledge that Fancy was never meant to be his.

Fancy smiled sweetly for she, too, remembered the day he'd told her farewell. Only later did she wondered if Sean's feeling for her went deeper than she'd realized at the time. Suddenly an idea came to her. After all, this was such a joyous occasion. Why not, she decided?

Her dark eyes darted in Nick's direction for one fleeting moment, then back to Sean, as she retorted flippantly, "Well, one will be named Sean in about . . . say, seven more months. So just be patient, Sean Sullivan."

Nick's mouth gaped with shock, but his green eyes flashed utter delight. She'd done it to him again . . . the little vixen! She was the most tantalizing woman in the world, he'd swear to that. She always seemed to surprise him, and she was the source of endless ecstasy and joy. Dear God, he loved her so!

Not caring that the others were watching, he leaped up out of his chair and crushed her in his arms. He kissed her long and lingeringly, and then he whispered to her, telling her the depth of his love for her.

This was a day Fancy would remember — a cherished time. It was no wonder the feisty mare, Fancy's Folly, came in first at the racecourse later.

When Fancy and Nick were finally alone in their bedroom, Fancy looked seriously at her husband and asked, "Why did you name the mare that, Nick? Fancy's Folly?"

A broad smile creased his face and his eyes mellowed with love, for to him she looked so sweet and innocent he could hardly believe she was the mother of twins and expecting another child. Wide-eyed and with her lips half parted, she sat up in bed, looking at him and awaiting his answer.

His deep voice replied, "Because, my love . . . I was already so foolishly in love with you, I wondered if you would prove to be my folly."

"Perhaps, I am, Nick Dubose, but I shall love you forever and ever — your folly and your Fancy!"

THE BEST IN HISTORICAL ROMANCE
by Sylvie F. Sommerfield

BETRAY NOT MY PASSION   (1466, $3.95)

The handsome sea captain's hands felt like fire against the raven-haired Elana's flesh. Before giving her heart she wanted his pledge of everlasting love. But as the prisoner of his fierce desire she only prayed . . . BETRAY NOT MY PASSION.

TAME MY WILD HEART   (1351, $3.95)

Fires of love surged through Clay's blood the moment his blue eyes locked with the violet of Sabrina's. He held her bound against him with iron-hard arms, claiming her honeysweet mouth with his own. He had bought her, he would use her, but he'd never love her until she whispered . . . TAME MY WILD HEART!

CHERISH ME, EMBRACE ME   (1199, $3.75)

Lovely, raven-haired Abby vowed she'd never let a Yankee run her plantation or her life. But once she felt the exquisite ecstasy of Alexander's demanding lips, she desired only him!

TAMARA'S ECSTASY   (998, $3.50)

Tamara knew it was foolish to give her heart to a sailor. But she was a victim of her own desire. Lost in a sea of passion, she ached for his magic touch — and would do anything for it!

DEANNA'S DESIRE   (906, $3.50)

Amidst the storm of the American Revolution, Matt and Deanna meet — and fall in love. And bound by passion, they risk everything to keep that love alive!

Available wherever paperbacks are sold, or order direct from the Publisher. Send cover price plus 50¢ per copy for mailing and handling to Zebra Books, 475 Park Avenue South, New York, N.Y. 10016. DO NOT SEND CASH.